*To James!
Thanks for your
friendship & support.
May your dreams come true
as well*

— Nick Poff

The Handyman's Dream

by
Nick Poff

authorHOUSE™

1663 LIBERTY DRIVE, SUITE 200
BLOOMINGTON, INDIANA 47403
(800) 839-8640
WWW.AUTHORHOUSE.COM

© 2005 Nick Poff. All Rights Reserved.

No part of this book may be reproduced, stored in a retrieval system, or transmitted by any means without the written permission of the author.

First published by AuthorHouse 09/27/05

ISBN: 1-4208-7569-8 (sc)
ISBN: 1-4208-7570-1 (dj)

Library of Congress Control Number: 2005907250

Printed in the United States of America
Bloomington, Indiana

This book is printed on acid-free paper.

Grateful acknowledgment is made to the following for permission to include copyrighted material:

One Man Band
Words and Music by Billy Fox, Tommy Kaye and January Tyme
(c) 1968, 1970 (Renewed 1996, 1998) SCREEN GEMS-EMI MUSIC INC.
All Rights Reserved   International Copyright Secured   Used By Permission

Acknowledgements

A huge thanks to some of the most wonderful friends a guy ever had: Tim Gibson, for being my best bud; David Marbach and Jerry Stinnett, who have always been there for me, and gave the town in this story its name; Andy Eastman and Chris Seagle, who were the very first to read the story of Ed and Rick, and gave me the book's title; Cari Arnold Kyle, who always seems to be there when I need her; Ed Didier, Ed's namesake, and a damn fine handyman in his own right.

Gratitude is the word that most comes to mind when I think of Skip Carsten, my guardian angel, who got me to admit I wanted to quit my job and write stories. You can take some quiet pride in this accomplishment, friend.

Here's a big shout out to the whole gang at WAJI & WLDE - the kind of co-workers who made me the envy of my friends. To my awesome bosses, Barb Richards and Lee Tobin: thanks for allowing me to check out of - but not leave - The Hotel California. The work you threw my way helped pay the bills while this book was coming to life.

Thanks to Casey Kasem, my number one radio hero, who always said, "keep your feet on the ground, and keep reaching for the stars."

To Edgar Huntington: many thanks for your encouragement, support, and ideas.

And finally, I am extremely grateful for Lisa Collins, the absolute best line editor this first-time novelist could have had.

Dedication

For Annette Owens (Anj) *the* best friend anyone ever had: There ain't a woman that comes close to you.

And in loving memory of Steven Purdy, who taught me a thing or two about romance, fulfilling dreams, *Harold and Maude*, and handymen in general. I wish you were here for this.

The Handyman's Dream

Prologue: Autumn, 1980

The first time Ed Stephens saw him was at the end of September.

Ed had just celebrated his twenty-eighth birthday. He'd spent a dull and obligatory birthday with family and had wasted the days since then turning the idea of being twenty-eight upside down, inside out, and round and round, as Diana Ross did in that new song of hers they were playing on the radio. A slave to the radio Top 40 since adolescence, Ed often thought of his life in pop song lyrics. He couldn't seem to find any significance in the number, though, or in the amount of years he'd put in on Planet Earth. The best he could do was to say he was two years from thirty, and since that was just plain depressing, he finally gave up the whole thing with one big mental shrug.

Until he saw the mailman.

Ed was, as usual, eating lunch at home. He'd finished off a sandwich and was absentmindedly making his way through a handful of M&M's as he walked to his front steps to see if the mail had arrived. No, either he wasn't getting anything that day, or it hadn't arrived yet. He looked westward on Coleman Street and thought he saw someone wearing a blue uniform, so he decided to sit down in his living room and give his feet a rest while he waited.

He sighed, sprawling full length across his sofa. Eventually he had to make an appearance at Louise Marlowe's house to check on a leaky pipe in her basement. Ed was a handyman, and he usually enjoyed tinkering with the problems his clients gave him, but he admitted only to himself that he found plumbing chores boring, so he wasn't in a particularly big hurry to look at Louise's leak. It could wait until after he'd looked at his mail.

He wiggled his toes in his heavy work boots. He wanted to take them off, but knew if he did he'd never muster the energy to put them back on and drive to Louise's house. He glanced out the window, pleased to see the mailman approach. He frowned, though, as he didn't recognize this guy. Ed's dad had been good friends with the Porterfield postmaster, and as a result, Ed knew most everyone who carried mail in his Indiana town. As the unfamiliar mail carrier approached, Ed's eyes widened.

The mailman was tall, taller than Ed's six feet, it appeared. He was broad shouldered and fit his uniform well. Like Ed, he was neither too heavy nor too thin, but happily in the land of just right. His thick, dark hair was cut short, and a well-trimmed beard framed his ordinary—handsome in Ed's eyes—face and accentuated his strong jaw. Ed couldn't see the mailman's eye color through the window, but guessed they would be brown, also like his own, but perhaps a shade darker than the almost-hazel color of Ed's.

Ed watched as the man pulled a handful of envelopes from the bag thrown across one of those broad shoulders and put them in Ed's mailbox. He shut the lid, turned, and headed back down Ed's front walk.

Ed, tired feet forgotten, rolled off the sofa. He opened the door and watched the mailman cross Grant Street.

"I'll be damned," he mumbled. "Who is that, and where did he come from?"

The mailman walked toward the first house on the next block with a casual, easy stride. He may have been new in Porterfield, but Ed suspected he wasn't new at delivering mail. He had the casual ability—and the tan, Ed noticed—of someone who'd been at his job for some time.

The music playing on his stereo's radio in the living room penetrated Ed's thoughts. It was a recent song from the Rolling Stones, "Emotional Rescue." Although Ed had always liked the Stones, he had a tendency to snicker to himself when he heard this one. Considering Mick Jagger's track record, the idea of him being someone's knight in shining armor struck Ed as being pretty funny.

Now, though, Ed wasn't laughing. *Damn, I sure wouldn't mind being rescued by that mailman.*

Suddenly, Ed knew what was bothering him about turning twenty-eight. He was tired of being alone.

Ed had lived all his life in Porterfield. Granted, it probably wasn't the best place for a single gay man to live, but he'd never given the idea of leaving much serious thought. His job and his house had kept him busy the past few years, and he had not allowed himself to dwell on his singleness. Now, however, his business was established, and he'd done everything to the house he felt like doing for the time being.

No one likes to admit it, but most people are looking for the person who can rescue them from being alone, especially a single gay man stuck in a small Indiana town. That afternoon, Ed knew if someone were to back him into a corner, he'd admit it. Oh, he'd made a few halfhearted attempts at finding a man of his own, but the results had been less than encouraging.

Ed stood on his front walk, his gaze on the mailman now half a block away. He told himself he was crazy, but he had a weird feeling the knight coming to rescue him wore a blue postal service uniform.

Chapter One

Ed couldn't help it. In the days that followed, he couldn't get the new mailman out of his mind. From the time he had broken up with Cathy Carroll after high school graduation and had devoted himself exclusively to the pursuit of those whose body parts matched his own, Ed had had an image in his mind, a full-blown mental picture of the perfect guy. That first day, when the new mailman dropped a handful of bills into Ed's mailbox, Ed knew he had found him.

Ed, a practical and pragmatic kind of guy, was well aware of a few drawbacks. He didn't know the mailman's name. He had never had a conversation with him. He had never seen him more than a few moments at a time. And, Ed admitted to himself, he didn't know the answer to the thorniest of questions: whether the mailman was interested in guys like Ed or preferred somebody with boobs and a skirt. No matter. From the moment Ed had set eyes on the hunky postal carrier—tall, dark, bearded, and handsome—he was overwhelmed with desire. Every time the mailman came striding up Ed's front walk, "You're the One That I Want" from the *Grease* soundtrack played in Ed's head.

Ed himself was not a bad-looking guy. At twenty-eight he had finally lost the boyish gawkiness that had haunted him for most of his life. He was tall and broad shouldered, and if he wasn't as well built as the guys he occasionally drooled over in *Honcho* and *Mandate*, he at least had the look: lots of denim, flannel, and boots, thanks in no small part to his work as a handyman. His sandy brown hair was cut short, his mustache thick and well trimmed. His eyes were warm and brown. He had inadvertently copied the "gay clone" look of 1980 and would have fit in well in San Francisco, but he was stuck in Porterfield, a small dot on the map of northern Indiana, where few men of his kind lived who would appreciate him. He was also rather shy, so he had a hard time connecting with the men he did happen to meet.

His love life sucked, Ed thought. Every now and again he managed to connect with someone he met at Carlton's, a gay bar in Fort Wayne, a city about thirty miles from Porterfield. He'd had some pleasant experiences, and even a few hot ones, but nothing had ever really developed with any guy, except for one older married man who had pursued him so fervently Ed had needed to take a two-month break from trips to Carlton's. He'd even been on the verge of changing his phone number when the married guy finally gave up.

He told himself that his feelings for the new mailman were simply a reaction to the lack of romance, not to mention sex, in his life and that he needed to get a grip, and fast. Even though nothing at all was out of the ordinary about his wistful dreams of sharing his life with another man, his practical nature told him he probably had about as good of a chance of fulfilling this dream with this particular man as he did of winning the Publishers Clearing House sweepstakes.

Every day, though, Ed found an excuse to be near the front of the house so he could watch the man of his dreams deliver his mail. He memorized every detail of the mailman's appearance for later bedtime fantasies. After three weeks of such fantasies—everything from wild, sweaty sex to homier visions of shared dinners and putting up the Christmas tree—Ed decided he needed to either see a shrink or make some kind of a move.

Fortunately or unfortunately, Ed's self-employment allowed him to arrange his day around the mail delivery. He had inherited his father's skill with basic home repairs, and when Ed had been laid off from his job at the electric motor factory in town, he'd gone into business for himself. If any of his regular clients, mostly older retired folks, noticed he never seemed to be available between one and two each day, they didn't bother to mention it. Once Ed finally worked up the courage to take action, he was relieved that he didn't have to worry about a set work schedule.

The first thing to do, he decided, was to try to have a conversation with the mailman. Either that or stalk him on his mail route, and after his own experience of being stalked by that insistent married man, Ed didn't think that was such a hot idea.

Ed chose a warm, sunny Monday afternoon in October, when his yard was full of leaves that needed to be raked. Ed dressed a good deal more carefully than he usually did for yard chores. Rake in hand, he walked into the front yard of his little white two-story house on the corner of Coleman and Grant Streets. Golden leaves from Ed's maple tree were lazily falling to earth, and he halfheartedly began to rake a few of them. Once he saw the mailman on his block, he thought he'd move closer to the front walk, meet the guy halfway to the house, and say hello. After that, he had no idea what he was going to say, but figured he had to start somewhere.

About one-thirty Ed saw a blue-clad figure walk onto his block. He squinted, looked closer, and almost threw his rake down in disgust. It wasn't his mailman! It was old Ralph Graham, who'd worked for the Porterfield post office as long as Ed could remember.

"Boy, wouldn't you know," he muttered, drumming his fingers on the rake. A thoughtful look came over Ed's face. Maybe this wasn't such a bad thing after all.

He was industriously raking away when Ralph entered his front walk.

"'Lo there, Ed," Ralph called.

"Hey, Mr. Graham," Ed said, looking up. "How are you today?"

"Oh, can't complain, can't complain," Ralph said, cheerful as always. "Kind of nice to be out on the street for a change."

"Yeah," Ed said. "You're not the guy who's been doing this route lately. Where's he at today?"

"Rick? Oh, just a day off. He'll probably be back tomorrow." Ralph shuffled through his mailbag.

"He must be new. I thought I knew most everyone who worked for the post office."

"Yep," Ralph said, handing Ed his mail. "You know Bill Metzger retired. Rick moved up here from Indy and took over his job. Nice boy, Rick. Gets along well with everyone."

"Wow, imagine that. Someone moving into Porterfield instead of out. That's different."

"Shame to say, but you're right. Well, I think he has family up here. That probably had something to do with it."

"Married?" Ed asked bluntly.

"Hmm?" said Ralph, looking puzzled. "Oh, you mean Rick. No, don't think so."

Well, there's some hope, Ed thought, deciding he'd better shut up before Ralph became suspicious.

"Good to see you, Ed!" Ralph turned back toward the street. "Looks like you got quite a job there with those leaves! You want to come over and take care of mine?"

Ed laughed. "I think I have as much as I can handle right now. Take care, Mr. Graham."

Ralph walked across Grant Street while Ed leaned on his rake, thinking. The mail Ralph had handed him slipped out of his fingers and fell into the leaves.

"Aw, crud," he muttered, stooping over to pick up the envelopes, mostly junk it appeared. "Well, the hell with this. Raking these leaves can wait until tomorrow afternoon. No sense in finishing it now." Surely he'd get to see Mailman Rick tomorrow. *Rick*, he said to himself, smiling. *I've always liked that name.*

⋄•⋄

The next day Ed awoke to what sounded like rain. He hauled himself out of bed and pushed aside the blind. It was indeed raining, a slow, steady kind of rain that would probably last all day. He wouldn't be able to work in the yard, and probably wouldn't be able to do it the next day either, as the leaves would still be soggy and heavy.

"Someone up there hates me," he groaned.

He sighed, dropping the blind. Rain or no rain, on Tuesday mornings he was due at Mrs. Heston's. The old woman could get around only with the aid of a walker, and she counted on Ed to stop by every Tuesday and help with her grocery shopping. Usually he didn't mind the slow trek though the aisles of the local IGA. She had been one of his first regular clients and an ardent supporter of Ed's handyman service, but his mind just wasn't on it today.

What with the grocery shopping and hauling some odds and ends out of Mrs. Heston's basement, Ed didn't get home for lunch until almost one. He made himself a ham sandwich, grabbed a bag of potato chips, and took his food into the living room where he could see out the front door. He was about to sit down when the phone rang. He debated for a moment whether to let it ring, but figuring it might be a client, he picked it up.

"Hello?"

"Ed? It's your mother."

Ed rolled his eyes. Yeah, like he wouldn't know that voice anywhere.

"What's up, Mom?"

"I'm making a big roast for supper, so I want you to come over. It'll go to waste with just me here."

Since Ed's father had died two years earlier, she called at least once a week inviting him for a meal. Somehow Norma, his mother, had been unable to get used to the idea of cooking for one. She also thought that Ed, since he was unmarried, should sell his house and move in with her. Between that and constantly telling his sister, Laurie, how she should raise her children, she managed to drive both siblings crazy.

"Okay, Mom. I'll be there," he said, sighing.

"Good. Be here by six. And if you want some of that awful pop you like so much, bring your own. I won't buy it. Speaking of buying, do you know what that ungrateful sister of yours said to me this morning? She said—"

"Hang on a minute, Mom," Ed interrupted.

He'd just seen a flash of blue by the street. He dragged the phone by its cord over to the door. Mailman Rick stood in front of Ed's house on the street sidewalk. He looked through his bag, then moved on. Obviously he didn't have anything to put in Ed's mailbox this rainy Tuesday.

"Crud!" Ed muttered.

"What's that? Edward, what are you mumbling about? I was trying to tell you that your sister told me I had no business—"

"Hey, Mom," he interrupted again. An idea had jumped into his head. "When you send someone a certified letter they have to sign for it, don't they?"

"What? A certified what? What's the matter with you today? I try to tell you about your sister and you're talking about the mail?" Norma's voice squawked through the phone.

"I just saw the mailman walk by so I happened to think of it."

"Well, go ask the mailman then! How in the world should I know?"

"It's raining, Mom. I don't want to go out there."

"Then call the post office! Who do you think I am, the postmaster general? Do you want to hear about your sister or not?"

"Oh, Mom, can't you tell me about it tonight? I really need to get going," he lied.

"All right, all right," she said, all aggrieved now. "Honestly, the two of you are going to send me to my grave. Just be here by six!"

"I will, Mom," he said patiently. "Bye."

"Good-bye!" she said, slamming the phone down.

Ed, out of habit, moved the receiver away from his ear.

Hmm. If someone sent me something I had to sign for, that just might be a way to get to talk to him. Not bad, not bad at all, he congratulated himself. It was definitely time to call Glen.

Ed had become friendly with Glen Mercer several years earlier during one of his trips to Carlton's bar. Glen had made a few trips to Porterfield, but Ed usually drove into Fort Wayne to see Glen. They would go out to eat, occasionally to the movies, and would hit the bar together. Ed hadn't seen much of Glen since the beginning of Glen's hot and heavy romance with a young college guy named Mike. Ed couldn't decide if he was jealous of Glen, or if he just plain didn't like Mike. Either way, he'd been avoiding Glen since late summer. That night, when he finally escaped from his mother's house, he called Glen.

"You want me to do *what?*" Glen asked.

"I need you to send me a certified letter. I don't care what it says. I just want the mailman to come the door and ask for me to sign for it."

"I think it will say 'you're a jackass.' Are you trying to tell me you have the hots for your mailman?" Glen's voice seemed to carry a smirk.

"Look, I'll pay you back. I'm just asking you to do me this one favor. I'd do the same for you."

"Ed Stephens, you have been lonely far too long. Do you even have a clue if the mailman is *gay*?"

"I'm hoping this will help me to find out."

"Good God! Ed, you need to move. Do you think I would have ever met Mike living in a town like that? No, I'd probably be chasing after the mailman!" Glen's laughter cascaded through the phone line.

Ed had noticed that Glen had gotten ever so smug since Mike had come along, and frankly, since Ed didn't consider Mike any great prize, he didn't have much patience with it.

"I really appreciate what you are doing for me, Glen," he said calmly. "You really are a good friend."

"Yes, I am. Because I'll do it, only because I want to hear what happens. I'll stop by the post office tomorrow on my lunch hour. And then you have to promise to call me the minute you talk to this guy, you hear?"

"I promise."

"Good. Let me know, okay?"

"Yeah, yeah," Ed said. "Thanks, Glen."

Glen carried on for a while longer, mostly talking about Mike, and Ed listened with half his mind. The other half was thinking about the day Mailman Rick would knock on his front door.

⋘•⋙

If Glen went to the post office on Wednesday, Ed figured he'd get the certified letter on Thursday. Still, he didn't see any reason not to stay around home on Wednesday afternoon. It wouldn't hurt to get another look at Mailman Rick.

The weather was still rainy and gloomy Wednesday afternoon. Ed settled in on his old sofa, a hand-me-down from his mother. He pulled the curtains back just enough to see out the window. The phone rang. Ed groaned, again debating whether he should answer it. Surely Norma wouldn't call to bitch about his sister two days in a row. Then again, Ed realized, she just well might. The phone rang on, six, then seven times. He finally got up and answered it.

"Ed? I need you to come over right away and look at this lamp my daughter gave me." The caller was Mrs. West, one of his most elderly clients, a bit of a character who was given to making mountains out of molehills.

"What's the matter with it?" he asked, his eye on the front door.

"Well, I went to turn it on and it gave me a shock!"

Ed waited. She didn't say anything more. "Is that all?"

"Isn't that enough? I want you to come over and make sure it isn't defective. The last thing I need is to get electrocuted."

Mrs. West lived in mortal fear of electrocution. You'd think someone had once threatened to send her to the chair, Ed often thought.

"Okay. I'll be over later this afternoon."

"Ed Stephens, you know very well that I get my hair done every Wednesday afternoon at four. You need to come over now."

"Now?"

"Yes, now. It's so dark with all this rain I need to turn a light on in here. Goodness me, I depend on you to take care of these things for me. What would your mother say?"

Aw, crud, Ed thought. It wasn't beyond Mrs. West to call his mother and complain, so he knew he had no choice. Norma already thought he was acting oddly, so he didn't want to give her any more ammunition.

"I'll be there in a few minutes," he said, and sighed.

Ed shrugged his jacket on and headed out the back door. Once in his truck he went out of his way to drive down his own street, looking for the mailman. Sure enough, Mailman Rick was just a block away from his house. Ed slowed down, watching him walk with that casual, easy stride. *Oh, he is so sexy.* Ed almost drove into the curb, his eyes on the mailman. He jerked his eyes, and the steering wheel, back to the left. Oh, well. Surely he'd see him tomorrow, and under no circumstances would he answer the goddamned phone.

That night Ed restlessly paced off the rooms of his house, from the kitchen, through the living room, and into the bedroom at the back of the house. He even went upstairs, something he seldom did, as he used the one big room on the second floor mostly for storage. He sat down on the battered brown hassock from his boyhood room in his parents' house. He gazed at the odds and ends scattered around the room with the sloped ceilings, and pondered his life and the silly plan he had to meet the new mailman.

He wasn't at all sure why the idea of having a boyfriend, or a lover, had taken such a serious hold on him. Oh, he'd always hoped he'd meet someone nice someday, but he didn't carry on about it, the way Glen or some other guys he knew did. Despite his fondness for all the romantic songs he heard on the radio and played over and over again on his stereo, he'd been more content all these years to simply dream about a wonderful guy, the Dream Man he'd conjured up while still in his teens. His practical nature being what it was, he never really thought he'd meet the Dream Man, who was just something to think about in the lonelier hours when Ed had nothing better to think about. He'd always assumed that some day he would meet a nice guy, and hopefully something good, and maybe even permanent, would grow between them.

That had all changed the moment he first saw Rick. The new mailman simply *was* the Dream Man, and for the first time Ed allowed himself to believe that a Dream Man—if not Rick, then some other guy—actually existed. Ed, who'd always made the best of what life had offered him, suddenly began to believe that maybe, just maybe, dreams sometimes come true.

He stood up and began pacing the room, dodging the boxes he'd moved from his parents' house to his. He paused at a box of his father's things, given to him by his mother after Tim Stephens's death. He rummaged idly through the items in the box—a bowling trophy, an old photo album, the Alistair MacLean books his father had enjoyed reading—and thought about his parents' marriage. Despite their personality clash—Norma, autocratic and sharp-tongued, and Tim, gentle and easygoing—it had been a good marriage.

Ed had never really thought of himself as getting married, as straight people did. He didn't know if he carried a residue of shame over being gay that kept him from thinking about such a relationship between two men, or if he'd simply never met a guy who seemed a likely partner. He was thinking about it now, though. All those pop songs on the radio, filled with all kinds of yearning, were hitting Ed's ears differently these days. Whether the desire for a relationship was ignited by turning twenty-eight or by seeing the Dream Man, Ed realized it was something he wanted very much for himself: to grow older in the company of another man, to jump off the sexual roulette wheel of the gay bars.

A thought occurred to him suddenly. Perhaps the reason he'd never given serious thought to leaving Porterfield was because all this time he did unconsciously desire the same kind of relationship his parents had enjoyed all those years.

"Jesus," he mumbled to himself. "I've been brainwashed by *Leave It to Beaver, Father Knows Best,* and *Ozzie and Harriet. And* Porterfield. Some great gay liberationist I am."

He shrugged. Maybe wanting a conventional relationship wasn't the trendy, gay way to be in 1980, but he was relieved to realize he now knew himself a little better than he had before the new mailman had arrived on the scene. If Mailman Rick wasn't available for a guy like Ed, at least now he knew what he was looking for.

⋖≽•≼⋗

Thursday morning was blessedly quiet for Ed. He didn't have any appointments scheduled and the phone didn't ring. That gave him plenty of time to prepare for the mail delivery, and to be a nervous wreck.

He felt as though he was dressing for a date. He shoved clothes around in the closet, tried on several different shirts, and fussed over which pair of jeans made his ass look its best.

"This is so dumb," he kept muttering to himself, looking at the rejected outfits thrown on the bed. "This could be this dumbest, biggest waste of time in your whole life."

Still, even if Mailman Rick turned out to be straight and completely immune to Ed's charms, Ed decided he might as well look his best. In some way, he thought, it really *was* a date. He just hoped he wasn't dressing to impress Ralph Graham.

By one o'clock Ed was sitting in a chair out of sight of the front door. He anxiously flipped the pages of a magazine. He didn't want to give the appearance of expecting a knock on the door. He looked at his watch, riffled through a few more pages of *National Geographic,* and thought about going to the bathroom. The anticipation seemed to be doing a number on his bladder.

The mailman hadn't appeared by one-thirty. By this time Ed really did need to pee, so he tossed the magazine aside and was about to get up when he thought he saw some movement on the sidewalk. He gripped the arms of his chair, took a few deep breaths, and told himself to calm down.

A few moments later Ed heard a knock at the front door. He closed his eyes and prayed: *Please don't let it be Ralph Graham!* He got up and opened the door. Relief flowed through him. Mailman Rick looked up from the letter in his hand and smiled.

"Mr. Stephens?"

"Yes, that's me."

Oh, my God, Ed thought. Rick was just as handsome up close as he was from a distance. Although the guy would probably never be asked to model for a magazine ad, the simple and direct masculinity in his face completely appealed to Ed. He had guessed correctly, as Rick's eyes were indeed a dark shade of brown. They were direct, friendly, and looking right at Ed.

"Certified letter for you, Mr. Stephens. I need to have you sign for it." He held up an envelope with a postal service form of some sort attached to it.

Ed reached for it, along with the pen Rick offered, noticing Rick's strong-looking hands and thinking that the dark hair on his hands and wrists hinted at much more to be found under Rick's well-fitting uniform. *Hairy, too. Can ya believe it?*

"Sure," said Ed. "Won't you come inside for a moment?" He had rehearsed that line over and over.

The mailman nodded and stepped inside. Ed put what he hoped was a friendly grin on his face. He took a few steps to an end table and laid the letter down, looking for the signature line.

Rick reached from behind Ed and pointed. "There's where you need to sign."

Ed was so overwhelmed to have the guy that close to him he wondered if he could manage to write his name. Willing his hand not to shake, Ed carefully wrote *Ed Stephens* on the form, then turned to hand it back to Rick. He was about to say thank you, but when he looked into Rick's face the words died in his throat.

Glen often claimed certain gay men knew when they were in the presence of another gay man. Ed told himself it was just wishful thinking, but nonetheless, whatever sensitivity to this he happened to have was tingling.

Rick was looking directly into Ed's eyes, and Ed forced himself to look back. A shot of what felt like electricity ran through his body. *If I was Mrs. West, I'd be calling an ambulance.* With his own brown eyes locked on Rick's darker brown eyes, Ed handed the letter to him.

A faint smile appeared above Rick's beard. He detached the form from the envelope, then handed the letter back to Ed. "Thanks."

"Thank *you*," Ed said. His mind raced as he tried to think of something else to say.

And then the damned phone rang.

He broke his gaze with Rick and turned to the phone, glaring at it in frustration. Rick, who had been standing still, looking back at Ed, seemed to come to life.

"Well, I should let you get that," he said, moving toward the door.

"Uh, yeah," Ed muttered, watching Rick's retreat.

The mailman pushed open the screen door, paused, and turned back to Ed with a smile. "You have a nice day, okay?"

"Oh, yes. You too," Ed said, a bit too brightly.

Rick nodded, letting the screen door close behind him. He walked down Ed's front steps, but suddenly stopped halfway down the walk and turned around.

"Hey," he called. "I forgot to give you the rest of your mail!"

He hurried back up the steps. Ed opened the screen door, and the mailman handed him two envelopes and a grocery store circular.

The phone continued to ring as Ed and Rick once again looked at one another. Rick glanced at the still ringing phone, smiled, then headed back down the front walk. Ed let the screen door slam and turned to the phone, wishing he had something other than two envelopes and a grocery store circular to throw at it.

"Aw, crud!"

<☆•☆>

Ed moped around the house that night, endlessly replaying his scene with Mailman Rick in his head. He pushed leftover pot roast around his dinner plate and saw Rick's face in the potatoes and carrots. *Is he or isn't he*, he wondered. *Am I crazy, or did he really look at me like I looked at him?* He scraped most of his dinner into the garbage, unable to work up an appetite for food.

He worked hard to convince himself his wishful thinking had misread the mailman's interest. Rick was merely a hardworking government employee doing his best to keep the customer satisfied. Ed could think of lots of ways that satisfaction could be achieved with this particular customer, but doubted they were included in the postal regulations.

He shuffled through his records, looking for something to play that would not make him think of Rick. The thing was, he realized, declaring an end to the whole thing would have been easier if Rick had been brusque or unfriendly in any kind of way. If he'd been obviously straight, wearing a goddamned *wedding* ring or something, Ed could have dismissed the mailman from his mind once and for all and hopefully looked elsewhere for companionship. He flipped over a Carpenters album with "Please Mr. Postman" on it and groaned. Nothing in his record collection was helpful. The only song he could think of that seemed appropriate was "They're Coming to Take Me Away, Ha-Haaa!"

He knew he had to call Glen, but kept putting it off. Telling Glen what had happened would be easy enough, but he knew Glen would encourage him to make another move, and Ed was so torn by indecision that he couldn't see himself doing anything Glen might suggest.

That awful phone rang. Figuring it would be Glen, he reluctantly answered it. "Hello?"

"Well?" Glen said impatiently. "What happened?"

Ed let out a deep sigh. "Nothing," he lied. "The guy's totally straight. But at least we tried. Thanks, Glen."

"Oh. Well, shit. I'm sorry, Ed. I was really hoping you were on to something."

"Me too. But, hey, this is Porterfield, right?" Ed's laugh was rueful. "Maybe I should move, right? That's what you keep telling me."

"Aw, Ed, don't get bummed out. You tried. That's more than some guys would do. And don't worry. You'll meet someone one of these days. And when you do, it'll just be that much sweeter." Glen paused, then changed gears. "Hey, tomorrow is Friday. Why don't you come into town? Mike and I have plans for most of the evening, but we might hit Carlton's later on."

"Thanks, Glen. I just might do that." *Why not. It's not like I have anything better to do.*

But that was the problem. Ed hoped he did have something better, and a lot closer to home. He was just afraid to find out for sure.

Chapter Two

Ed was debating whether to hang around the house Friday when another phone call solved the dilemma. Mr. and Mrs. Hauser called late in the morning and asked Ed to come over and look at their backed-up toilet. He managed to spend enough time with the Hauser toilet that he didn't return home until late afternoon. He checked the mailbox and found it empty. So, Mailman Rick hadn't even stopped at his house that day. Ed didn't know whether to be disappointed or relieved.

That night he sat in his quiet house, still thinking about the mailman. By this time he was ready to consider seeking psychiatric help and wondered if he could find a shrink as cheap as Lucy in *Peanuts*. He was beginning to worry that his preoccupation with the mailman was turning into obsession. *This is not good,* he told himself, at that moment realizing he'd been sitting in the dark. He switched on a lamp and started pacing.

Perhaps the thing to do was take Glen up on his offer of meeting at Carlton's. Maybe if Ed met some other guy, he could put the mailman out of his mind, at least for the evening. Although he had little faith in the idea he might actually meet some runner-up Dream Man that night, whoever he might meet had one big advantage over Mailman Rick; Ed could rest easy knowing the man was gay.

He paced into the bedroom and pondered the clothes hanging in his closet. He never knew what to wear to that place. His usual handyman clothes embarrassingly pegged him as a guy trying too hard to be macho, but he felt foolish in anything dressier. Glen had tried on several occasions to get Ed into trendier clothes, but had finally given up. If someone would have asked Ed to identify International Male clothing, he would have been thoroughly stumped. *Oh, what the hell,* he thought, and put on what he considered to be his best macho-gay-man outfit, flannel shirt and all.

Ed climbed into his truck and headed out of Porterfield. The weather had finally cleared, resulting in a beautiful autumn evening. As Ed drove along Highway 401, he listened to the radio and tried to avoid thinking about the past week. The Larsen-Feiten Band came on with "Who'll Be the Fool Tonight."

"Probably me," Ed groaned.

Although he had made numerous trips to Carlton's over the past few years, he still felt nervous going there. It had nothing to do with the fact that Carlton's was a gay bar in a city where being gay wasn't all that cool. After all, Ed reasoned, things had changed a lot for gay folks in the past few years. No, he froze at the idea of all those men, posing and looking. Ed had not perfected the fine art of cruising, and wondered if he ever would.

He thought back to the first night he'd finally summoned up the courage to go in. When he had seen the small neon sign reading CARLTON'S over the door, all he could think of was Rhoda Morgenstern's unseen doorman. That drunken, moronic voice played over and over in his head: "Hello, this is Carlton your doorman." To make conversation he said as much to the bartender, who turned out to be Carlton himself and who had obviously heard that line more than once. Ed had almost died of embarrassment. But Carlton was a decent sort, not to mention a good businessman. He had smiled and told Ed his screwdriver was on the house. Ed had warmed to Carlton, but never quite to the bar itself.

Ed walked in just after ten o'clock, still rather early for a gay bar on a Friday night. A few guys were playing pool, and some of the regular barflies were parked on their usual stools. Music thumped in the makeshift disco room. "A Lover's Holiday," a song Ed liked, was playing in the empty room. It was such a joyful tune, and the idea of a man rescuing him from a dull party fit into the thoughts he'd been having lately.

He glanced around the bar, taking in his potential rescuers, and thought he might be better off stranded for a while. *The night's still young,* he thought, sighing to himself.

He picked up his usual screwdriver at the bar and wandered beyond the pool table to where a jukebox was playing, competing with the music from the other room. He leaned against the wall, sipping his drink and watching the pool game. *What the hell am I doing here?* he asked himself, as he always did. He looked toward the door and almost dropped his drink in surprise. *Oh, my God! I was right!*

Mailman Rick had just walked in.

He wasn't in his postal uniform, of course. He was dressed pretty much like Ed, but Ed had that face so memorized he knew it was Rick. He watched Rick approach the bar and buy himself a beer. Ed was so undone he turned around and faced the jukebox. For the millionth time he wished he had the balls to just walk up to a guy and start a conversation. He stood, frozen, looking over the song titles on the jukebox. When he finally summoned up the courage to turn around, he saw Rick sitting at the bar, talking to a regular named Russ who was devastatingly handsome and well aware of it.

"That figures," Ed muttered under his breath.

Ed, with a shaking hand, raised his drink to his mouth and took a sip, still watching Rick and Russ. Rick laughed at something Russ said. *Not only handsome but witty,* Ed thought, wishing the guy would drop dead on the spot.

The bar was getting a bit more crowded. Several younger guys walked to the end of the bar, blocking his sight of Rick. Ed took another gulp of his drink, trying to convince himself to move away from the jukebox. He wanted Rick to see him, but was terrified Rick would not acknowledge him. Not only that, but he realized he needed to pee rather badly. *Aw, crud.* At least the men's room was in the opposite direction. Surely he could make himself walk that far.

Ed slipped around the jukebox and hurried into the empty men's room. He took care of business, then stopped to wash his hands. He looked at himself in the smudged mirror over the sink. Was there something in his face that did, or would, appeal to the mailman? Glen had insisted over and over that Ed was a nice-looking guy, but at this moment Ed didn't believe it.

He pushed open the door to walk out and almost knocked over someone trying to walk in—Rick. Ed was so surprised he could only blink nervously and stare into the face of the man he'd been thinking about for weeks. *Now what?*

Rick regained his balance and said, "Whoops! Sorry!" He glanced at Ed, then looked closer in the dim light, frowning. "Don't I know you?" he asked.

"Uh . . . ," Ed said, still blinking.

A smile suddenly lit up Rick's face. "The certified letter! I knew I recognized your face. Well . . ." Rick paused a moment, still smiling. "Not that I'd forget it."

Ed couldn't believe it. Unless he had completely lost his mind, Rick was flirting with him. *Any moment now Rod Serling's gonna walk in here and say, "Ed Stephens doesn't know it, but a big joke is being played on him in* The Twilight Zone."

"I'd certainly know yours anywhere," Ed managed to say.

Rick laughed. "Small world, isn't it? Imagine, running into someone else from Porterfield here." Rick shifted his eyes from Ed's face to the floor. "I, uh, I kinda need to get in there," he said, looking back at Ed, his smile changing into an embarrassed grin.

"Oh!" Ed moved out of the way.

"But, hey," Rick said, reaching for Ed's arm. "When I come out, could I buy you a drink?"

A warm tide of relief swept over Ed, washing away his anxiety. He looked at Rick's hand on his arm, then up at Rick's face. He laughed suddenly, surprising himself.

"Actually I'd like that a lot."

Ed walked, on legs suddenly weak, back to his spot next to the jukebox. He propped himself against the wall and looked for the drink he had left behind on his trip to the men's room. It was gone, probably picked up and discarded by a passing waiter. Oh, well, at least I'll be empty-handed and ready for another when Rick comes back. Rick! The name bounced around his brain in a constant echo. *I am not crazy. He really did look at me the way I think he did. Screw the Publishers Clearing House sweepstakes. I think I just hit the jackpot I really want.*

His thoughts suddenly veered off in another direction. *What if,* he asked himself, *the guy is a creep? Then what? I don't care how cute he is, I am not dating a creep, and I certainly won't get naked with one.* Ed very much wanted to know if Rick was as hairy as he thought he was, but also realized he didn't want to know badly enough to risk spending time with someone who might have the personality of dryer lint or who was overly impressed with himself. After all, most of the guys Ed had experienced were all graduates of the Fuck and Ask Questions Later school of thought. He was an average guy, with the average guy's above-average sex drive, but since the first time he had seen Rick, Ed knew he was looking for something much more than a quick romp.

Rick walked out of the men's room and smiled when he saw Ed. Ed couldn't help but think that even if the guy turned out to be a creep, he had one hell of a nice smile.

"Hi, again," Rick said.

Ed looked into Rick's eyes, and that same electric charge he'd felt the day before ran through his body.

"Can I buy you that drink now?" Rick asked.

"Sure," Ed said, dropping his eyes, embarrassed at the way he had been staring at Rick.

"Tell you what, why don't you grab that last table over in the corner, where it's quiet, before someone else does?" Rick said, pointing. "I'll get us something to drink, and meet you there. What'll you have?"

"Uh, screwdriver," Ed said, looking up again.

Rick's smile now wasn't much more than a small grin, but unless someone had slipped something into Ed's first drink, he could tell Rick was pleased to be with him.

"You got it. One screwdriver coming up." Rick's grin broadened back into his warm smile as he turned to the bar.

Ed stumbled around the pool table to the small, round table Rick had indicated. He pushed aside some empty beer bottles and an overflowing ashtray, then sat down where he could watch Rick at the bar. Ed saw Russ approach Rick, then Rick smiled and shook his head. *Damn! Rick's blowing off the hottest guy in the bar for me?* He found himself shaking his head, as well. *At some point very soon I am going to find myself at home, alone in my old double bed, waking up from this dream.* He looked around the room. No, Rod Serling still wasn't in sight.

Rick brought Ed's drink and his own beer bottle to the table. He pulled out the beat-up chair on the other side of the table and flopped on it with a sigh.

"I tell you, it feels good to sit down after a day on my feet!"

"I can imagine," Ed said, feeling a smile racing across his face.

He couldn't have explained it if he tried, but for some reason he had a sudden desire to holler out loud and dance around the pool table, and Ed was no dancer. Somewhere deep inside of him a big bubble of joy was growing, and he felt its warmth spread though his body much more than the warmth of the vodka from his drink.

"Well." Rick seemed to be at a loss for words. "Uh, how 'bout a toast to, uh, Porterfield?" He raised his beer bottle, looking a bit sheepish. "Sorry. That's all I could think of."

Ed chuckled and raised his glass. They clinked, glass to beer bottle, and drank to Porterfield.

"Actually, it's not a bad toast at all. You are definitely the first person from home I've ever seen here. Sometimes I think I'm the only gay man in that town."

Rick nodded, smiling. "Me too. Moving there was a bit of a culture shock, let me tell you."

"Where are you from?" Ed asked, taking another sip of his drink.

"Indianapolis. Born and raised, and probably would have died there if fate hadn't've stepped in and sent me off to good old Porterfield."

Ed looked at him questioningly.

"Oh, it's a long story," Rick said, settling back in his chair. "How do you feel about long stories?"

"I think I'm up for one." Ed hoped it would indeed be a long story, as it might give him time to calm down.

"Okay! Well, my sister, Claire, lives in Porterfield with her three kids, Judy, Josh, and Jane. Her husband lived there, until recently, when he packed a bag and disappeared one night. Are you familiar with the name Hank Romanowski?"

Ed thought a moment. "Yeah, I remember him. He was about two or three years ahead of me in school, a big, good-looking guy. Kinda rough around the edges," Ed said, not revealing that Hank had been a first-class hoodlum in high school.

"That's Hank. Although *rough around the edges* is putting it nicely. He met Claire when he was doing highway construction work down in Indy. He swept her off her feet, and the next thing you know, Judy is on the way. They got married, and he insisted they move back to his hometown. My parents about died, let me tell you. They're both teachers, incredibly liberal, but when Claire brought Hank home for the first time, I thought they were gonna call the cops. They took my being gay a hell of a lot better."

He caught Ed's surprised look. "Oh, yes, they know. Like I said, they're both liberals, used to march in the antiwar protests and all that. Hell," he said, and chuckled, "they probably would have stood up at Stonewall, if they'd known about it. That's just the way they are. Compassionate to a fault where a cause is concerned, but definitely not where Hank Romanowski is concerned. They smelled him from a mile away. So did I, for that matter, but Claire was pregnant, and determined to marry this guy.

"Funny thing was, things went really well for them for a long time. Claire finished school here in Fort Wayne and got a job as a dental hygienist in Dr Wells's office in Porterfield. She had two more kids, Hank had a decent job doing construction, and it all looked good from the outside. Inside, it was getting ugly. Hank began to cheat on Claire, and his drinking got a hell of a lot worse. Mom, Dad, and I suspected things were falling apart, but Claire wasn't talking. Finally last winter, ole Hank just took off. Jumped in his crappy old Firebird and blew town. No one's seen or heard from him since.

"Well, at first I was all for hiring a private dick and tracking him down, at least so I could beat the snot out of him, if nothing else. But I began to think that Claire was probably a lot better off without him. Mom was all for Claire moving back to Indy, but Claire wouldn't hear of it. She had her job, and she thought the kids had been through enough without having to change towns and schools and make new friends.

"Still, Hank's taking off like that flattened her. I think she'd been through so much already, she just . . . oh, she didn't fall apart, but she was really having a hard time adjusting to being a single parent. We were talking on the phone one night, and she kinda jokingly said she was going to see if they had any openings at the Porterfield post office. At first I thought she was crazy, but then the more I thought about it, the more the idea appealed to me. My nieces and nephew are great kids, and it began to seem like a good idea, me moving up here to help out, as opposed to Mom getting her way and uprooting the bunch of them. Plus, I had my own reasons for thinking a change of scenery wouldn't be such a bad thing.

"Anyway," Rick said, grinning, "to try to make this long story a little shorter, I moved up here in July, got a job at the post office, and began delivering mail on your street about a month ago. Claire's life has suddenly gotten a lot easier, and the kids are thrilled to have Uncle Rick around full-time. It seems to be helping everyone, except my mom, who's now added me to her worry list. But that's nothing new."

"Wow," Ed said softly. "That's quite a story. I mean, that you'd be willing to do that for your sister and her kids. My sister is the greatest, and her kids are okay, but I don't know if I could do that. But then again, her husband's a pretty cool guy."

"There was nothing cool about Hank Romanowski," Rick said flatly. "Look up *asshole* in the dictionary, and there he'll be! Oh, it may seem like some great noble sacrifice I'm making, but for the kids' sake, I'm glad to do it. Besides, you do what you gotta do for the people you love."

Ed's admiration of Rick grew. Nope, the guy was no creep.

"Man," Rick said, looking embarrassed again. "Here I am, hogging the conversation! What about you? I don't know anything about you except your name is Ed Stephens, you live on Coleman Street, and"—Rick dropped his eyes to the table, then raised them to Ed's—"you're awfully cute. By the way, my name's Rick Benton. I just realized I never introduced myself. Hell, I feel like I already know you!"

Ed was blushing from Rick's observation, not to mention the fact he already knew Rick's name, or at least his first one. *My God! He thinks I'm cute. The Dream Man thinks I'm cute.* Somehow Ed managed to get past that to say, rather casually, that Ralph Graham had told him Rick's name in passing.

"I guess I felt like I knew you already, too," he said, looking again into those beautiful, dark brown eyes.

Rick looked steadily back. Ed knew he was not fooling himself. Something was definitely growing between them, not unlike the something currently growing in his jeans.

"I'm a handyman," he finally managed to say. "I used to work for Marsden Electric, but I'm self-employed now. Like it a lot better, too."

"A handyman," Rick said, admiration in his eyes. "Wow! You mean you really go around, toolbox in hand, fixing things for people?"

Ed nodded, a fresh blush on his face.

"How 'bout that? A gay man who can fix things. That is so cool. Well, I know I already kinda said this, but I'll say it again. You have got to be the cutest handyman in Porterfield, Indiana."

Ed's blush deepened, reddening his fair-skinned cheeks. He bolstered his shaky self-confidence and was able to reply, "I know *you* are absolutely the cutest guy who ever delivered mail in Porterfield."

Rick lowered his eyes and smiled. "Thanks."

"How'd you find this place?" Ed asked, to change the subject.

"Oh, Claire told me about it," Rick replied, his gaze once again upon Ed. "Just like my folks, she's cool with the gay thing. I think she's worried about me, since I haven't had much social life outside of her and the kids since I moved here. She all but pushed me out of the house tonight, telling me to have some fun if it killed me."

"You're looking pretty alive and well to me," Ed said, shocking himself at his own boldness.

"You too," Rick said quietly, smiling again.

The bar was getting crowded. Ed noticed a long line of guys waiting for drinks at the bar, and he could just make out the bobbing heads of the dancers in the disco room. "Upside Down" was playing. Ed, who was not typically gay about some things, was definitely a gay man when it came to Diana Ross. He'd loved her since he'd first heard the Supremes on the radio years before. His foot tapped the beat against the floor, and he thought about asking Rick to dance.

"I love this song," he commented.

"Me too."

Rick's smile became bashful.

"I'd ask you to dance, Ed, but I'm not all that good at it. Besides, I'd much rather dance to something slow with you."

At the idea of actually touching Rick, that electric charge went through Ed again. "That would be nice," he said softly. "And don't worry, I'm not much of a dancer either!"

They both laughed. Rick took a long sip from his bottle of beer, and Ed raised his glass to his mouth, surprised to see that the ice had almost melted while they had been talking. He knew beyond any doubt that he wanted to get to know Rick Benton better—hell, a whole lot better—but wasn't sure how to go about it. He didn't want to do anything to offend Rick, and more importantly, he wasn't sure he wanted to rush whatever was happening between them.

"I really like the music they play now," Rick was saying. "But sometimes I miss the music from my high school days, in the late sixties."

"Me too." Ed couldn't help but wonder what else they had in common. "I graduated in 1970. How about you?"

"Broad Ripple High, class of '69," Rick said mock proudly, "which makes me twenty-nine. And you're . . . what? Twenty-eight?"

"Just turned, yes. Porterfield High for me! We had one hundred and seven kids in our graduating class. I'll bet yours was a lot bigger!"

"Oh, yes. I tell you, I can't imagine what it would be like to grow up in a small town, but you know? I really kind of like living there. Everybody's so friendly, especially the people on my route. Why, I can't tell you how many of them have stopped to make conversation while I'm delivering their mail. Hell, that hardly ever happened when I was working on the north side of Indy."

Ed snickered. "Oh, I don't know if they're being friendly or just nosy. There's a lot of *that* in a small town, believe me. Just be glad my mom's house isn't on your route. She'd have your whole life story by now."

Rick laughed, then tipped his beer to his mouth for the last few drops. He set the bottle down carefully, studying it. He looked up at Ed and studied him as well.

"You know, when I delivered that letter to you yesterday, I was really hoping I'd get to see you again. I mean, I told myself I was imagining things, but I just had the feeling, you know?"

"Me too. My friend Glen calls it fag intuition, but I just call it wishful thinking."

Rick laughed again. "Yeah, that's right! But I never, ever guessed I'd run into you here tonight. You didn't get any mail today, you know. I can't tell you how disappointed I was."

Ed, blushing once again, couldn't think of anything to say.

"I think that's why I let Claire talk me into coming out tonight. When I saw you yesterday, it hit me that I'd been awfully lonely lately. So I came here . . . oh, hoping to . . . well, whatever. You know how these places are."

"Yeah, I know. Thing is, I think I came here for the same reason, after seeing *you* yesterday."

Rick looked at him in surprise. "Then it wasn't my imagination? I mean, that maybe it wasn't so much the intuition thing as . . . " He trailed off, looking at the floor.

"Rick," Ed said, thinking how good it felt to say his name, "as far as I'm concerned, it wasn't your imagination."

Rick looked up to meet Ed's eyes. The music was thumping even louder from the disco, Freddie Mercury hollering his way through "Another One Bites the Dust," but Ed was so lost in Rick's eyes he could not have said what was playing.

Rick slowly put his hand on the table, palm up. Ed reached out, tentatively, to take it in his own. He almost gasped when they touched. That electric shock roared through him again. Rick looked at his hand in Ed's, then looked up at Ed.

"Damn," Rick whispered hoarsely. "I wish I could kiss you right now, right this very minute."

"Me too."

But neither one of them moved. They sat, hands lightly clasped, looking at each other across the table. For a moment they seemed to be the only two people in the place, but then someone drunkenly bumped into their table. Rick's empty beer bottle tipped, and his free hand reached out to grab it. He carefully steadied the bottle.

"If I'm going to kiss you, I don't want it to be here," he said to the bottle.

"I . . . I don't know how you'd feel about this," Ed stammered. "But we could go back to my place."

Rick looked up, his face relieved. "I thought you'd never ask."

They both laughed now, their grip on each other's hands tightening.

"After all," Ed said, just as relieved. "We both have to go back to Porterfield."

"This is true. I really want to get to know you, and this just ain't the place to do it."

"Then what the hell are we waiting for? It's a long drive."

The words of "A Lover's Holiday" went through Ed's mind. He wished he could hear the song again. *Geez, I'm really being rescued!*

They both stood up, and Ed reluctantly let go of Rick's hand. Rick immediately put his arm around Ed's waist, and Ed sighed happily. Oh, if this was a dream, it was the most vivid one he'd ever had.

Glen and Mike walked through the door as Ed and Rick were on the way out. Ed slipped his arm around Rick, and both Glen and Mike stopped dead, mouths open in shock.

"I'll call you tomorrow, Glen," Ed said nonchalantly as they passed, his arm firmly around his mailman's waist.

Once they were in the parking lot, Ed waved at his white Chevy pickup. "That's me."

Rick glanced at a worse-for-wear burgundy Monte Carlo. "That's my poor old ride. She don't look like much, but she gets me where I need to go."

"Well, as long as it gets you back to my house tonight, that's all I care about right now. You know where I live, but go around the corner onto Grant Street. That's where my driveway is."

Rick nodded, pulling his keys out of his pocket. "Cool. So, I'll see you in about a half an hour, okay?"

Ed turned to unlock his door, but suddenly turned back to look once more at Rick. He was standing by his car, looking at Ed. They smiled reassuringly at each other, then got into their vehicles.

All the way back to Porterfield, Ed kept glancing in his rearview mirror to see if Rick was still behind him. Ed did his best to gauge the traffic lights so Rick would never get caught on a red without Ed.

Once he was heading south on Highway 401, he had to restrain himself from flooring it because he wanted to be home with Rick so badly, but he kept the speedometer right above fifty-five all the way. Heart came on the radio singing "Crazy on You."

"Girls," he said, "you don't know the half of it!"

The lights of Porterfield finally appeared in the night sky. Ed carefully drove through town and turned onto his street. Rick was still right behind him. As they pulled into his driveway, Ed clicked his garage door opener, then drove the truck into the garage. When he stepped outside the side door, Rick was waiting for him.

"Hi, again," Rick whispered, a warm smile on his face.

"Hi to you too," Ed whispered back.

He led Rick in through the back door, then two steps up to his small but efficient kitchen and dining area, and flipped on the light.

"Can I get you something?" Ed asked. "I think I have some beer, but I know for a fact I have Pepsi."

Rick laughed. "Kindred tastes. Oh, yeah, I took the Pepsi Challenge last summer. I know the difference between Pepsi and Coke."

Ed shook his head in amazement as he pulled two cold cans out of the refrigerator. Something else they had in common, he thought. He handed a can to Rick, who murmured his thanks.

"Well," Ed said, "shall we go sit down?"

Rick looked solemnly at Ed, not answering his question. He carefully set the Pepsi can on Ed's kitchen table.

"You know, I think we have some unfinished business from that place. I don't know if it's right or not, but if I don't get to kiss you, and soon, I'm gonna go crazy."

Ed's Pepsi can joined Rick's. He turned to Rick. Standing this way, he saw for the first time that Rick was indeed taller than him, a good two inches, at least. Ed looked into Rick's eyes, and again that electric shock jolted through him. Ed had kissed his fair share of men, but never before had he seen a man look at him with such longing.

Ed reached out to him, and Rick gently took him in his arms. Ed's arms slipped around Rick, rustling his nylon windbreaker. Their lips came together, tentatively, then with more confidence. Ed's mind began to whirl. He crazily had an image of Sally Field as Gidget, writing about a pretend kiss with her boyfriend Jeff, in her diary. "I sank into nothingness," Gidget had written, and Ed suddenly knew exactly what that felt like. He would have sworn in any court of law this was the first time he'd ever been kissed by a man, because it felt like the first time. His arms tightened around Rick, and he felt Rick's tighten in response. How long they stood there, holding each other, mouths tenderly together, Ed couldn't have said, but when they reluctantly broke apart, it seemed like a lifetime.

They stared into each other's eyes.

"Wow!" Rick finally broke the silence. He smiled at Ed in astonishment. "Oh, I knew that would be worth waiting for, but—"

"I know." Ed was feeling quite weak in the knees. "Man, I gotta sit down."

They both laughed, relieving the tension. Ed helped Rick off with his windbreaker, which he carefully put over the back of a kitchen chair. He led him into the living room, gesturing for Rick to take a seat on the sofa, while he turned on a nearby lamp. He turned back to Rick, who had one arm thrown against the back of the sofa. Ed sat down next to him, and Rick's arm slid down around his shoulders.

"I'm so glad you're here," Ed said, feeling the words were inadequate to what he was feeling. "And I left our pop on the kitchen table."

Rick chuckled. "I don't need it right now. I just need to sit here and pinch myself, like, a hundred times to make sure this is real."

"If this is a dream, I'm gonna be really pissed."

Rick turned Ed's face to his for another kiss. This one was even better than the first, if that was possible. Rick's hand came up to lightly stroke Ed's cheek, and Rick made a soft sound deep in his throat.

The lingering kiss ended, and Rick slid forward, yanking on his jeans. "Sorry," he said, obviously embarrassed as he tried to adjust his crotch.

Ed pulled on his own tight jeans. "I've got the same problem."

"I don't know what to do," Rick said, stroking Ed's mustache. "I honestly came back here with the intention of sitting up all night, talking, but that isn't what I want to do right now. I mean, I really do want to get to know you better, but I also . . . well, you know," he finished sheepishly.

Ed reached over to run his fingers through the dark hair he'd admired for so many weeks. "I know what you mean. I think it's okay, though. I have a feeling you won't be putting on your coat and leaving right afterward."

Rick shook his head. "I'm not going anywhere. You can count on that. Ed, would you please make love with me? Tonight? Right now?"

"Yes."

Ed stood up and put out his hand. Rick took it and pulled himself off the sofa. Ed led him from the sofa, past the stairs, and into his small, but cozy bedroom at the back of the house.

"Boy, am I glad I don't have to work tomorrow," Rick murmured gratefully.

"Me too, Mister Mailman, me too," Ed responded, lifting his head for another of Rick's perfect kisses.

"Cumma, cumma, cumma, cumma, come, come, Mister Handyman," Rick sang softly in a bad—but wonderful to Ed's ears—imitation of James Taylor. "The mailman has a special delivery for you."

⋖☒●☒⋗

"Spent and content," Rick whispered against Ed's ear much, much later. "I don't know when I've felt as good as I do right now."

Ed pulled himself closer to Rick, smiling. "I can answer that question for myself. Never."

Rick sighed. "Oh, Ed . . . Ed, baby, you are something else, you know that? If I would have known about the cutest handyman in Porterfield, Indiana, believe me, I would have moved here long before Hank ran off."

"You really mean that?"

"Absolutely."

Ed toyed with the idea of telling Rick the truth about the phony certified letter, but decided to wait until he knew Rick better, as he was convinced he would soon be getting to know Rick a lot better.

"The first time I saw you at my front door," he said slowly, "I couldn't believe it. I walked out the door and watched you walk down the street, just thinking, 'who is that?' and 'how can I get to know him?'"

"I wish I'd known," Rick said, kissing him again. "Why didn't you holler at me? Why didn't you scream, 'Hey, you, in the blue? I need more than just my mail!'"

"Sheer terror. How was I supposed to know?"

"I know. That's exactly how I felt yesterday, giving you that letter. I was so blown away by you I told myself that you had to be some straight guy, home for lunch, watching the kids, or something."

"No kids here," Ed said, stroking Rick's back. "Just a lonely handyman."

"That's good. I've got plenty of kids at home. And trust me, if you don't want to be lonely anymore, I'd be very, very happy to keep you company."

"I'd like that more than anything in the world," Ed said, sighing with ... relief? joy? amazement? Oh, hell, they all applied. "You know, I'm hoping tonight isn't the only special delivery I get from the new mailman."

"I'll have to check back at the post office, but I think there's another one waiting for you for tomorrow." Rick looked thoughtful. "Matter of fact, I think there's one for the next day, too."

Ed chuckled. "There's no mail delivery on Sunday."

"There is now, baby," Rick said, hugging him. "You can get a special delivery anytime you want."

Ed sighed, thinking that although no manger, stable, or shepherds were involved, a miracle of some sort had taken place in Porterfield that night. The refrain of an old Chicago song went rolling through his mind. *It's only the beginning,* he thought. He knew in his heart this was indeed only the beginning for Rick and himself.

Chapter Three

Ed's clock radio snapped on at ten o'clock. He slowly came awake, trying to push his tired eyes open. He looked around his bedroom in confusion, bleary eyes coming to rest on the clock radio, which was blaring Air Supply's "All Out of Love."

"How inappropriate is that?" he mumbled, reaching to shut it off.

He rolled over, groaning, then smiled as his head landed on the pillow Rick's head had lain upon several hours earlier. Ed had experienced some of his usual weird dreams while he slept, but he knew it was no dream that Rick Benton, the new mailman, had been with him. Rick had left around four, saying he thought Claire and the kids might worry if they woke up and he wasn't home. Ed sniffed the pillow richly, thinking it still smelled of Rick. *Oh, man, you can shake me, but don't wake me from whatever is going on with him and me,* he said to himself happily, paraphrasing an old Four Tops song.

Ed crawled out of bed and reached for his ratty old bathrobe. He wondered if Rick had managed to get any sleep on this Saturday morning in a house that held three kids. He imagined Rick in the room he had told Ed he shared with his nephew, pillow over his head, as a cartoon program blasted from a nearby television. He hoped Rick was getting *some* rest after their long night. Ed's smile became a frown, as he wondered if Rick's rather unique living arrangement would create any problems in their budding relationship. But Rick had promised to return to Ed's house that night around six for dinner and whatever else they may think of to do with the evening. He'd even hinted he might be able to spend the night.

Ed shuffled into the bathroom half-awake, imagining them together the next morning, thinking of his new mailman making a Sunday delivery. He counted the hours until he would see Rick again and knew that the day would not move fast enough. Still, he wouldn't be sitting around waiting. He had promised his sister, Laurie, he'd be over early in the afternoon to install her new dishwasher.

"More plumbing," he grumbled, walking into the kitchen.

He was both tired and excited, and he had no interest in fixing a nutritious breakfast. Half-convinced his mother would fly into the room at any moment, he snuck a Hostess cupcake out of a cabinet and wolfed it down with guilty relish. He grabbed an overripe banana off the counter, then poured himself some orange juice.

He halfheartedly peeled back the banana. When it came to fresh fruit, Ed's imagination seldom went much past bananas. He wasn't all that crazy about them, but found them wonderfully convenient and portable, an easy snack to grab while he was working on a long job.

His thoughts turned to his job and the motley crew of people he routinely helped. Ed's almost boyish shyness, his warm smile, and his easy grace with older folks had made him extremely popular with the senior set in Porterfield. They knew they could depend upon him for the largest of tasks, such as house painting and appliance repair, all the way to the simplest of things, such as oiling squeaky doors and hauling heavy bags of water softener salt. A good deal of what he did wasn't so much fixing as maintaining, and more than one of his regulars had claimed he kept them out of the nursing homes they all seemed to dread. Such remarks made Ed think he was doing his part to make the world a happier place.

He wondered, though, how this remarkable new turn his life had taken would affect his work. Although Ed hadn't specifically told even his own family he was gay, he didn't particularly think of himself as closeted; rather, his up-to-now discreet social life had simply never caused any reason for raised eyebrows. He knew he wanted to spend as much time as possible with Rick and was convinced Rick felt the same way, but Ed was a little uneasy about developing such a relationship in Porterfield, "the Peyton Place of Indiana," as his sister once referred to it. He shrugged it off. *Hell, we haven't even had our first real date, and already I'm worrying. Let it go and enjoy it. Through some unbelievable miracle you got the guy you wanted, and he's coming back tonight, and you are the luckiest guy in the world. Just let it happen, for God's sake!*

By one o'clock he was in his truck, on his way to Laurie's house, determined to keep his thoughts only on the task before him. A good deal more tranquil and affable than his mother, Laurie was just as shrewd as Norma, however, and more than once she had ferreted information out of Ed he had wanted to keep to himself.

He pulled up in front of her comfortable, green two-story home on West Elm Street. Laurie and her husband, Todd, had bought it for a great price at an estate sale. It had been well modernized by the elderly couple who lived there previously, and though it wasn't quite ready for the eighties, it was up-to-date by seventies standards. Ed, who considered his own home not much more than a bachelor pad, was a trifle envious. He wondered what kind of houses Rick liked best, then shook his head.

"You barely know the guy," he snorted, parking the truck. "Get a grip, Stephens!"

Toolbox in hand, Ed entered the house through the front hall. He peered into the family room, where his brother-in-law was parked in his recliner, intent on a televised football game. Todd Ames, a short, dark-haired, attractive man, was usually just as calm and good-natured as his wife, which was an asset to his job as a loan officer at Porterfield First National, but he was looking a bit surly at the moment.

"How's it going?" Ed asked, glancing at the TV.

Todd scowled. "Oh, IU is losing, as usual. Stupid bastards," he hollered at the TV.

Ed, who didn't know a first down from a fourth, merely said, "That sucks," and walked into the kitchen, and familiar territory. His five-year-old niece, Lesley, was running around the kitchen table, whisk broom in hand, dressed in a witch's costume.

"How do you expect to fly anywhere on that?" he asked her.

Lesley paused in her circles and glared reproachfully at her mother, who was taking clothes out of the dryer.

"This is the only broom Mommy will let me have." She approached Ed from behind and slapped his butt with the whisk broom. "I'll get you, my pretty, and your little dog, too!" she screamed, taking off for the family room.

"Lesley, I told you to quit hitting people with that broom! Now go put it away for the rest of the day," Laurie shouted.

Ed looked at his sister, who rolled her eyes at him. "Isn't Halloween still a week away?" he asked her.

Laurie sighed a mother's sigh. "Not around here. It started a week ago, and she'll probably still be wearing that outfit when we carve the Thanksgiving turkey."

Ed laughed as he inspected the secondhand dishwasher Laurie had convinced Todd to buy to replace the old one, which was still under the kitchen counter.

"I made Todd promise to help you haul that thing out back when you're done," Laurie told him.

"Well, first I need to turn the water off. I hope your laundry's done," he said.

"Yeah, this is the last of it. Just let me get some water for coffee, then it's all yours."

When Ed returned from the basement the coffeemaker was going and a glass of Pepsi waited on the counter near the dishwasher.

"Since I knew you were coming, I bought a carton of bottles on sale at the IGA," Laurie said, indicating the Pepsi. "I'm about half-tempted, though, to let you take the rest of it home before the kids, or Mom, finds it. The kids are wired enough as it is, and I can just hear Mom. 'Do you want your kids to spend as much time at the dentist as you did?'"

They both laughed. Ed looked fondly at his sister, just a year and a half younger than himself. Through the mysteries of genetics, Laurie had inherited their mother's short stature, but their father's dark hair and coloring. Ed was even taller than Tim Stephens had been, but had his mother's sandy-brown hair and light complexion.

"I'd be happy to take all the pop you have," Ed said, thinking of his dinner company and the cans of pop he and Rick had never got around to drinking the night before. He turned to the old dishwasher, smiling.

Laurie looked puzzled for a moment, then smiled back at him. Ed was still occasionally surprised at how close they had become as adults. To his recollection, they had passed the years 1961 through 1966 in their own form of the Cold War, speaking to each other only when absolutely necessary, then mostly in threats and demands. He happily settled to work, grateful for his sister's friendship and their collusion together against their mother's bossiness.

"Where's Bobby?" he asked now, noticing he hadn't heard or seen his seven-year-old nephew.

"Oh, he's next door at the Schmidts'," Laurie said, folding towels. "He's totally hooked on that Pong game they have on their TV. I don't get it"—she shrugged—"just bouncing a dot back and forth on the screen, but he loves it. Who cares, though? If the Wicked Witch of the West stays out of here, I may actually get some work done."

Intent on disconnecting the old dishwasher, Ed chuckled, his back to Laurie.

"What's up with you today?" she asked. "No offense, but you look like crap, as though you didn't get any sleep at all, but you're in an awfully good mood."

"Is that a crime?"

"No. But it wasn't that long ago we lived in the same house. I don't recall you being so sunny when you're short on sleep."

Ed sighed. *Here it comes.*

"You have a big night last night?" she asked.

"Oh, I was hanging out with a friend," he mumbled, head under the counter.

They'd never talked about it, but he wondered if Laurie knew the score with him. She'd been friends with some gay guys in business school, and she'd dropped a few subtle hints over the years.

"Aha!" Laurie crowed, pouring herself a cup of coffee. "That explains it. All bleary eyed, but afterglowing all over the place. Is it someone from town?"

"Geez, Laurie," he protested, glad she couldn't see his face.

"Oh, come on," she said impatiently. "I may be a mom, and Norma Stephens's daughter, but I know afterglow when I see it. Heck, I could tell the minute you walked in here. So who is he?"

"Um . . ."

"Oh, Ed, get over it! I had you figured out the minute you broke poor Cathy Carroll's heart. I don't care if it's another guy. Come on! I'm your one and only sister. Details!"

Ed pulled himself from under the counter, sighing. "First of all, I did not break Cathy Carroll's heart. She'd pretty much written me off when I told her I was going into Marsden with Dad instead of going to college. The only reason she hung on to me was for a date to the senior prom. Secondly, I just met this guy, and I don't want to jinx anything. So don't make a big deal out of it, okay?"

Which, unfortunately, piqued her interest even more. "Wow! You mean this is someone special?" she asked, eyes bright.

Ed sat on the floor, resigned to telling her the whole story, which he did, ending with Rick's reasons for living in Porterfield.

"Wow," she repeated, impressed. "I didn't know they made men like that. We go to Dr. Wells, you know. I think his sister has cleaned my teeth. Awfully nice, as I recall. And good at her job. I had no idea she was married to Hank Romanowski. Well, for her sake I'm glad her brother's here for her. And even gladder her brother is here for *my* brother."

"Aw, crud, Laurie, we barely know each other. Don't go picking out wedding presents yet."

"Still," she said, looking at him wisely over her coffee cup. "If the look on your face when you say his name means anything, I have a feeling he'll be around for a while."

Ed's usual blush spread over his face. He returned to his dishwasher chore. "If we're going to be all open and honest here," he said, inspecting the hoses on the new dishwasher, his back to her, "I'm glad you're okay with all this, but what do you think Mom thinks about it?"

She didn't say anything, so Ed turned around to face her. "Well?"

Laurie shrugged. "I don't know. We've never talked about it. Your guess is as good as mine. But I wouldn't worry about it."

Ed stared at her in disbelief.

"Oh, I know Mom's loud, opinionated, and whatever else you want to call her," she said with a sigh. "In spite of it, though, all she really wants, like Dad did, is for us to be happy. You know she's not any Bible-banger. Heck, she hasn't set foot in church since Pastor Garnett had that affair with Mrs. Wheaton. Mom would rather be a heathen than a hypocrite, she always says. I think if you bring a guy to her house who can charm her and who praises her cooking, she won't even notice it's a guy and not a girl."

"Easy for you to say," Ed retorted.

"Yes, it is. But if I was really worried about it, I'd tell you."

Ed took a sip of his Pepsi. "All the same, I'd like to put that off as long as possible!"

"Can't say as I blame you. Poor Todd still has nightmares about the first time I took him home to Mom." She looked affectionately at her brother. "Now, get that thing hooked up and get out of here so you can get ready for your date, okay?"

Ed smiled at her in gratitude. "You know, you're not bad, for a little sister."

"I'm the best damned sister in the world! You get down on your knees and thank God you got me, ya hear? And you can just tell this Rick Benton for me that he'd better be good to you, or he'll have me to deal with."

⊰•⊱

The phone was ringing when Ed entered his house later that afternoon.

"It's about time you got home," Glen complained when Ed answered. "Why didn't you call me, and who was that last night?"

Dragging the phone with him, Ed threw himself on the sofa. "I'm sorry I haven't called, but I was at Laurie's, putting in her new dishwasher. And as for that guy last night, he was"—Ed paused dramatically—"the new mailman!"

"What?" Glen squawked. "You said he was straight."

"Well, when I'm wrong, I'm wrong," Ed said, taking great pleasure in smugness.

"Are you shitting me? What's going on in that town anyway?"

"Look," Ed said, stretching out on the sofa. "I wasn't at all sure when he came to the door Thursday, and I knew if I said I thought that *maybe* he was one of us, you'd have me chasing him all over town, and I didn't want to do that. He just happened to walk in there last night, we just happened to bump into each other, and it just so happens that he likes me as much as I like him."

"Well, slap my ass and call me Anita Bryant. Ed Stephens with a boyfriend! The eighties are definitely starting off with a bang. And in that town! Christ! Did you move to the Magic Kingdom or something? Are you still in *Porterfield*?"

"I was when I woke up this morning," Ed said, still smug.

"My God. You saw the guy, you wanted him, and you got him. That's unreal. Maybe I should move to Porterfield."

"Problems with Mike?"

"Oh, no. But, Ed, things like this don't happen very often."

"I know. I still can't believe it. It's like a dream."

They were both silent a moment, then Glen asked, "So when are you seeing him again?"

"Tonight."

"God!" Glen sighed, stunned once again into silence.

"Listen, Glen, I really need to get ready for him. He's coming over later. Can I call you back this week?"

"You'd better," Glen shouted. "I want every last horny, dirty detail. I may even drive out to that stupid town to see you. This is better than *All My Children*."

Ed hung up the phone, knowing he'd just experienced a first: He had managed to impress Glen Mercer into silence. *Things are definitely changing around here. My knight in shining blue cotton is really coming here again.* He looked at his watch. Only three-thirty. Crud! He still had over two hours before Rick was due to arrive.

He pulled himself off the sofa and looked critically around the room, wishing he was Samantha Stephens instead of Ed Stephens and could make it immaculate with the twitch of a nose. On the other hand, Rick seemed to be quite easygoing, and living in a house with three kids, he was probably used to a little dust and clutter. Still . . .

Ed tracked down a dust cloth and made a half-assed circuit of the living room furniture. He then hauled a battered old Hoover out of the kitchen closet and pushed it around for a few minutes.

"Good enough," he mumbled.

He looked at his watch again. Well, he'd used up a whole twenty minutes. Now what?

He'd already decided to have a pizza delivered for their dinner, as Rick had mentioned he liked pizza as much as Ed did, so he didn't have any food preparation to do. He didn't know what they would end up doing all evening, besides eating, talking, and—he let out a big sigh—maybe repeating last night's lovemaking in the bedroom.

He went to his record cabinet and pulled out an album of Carly Simon's greatest hits. Soon "Anticipation" was pouring out of the speakers. He paced around the room, wondering if Carly Simon had ever felt this nervous and excited about James Taylor. He couldn't imagine that anyone who was cool enough to write "You're So Vain" ever felt as dorky as he did. As Carly sang about how right it feels to have her lover's arms around her, Ed remembered exactly how it felt the night before with Rick's arms around him.

He shook himself back to the present. *Just look at you,* he told himself sternly. *It was bad enough you were channeling Gidget last night when he was kissing you, but now you're* acting *like Gidget. You may be queer, but get a grip already.* He laughed, a loud happy laugh. Oh, what the hell. Even if things crashed and burned with Rick, he knew he'd always remember how he felt right now. It was a grand feeling, and Ed decided to enjoy it.

He dreamed through two sides of Carly Simon, then decided it was late enough to hit the shower. It would be his second shower of the day, but he wanted to be as fresh as possible when Rick arrived. He scrubbed himself with a worn-down bar of Dial and joyfully butchered "Anticipation."

Ed wiped the steam off the bathroom mirror, then carefully studied his face. What on earth did Rick see in him? The same old Ed Stephens looked back at him, and all Ed could do was shrug at himself. He didn't know what Rick saw, but Ed was just glad Rick saw something.

"Son of a gun," Ed whispered to himself, switching from "Anticipation" to "You're So Vain." Hell, Carly could have James Taylor, and she could have Mick Jagger singing backup for her. Ed didn't envy her. He was more than content with the idea of Rick Benton coming to see him.

Towel around his waist, he went into his bedroom and wasted a few more minutes deciding what to wear. Rick seemed to enjoy the whole handyman thing, so Ed dressed as he usually did, relieved that Rick didn't seem to have any more fashion sense than he did. He glanced at the clock radio. Almost five-thirty. He dressed slowly, then wandered into the kitchen to help himself to some of the Pepsi Laurie had sent home with him. How was he going to survive these last few minutes?

He took his pop into the living room and wondered what kind of music Rick would like to hear. They seemed to have about the same tastes, but Ed wanted something special playing when Rick arrived. He flashed back to the night before and his thoughts of Chicago's "Beginnings." Perfect, he thought, substituting Chicago's greatest hits for Carly's on the turntable. He was about to place the needle on the record when he saw a burgundy car round the corner and enter his driveway. Rick! He looked at his watch, and smiled. Ten minutes early, even. Maybe Rick was anticipating the evening as much as Ed was. Ed dropped the needle carelessly on the record and hurried to the kitchen window.

"Carly," he muttered, watching Rick reach for something on the passenger seat. "Take your anticipation and get the hell out. He's finally here!"

Chapter Four

Ed moved away from the kitchen window before Rick could see him. He didn't think Rick needed to know just how anxious Ed was about the evening ahead. He crept back into the living room, where Chicago was playing. "Make Me Smile" was the first cut on the album side, and Ed was indeed smiling.

He heard a polite knock on the back door. He closed his eyes and took a deep breath before he walked slowly to the door. He opened it, and there was Rick, looking just as wonderful as he had when he had left Ed's place very early that morning. Rick was smiling over—Ed could not believe it—a bouquet of roses. Needless to say, no one had ever given him flowers of any kind before. Right then and there he threw in the towel and decided he didn't care how feminine it might be; he was deeply touched that Rick would spend his hard-earned money on something so romantic for him.

"For the cutest handyman in Porterfield, Indiana," Rick said bashfully, handing him the seven deep-red roses done up in green florist's paper.

"I'm . . . I'm blown away," Ed said, taking the flowers. "I mean, thank you. I'm just so surprised."

Rick grinned, obviously pleased at Ed's response. "I hoped you would be. Since this is kinda our first official date and all, I wanted to do something special."

"It's very special," Ed said, brown eyes glowing. He felt like some silly-ass beauty contest winner. Hell, all he needed was a crown and scepter. He laughed. "I don't even know if I have a vase for them."

Ed laid the roses on his kitchen table, then turned back to Rick, who was dressed as casually as Ed had hoped he'd be, in a faded IU sweatshirt and jeans. Ed didn't care if he ever saw the guy in a suit. Rick couldn't possibly look better than he did at that moment.

"You know," Rick said, a mischievous look in his eyes, "I had another motive with those flowers. I was hoping they might buy me another kiss from you."

Ed found himself grinning at Rick. "Just one?" he teased. "How about one for each rose?"

"Mmm," Rick moaned, taking Ed in his arms. "I like the way you think, Mr. Stephens."

Ed wasn't sure just how many kisses those roses bought for Rick. He lost count somewhere way past seven. The evening, he decided, was getting off to a very good start. At some point Ed managed to free his mouth long enough to ask if Rick was hungry.

Rick chuckled. "Well, actually, I'm starved. I haven't had much to eat today. Do I remember you promising pizza?"

"I sure did," Ed said, reluctantly letting Rick go and heading for the phone. "I'll call Gino's. They probably know the way to my house blindfolded."

Once the pizza was ordered, Ed poured Pepsi for both of them and got Rick settled comfortably in the living room. Ed then scouted around for a vase for the flowers. Much to his surprise he found something appropriate in the basement, obviously left behind by the previous owners.

After arranging the flowers and placing them on the kitchen table, Ed joined Rick in the living room.

"I hope the pop is okay. I've got something stronger if you want it."

"Nope," Rick said. "Pepsi is perfect with pizza, and I don't drink all that much anyway."

"Me neither," Ed said, again struck by how much they seemed to have in common. "Ever since I barfed all over the interior of my friend Ted's car in high school, I've never been able to get too excited about it."

"For me it was a New Year's party in college," Rick said, sneaking an arm around Ed's shoulders. "I felt so shitty that New Year's Day, I vowed I'd never get that bombed ever again. I knew a lot of guys who drank too much in Indy, too. It really kind of turned me off the whole thing."

Ed was curious about those Indy guys, but figured he'd hear about them soon enough. "I'm glad you like pizza," he said, changing the subject. "I'm not much of a cook, and frankly, I would have been a nervous wreck, trying to make dinner for you!"

Rick threw his head back and laughed. "Oh, man, don't worry about it. Hell, I'm so glad to be here you coulda given me a baloney sandwich and I would have been happy. Besides, I think pizza is about my favorite food.

Well, next to breakfast. I do like a good breakfast. I cook a pretty mean breakfast, too."

Ed looked shrewdly at him. Was that a hint about spending the night? "I think I have some eggs in the refrigerator."

"Would you like me to make you breakfast in the morning?" Rick asked coyly.

"If that means you'll be here between now and then, yes."

A look of relief passed over Rick's face, and his arm tightened around Ed's shoulders. "Man, I was hoping you'd say that. All day I was thinking about how much I hated to leave you this morning, and how much I wanted to fall asleep next to you."

"Tonight's the night," Ed said, smiling at him.

"Everything's gonna be alright," Rick said, reading Ed's mind.

Ed shook his head in amazement. Anyone who knew the Top 40, past and present, well enough to throw that line out was okay in his book. The whole thing was getting downright spooky. *I'd better watch it, or I'm gonna start looking for all the flaws.* He was sure Rick had some, but Ed just didn't want to know what they were yet.

"I'll have to go get something out of the car, though, before then," Rick was saying.

Ed looked puzzled.

"Oh, just my glasses," Rick said sheepishly. "That was another reason I had to leave this morning. My contacts were killing me."

Ed chuckled. He was glad to know Rick was self-conscious about something.

By the time they were settled at the kitchen table over a Gino's Special—everything but the anchovies—they had both begun to relax. Food had a way of doing that, Ed had learned over the years. After the edge had been taken off their appetites, they began to talk, filling in the blanks of each other's lives.

Rick was curious about what growing up in a small town was like, so Ed told some stories, some funny, some not so funny.

"I had a lot of friends in high school," Ed said. "Oh, I wasn't popular, but the other nerdy types liked me well enough. We had our own little gang, and I think it helped us get through. I was really grateful to them, but at the same time, I thought I was the only guy in the world who felt like I did. I remember guys talking about 'queers' and 'fags,' but I never really put it together. Once I did, I felt even lonelier, wondering if I was going to have to spend my whole life lying about how I really felt. I remember being so scared someone would figure it out. I lost track of almost all of those guys I ran around with back then. It was easier to let them go than tell the truth."

Rick toyed with a pizza crust on his plate. He looked up at Ed. "Did you ever think about killing yourself?" he asked bluntly.

Ed looked back at Rick. A bond that can only be understood by two gay men began to form between them. "Yes," he said quietly. He didn't need to say anything more.

Rick sighed. "Well, I didn't have a lot of friends back then. I was a bookworm with big, thick glasses, and pretty much everyone left me alone. Plus, I had to cope with being the younger brother of Claire Benton, one of the most popular girls at Broad Ripple. I just assumed everyone thought of me as Claire's loser brother."

Ed looked at him in surprise. "You were unpopular in school? Man, that's hard to believe."

Rick laughed, but there wasn't much joy in it. "Oh, yes. Just looking at this pizza here reminds me of Claire's favorite nickname for me back then: Pizza-face. I had horrible zits and wanted to wear a ski mask to school. Nothing I tried seemed to help. The money I wasted on Clearasil! Then there was the fact that I was so tall. Everyone thought I should go out for basketball, but there was one problem with that: I hated it. I wasn't tall and graceful, just tall and awkward.

"I remember going for long walks around our neighborhood late at night, when I thought no one could see me, just thinking about how lonely I was, and that no one else in the world could possibly feel the way I did. I also had a sneaky feeling that I liked boys a hell of a lot more than girls, and believe me, that didn't help.

"I remember the summer after graduation. My parents all but forced me into the car and dragged me down to Bloomington for my freshman year at IU. They told me about a million times that college would be better, and sure enough, they were right. Not at first, though. I was miserable through that first semester, but eventually I got to know some people, and for the first time I felt like I fit in somewhere."

"How did you end up in the postal service?" Ed asked.

"Well, I lasted two years at IU as an English major," Rick said, getting up from the table to refill his glass. "For someone who read as much as I did, it seemed appropriate. But I didn't know what I wanted to do with it. I didn't want to teach, like my folks, and I never really had any ambition to write. The summer after my sophomore year, when I'd survived the draft lottery, I took a summer job doing vacation fill-in for mail carriers at one of the Indy post offices. I loved it! Those long walks I mentioned? Well, this was just like that, only I was getting paid for it. I loved being outside, being on my own for most of the day. When I was offered a full-time job, I just stayed. My parents about died, let me tell you, but eventually they came around when they saw I was doing what I really wanted to do.

"Too, I was still struggling with the whole gay thing, and more than anything I wanted to be on my own to figure it out. I had my own job and my own apartment, and I think I really began to learn just who Rick Benton was. Oh, that wasn't the end of the story. I had some big screwups ahead of me, but at least I was alive, living my life. For a long time I wondered if I'd make it that far."

Ed nodded, chewing on his pizza. "Yeah, I remember feeling like that. When I got laid off at Marsden I moved back in with my parents. Geez, what a disaster! When I had the handyman thing going well, I bought this place, and it was a lot better. That's when I started sticking my nose out of Porterfield, looking to see if there were any other guys like me around. It was such a relief, too, to be out of that factory. I mean, there I was Tim Stephens's boy, and no one messed with me too much, but I could just imagine them all finding out I was a fag. I don't think I would have survived it."

"Yeah," Rick said. "I've been pretty lucky with the postal service. Oh, it's no gay-friendly place, but I've always gotten along well with everyone, and no one's ever given me any grief. Plus, the rest of my body finally caught up with my height sometime in college. I began to realize that most guys won't mess with a big, tall guy. Thank God for stereotypes! Why would anyone think a six-feet-two, two-hundred-pound guy who doesn't swish when he delivers mail would be queer?"

They both laughed.

"You had me fooled," Ed said, reaching for more pizza. "I had to see you in that bar last night to know for sure."

Rick shook his head. "Oh, me too. When I saw you coming out of the restroom it took me a moment to figure out who you were. I mean, surely that sexy guy with the certified letter *couldn't* be gay. No one I reacted that strongly to could be interested in me."

Ed was blushing as badly as he had the night before. Fair skin can be a real bitch sometimes. "You really thought that?"

Rick nodded. "Walking my route the rest of that day, I kept thinking, if that guy would be gay, moving to Porterfield would be totally worth it. And you are. And right now it is—worth it, I mean." Rick dropped his eyes from Ed's. "I barely got any sleep at all this morning. I couldn't stop thinking about you, and how much I wanted to see you again. Hell, I was ready to come over here about two hours early. I drove around town, wasting gas, until I thought I could show up without looking too eager."

Ed laughed, thinking of his afternoon spent with Carly Simon and all the anticipation. "Considering the afternoon I put in, I wish I'd known."

Now they both laughed, and whatever pretense had been left between them fell away. Ed knew two people seldom get to that point so quickly, but whatever fates had thrown Ed and Rick together continued to bless them.

They continued to talk, the pizza growing cold on the table before them. Rick told Ed about his ex-lover, Jack.

"Oh, I thought I was grown-up when I started that disaster, but I found out I was still pretty young and stupid." He recounted the relationship, a story that both horrified and fascinated Ed, who'd never experienced anything like it. "It went on for about two years before it was finally over. But he would still drop back into my life from time to time. That was the other reason I thought a move to Porterfield would be a good idea. It's a lot harder for him to find me here."

When Rick talked about Jack, a shadow of doubt fell across Ed's mind. The pain in Rick's face was too obvious to miss, and Ed wondered if this Jack was someone he had to worry about. The doubt faded, though, when Rick, done with his story, looked at Ed. It was also obvious that Rick was here in the present with Ed, and very happy about it.

Rick insisted on doing cleanup. He told Ed he could have his turn the next day after breakfast. Rick moved around the kitchen foreign to him with a casual assurance Ed almost envied. He wondered when that tall, awkward teenager Rick had told him about had vanished, leaving behind this strong, confident man.

Ed went into the living room and put on Elton John, a request from Rick. He was glad to be away from Rick for a moment. He had thought he was in love with the new mailman when he didn't know a thing about him, but now, watching this man washing dishes at his sink, Ed thought the cliché "falling head over heels in love" suddenly made sense. *It's just infatuation,* he scolded himself. *This is going better than anyone could have hoped, and you're just overwhelmed by it. You've know him only about twenty-four hours. Get a grip, Stephens.* Oh, he could scold himself all he wanted, but Ed knew he had forgotten about the fantasy mailman and was beginning to feel something strong for the real-life Rick Benton.

The domesticity of the evening probably had something to do with it as well, Ed thought. They weren't sitting in some restaurant, awkwardly watching their words, being interrupted by a waiter. They were at home—Ed's home, of course, but still at home—and it felt natural. This was one of the rare times Ed had experienced having a man he barely knew in his home, and it was also the first time he felt completely comfortable with the situation.

Dishes done, Rick joined Ed in the living room.

"This is nice, just hangin' out," Rick said, making himself comfortable on the sofa next to Ed. "I'm glad we decided to do this instead of going somewhere."

"You still look a little tired to me. I may have to put you to bed early tonight."

"I don't have a problem with that," Rick said, one arm around Ed, the other hand tracing the stripes on Ed's flannel shirt. He nodded to the stereo. "I'm sorry, but Elton's got it wrong tonight. *This* Saturday night is alright for lovin', not fightin'."

Ed snuck one hand under Rick's sweatshirt.

"Mmm, you like your men hairy, don't you?" Rick untucked Ed's flannel shirt and T-shirt and snuck in a hand of his own. "Me too! I can't tell you how good you feel."

"You can try."

"The hell with talking. I'll just show you!" Rick squeezed Ed underneath the shirts. Rick's sigh sounded contented, but to Ed's eyes he looked a little troubled.

"Is something wrong?" Ed asked.

Rick pursed his lips, looking at the ceiling, but didn't say anything.

"If something's bugging you, I wish you'd tell me."

Rick shook his head. "No, nothing is wrong, really. I'm just wondering, though . . . Ed, what we did last night, is it okay with you?"

"What do you mean?"

Rick shifted on the sofa, taking his warm hand away from Ed's chest. "Oh, the fact that we had barely met and I was dragging you off to bed. I feel a little bad about that. I just didn't want you to feel that was the only reason I was here."

"You didn't exactly drag me."

"I know. But I didn't want you to think I was just one of those bar guys, looking for nothing but sex. I went there last night because I was lonely, and tired of being alone. I hadn't counted on running into the cutest handyman in Porterfield, Indiana. I was so excited about meeting you, I couldn't wait to spent some real time with you outside of that place. So what did I do the minute we got back here? Said 'Let's do it,' and had your clothes off in no time! I really did want to get to know you, and still do. More than you know. But when we kissed last night . . "

"Hey, I was there. I felt it, too." Ed ran his hand in lazy circles across Rick's chest. "I also seem to recall saying something about the fact that I wasn't worried about you running off afterward. I wasn't, and I'm still not worried." He sighed. "I know what you mean, though. It's so easy to just grab some guy and go for it. I've done that. But last night was different. And by the way, you didn't say, 'Let's do it.' You said, 'Will you make love with me?' There's a big difference. If some other guy had said that, I probably would have laughed, but I knew you meant it. I knew our sharing that was just part of getting to know each other. I didn't want to wait, and I don't regret it."

"Just a couple of horny guys doing what comes naturally," Rick said lightly, then sighed. "Ed, I just wanted to be close to you so badly. I don't remember a time I wanted to be with someone so much. Thing was, it wasn't about the sex; it wasn't about being horny. I just wanted to be with you, and I guess that's how we've been programmed to respond to a desire like that. Get naked and do it."

"I think you're being a little hard on yourself," Ed said tentatively. "Do you wish now that we had waited?"

Rick looked thoughtful for a moment. "I really don't know. A part of me wishes that, yes, we'd waited awhile. I knew when we got back here last night that I'd be seeing you again, seeing you as often as you would let me. Then again, I feel so much more comfortable with you tonight, and I think part of that is because of what happened last night. I know how beautiful you are, in and out of your clothes. I don't have to worry about whether we'd be okay together in bed. I know we are, and I'm looking forward to the next time, whether it's tonight or . . . hell, whenever."

Ed did some thinking of his own. "I think maybe all that waiting jazz is overrated. I think we get confused, trying to play by the straight rules, then trying to play by the gay rules. I felt a connection between us last night, and I was ready when you asked. I've been awfully lonely myself, you know." He shrugged. "I'm just a simple handyman. I can't figure it all out. I do know this, though. When it comes to tonight, the thing I'm most looking forward to is just being with you all night, knowing you don't have to leave, and you don't want to leave. Is that wrong, too? Should I send you home like Ann Marie used to do to Donald Hollinger on *That Girl*?"

Rick laughed. "I loved that show. I'm so queer!" He laughed again. "I always wondered about those two, if they ever did it. Oh, hell, I give up. What's that old song, something about 'if loving you is wrong, I don't want to be right?'"

"Well, I think he was singing about having an affair even though he was married, but I get your point," Ed said, grinning at him. "I sure hope you stay, though. I'm feeling greedy. Now that I've got the mailman in my arms, I don't want to waste any time I get."

Rick looked at Ed, shaking his head. "I don't have that kind of willpower. I'm afraid you're stuck with me for the night." His hand returned to Ed's side, and he leaned over for a kiss.

"Did anyone ever tell you that you are the best kisser in the whole world?" Ed asked him.

"No, baby, I'm the runner-up. *You're* the best kisser in the whole world."

"Maybe you don't get good at it until you're kissing someone you really want to kiss," Ed murmured, "and I think it will be a very long time before I get tired of kissing you."

"Me too, baby, me too," Rick said, proving it.

The record ended on the stereo. The tonearm lifted off and silently glided to the side of the turntable.

"Do you want to hear something else?" Ed asked in the sudden silence.

Rick was about to answer, when he glanced at his watch. He shook his head in disbelief. "Do you realize that we have not even officially known each other for twenty-four hours yet?"

Ed grabbed Rick's arm to look at his watch. "Aw, that can't be. I feel like . . . like . . ."

"I know," Rick said, kissing him again. "I gave up believing in magic when *Bewitched* went into reruns, but I think someone put a spell on us."

"It must have been Uncle Arthur," Ed replied, snickering. "I always thought he was a big fag."

Rick roared with laughter. "Must have been," he hollered. "Oh, but I sure am glad, baby."

"Hey," said Ed, still laughing. "You didn't answer my question. More music?"

Rick shook his head. "No. I don't need it. You were right about one thing, I really am tired. I'd love nothing more than to just go lie down and hold you next to me. I have a feeling I'll sleep a lot better than I did this morning."

"Well, don't forget your contacts," Ed teased him, "and those glasses in the car. I don't want you tripping and falling over something in the night."

Rick joined Ed in the bedroom a few minutes later, looking self-conscious about the glasses he was now wearing.

"Talk about male vanity! I don't know what you're upset about. You look just as good with glasses." Ed reached up and traced the wire-rimmed frames. "Actually, they make you look even sexier, if that's possible."

Rick shrugged. "Those high school scars run deep. That's all I can say." He watched Ed take off his flannel shirt, then pull his T-shirt over his head. "You know, I meant what I said. We don't have to—"

Ed put his hand over Rick's mouth. "Stop worrying! Look, if something happens, it happens. Right now I am getting undressed to go to bed, to lie down with my new boyfriend, 'cause I want more than anything to go to sleep in his arms." He took his hand away. "Is it okay I called you my boyfriend?"

Rick pulled Ed to him, stroking his bare back. "It's an honor to be your boyfriend. Off the top of my head, I can't think of anything else I'd rather be right now."

Rick undressed for bed, then they made themselves comfortable in Ed's old creaky bed.

"I think it's only fair to warn you," Rick said, his face against Ed's neck. "I snore."

Ed rolled over to face Rick. "Now you tell me. Get the hell out! I've changed my mind."

Rick smirked at him. "I'm not going anywhere."

"Well, thank God for that." Ed kissed him.

They both laughed and settled down again. Now that he was lying down, Ed had to admit to himself that he was tired, too. The day had been long, with a lot of emotion. He was about to reach over and turn out the light when he felt Rick stir beside him.

"Good night, Ed. And thank you."

"Thank you?"

"Yeah, thank you. For being my new boyfriend, too, and for just being you. Not only are you the cutest handyman in Porterfield, Indiana, but you're the nicest as well."

Ed looked at Rick and couldn't believe how sweet and vulnerable he looked without any visual aid. Ed decided to keep that information to himself for the time being, though. "Good night, Rick. Thanks for being the nicest mailman in Porterfield, Indiana."

Ed turned out the light. He lay down, and Rick's arms enclosed him once again.

Ed had never been scared about living alone or sleeping alone. Weird noises in the night seldom bothered him, and he never worried about burglars. Just the same, falling quietly asleep in Rick's arms, he felt safer in his own home than he ever had before.

Chapter Five

Ed carefully pulled the old comforter he used as a bedspread over the rest of the covers, making them even. It had been given to him by one of his clients, and the blue and white stripes were faded from age, but Ed loved it because it was, well, comforting. He couldn't imagine having some perfect, designer spread you were afraid to sit on across his bed, as Glen did. Ed firmly believed that a bed, along with everything else in one's house, should be as comfortable as possible.

He paused by the bed a moment, listening to the sounds of Rick making their breakfast in the kitchen. It was a weekend of firsts, all right. Ed had never had a man spend the night, and he certainly had never had a man eager to make breakfast for him.

Ed was a little ashamed to admit to himself that the few brief relationships he had experienced had been based on restaurant dinners, recreational activities, and a good deal of sexual satisfaction. No wonder his life had begun to seem so empty. He sent a quick prayer to the heavens for sending Rick to him, who had made it quite clear that he wanted their relationship to be deeper and stronger. Ed recalled one of his clients—a calm, thoughtful woman named Hilda Penfield—telling him once that life usually sent a person what he needed when he was ready for it. He thought he was ready for what seemed to be developing between Rick and himself, at least he hoped he was.

"Grub's up!" Rick hollered from the kitchen.

Rick had carefully set the table with what passed as good china and flatware at Ed's place, mostly castoffs from his mother. Last night's roses were strategically placed in the middle of the table, but off to one side so the two men could see one another. A cup of steaming coffee sat by Rick's plate, but for Ed, who'd never acquired a taste for the stuff, a glass of orange juice from the carton in the refrigerator waited.

"Wow!" he said in appreciation.

Rick looked bashfully pleased. "Well, I did the best I could. I guess I've been at Claire's so long I've forgotten what it's like to make a meal in a bachelor's kitchen. And, baby, if I'm going to spend any more time around here, we've got to get you a coffeemaker. I don't deal well with this instant stuff."

Ed laughed, contemplating more Sunday mornings like this one. "I've never had to worry about it before. But I think I can track one down. Hell, I'll even buy the coffee for it. This looks great. Thanks!"

Rick spooned eggs onto Ed's plate. "Well, it's not much, but I found some cheese to grate in the eggs. Even found a cheese grater, much to my surprise. Ed, don't you cook here at all?"

Ed reached for his juice. "Oh, sometimes. The cheese grater is for when I make spaghetti. My mom brainwashed me into believing that parmesan out of a can is poison, and if the cheese isn't fresh grated, it ruins the sauce. Her sauce, I should say. From scratch. If she found a jar of spaghetti sauce in my fridge, she'd probably throw it at me."

"Your mom sounds like a real character," Rick said, sitting down.

"Well, that's one way to look at it," Ed said, tasting the eggs. "Oh, this is good! I can't believe you pulled this together in my kitchen. Anyway, Mom takes great pride in her cooking. She has me over for at least one meal a week, then loads me down with leftovers, so I'm usually just finishing one batch when she dumps more on me. I had good intentions of becoming a better cook when I moved here, but with all her good food around, I've gotten lazy."

Rick, buttering a piece of toast, chuckled. "I'm no chef, but I know my way around a stove. I got sick of the McDonald's–Burger King routine when I was living alone, so I learned to how to feed myself. My mom, bless her heart, has many talents, but I wouldn't call cooking one of them."

"Well, this is really good," Ed said, savoring eggs better than anything he'd ever scraped out of a skillet. "You can make breakfast for me anytime."

"Then remind me to hit the grocery store before I come over here again." Rick laughed.

"Did you sleep okay?" Ed asked.

"Not too bad. Did my snoring keep you awake?"

"Just a little bit," Ed answered, not wanting to admit having someone else in bed with him might take some getting used to, even if it was Rick.

"I guess we're even then," Rick said. "Do you know you thrash around when you're dreaming? You slapped me right across the head about four this morning."

"I did? I'm sorry!"

Rick grinned at him. "I'll live. I just wondered who you were mad at. Hope it wasn't me."

Ed thought for a moment, but none of last night's dreams came back to him. "I know it wasn't you. Probably one of my crabby clients."

Rick wanted to know about his clients, so Ed described a few.

"I'm impressed," Rick said. "You know, you really provide a great service for some of those old folks. They're really lucky to have you."

"It works both ways," Ed said, pleased at Rick's words. "I'm lucky to have *them*. They keep me out of that factory, and keep a roof over my head."

After breakfast had been eaten, and the kitchen put to rights by Ed, he saw Rick glance at his watch. Ed's stomach tightened. He knew Rick would have to leave at some point, but hoped it wouldn't be so soon.

Rick took Ed in his arms for a hug and sighed. "I guess I'm good for a couple of hours at least, if you want me hanging around. At some point I'm going to have to go home. The kids think I'm having a 'sleepover' with a friend, which they think is very neat, but I've got homework to check before tomorrow."

"You check their homework?"

Rick chuckled evilly. "Oh, yes. It's my way of getting revenge on Claire for making fun of me for being a bookworm in school. I never pass up an opportunity to make her look stupid. I have a long memory, and revenge is sometimes very sweet."

"Aw, and here I just thought you were some kinda saint."

"They don't come any more human than me, baby," Rick said, kissing him.

They settled on the sofa for more conversation.

"We can go somewhere if you like, but there's not much to do in Porterfield on a Sunday afternoon," Ed said apologetically.

"No, this is fine. It'll be noisy when I get home, and tomorrow's Monday, so I'm content to just sit here, getting to know you better, and maybe kissing you every five minutes or so."

"Five minutes? Can't you whittle that down a little bit?"

Rick heaved an exaggerated sigh. "Just became my boyfriend last night, and already he's making demands on me. Shit!" He wearily pulled Ed to him for a lackluster kiss.

Ed pouted. "You can do better than that. I know you can."

Rick smirked at him. "I know I can, but be careful what you wish for, baby. I could get you into all kinds of trouble this afternoon."

"I'll take my chances," Ed said, smirking back at him.

By midafternoon Rick was looking at his watch every fifteen minutes, and Ed knew soon he'd be in the house alone.

Finally Rick not only looked at his watch, but stared at it, groaning. "Oh, I don't want to go. But I have to, I really have to." He looked at Ed with affection. "I've had a great time, baby, absolutely great. I can't wait to do this again, but duty calls. If nothing else, I'll see you tomorrow afternoon."

"You will?" Ed asked, puzzled.

"Of course! When I deliver your mail. I'm still your mailman, you know."

"Oh," Ed said, laughing. "I'd forgotten. That all seems like such a long time ago. Well then. I'll make a point to be home around that time, okay?"

"Okay. That will give me a chance to see what disasters are brewing at home, and then maybe we can make some plans." Rick looked carefully at Ed. "This whole thing I've got going, living at Claire's, helping with the kids, does it bother you?"

Ed shook his head. "No. I think it's great. When you told me that whole story the other night, I knew right away that you were a good guy. I don't think very many people would do what you're doing."

Rick shrugged that off. "Maybe. Thing is, now that I have my very own handyman boyfriend, I intend to spend as much time with him as I can, when I can work it in, between checking homework, making peanut butter sandwiches, and playing Candy Land."

"I'll be here," Ed said, smiling at him.

Rick grabbed him and pulled him across the sofa for a kiss that was anything but lackluster.

"Thanks, baby. I'll make sure the cutest handyman in Porterfield, Indiana, gets as much attention as I can give him."

After Rick left, Ed contemplated the nickname Rick had begun to use for him more frequently as the weekend had progressed. "Baby," he mumbled to himself. Rick had first called him that Friday night, and by Sunday afternoon, it had almost entirely replaced "Ed."

Ed, who'd never been called anything but Ed, Edward, or Eddie, wasn't quite sure how he felt about it. He certainly preferred it to jerk, asshole, or loser—all names thrown at him and the other unpopular kids in his school days. He also knew he liked it a lot better than fag, homo, or fairy—names he feared would be hurled at him from time to time. Still, even if he was rather puzzled at the idea of being someone's baby, he knew Rick meant only the greatest of affection when he used it, and for that reason alone, Ed thought he was beginning to have a sneaking fondness for it.

He thought of all the songs he liked with the word *baby* in the title: "Baby Love," "Baby, I Love You," "Baby, I Love Your Way," to name just three. If being Rick's baby meant Rick was beginning to love him, then it was okay with Ed.

He wished he had something similar to use for Rick, but nothing came to mind. He'd never call Rick "honey." He knew too many gay guys who called each other that. Ed's brow furrowed as he tried to think of something appropriate, but he finally decided that if a term of endearment existed for how he felt about Rick, it would come to him, as Hilda Penfield would say, when he was ready for it.

◈

Ed spent a busy Monday morning running from one small job to the next, but made it home by lunchtime. Since he was free for the afternoon, he decided to go back to the chore he had started exactly one week ago, raking leaves. Could it have been only a week ago, he thought, that he was plotting to meet the new mailman while raking leaves? He lightheartedly carried his rake to the front yard, amazed to think that the new mailman was now his new boyfriend.

Does Rick like me as much as I like him, or am I in a coma somewhere, dreaming this whole thing?

The day was cool, but no rain had fallen since Wednesday, so the leaves were light and easy to rake. Ed blessed a nice breeze blowing from west to east, making it even easier to rake them onto Grant Street for city pickup. Ed loved the smell of burning leaves, but the town council had outlawed leaf burning within the city limits. He felt vaguely cheated now each autumn. It didn't seem fair to go to all that work, then not have a bonfire. He put on his work gloves, then settled in for a long afternoon of raking, pausing occasionally to see if Rick was coming.

Rick appeared a half hour later. Ed watched him approach, and was pleased he now knew what the mailman looked like without the uniform. Rick raised a hand in greeting, smiling as well.

They met at Ed's front walk, and Ed found himself automatically reaching for Rick, but stopped, suddenly aware they were outside. Rick noticed and looked uneasy.

"Hi, Ed."

Ed looked around, wondering if anyone was watching. The Hendricksons, next door, were a middle-aged, empty-nest couple who both worked full-time, but Mrs. Van Vleet, across the street, was probably home. The cranky old broad had never availed herself of Ed's services, telling him once with a sniff that she had a son for that sort of thing. Considering how run-down Mrs. Van Vleet's house was, Ed didn't have too high an opinion of either her or her son.

"Can you come inside for a minute?" Ed asked, feeling as though curtains were being pulled back in every house on the street to watch them.

Rick nodded, then followed Ed up the front walk. Ed took one quick glance across the street, but then remembered that Mrs. Van Vleet would be glued to her tube, more interested in the small-town doings on *As the World Turns* than what was happening right outside.

Once inside, Rick dropped his mailbag and immediately grabbed Ed for a bear hug and a kiss. "Mmm, I've been looking forward to that all day."

"You and me both," Ed replied, kissing him again. "Any chance I might get to have an extra mail delivery tonight?"

Rick looked uncomfortable. "I kinda doubt it. I'm really sorry, baby, but this whole week is pretty much screwed for me with family stuff." He shrugged helplessly. "How did I know before last Friday night I'd have better things to do? There's a lot going on, and the kids are all excited about Halloween. I promised to take them trick or treating Friday night. The weekend is messed up, too. I have to work Saturday, and I promised Claire I'd stay home and watch the kids that night so she could go out with her girlfriends."

"Oh." Ed was disappointed. He didn't know what to say.

"I promise to call you every night, though. And we can do something on Sunday. I have the whole day free, just for you, if you want me." Rick looked as though he thought Ed would tell him not to bother.

Ed realized how guilty Rick felt. Ed gave him a reassuring smile and another kiss. "Sunday it is. That gives me something to look forward to all week."

Rick looked somewhat relieved by that, but still worried. "It won't always be like this, I promise. But all this stuff came up before we met. If you want, I'll come over early on Sunday and make you breakfast again, and we can spend the whole day together."

"I'd like that. Don't worry about it, okay? You're worth waiting for."

Rick seemed unconvinced. "I'm glad you think so." He tightened his grip on Ed. "But if I was some other guy, you wouldn't have to—"

"Stop that! I don't want some other guy. I want you. This is all still really new, and we'll figure it out. *Please* don't worry. I'm cool, okay?"

Rick looked at him quietly for a moment, then broke into a broad smile. "You're something else, baby. My gut told me you were something special, and it was right." He kissed him again. "Thanks for understanding."

Ed changed the subject. "So about this trick or treating. What kind of costume will you be wearing? Your postal uniform?"

"No, I think I'll just dress up as the handyman's boyfriend. That's my favorite costume right now. Do you want us to stop by your house?"

Ed shook his head. "I probably won't be here. Mom'll probably call and insist I come over and help her hand out cookies. She makes a ton of them, and all the kids on this side of town know about it, so it gets a little crowded at her front door." Ed rolled his eyes. "The costumes give her fits. I always have to explain to her who Darth Vader is."

Rick laughed, and Ed was glad to see him back to his usual self. "I'll call you this evening, I promise." He gave Ed one last hug and kiss. "But now I have mail to deliver."

Ed reluctantly let him go. Rick returned to his route, and Ed returned to his yard full of leaves.

He'd been hard at it for another hour when he saw Laurie's car turn into his driveway. He dropped his rake, grateful to take a break.

"Hey, you," he called, as she slammed her car door and started across the yard toward him.

"Hey, yourself," she said, kicking away the leaves. "You wanna come do my yard?"

"Hell, no," he retorted. "Get your husband to do it."

"Yeah, right," she said, meeting him under the maple tree in his side yard. "I'll probably end up doing it myself." She took a deep breath of the autumn air, opening her arms to the breeze. "It was so stuffy at work today. This feels great." Laurie worked part-time as a secretary in a law office downtown.

"What brings you over this way in the middle of the afternoon?"

"I left work early to pick up Lesley from kindergarten. I have to take her for a checkup, so since I had a few minutes, I wanted to stop and see how you are and how your weekend went."

Ed blushed, and Laurie giggled with delight. "Oh, you still blush as good as you did when we were kids. Hmm, I guess the weekend went pretty well."

"Yeah," he mumbled, looking at the ground.

"Good, I'm glad." She looked fondly at her brother, who was smiling at the ground, shuffling the leaves with his work boots. "You're really stuck on this guy, aren't you?"

"Is it that obvious?" he asked, looking up.

"Yeah. I don't ever remember seeing you like you are these days." She sighed. "Oh, Ed, I can only imagine how hard it's been for you all these years, so I'm really glad you're having a good time with Rick. Just be careful, though, okay?"

Ed looked surprised. "What do you mean?"

"I mean it's okay to think you're in love and all that romantic stuff, but don't get too carried away until you've known him for a while. Make sure he's all you think he is before you get too serious about it."

"When did you get to be Ann Landers?"

"Since I've been watching my high school girlfriends getting divorced, that's when. I sat and watched my friends all get married right out of high school to guys that weren't ever going to be anything more than they were in school. I vowed I wouldn't do it, but look what happened: I met Todd and we got married before I was even through secretarial school. I was lucky, 'cause Todd's a genuinely good guy, but some of my friends are still dealing with regret, and kids they have to raise on their own."

As a breeze blew more of the yellow leaves off the tree, Laurie sighed again. "I don't care if you're gay or straight, relationships are hard work, and let's face it: I've got eight years experience to your zero. So, yeah, I feel qualified to give you advice. Be as crazy about him as you want to be, but give it time to grow."

"We don't exactly plan to run off to Vegas or anything," he grumbled.

"Look, don't get all defensive. I'm just playing sister here, because I strongly suspect you don't have anyone else to talk to about this, or at least anyone who cares enough about you to be as honest as I am. Give it time. Eventually you'll either get tired of him, or you'll find out how much you really care about him."

Ed sighed. "You're right. I guess I am feeling a little carried away by the whole thing. I wish you knew him, though. You'd see why he's worth getting carried away over."

"Bring him by the house sometime. And don't worry about Todd. I'm sure he won't have a problem with it. One of his cousins in Chicago is a lesbian, so it's nothing new to him."

"I'll do that," Ed promised. "That is, when I get over wanting him all to myself."

Laurie rolled her eyes. "Oh, brother. You've got it bad. Okay, you do that, when you start getting bored enough to remember you have a sister. Meanwhile, I've got a date at the pediatrician with the Wicked Witch of the West. I hope she doesn't try to slap his ass with a broom, too!"

⋘•⋙

Rick did call that night, and they spent a half hour on the phone, just talking.

"At least I'll be able to see you every day when I drop off your mail," Rick said.

"Not tomorrow," Ed said sadly. "Mrs. Heston has me for the whole day. After I deal with her groceries, I'm spending the rest of the day raking her leaves, after I spent all afternoon today on mine. She's even making lunch for me. Can you believe that? A seventy-nine-year-old woman who uses a walker is making *me* lunch. You gotta love the old girl."

"How many other yards do you have to do?"

"None. Oh, I try to make it clear to them that I'm not a lawn service. If I raked and mowed and pulled weeds for all of them, I'd never get anything done, but Mrs. Heston is special. I probably wouldn't have this business if it wasn't for her support in the beginning. I know she won't tell anyone else about it, either. I'll shovel their snow in the winter, but they're on their own the rest of the year."

"Well, I'm disappointed I won't see you tomorrow, but I'll call you tomorrow night," Rick said before hanging up.

◆

The week passed quickly, a lot faster than Ed expected. They had brief visits when Rick delivered the mail, and phone calls in the evening, but Ed couldn't wait to spend some serious time with Rick. As good as his word, Rick hauled a bag of groceries into Ed's house Sunday morning and made a huge breakfast that Ed thoroughly enjoyed.

"Is there anything special you want to do today?" Ed asked him, clearing the table. He groaned. "Oh, I ate too much. But it was wonderful, every bite."

Rick patted Ed's belly. "Nothing like a well-fed handyman. Oh, there's nothing really special I'd like to do, but I was thinking about something."

"What?"

"I was thinking it would be fun for you to show me Porterfield, or at least the Porterfield you know. Where you went to school, the house where you grew up, that sort of stuff."

Ed snickered. "A tour of Ed's Porterfield. That should take about five minutes."

"Okay. How 'bout this? After that five minutes we can drive out in the country, find a deserted road, and neck for a while. What do you think?"

"You mean, like we were in high school or something?"

"Yeah! I never got to neck with anybody in high school. I'd love to pretend I was in high school, and you were my boyfriend, and we were sneaking around behind everyone's backs. I always felt like I missed something."

Ed paused at the sink, staring out the window. He turned to Rick and smiled.

"I know just the place."

"A cemetery?" Rick asked in disbelief. They were in Ed's truck, sitting on a narrow gravel road several miles west of Porterfield. He looked through the wrought-iron gates of the small, country cemetery and frowned. "I was picturing a cornfield or something. Cemeteries we have in Indianapolis."

"First off, city slicker, if you were paying any attention to the scenery, you would notice that all the corn has been harvested and we've passed nothing but fields full of stubble. Secondly, this isn't just any cemetery." Ed put the truck in gear and drove through the open gates. "Up here by the road is the modern part, but back behind that hill is the old part. All the graves are from the 1800s, and no one ever goes back there. You can't see it from the road because of the hill, and the trees hide it on the other three sides. We used to come out here in high school to drink and smoke and act like idiots. It's perfect. You'll see."

Ed drove past rows of tombstones, over a gentle rise in the land, and below them was an old, tree-shaded graveyard.

"My great-great-grandparents are buried back here. That's how come I've always known about it."

He parked the truck behind a tall, spreading pine tree. When he shut off the engine the only sounds they could hear were a couple of feuding crows and the wind in the trees.

Rick looked around, taking in the leaning tombstones, their engravings almost worn away, and the sheltering trees. He nodded, smiling. "You were right. It's perfect. I'll never doubt you again."

Ed reached out a hand to him. "How about you slide over here a little closer to me, huh? It's kinda cold out there today."

Rick obliged, sliding across the seat, kissing him when he was by Ed's side. "Man, this is great. I really feel like we're in high school, hiding out here from everyone."

Ed turned the key to accessory so they could listen to the radio. "Well, if it's high school, I sure wish I could hear some Guess Who or Blood, Sweat and Tears or something," he said.

Casey Kasem, one of Ed's radio favorites, was counting down the biggest hits in the land for that week. Casey was up to the Devo song "Whip It" and described why the group wore flowerpots on their heads. Ed punched his other FM presets, but the sounds of 1980 were dominating the airwaves.

"You need a cassette player in here, baby," Rick murmured, kissing him again.

"Well, come to think of it, all we listened to back then was AM."

Ed switched the radio. He dialed past a football game and a church service, then to their great joy and surprise, landed on the Beach Boys' "Good Vibrations."

"I love this song," Rick said. "Remember *Pet Sounds*? I had that album. I think someone stole it from me in college. Now, this is more like it. I always wanted to make out with a cute guy to this song."

"I'm right here."

Ed moved closer to Rick. They blissfully indulged in some serious high-school-style necking through the Beach Boys, the Mamas and the Papas, and Del Shannon. They had stumbled onto a Sunday afternoon oldies show on a weak AM station from the next town over.

They both sighed when the Four Tops came on with "Baby I Need Your Loving."

"Oh, baby, I do indeed need your lovin'." Rick ran his hands under Ed's sweatshirt, kissing him hungrily.

Ed kissed him back, just as hungrily. He reached for Rick more aggressively than he had allowed himself for over a week.

Rick moaned, saying, "Are you sure, baby? Here and now?"

"It's okay. Our parents don't know where we are. And I've spent a whole week dreaming about being this close to you."

The world outside of Ed's truck faded away. The old songs washed over them from the static-filled AM radio signal as they did things they could only dream about when those songs were new.

Later, as they huddled together by the steering wheel, Ed started the motor to get the heater going. They had created quite a bit of their own heat, but the sky was clouding over, the wind was blowing harder, and it was becoming much colder.

"Almost seems like it's going to snow," Ed remarked, watching the gray clouds racing across the sky.

Rick sighed and snuggled closer to Ed. "Baby, being with you is so incredible. It was worth waiting for all this week. Oh, I could have snuck out of the house, gone to your place for a half an hour, but that would have just been some physical thing. This afternoon, right here, was the real thing. I'm so glad I found you."

It was on the tip of Ed's tongue to say "Me too, Rick," but the Beatles song playing on the radio caught his ear. "Me too, darlin'," he said, as "Oh! Darling" fought through the radio static.

Rick smiled. "Good old *Abbey Road*."

"Remember all the 'Paul is dead' rumors?"

"Just because we're parked in a cemetery is no reason to talk about death," Rick said, still smiling. "And anyway, am I really your darlin'?"

"Yes." Ed kissed him. "And I'm your baby, right?"

"Absolutely," said Rick, returning the kiss.

The air blowing from the vents warmed Ed, but not as much as the words they spoke. As light snow began to fall over the long-neglected cemetery and they sat together quietly, serenaded by the songs of their past, Ed thought of their future together.

Chapter Six

The following Tuesday, Election Day, Rick was making his regular early afternoon stop at Ed's.

"Let the rest of the world have their coffee breaks." Rick squeezed his handyman. "I've got me a kissin' and huggin' break."

"Considering how I feel about coffee, that's fine for me," Ed said, squeezing back. "But you know, darlin', if you want, now that I have that coffeemaker, I could slip you a cup every afternoon."

Rick sighed with regret. "That would be great, but I don't think it's such a hot idea. I'm pushing it as it is, stopping here almost every day. Oh, there's nothing wrong with saying hello to a friend while I'm on the job, but I don't want anybody beginning to notice, if you know what I mean."

Ed nodded. He knew exactly what Rick meant. "Anyway," Ed said, not wanting to dwell on any potential disapproval of their growing relationship, "I won't be home tonight, so don't bother to call. Mom's invited me for dinner so she can have someone to bitch to about the election. I'll end up hanging around there, keeping her from throwing something at the TV when Indiana goes to the Republicans, like it always does."

"Democrat?" Rick queried, eyebrows raised. "I would have guessed the opposite."

"Oh, no. Not my family, or my mom's family anyway. The Beales go way back around here, all the way to those graves I mentioned the other day at the cemetery. They're all hard-core working-class types, and they have no use for Republicans. Why, my grandparents were so devoted to FDR they had a picture of him in their living room. Mom's brother, my uncle Chester, says that if you don't know who to vote for, vote Democrat, and you can leave the booth with a clear conscience."

"Well, just don't tell your mother I'm voting for John Anderson today. I like the idea of someone challenging the two-party system, but there is no way in hell I'd vote for Reagan."

"I voted this morning, for Carter. If I had voted for anyone else, I'd be cut out of the family."

"Man, they'd love my folks then." Rick chuckled. "Well, if we ever get to the point of showing up together at family gatherings, I don't have anything to worry about then."

Ed looked at Rick, but didn't say anything. At this point, the idea of anyone in his family other than Laurie knowing about Rick made him uneasy. Although Ed tried to hide it, Rick apparently noticed his discomfort.

"Oh, don't worry about it, baby. I'm just talking. I will say, though, I'm kinda planning on being around for a while, so it may be something we have to deal with. My folks are no problem at all, of course. I already know they're gonna think you're great. But what about your mother? Will she think I'm great?"

Ed shrugged, looking away. "I don't know. Laurie's dying to meet you, so that's no problem, but Mom? Right now, I'd like to *keep* you around, so maybe we can put that off for a while, okay? I don't want her scaring you off."

Rick laughed, hugging Ed again. "I'm not scared. Hell, after hearing about her, I'm looking forward to meeting her. She can't be too bad. After all, you turned out pretty good."

"Just let me get through tonight first, okay?" Ed said nervously.

"Yes, sir. No more family talk, I promise. I'll see you tomorrow, same time, same place. Is it a date?" Rick asked with a kiss.

"I'll be here," Ed said, smiling at his mailman, still amazed this dream was in progress. "And I'll stock up on hugs and kisses, just for you."

⋰•⋱

Ed tried to keep his thoughts away from Norma's possible reaction to his relationship with Rick when he joined her for dinner that night. He sat at his usual place at her dining room table, happily serving himself his mother's stew and fresh baked biscuits. Looking at the brimming serving bowl, he knew he'd be eating stew for the rest of the week.

Norma Stephens bustled into the dining room with butter for the biscuits. She was a short, slender woman, her hair the color of Ed's, although Ed suspected it was quite gray under the Miss Clairol. At fifty-one, middle age was creeping onto her face, but Norma fought it as much as possible. "Just because your father's gone is no reason for me to let myself go," she often said.

Tim Stephens had died two years earlier at the tender age of fifty, the victim of a heart defect he'd never known he had. Ed missed his gentle father, missed the time they had spent together in Tim's basement workshop, and his never-ending patience with his children. Norma's occasional overbearing personality had always been counterbalanced by Tim's quiet understanding, and his wry sense of humor with Norma had always let Ed and Laurie know they didn't have to take her too seriously.

Why Norma and Tim had been so compatible was still a mystery to Ed, but he knew, despite whatever Norma might say, that she missed him as much as Ed and Laurie did.

"Eat up, eat up," Norma commanded, as she always did. "There's plenty. I'll have some for you to take home, unless I decide to take the whole pot downtown and throw it through the door of Republican headquarters. Oh, I know those smug so-and-so's. Probably whooping it up as we speak, convinced they've got that second-rate actor elected. Honestly. I can't believe how stupid the people of this state are, or this country. Didn't anyone ever see any of his movies? He can't act. Why would anyone think he's fit to run the country, or even a garbage truck? Old, too. He needs to be put out to pasture."

Ed smiled. He enjoyed his mother's harangues when they weren't directed at him.

"Why, he ruined *Dark Victory* for me. Imagine, putting that flop of an actor in a movie with Bette Davis! What was Jack Warner thinking? I cannot to this day watch that movie, and I've seen every other movie Bette Davis made at least twice."

"You forgot *What Ever Happened to Baby Jane?* You didn't see that one twice, Mom."

"Humph," she sneered. "That wasn't a movie, that was a horror show. I meant Bette Davis when she was *Bette Davis,* not the mess she is now. Well, I'll say one thing for her: At least she's not dumb enough to think she can run the country." She narrowed her eyes at Ed. "You voted today, didn't you? For Carter?"

"Oh, Mom. Of course I did. Would I be sitting here eating your stew if I hadn't?"

"Just checking," she said, giving him a suspicious look.

After dinner they moved into the living room to watch the election returns on the big color console television on which Ed had, years before, watched the first moon landing. When it became apparent that Ronald Reagan would indeed take office in January, Norma slapped the arms of her chair.

"Well, that's that. Fools! Didn't anyone learn anything after Nixon and Watergate? Why, this country won't be fit to live in four years from now."

Ed slowly counted back in his mind. "Mom, you've lived through, by my count, at least three Republican presidents. I'm guessing you'll survive this one, too."

"Sleazy money-grubbers in ugly golf clothes, all of them. Nothing but a bunch of greedy old men," she grumbled. "And it's four. I know you. You forgot Hoover."

Ed gave up. Norma could not be pacified tonight.

"You're taking this awfully well," Norma said, eyes upon her son. "Why, if your father was here, he'd be agreeing with me."

"Like he'd have a choice."

"Watch your mouth. Seems to me you've been in an awfully good mood for quite a while now. The way you were moping around after your birthday, I was beginning to wonder if you were having some silly man's problem, worrying about getting old or some such nonsense."

Ed shrugged, trying for innocent nonchalance. "I'm not worried about anything, and I am in a good mood these days. I've always liked this time of year, with the leaves changing and all. You know that."

"The leaves are almost gone, Edward," she said, beginning to zero in on him. "Most people get depressed in November."

"Well, you always said I was different from everyone else."

"Humph. Sometimes I wonder," she said, still looking at him intently. "By the way, where were you Sunday afternoon? I tried to call three different times and you weren't home."

Ed commanded himself not to blush, thinking about what he and Rick had been doing at that time, not far from his ancestors' graves. "I was hanging out with a friend. Do you have a problem with that?"

"Who with?" she demanded. "That character from Fort Wayne who uses hair spray?"

Ed had to smile at Norma's description of Glen. "No. Just a guy I've gotten friendly with here in town. Actually, he delivers mail on my street. We got to talking one day when I was out front, raking leaves." The white lie came easily.

"A mailman! Not one of those drunken hooligans your father used to play cards with?"

"Oh, Mom. Dad's friends were not drunks. I never saw Dad have more than three beers in his life. You just resented the fact that he was off somewhere having a good time without you. And, no, this guy is new in town. You know I haven't really had any friends around here since all the guys I knew in high school moved away, so I'd think you'd be glad to know I have someone to hang out with sometimes."

He knew Norma couldn't argue that fact, but she still found something to throw at him. "New in town, you say? Why on earth would anyone move here to be a mailman?"

Ed sighed, and told her about Rick's family.

"Romanowski," she exclaimed, scandalized. "Why, that family was nothing but trash. This town is well rid of that Hank Romanowski, I'll tell you. He was probably stealing hubcaps when he was still in diapers. What was this man's sister thinking, marrying him?"

"Not everyone gets lucky in love, Mom." He shifted uncomfortably in his dad's recliner. He had forgotten Norma would have some choice words for good old Hank.

"There's unlucky, and there's stupid," she grumbled. "Oh, well. Good riddance to bad rubbish. At least this woman is trying to raise her children right. I guess I'll just have to meet this Rick, this friend of yours, though. He's either a decent, good man, helping out his family that way, or an absolute fool. I'm not sure which."

"Rick *is* a good man, Mom. It's been a pleasure getting to know him. I've enjoyed having someone to buddy around with lately."

Norma looked thoughtfully at her son. "Nothing wrong with men getting together, doing men stuff, I suppose."

Ed sensed something more behind her words, but decided to ignore it. "Well, if nothing else, he hates the Republican party as much as you do."

Norma's eyes lit up. "That doesn't surprise me one bit. A man who'd be good enough to help raise his sister's children couldn't be a Republican. You bring this Rick over for dinner some night, you hear?"

"Yes, Mom," he said obediently, hoping that night was still a long way in the future.

⊱●⊰

Wednesday evening, after a bowl of Norma's leftover stew, Ed went digging in his record cabinet. It was an especially nice cabinet, a product of Tim Stephens's basement workshop. Noticing that his son spent most of his allowance and lawn-mowing money on records, Tim had built the cabinet for Ed's thirteenth birthday. It was big and sturdy, with two sliding doors on the front and designed to hold a large number of the 45 rpm records Ed had bought almost compulsively well into adulthood. Other boys may have had sports, but Ed had the music he heard on the radio. He often thought his business kept the downtown Woolworth's record department thriving through the sixties and seventies.

In recent years, Ed had gotten into the habit of listening to albums, but the music he had heard Sunday afternoon with Rick had whetted his appetite for his older records. He had tuned in that low-power radio station several times since, mostly catching farm reports and Andre Kostelanetz records. The oldies show they'd heard must have been a Sunday-only program.

The cabinet now held one small row of 45s, records Ed had purchased since he had moved into his house, but albums took up the rest of the space. He scooped up a stack of albums and carried them upstairs to his storage area, then returned to the cabinet, staggering under the weight of a cardboard box overflowing with 45s. He happily began to paw through them, murmuring to himself as old favorites appeared. Setting some aside to play, he carefully arranged others in the cabinet. He couldn't find "Good Vibrations," but the Four Tops were well represented, and soon "Baby I Need Your Loving" was pouring out of the speakers.

He leaned back against the cabinet, sighing, replaying Sunday afternoon in his mind. Oh, he totally understood the yearning in Levi Stubbs's voice now. Ed felt so damned lucky he had found Rick. He was almost overwhelmed by the joyful companionship and the growing intimacy between them. He'd never been so excited by, yet so completely comfortable with any other person before.

He listened to the powerful, haunting song and remembered all the years he'd been alone, doing his best to ignore the loneliness. Thinking of Rick, thinking of how quickly he found himself caring deeply for Rick, brought tears to his eyes.

"I wish I could tell him that I love him," he whispered to himself. "But I know it's too soon. It's too soon to say it, too soon to know for sure. But I do, I know I do."

The phone rang, interrupting his thoughts. Sure it was Rick, he leapt to his feet, answering the phone with a cheery "Hello!"

"Hello to you, stranger." Glen sounded rather annoyed. "So busy with your mailman you've forgotten your friends?"

Glen's tone, and his words, made Ed feel a little annoyed himself, especially since he was hoping for Rick. "I have to pay for every call I make to Fort Wayne," he said coldly. "I'm trying to keep the phone bill down."

"Well, if you got a real job, you wouldn't have to worry about it," Glen said, all snippy now. "I don't seem to have a problem calling *you*. How is the great postal carrier anyway?"

Ed's annoyance grew. "I do have a real job. Just because I don't get dressed up and spend the day in some office doesn't mean I don't work, or make enough money to live on. And as I recall, when you first started seeing Mike, I didn't hear from you for over a month."

"Touché, touché." Glen was laughing now. "I give up. You made your point. C'mon now, really. How's it going?"

Ed felt only partially assuaged. "It's going very well. Rick and I are having a wonderful time."

"That's not what I meant, and you know it."

"I do?"

"Yeah, I want the real dirt. What's he like in bed?"

Ed snorted. "Like I'd tell you."

"*I* tell you."

"Well, I'm not telling you. And, no, Glen, I'm not gonna tell you how big it is, either. If you want to blab all the gory details of your sex life, that's your business, but I don't feel comfortable sharing that stuff with other people." He went to the stereo and turned the volume down.

"Okay, so be that way. My God, it must be love, if you're acting all secretive and protective," Glen said crankily. "What are you listening to, anyway?"

"The Four Tops, and if it *is* love, I'll let you know!"

"Four Tops? Are *they* still around? Well, anyway, I think I need to meet this Rick. Why don't the two of you come into town Friday night? The four of us can have dinner together."

"The four of us?" Ed asked, stalling for time. Four meant Mike was involved, and Ed wasn't sure he was up to an evening with Glen's young, arrogant boyfriend.

"Well, of course. It'll be a double date. We've both got men now, so we should start doing couple-type things."

Ed admitted to himself that spending the evening with another couple could be fun, but doubted the fun factor of this particular group, seeing as how one of the members—Mike—had a tendency to start every sentence he uttered with "Oh, please."

"I'll have to ask Rick. He may not be free on Friday night. We haven't talked about it yet."

"Why wouldn't he be?" Glen wanted to know.

Ed hadn't bothered to fill Glen in on Rick's family situation, knowing what kind of response he was likely to get.

"You tell him I won't take no for an answer. We'll meet you at North Side Fish Market at seven, okay?"

"North Side *what*?"

"Oh, Ed, you are so out of it. It's the coolest new restaurant in town. It's where Martino's used to be. You remember that place. I'll make a reservation, 'cause they're always packed on the weekends."

"Do they have anything other than fish?" Ed asked with suspicion.

"Oh, for God's sake. Grow up, Ed. You're a gay man. Learn to eat like one."

"Where in the gay rule book does it say you have to eat fish to be gay?" Ed demanded.

"I just mean you should be willing to try new things, expand your horizons a little bit. God, you need to get out of that town."

"Yeah, like Fort Wayne is the gay mecca of the Midwest."

"Maybe it isn't, but it's a big step up from Porterfield. And, yes, I suppose they have a piece of steak or two in the kitchen for guys like you."

Ed sighed. Until he met easygoing Rick, it hadn't really occurred to him how pushy Glen could be. "Okay, but I have to talk to Rick first. I'll call you tomorrow night, okay?"

"Think your phone bill can handle it?" Glen sneered.

"Yeah. I'll just rob one of my old ladies' cookie jars tomorrow!"

"*That's* the Ed I know," Glen said, pleased. "I look forward to hearing back from you."

Aw, crud, Ed thought, hanging up the phone. *First Mom and now Glen. I'm going to be so busy hauling Rick around to meet people, I won't have him to myself at all.*

⋰•⋰

Ed carefully pulled his truck into a space of the crowded North Side Fish Market's parking lot that Friday evening. The fact that he was dressed up and about to have an expensive dinner in a fish restaurant with Glen's snotty boyfriend, *and* the fact that Rick was amused by it all, was making him rather irritable.

"It's not gonna be that bad, baby," Rick said, squeezing Ed's hand. "If this guy is as affected as you say, we'll just have something good to laugh about all the way home."

Inside, Ed told the hostess barricading their way into the dim dining room that they were meeting friends. He spotted Glen and Mike sitting next to each other in a booth, facing the entrance. Glen raised his hand for a discreet wave. Ed's eyebrows rose a bit as he took Glen's and Mike's appearance in. They both had their hair swept back from their foreheads in the current style, and as Norma would be quick to point out, a good deal of hair spray had been used to achieve it. They were dressed much the same as well, both wearing pastel dress shirts and skinny black ties.

"Man! What do we have here, the Doublemint twins?" Rick asked under his breath.

Ed snorted with laughter, then tried to compose himself as they walked to the table.

Greetings and introductions were passed around as Ed and Rick slid into the other side of the booth. Ed noticed both Glen and Mike checking Rick out, obviously more impressed than they were willing to let their faces show. Feeling a bit smug, Ed opened his menu and scanned past a multitude of seafood entrées, looking for something a good meat-and-potatoes guy could enjoy.

A slim young man with a gold stud in one earlobe glided up to their table. "Hi, I'm Craig, and I'll be your server tonight. How are you gentlemen this evening?" he asked, with a lingering look at Rick.

Ed found himself experiencing his first attack of possessiveness. "We're just great, Craig." He moved closer to Rick, making sure Miss Thing with the earring noticed.

Server Craig ever so slightly raised his eyes at Ed, but maintained his let's-all-be-friends demeanor. He went into a long description of the night's specials, kidded with them while taking their drink orders, then left for the bar, saying, "I'll be right back with those, boys."

"Geez," Ed mumbled.

"When did waiters get to be servers?" Rick wondered.

"Oh, please. Servers work in fine restaurants, waitresses and *waiters* work in diners," Mike said, sniffing.

"Do tell," Rick said, smiling at Mike's pretension.

"It's an eighties thing," Glen said with a shrug.

"If I wanted a friend, I'd buy a dog," Ed said, watching Craig at the bar, who was still eyeing Rick. "At a restaurant, I just want someone who can get the food on the table without spilling it in my lap."

"Oh, please," Mike said. "Servers take their jobs very seriously, trying to make sure you have the best culinary experience possible. That's what dining in a fine restaurant is all about."

"Then I suppose the potential size of the tip has nothing to do with it," Rick said, laying his menu down. "Although, I have to admit that salmon he mentioned sounds pretty good."

"I think I'll stick with the prime rib," Ed said.

Glen sighed. "So what else is new? Well, go ahead, get your prime rib, but if you don't stop glaring at that queen you probably *will* get it in your lap."

"How are we supposed to share a good bottle of wine if Ed gets red meat?" Mike whined.

"I'll just drink my Pepsi—no, make that *Coke,* according to our buddy Craig—and you three can split the wine," Ed said, moving his perturbed look from Craig to Mike.

Mike snorted with impatience. Glen looked amused by his boyfriend. "Now, be nice, Mike. Ed's just a small-town boy, and if he wants to stick to what he knows, that's his business."

Mike nudged him. "I *told* you I want to be called *Michael* now."

"Sorry, hon, I forgot," Glen said, looking at him affectionately.

"Well, since *Edward* here is driving, I think it's fine if he sticks to pop, but I'd be happy to take a glass of whatever wine you suggest, Michael," Rick said, winking at Ed, who tried not to laugh.

Mike/Michael looked balefully at both of them, then turned his attention to the wine list.

Ed felt a strong kick from the devil on his shoulder. "Are you even old enough to drink?"

Rick almost choked on his water. Glen looked distressed, but Michael merely gave Ed a frosty smile.

"My ID says I'm twenty-five."

"Better watch out," Rick said teasingly. "They'll be calling you a troll before too long."

Michael looked horrified at the very notion.

"He's just joking," Glen said soothingly to Michael. He turned to Ed. "Your mailman's quite a cutup, isn't he? I'll bet he had some laugh when you told him about that phony letter I sent you."

Ed gave Glen a stricken look. He still hadn't told Rick about the scheme he had engineered to meet him.

Rick looked questioningly at Glen. "What are you talking about? What letter?"

Glen's mouth opened in surprise. "You mean he hasn't told you yet? Ed, you rascal, I was sure you would have confessed to that by now."

Ed found himself blushing a deep, fiery red. Michael put aside the wine list long enough to smirk at him. Rick, though, was still looking at Glen, not comprehending what he was saying.

"That certified letter," Glen explained, chuckling. "That was from me. Ed called me and asked me to send him a certified letter so he'd have an excuse to talk to you. At the time I thought it was kinda stupid, but it certainly has paid off, hasn't it?"

Ed was ready to crawl under the table. Server Craig reappeared at that moment, setting down drinks. Ed kept his eyes away from Rick as he mumbled his order after the other three. Craig gave him a condescending smile as he slowly and distinctly asked if Ed wanted his prime rib "well, medium well, medium, or rare."

"Medium." Ed was all set to knock Craig and his order pad into next week.

Suddenly he felt Rick's hand slip into his. He looked up at Rick, who was smiling at him. Ed relaxed, knowing by Rick's smile that everything was okay.

Craig's smile slipped a notch or two. "I'll be back as soon as possible with your appetizers," he said, fleeing toward the kitchen.

"You set that whole thing up just so you could meet me?" Rick whispered, still smiling.

"Yeah," Ed mumbled, still blushing.

"Thanks, baby," Rick whispered, saying no more.

Glen and Michael watched this with a great deal of curiosity, but when it became clear that Rick had no desire to pursue the subject in front of them, they settled for exchanging the smug smiles of people who have a lot of speculation to do later in the evening.

Rick turned his attention to the couple across the table. "Well, how 'bout that! How'd you two happen to meet? Can you beat that story?"

⋖⋗●⋖⋗

"Now *that* was a trip," Rick said once they were back in Ed's truck.

They had said their good-byes with Glen and Michael in the parking lot. Glen and Michael were on their way to Carlton's, but Rick had begged off, as he had to be at work Saturday morning.

"Hope to hell that boy has his fake ID on him. Twenty-five, my ass! He can't be a day over nineteen."

"Well, Glen likes 'em young." Ed was just relieved the evening was over.

"Man," Rick snorted. "How he can cram that much pretension into that skinny little body is beyond me. I can just see him ten years from now, duking it out with Craig the server for the title of most refined gay man in Fort Wayne."

Ed howled with laughter. "Oh, man. Can't you just see them clawing and hissing at each other, trying to claim the crown for Miss Pretentious 1990?" He shook a limp wrist in Rick's face.

"Let's face it, baby. We were both losers in high school, and we're still losers, trying to fit in with that kind of gay men. I think we *belong* in Porterfield."

Ed, taking advantage of the dark parking lot, gave Rick a quick kiss. "I never knew being a loser could feel so good."

Rick grabbed Ed for a more serious kiss. "I still can't believe you got him to send you that letter, just so you could meet me. I can't even say how touched I am that you would do that. Why didn't you tell me?"

Ed shrugged. "I was embarrassed. I guess I didn't want you to know how anxious I was to meet you."

"But, baby, don't you see? That letter brought us together. I wouldn't have recognized you at Carlton's that night if I hadn't've given you that letter the day before, and I know you well enough already to know you wouldn't have approached me in that bar, right?"

"Probably not," Ed muttered, feeling his face go red again.

"So it worked. It was sheer genius! Why, if you hadn't've done it, we'd both probably be sitting at home alone tonight in Porterfield, feeling sorry for ourselves. Instead, here we are, outside this pretentious, overpriced fish shack, me digesting some of the worst salmon I ever ate, and you still ready to clobber that damned server with a wine bottle."

Ed looked at him for a moment, then broke into more howling laughter. Rick joined him, and they both laughed so hard they steamed up the windshield.

"Oh, man," Ed gasped. "We gotta cut this out, or I'll never be able to drive us home."

Rick calmed down, wiping the tears out of his eyes. "If anybody would have told me back in Indy that I'd end up here, I would've told them they were full of shit. But I am so happy, baby, so happy I'm here with you."

"Me too," Ed said, collapsed against the seat, exhausted from relief and laughter.

"Let's blow this clambake, shall we?" Rick asked, setting Ed off on more giggles.

They managed to calm themselves down for the long drive back to Porterfield. Rick kept his hand firmly and possessively on Ed's leg the whole way, and whenever Ed glanced over, the look on Rick's face told Ed he had found the man he could always be himself with, even in a trendy, tacky fish restaurant.

When they pulled into Ed's driveway, Rick took his hand away from Ed's leg to get out of the truck, then turned back to Ed and asked, "Can I come in for a while?"

"Sure," Ed said, surprised. "But you have to get up so early."

"I know. I'm just not ready to let go of you yet."

Ed took Rick's hand and led him into the house.

Once inside, Rick's attention was drawn to the stacks of records around the stereo. "What's all this?"

"After hearing all of those old songs last Sunday, I decided to get all my 45s out and listen to them. I've had them going all week."

"Cool." Rick shuffled through a few, checking out the titles. He paused over one, smiling. He handed it to Ed. "Can we hear this one?"

Ed looked at it in surprise. It was Andy Kim's "Baby, I Love You," one of the songs he had been thinking about long before he pulled the records out of storage.

"Sure," he said, placing it on the turntable.

"They were playing this one on the radio the summer after I finished high school," Rick said, pulling Ed onto the sofa next to him. "I remember hearing it late at night, wishing I had someone to love, wondering if I'd ever meet someone I could care about that much."

Ed looked at him as the phonograph needle connected with the scratchy record, his heart beating faster as he sensed what Rick was trying to say to him.

Rick softly sang along with the record. He stumbled a bit over the lyrics, but Ed heard what he needed to hear. "Baby, I love you" came through to his ears loud and clear.

Rick looked into Ed's eyes. "'Cause I do, baby, I really do. If I had any doubt before, I don't now, after finding out about that letter. And like the damned song says, I may start crying, just thinking about how much I love you." Indeed, tears were in his eyes, and they weren't from the laughing they'd done together.

Ed looked back at him, tears coming to his own eyes. "I love you, too, darlin', I . . . I . . ."

Rick silenced Ed's stammering with a kiss. "My heart really couldn't wait another day to tell you," he said, his cheeks wet. "I've been wanting to tell you so bad, but I kept telling myself to wait, that it was too soon."

"Me too," Ed whispered, convinced Rick was reading his mind.

"Two weeks ago tonight," Rick gulped, trying to choke back the tears, "I swear my life changed forever. I knew the first time I kissed you. I always thought love at first sight was bullshit, but it's not. Do you really love me too, baby?"

"I loved you even before I knew your name," Ed told him, his fingers gently wiping the tears on Rick's face. "That letter? Why do you think I did that? I had to know if you really were the man I'd been dreaming about all these years, finally coming to rescue me."

"Am I? That man?"

"Yes," Ed whispered, as his own tears began to fall.

"Oh, baby, baby," Rick murmured, holding him close. "I'm so glad I'm that man."

The record began to play again as Rick brought Ed's lips to his. His hand went to Ed's face, his turn now to brush away the tears.

"Baby, I love you," he repeated. "I have a feeling I'm gonna love you for the rest of my life."

Chapter Seven

Ed stretched happily in bed the next morning, enjoying the rare November sunshine streaming through the blinds. He relived the evening before, still amazed that a night he was originally dreading turned out to be one of the most important ones of his life.

He frowned a bit. Oh, common sense told him that an open declaration of love between two people was one thing, but maintaining it over time was something else altogether. It was, he knew, still too soon to know for sure that he and Rick were, as they used to say in school, "meant for each other." Still, if Rick seemed to think he was going to love Ed for the rest of his life, Ed was, for the time being, more than willing to give Rick the rest of *his* life to prove it.

He looked at the clock and thought of Rick, already up for hours, preparing for the day's mail delivery. Ed had work himself to do that afternoon, so he wouldn't see Rick when he came down his street. He didn't care, though. Rick had arranged for another "sleepover," and this time tomorrow morning Rick would be right where Ed wanted him: next to him in this bed.

When Ed made it as far as the living room in pursuit of some breakfast he stopped and looked foolishly at the stereo. "Baby, I Love You" was still on the turntable. Feeling even more foolish, he hit the stereo's power button, then flipped the turntable's automatic switch. The record began to play as he went to the refrigerator for his usual glass of OJ.

"Stephens, you big dork, you've got it bad," he mumbled to himself, still hearing Rick's soft, sure voice over Andy Kim's.

With a bounce in his step, Ed trotted up Hilda Penfield's front steps that afternoon. Mrs. Penfield lived a few blocks north of Ed's place on Spruce

Street in an old brick Victorian home, and Ed enjoyed being responsible for the smaller aspects of its upkeep.

Today, however, Mrs. Penfield had asked him to help her pack up some books she was donating to a library fund drive. She warmly greeted Ed at the door, then led him to an upstairs bedroom lined with floor-to-ceiling bookshelves. In addition to the full shelves, books were piled on the floor, along with numerous cardboard boxes.

"Geez, Mrs. Penfield. Why don't you just move the library over here instead?"

"Well, Ed," she answered with a chuckle. "What else would you expect from a retired English teacher?"

He looked fondly at the old woman. Mrs. Penfield had presided over Ed's English class his sophomore and junior years in high school and was one of the few teachers he remembered with any amount of admiration and respect. He believed he had learned more in her classroom than any other, and her persuasive encouragement had turned Ed into an avid reader through his high school years. It was a habit he had let go in adulthood, but now, looking at what seemed to be a lifetime's worth of good reading in one room, he felt an urge to rekindle it.

"George and I," Mrs. Penfield said, referring to her late husband, "didn't drink or smoke, but as you can see, we had one serious vice: books. It's a wonder this house hasn't crumbled under their weight. I think, though, the time has come to share these with the rest of the world."

"Isn't it hard to let them go?" Ed knew Mrs. Penfield's belief in the power of a good book.

She shrugged. "At my age I certainly don't plan to read them all again. The ones dearest to me are downstairs, in easy reach. If the sale of these will help keep the Porterfield Public Library going, then I'm more than happy to part with them."

Ed smiled. "Considering how many kids you sent there over the years for library cards, I guess that's not a bad idea."

Ed got to work, packing as many books as he could fit into each box, then hauling them out to his truck. He'd been at it for an hour or so when Mrs. Penfield reappeared with a glass of water for him.

"Thanks," he said, thirstily chugging.

"You've made good progress." She nodded approvingly at the emptying shelves. "And, Ed, if you see something you might like for yourself, please take it, or them, home with you. The Porterfield Library can survive the loss of a few of them."

"Thanks again." He indicated a small stack off to the side. "I was wanting to look closer at those when I took a break. I think that Ri—I think that I would like these. Especially this one." He picked up a book he actually had put aside for himself. It was a novel by someone named Anne Tyler. "It was written when I was in high school. I would have loved it back then, a story about a girl who falls in love with a small-town rock singer."

Mrs. Penfield glanced at the book and smiled. "*A Slipping-Down Life*. Yes, you'll enjoy that. I recall you being a big fan of rock-and-roll music. Anne Tyler is always good company. I'm sure there are some others by her in these piles. Take as many as you want."

"I have to admit, packing all of these books is making me want to read again."

"Mission accomplished, then," said Mrs. Penfield with a mischievous grin—not unlike Rick's, Ed thought—on her wrinkled face.

"You set me up, didn't you?" Ed asked with a grin of his own.

"Not intentionally, but if I'm still playing a part in the process of getting you to open a book, then I'm delighted." Mrs. Penfield slowly lowered herself into the one straight-backed chair in the room, her arthritis obviously bothering her. "It's good to see you cheerful, Ed. Is there a special reason you're so chipper these days?"

Ed realized he was, yet again, blushing. "I'm in love," he mumbled, eyes on the books he was packing.

"Ah, that's it. I should have known. Love has its own special glow, but these old nearsighted eyes of mine aren't as sharp as they were when I was dealing with a room full of love-struck adolescents." She chuckled to herself. "I'm out of practice."

Ed looked up to see her smiling fondly at him. He looked into a face that had never shown him anything but kindness and compassion.

"Mrs. Penfield," he blurted. "I'm in love with another man."

Her smile grew larger. "I hope you weren't intending to shock me with that statement."

"No," he mumbled, eyes back on the books. "But I sure shocked myself."

"Oh, Ed." She sighed, her smile fading, but a look of quiet understanding remained on her face. "I've known since your high school days that a shadow of some kind was hanging over you. I was never sure what it was, though. I couldn't understand why a young man as bright and likable as yourself was hanging back, not participating as fully in life as possible. I think it's only been in the last few years, with the advent of the gay liberation movement, that I've begun to suspect that a great many of my former students were carrying that weight around."

Ed's eyes rose in interest.

"No, I'm not naming names. But, yes, others, even some in your own class, I'm sure of that. What troubles me as a teacher, though, is that homosexuality was such a taboo topic for so long that I had no way of knowing or understanding what was troubling *you*, or those other students. I can only hope that our colleges are better equipping teachers for that sort of thing these days."

"I kinda doubt it." Ed shoved some books into a box with more force than was necessary.

"I suspect you're right. That's a shame. It also troubles me to think there are teachers out there, teachers who think of themselves as good teachers, who have watched the same television programs I have and have read the same magazine articles I have and still won't bother to reach out to a young person who is obviously suffering."

"They don't make many like you, Mrs. Penfield," Ed said in gratitude.

"Well, they should. It hurts my heart to think of you carrying such a burden alone all of these years."

"Rick and I talked about it, what it was like in high school and how we got to where we are. I guess you just have to find a way to deal with it, to cope. You either find a way to survive, or you die."

"I'm sure many have died," Mrs. Penfield said quietly. "For my own selfish reasons, I'm glad you've become a survivor, Ed. But enough of this talk. Tell me about your young man."

"Well, he's not all that young. He's a year older than me."

"That is still very young to me."

He grinned at her. "Okay, okay." He stared off into space for a moment. "Rick's wonderful. I mean, you'd expect me to say that, but he really is. He's intelligent and funny. He reads a lot. In fact"—he gestured toward the growing stack of books by his side—"most of those are for him. He's strong. I don't mean he can lift a truck or something, but he's strong in the way that really counts. I think surviving being gay has made him strong."

"There are those who say what does not kill us makes us stronger."

"Yeah, that's right. That's Rick right there. He's also very kind. Right now he's helping his sister take care of her children. Her husband just took off," he explained, "and Rick moved up from Indianapolis to help her out. He says it isn't a big deal, but I don't know very many people who'd do that. He says meeting me was his reward for any sacrifice he made."

"And Rick? Is he your reward?"

"Yes, he is. I don't know what I did to deserve it, but yes."

"You've done more than you know, Ed," she said gently. "I could point out the specifics, but if you give it enough thought, it will come to you on your own."

"Thanks," he said, his blush returning to his face.

"I've no doubt that your Rick is everything you say, and I'm pleased to hear he feels for you what you obviously feel for him. If it is indeed love, time will tell."

"That's what Laurie said, that I wouldn't know for sure until I'd given it enough time."

Mrs. Penfield nodded in delight. "Your sister is a wise woman. I enjoyed her in class as much as I did you. Ed, do you think you're up to one more lesson from an old teacher?"

"As long as there isn't a quiz!"

"No quiz. Although I fully expect you to keep me updated on your progress." She frowned in concentration. "I'm not quite sure how to say this, but it strikes me that you and Rick have a bigger uphill battle to face than a man and a woman would have. I fear the disapproval you may have to face. If the love is real, it will give you the additional strength you'll need to fight those battles."

"You mean," Ed said slowly, "that if our love is as strong as I think it is—well, hope it is—that it will help us fight off those who think we don't have a right to be together?"

"Exactly. The love will grow stronger, as the two of you will. It occurs to me that you'll both need a good deal of strength, as well as patience, to cope with the unique problems you might face. Not to mention a lot of understanding and compassion for each other. That's more than a good many people are willing to bring to a relationship, but I believe it will be essential to your success."

Ed thought about what she had said. "We need to be there for each other during the bad times, and if we truly love each other, we will be."

Mrs. Penfield smiled at her former student. "Yes, Ed. It's adversity that tests our love for one another the most. If you and Rick can survive the adversity, and survive it together, than you'll both be stronger, better men for it. There. That's the lesson. The old lady is through with her sermon."

"Thanks for the lesson, Mrs. Penfield, and more importantly for not judging. Some part of me knew you wouldn't, so that's why I felt I could be honest with you."

"I'm glad of that, Ed. That means a great deal to me. Thank you for confiding in me. Perhaps Rick can accompany you on one of your jobs here. I'd like to meet him."

"Sure, I have a feeling the two of you would really hit it off!"

Mrs. Penfield slowly brought herself to her feet. "Well, I need to let you get back to work. Since I'm still as nosy as I was in school, there's a lot more

I want to know, but we can save it for another time. I'm really very happy for you, Ed. And don't ever doubt that you deserve it, because you do."

⊰⋅●⋅⊱

Ed was stretched out on the sofa, already engrossed in the Anne Tyler book, when Rick arrived that evening. He burst through the back door, and Ed threw his book aside to meet him in the kitchen.

Rick was carrying a large paper bag. It looked slightly greasy, and it smelled delicious.

"I have solved our dinner problem," he announced triumphantly.

"You did? What's in there?" Ed leaned over the greasy bag to kiss him.

Rick put the bag on the table, then reached for Ed and a much closer, more substantial kiss.

"When I left work today, I noticed the Porterfield Jaycees were having a chicken barbecue fund-raiser," Rick said when they'd had enough kisses for the moment. "I stopped by there on my way here and picked up two dinners for us. We've got barbecued chicken, baked potatoes, and everything else we could need, except the drinks, but I know my man always has plenty of cold Pepsi-Cola on hand."

"You mean you don't want a bottle of some *fa-a-abulous* white wine to go with it?"

"Oh, please. I'm sure *you* wouldn't have an appropriate vintage," Rick said in a prissy voice, making them both laugh, remembering the past evening.

They sat down to enjoy the chicken.

"I've got a surprise for you, too," Ed said.

"Oh?"

"Yeah, I'll show you after dinner. I spent the afternoon at Mrs. Penfield's, like I told you, and I brought home a little bonus. We had a great conversation, too. Were your ears burning?"

Rick looked pleased. "You mean you told her about us?"

"Yeah. I didn't set out to, if you know what I mean, but Mrs. Penfield was always pretty good at getting me to talk in class. Anyway, she's happy that we're together, and she'd like to meet you someday."

Rick shook his head, smiling. "Whadda ya know? Someone on our side. It's nice to know that when the villagers come chasing after us, torches lit, that someone will be supporting us."

"Mrs. Penfield talked about that, about how we need to be strong, and that our love will see us through if it's real."

"Really? She sounds like an amazing woman. I'd like to meet her, too."

Ed was about to reply when he heard a knock at the back door. They looked questioningly at each other, then Ed shrugged and went to the door.

"Surprise!" Laurie called out when he opened the door.

Ed mock-glared at her, hands on hips. "Man, you just couldn't wait, could you? Well, come on in."

She followed him into the kitchen, carrying a paper bag of her own. "I have a legitimate reason for being here. I have brought your dessert."

"I didn't know we'd ordered dessert," Ed said, as Rick got to his feet. "Rick, this is my supersnoop sister, Laurie, who cooked up an excuse to get her beady brown eyes on you."

Rick chuckled. "Well, that's okay. I've been wanting to meet her, too."

Laurie smiled at him. "It's good to meet you at last, Rick. Ed's right. My curiosity got the better of me. I really do have dessert, though, some of Todd's birthday cake." She slid a plastic-wrapped plate with two pieces of chocolate cake out of the bag.

"Aw, crud. I forgot it was Todd's birthday," Ed said, ashamed.

"Well, you've been busy," she said, glancing at Rick, who grinned rather sheepishly. "Anyway, rather than let my husband, who's put on entirely too much weight recently, finish it off, I decided to farm some of it out. And, yes, it seemed like a good sisterly excuse to drop in." She looked at the food spread out on the table. "Oh, the Jaycees. Is that any good? Todd brought home some tickets from the bank, but the kids insisted on dragging him to Fort Wayne for supper and the movies for his birthday, so I didn't bother."

"It's not bad," Ed said, taking the cake plate from her. "Thanks, though. This'll finish it off right."

"How'd you get out of going to the movies?" Rick wanted to know.

"Mommy decided that Daddy needed to spend some quality time with his children," she said with a smile.

"Translation: She wanted the whole goddamned house to herself for an evening," Ed said.

"You got that right! I'm going to go home, take a long, hot bubble bath, put some music *I* like on the stereo, and relax. Hell, I might even drink one of Todd's beers."

They all laughed.

"Well, I suppose I should ask you to sit down," Ed said. "I'm sure you have about a zillion questions for poor Rick here."

Laurie shook her head, smiling. "No, I don't want to interrupt your dinner. I think I just wanted to make sure he really exists, that you didn't make him up to fool me like you did when we were kids."

"Oh, I'm very real." Rick tapped himself on the chest.

"I can see that," she said, "and really cute, too, I might add."

"*Lau-au-aurie!* Geez." Ed's eyes rolled heavenward, as Rick grinned in embarrassment.

"Oh, I'd better get out of here before I really get in trouble. He's about ready to kill me," she said to Rick, giggling. "Get him to tell you about the time I hid the needle from his record player and he pushed me down the stairs. Mom about killed us both over that one."

"You pushed your sister down the stairs?" Rick tried to look horrified.

"Oh, he did a lot worse than that at one time or another. But he loves me, don't you?" she asked, hugging her brother.

Ed looked at Rick, shrugging. "Linus and Lucy. That's what Dad used to call us."

"If Claire were here, she could tell you some good ones, too, believe me."

Laurie let Ed go and looked appraisingly at Rick for a moment. She nodded. "Yeah, I think he's okay. That's what my female intuition tells me, anyway." She smiled. "You take good care of my brother, you hear?"

"Laurie!"

Rick laughed. "That is my intention, ma'am, to take the very best care of him possible."

Laurie reached out to give Rick a hug, too. "Welcome to the family then. And good luck. You'll need it when you get the pleasure of meeting Mom."

"Thanks," Rick said, returning the hug.

"Isn't it about time you went home?" Ed asked crankily.

"Ed!" Rick protested.

"No, he's right. My mission here is done. My curiosity is satisfied, and I've got a bubble bath waiting. Really, though, Rick, it is good to meet you."

"Likewise," Rick said, smiling at her with the warm, tender smile that Ed so loved. "Thanks for the cake, too. It looks great."

"You're very welcome," Laurie said, turning for the door. "Keep him around, you big dork. He could teach you some manners." She scooted toward the back door before Ed could grab her. "Good night all," she called as she fled out the back door, Ed in pursuit.

"I'll get you later, Shortshit," Ed hollered as she ran for her car.

"You can't catch me, you can't catch me," she taunted as she slammed the car door.

Ed flipped her the bird, and giggling hysterically, she backed out of the driveway, then roared away on Grant Street.

Ed returned to the kitchen, where Rick was shaking his head over their performance.

"Can you believe her?" Ed asked indignantly.

"Linus and Lucy indeed," Rick said, pulling him in for a hug. "And here I thought I was dating a nice, mature man."

"She can be such a pain in the ass."

"It's obvious she cares about you a lot. As a gay man, you can be damned grateful for that. And besides, all sisters are pains in the ass," Rick said, with a playful slap on that part of Ed's anatomy. He glanced at the cake. "How well does she bake?"

Ed snickered. "Well, if it's Mom's recipe, and I don't doubt that it is, it should be pretty good, although Mom would be sure to find something wrong with it."

"Man, I have fallen into a family of flakes. Where's my ticket out of here?"

"You," Ed said, locking Rick in his arms, "are not going anywhere."

"You're right," Rick said, the warm and tender smile for Ed this time. "I'm not."

Chapter Eight

After dinner, Rick adjourned to the living room to inspect the books Ed had brought him from Mrs. Penfield's, while Ed settled in for KP duty in the kitchen. Ed carefully washed Laurie's plate, torn between smashing it on the floor and taping a twenty-dollar bill on the back of it. He was annoyed with her for dropping in unexpectedly, but knew Rick was right: Her approval of their relationship was a great blessing.

Rick had put a stack of 45s on the stereo. Ed smiled, hearing the soft sounds of Lobo's "Don't Expect Me to Be Your Friend." He had forgotten he had that one in his collection. Ed still couldn't believe Rick enjoyed those old songs as much as he did. Plenty of people over the years had sneered at his taste in music, so Rick's enjoyment of it meant almost as much to Ed as his love did.

Drying his hands, Ed walked into the living room. Rick was sprawled on the sofa, engrossed in one of Mrs. Penfield's books. He looked up at Ed's entrance.

"You really did good, baby. These will keep me busy for weeks. You'll have to take me over there sometime so I can thank her myself."

"I'm glad you like them." Ed made room for himself on the sofa. "It occurred to me that since you read so much, maybe I should get back in the habit, so I'd have something to do when you've got your nose buried in some book."

"It would be nice to share that with you. I'll tell you, though," he said, taking Ed's hand, "I'm really impressed by your teacher. I can't think of any teacher I ever had who I would confide in."

"Mrs. Penfield is the best," Ed said firmly. "I know what you mean, though. If any of my other teachers called for handyman work, I'd probably tell 'em to drop dead."

"And your sister. Stopping by like that—"

"Barging in, you mean," Ed interrupted.

"*Politely* stopping by," Rick said, giving Ed a look, "not only with cake, but with her seal of approval for us. I'm guessing there are a lot of sisters out there, who, if they bothered to stop by their gay brothers' houses with cake, would lace it with arsenic." Rick sighed, sitting up so he could put his arms around Ed. "I worry, and I know you worry, about what people around here will think about us, so it means a lot to me to know we have people we can count on."

"Two down, eight thousand nine hundred and ninety-eight to go," Ed said, referring to Porterfield's population. "You're right, though. It's like Mrs. Penfield said: We gotta be strong, and I guess we should be grateful for all the outside help we can get."

"Being with you, baby, makes me strong," Rick said softly. "I feel as though I could take on the world when I'm with you. I don't care what anyone says. Finding you was the best thing that ever happened to me, and I'm not going to let anyone interfere with that."

Ed thought about that as another record dropped onto the turntable. Skylark's mournful "Wildflower" began to play. Oh, the girl in the song may have faced some hard times, but so had every man who'd ever loved another man.

"I know. I can't believe that anyone would hate us for loving each other, but they do. It isn't fair."

"Baby, I remember reading somewhere that life isn't fair, even, or equal. As long as we know we're right, that's all that matters. And if I haven't told you yet today, I love you very much."

Ed let go of the disturbing thoughts and allowed himself to relax inside Rick's arms. "I love you, too. Thanks for loving me. I think it's about the best present I ever got."

They spent the evening piling records on the turntable and leafing through the books. Ed thought a lot of gay guys would be horrified, Glen included, to know how they were spending a Saturday night so early in their relationship, but he was completely content. He understood that Rick's early morning work hours left him unenthusiastic for more glamorous nightlife activities, and as for himself, Ed was simply happy to spend a quiet evening in his own home—the home where he'd spent so many lonely nights—with the man he loved.

Ed glanced at Rick, who was snickering at Philip Roth's *Portnoy's Complaint*. Rick had exchanged his contacts for glasses shortly after dinner, Ed was pleased to note, glad that Rick no longer worried about wearing them around him.

Rick laughed out loud, closing the book. "Man, and I thought I was neurotic. Thanks again, baby. I meant to read this years ago, but never got around to it. How's your Anne Tyler?"

"Great. These people are so . . . I don't know. It all kind of reminds me of Porterfield, so I'm really liking it."

"A man who appreciates a good book," Rick said, and sighed. "I didn't know they existed. I'm glad, though. I've always thought you could learn a lot about how to deal with the haters out there if you read what other people had to say. But now," he said, standing up and stretching, "I'd like some serious face-to-face time with my handyman."

"Face time. Does that have anything to do with kissing?"

"You bet it does," Rick said, making no move toward Ed. He stood over Ed, studying him.

"What?"

"Oh, I was just thinking. I'm just amazed at how sexy you are, just sprawled out on the couch like that. I've seen tons of pictures of naked men trying to look like studs, but I don't think any of them ever turned me on the way you do, fully clothed, looking at me with those beautiful eyes of yours."

Ed, thinking similar thoughts about Rick, moved to the back of the sofa, inviting Rick to lie next to him, which he did. Arms tightly around each other on the narrow cushions, their lips came together gently and tentatively. The passion they both felt began to smolder, and the kiss grew stronger, the embrace tighter. Joe Simon's "Drowning in the Sea of Love" was playing on the stereo.

Rick came up for air long enough to mutter, "Baby, I am drowning. Drowning in you."

"Rick," Ed whispered, staring into Rick's eyes.

"What, baby?"

"I . . . I just love you . . . that's all. Just love you so damned much."

"Oh, Ed," Rick whispered, kissing Ed, caressing his face. "I love you so much it almost hurts. Like this couch. It's killing me. Can we go in the other room?"

They both laughed, relieved to take the edge away from the powerful emotion sweeping over them.

Once in the bedroom, though, bare skin to bare skin, it returned. The desire they'd had for one another since that first kiss, weeks ago, rolled over them unchecked—an ocean at a stormy high tide. Their mutual love revealed and expressed, they no longer had any doubt or uncertainty, only the wonder and joy of each other.

Every touch, every kiss was savored as they allowed themselves to explore, feeling boundless in their love. Rick rolled over to Ed's side, putting his arms around him, pulling Ed tight against him, kissing his neck, his hand reaching to stroke Ed's chest, his belly. Ed felt Rick's passion and his desire, amazed that it matched his own in intensity.

"Oh, baby," Rick whispered against Ed's neck. "I want to be inside you, want to be as close as we can be together."

Ed's body went rigid, his desire melting. His mind immediately flashed back to a painful experience with a selfish, aggressive man several years earlier. It had been frightening, even humiliating, and Ed had vowed never to go there again. He had shared the story with no one, only telling himself privately that he was no one's bitch, and that no man would ever have that access to him ever again.

"Ed?" Rick turned Ed around to face him. Comprehension came into Rick's eyes. "Some bastard hurt you, didn't he?"

Ed turned away, the old humiliation returning. "Yes," he muttered.

Rick forced Ed's eyes back to his. "Do you think I'd do that to you?"

Ed couldn't respond, the painful memory interfering with the present.

Rick pulled Ed back to him. "I'm sorry. We don't have to go there. I didn't know, but now that I do, the thought of anyone hurting you that way kills me. Oh, Ed, I wish the first time had been with me. I just want to show you how much I love you, how much I want to be a part of you. I want to show you how wonderful it can be to be together like that. I wanna make love with you the way two men should—no fear, just love."

Ed felt tears come to his eyes. "I don't want to disappoint you."

Rick gently brushed the tears away from Ed's eyes. "I don't think you could ever disappoint me."

Ed began to relax, realizing he was safe with Rick. "We could try."

"No, baby, I don't want to do anything that would scare you, or make you ever afraid of me."

Those words, the honest emotion behind them, freed Ed from the earlier humiliation. "It's . . . it's okay. I think I want to."

Rick kissed him, and although their kisses had been extraordinary up that point, Ed still felt something more, a promise he had never received from another man before. He knew he could give himself to Rick, and still be a man afterward.

"Baby, I promise, I'll be careful. If it isn't good for you, I'll stop. It'll only be good for me if it's incredible for you. You believe me, don't you?"

Ed nodded, tears gone, a smile coming to the lips Rick continued to kiss.

Afterward, after Rick's quiet reassurances and his ability to make Ed experience a pleasure he'd never known, Ed grew to believe even more strongly that Rick Benton was the man he'd been looking for all his life.

"We can flip that around whenever you want, you know," Rick said, arms tightly wrapped around Ed.

Ed looked at him questioningly.

"Baby, the only thing I can imagine being better than what we just had would be to feel you inside me that way, too; showing me your love the same way I showed mine. I wanna share it all with you, be every bit of a man with you. I don't want to control you, I just want to love you right. I know there is no bigger, better man in this world than you, and to be loved by you that way would be one of the greatest gifts you could give me, next to your love."

Their mutual declaration of love was still fresh, still new enough that it couldn't be said often enough, but Ed knew, looking into Rick's eyes, that no words were necessary right now. His love for Rick was shining back at him in Rick's eyes.

⋆●⋆

It was very late, but they were still awake. They lay side by side in the soft darkness of Ed's bedroom, Rick's arms protectively around Ed.

"I am so tired," Rick said against Ed's hair, "but so wide awake at the same time. I know you'll still be here when I wake up in the morning, next to me, but right now, even going to sleep feels like leaving you."

"I feel peaceful," Ed said. "I'm trying to remember the last time I felt like this. I thought love was supposed to make you run around in circles, like an idiot or something."

"Well, baby, I think we used up a lot of that energy earlier."

Ed snickered softly. "I s'pose you're right."

Rick kissed Ed's neck. "Are you okay?"

"Better than okay."

"Good. That's the most important thing to me right now. You know, I meant what I said . . . about, uh, taking turns."

"I know."

"Do you want to?"

"Yes."

"I'm glad, baby. I'd be the luckiest guy in the world, to get to have you that way."

"Thanks, darlin'. I feel the same way, now that I know . . ."

"Know what, baby?"

"That it . . . that it can be so good, so great. I'd love to make you feel the way you made me feel tonight."

"And I want you to feel what I felt. If I wasn't so damned tired—"

"No." Ed turned to smile at Rick. "When the time is right. It'll happen, I know it will."

"You're not afraid anymore?"

"No."

"What did he do to you? Do you want to talk about it? You don't have to if you don't want to. I just need to know you're okay with me. Whatever may happen outside of this room, I want you to know you can always trust me here."

"I do. Trust you, that is. I love you more now, if that's possible."

"I think it's possible. I love you more now, too. I want to kill that guy, though."

Ed sighed. "It doesn't matter anymore, after tonight. What happened was . . . well, it was as much my fault. I was stupid."

"We all get stupid sometimes, baby, but no one has the right to hurt you."

"It was about three years ago," Ed said tentatively.

"You don't have to tell me if you don't want to."

"I think I do. Just don't let go of me, okay?"

Rick's arms tightened around him. "I'm right here."

"Okay. Well, I went to Carlton's. I was lonely and I was horny. I was looking for sex, I admit it."

"Baby, if I didn't have the most incredible man in the world in my arms right now, I might be out looking for sex, too. Nothing to be ashamed of."

"Oh, I'm not. Not really, anyway. I think . . . I think if I'd been thinking with my head and not my dick, it wouldn't have happened, that's all.

"Anyway, you know I told you I don't drink very much. Well, I did that night, 'cause I was nervous, I guess. I was worried about driving home when this big, older guy started talking to me. He was hot, or at least I thought he was with all that booze in me. He asked me to go home with him. He told me he'd take me back to my truck in the morning. I was worried enough about driving, and drunk enough, to think it was a good idea.

"So he takes me back to his place, somewhere out on the north side of Fort Wayne. Hell, considering how much he'd had to drink, it was a wonder *he* didn't get stopped. Next thing I know, we're in his bed, going at it. No problem at all, until . . well, I said no, and he said yes. He kept telling me it would be okay, but it wasn't. I mean, I hate to admit this, but I really was a . . a virgin when it comes to that. I was always curious, but it had just never happened.

"I couldn't believe how much it hurt. He just got all impatient with me and said it was supposed to hurt. I didn't believe him, though. I knew enough to know that it would be fine if . . if . . . you did it right. I wanted to leave, but my truck was back at the bar. I was still half-bombed, and I felt trapped. What was I supposed to do? Go out and try to find a cab? At three in the morning? You ever notice how scarce they are in that town?"

"Oh, baby," Rick whispered, kissing Ed, rubbing his back.

"Anyway, so I tried to push him off me, but he decided I liked it rough or something, and he kept . . . well, kept pushing harder. I finally managed to knock him off of me. In fact, I pushed him so hard he fell on the floor." Ed chuckled, remembering the satisfaction of that moment.

"I hope to hell you picked up something and bashed his head in."

"I wanted to, believe me. I thought he'd come after me, but he didn't. I was stumbling around, trying to find my clothes, and he sat there on the bed and called me a cock tease, a pussy, and I don't remember what all. Told me I wasn't a man 'cause I couldn't take it.

"It was then that I noticed there were a lot of women's things scattered around. It hit me that he was married, and cheating on his wife with a guy. I was so . . . so green it never occurred to me that a guy would do that. Pretty stupid, huh?"

"A lot of guys aren't as brave as you, Ed, making the decision you made to be true to yourself. Then, not only do they mess up their own lives, but they mess up everyone else's, too."

"Did you ever think about getting married, to a woman?"

"No."

"Then you're brave, too."

"I guess. I just knew I couldn't do that, couldn't hide, or at least knew I couldn't hide it that well. So what happened when you realized he had a wife?"

"Well, at first I was just shocked. You know how I am." Ed laughed, and the laughter felt wonderful. "I just stood there, probably with a dumb look on my face, while he's calling me every name in the book. Finally I said, 'Well, at least I'm not married.'

"That shut him up, at least for a moment. He started saying something about—oh, I can't remember—something about his wife being out of town, and what she didn't know wouldn't hurt her."

"So he decided to hurt you instead, fucking bastard."

"Yeah. Well, that all sobered me up pretty fast. I told him he was the most miserable piece of shit I'd ever laid eyes on, and told him I was going to come back later and tell his wife."

Rick laughed. "Man! What'd he do?"

Ed felt even better, hearing Rick laugh. "Oh, he about turned green, let me tell you. He started to get off the bed, and I told him not to come near me, that I worked with my hands, and did he really want to mess with me, as mad as I was?"

"You do have very strong hands, baby." Rick admired Ed's hands, taking one in his own.

"I told him if he gave me twenty bucks and called a cab so I could get back to my truck, I'd never say anything to anyone. I guess he believed me, 'cause he got all nervous-looking. He gave me the money, called the taxi company, and I waited outside, convinced he was gonna sneak out and try to kill me—you know, so I wouldn't be able to get him in trouble. I guess I watch too much TV."

"No, I don't blame you a bit. Considering what a shit he was, anything was possible."

"Yeah, really. Well, it was early spring, and still pretty cold, at least at three in the morning. I don't know how long I waited, probably a half hour at least, but the cab finally showed up, and I got the hell out of there."

Ed sighed. "I got back to my truck and drove back here to Porterfield. Oh, the stuff I was thinking. I thought how a woman must feel, being raped. That's what it felt like. I felt like a total jerk, and I . . . well, it still hurt a lot, too. Before I even got home I vowed that no one would ever do that to me again, make me feel that way."

He looked at Rick. "And no one has, until tonight, but it didn't hurt. It felt the way it's supposed to feel, 'cause I knew you were loving me, not hurting me. And like I said, I love you even more now for showing me that."

Rick rubbed his tired eyes, then smiled. "If it's any consolation, my first time was pretty awful, too. Nothing like that, but I was young and scared, and the other guy was pretty bad at it. It took me a while to figure out the love part of it, too. I knew tonight, though, that it would be okay, because I've never loved anyone as much as I love you right now. Being that close to you . . . damn, Ed, I thought I was gonna cry I was loving you so much."

"Me too."

"So, you want me to go kill this guy? I will."

"No, he got what was coming to him. I heard later that his wife caught him with some other guy, and she sued the shit out of him. Took him for everything he had. I think he left town. He was some important guy in the city government or something, and he was ruined in Fort Wayne."

"Well, as much as I don't like to see that happen to any gay man, I think he got what he deserved." Rick yawned.

"I never told anyone that story until now, but I'm glad I told you. I don't think it'll bother me anymore."

"I know, baby. That's why I wanted you to tell me."

Ed poked him playfully. "Okay, Lucy. Do I owe you five cents now?"

Rick kissed him. "No. Just keep lovin' me. You think you can do that?"

Ed kissed him back. "I know I can do that."

"That's all I want, baby, is for us to love each other so much that we can . . . can always be there for each other." Rick looked at the ceiling, his face creased in thought. "Thing is, that some point in time, we're gonna hurt each other. Oh, I don't mean intentionally. I'll do something, or you'll do something, and someone will get his feelings hurt. I just want you to know that when I do something stupid, I still love you, and I love you too much to do something deliberate. And I love you so much that I would never, ever hurt you here, where we're the closest we can be. Do you believe me?"

"Yes. I believe that. And the same goes for me, too." Ed looked at Rick, who looked as though he was about to fall asleep. "Darlin', it's okay now. You can go to sleep. I know you're not gonna leave me."

Rick put his hand to his mouth to cover another yawn. "Well, if I ever do, then I'm an even bigger fool than that son of a bitch. Okay, baby. Good night. I love you, and when I get up, I'm gonna make you the biggest, best handyman's breakfast ever, you hear?"

"I hear. I love you, too, darlin'. Good night."

Rick was asleep in minutes, soon snoring away as he always did. Ed lay next to him, one arm on Rick's pillow, just barely touching his head. Ed looked at him, still wondering what he had done to deserve this wonderful man who loved him so much. Hilda Penfield had said that if he gave it some thought, he'd figure it out, but right now he was too tired for that kind of thinking. He whispered "thanks" to the universe, at that moment content just to be grateful.

Making sure Rick was indeed sound asleep, Ed rolled over on his side and put his arms around Rick. He fell asleep next to the man who wanted to share not only his body, but his love and his life with him as well.

Chapter Nine

Ed was just finishing a bowl of Campbell's soup for his lunch when he heard a knock at the front door. "Is it that late?" He dropped his spoon in the bowl. He walked to the door, and sure enough, Rick was making his usual afternoon stop.

"Looks like you got some mail today, Mr. Stephens," Rick said, rather suggestively, Ed thought.

"Well then, why don't you come in and give it to me?" Ed pushed the screen door open wide.

Rick walked in, dropped his mailbag, and took Ed in his arms for a kiss. Ed pulled Rick closer for another long kiss.

"Damn," Rick muttered against Ed's mouth. "I feel like I just came home from the war."

Ed reluctantly pulled his lips away from Rick's, but kept his arms around him in a firm grip. "I spent the morning messing with the Hausers' plumbing. As far as I'm concerned, I was at war."

"Ah, poor baby." Rick began to touch Ed in all sorts of private places. "Sounds like you could use a break."

He was about to kiss Ed again when the phone rang. They both glanced at it, rolling their eyes.

"Why is it," Rick said, "that your clients always seem to call when I want you to myself?"

"God hates me," Ed replied. "Well, at least I thought He did until a few weeks ago." He smiled at Rick, going in to finish the kiss Rick had started.

"Aren't you going to answer that?" Rick pushed him away.

"Nope. It's just Mom."

"Oh? How do you know that, Kreskin?"

"Because. Laurie called here earlier to bitch about her, so that's got to be Mom bitching about Laurie. It can wait."

"What did she do this time?" Rick asked, grinning. He loved Ed's Norma stories.

"Well, she was over at Laurie's, visiting last night. When no one was looking, she threw away the kids' Froot Loops and left a box of Quaker Oats in its place. That was her subtle way of saying she thinks Laurie and Todd are giving the kids too much sugar." Ed shook his head. "What's she going to do next, give the kids underwear for Christmas?"

Rick chuckled. "Grandma of the year, 1980."

The phone abruptly cut off in the middle of a ring. Ed sighed in relief. "Oh, well, she'll call back in about fifteen minutes. I'll talk to her when you're not around. Now, where were we?"

"I was taking advantage of the cutest handyman in Porterfield, Indiana. But unfortunately, I still have a lot of mail to deliver."

"Aw, crud," Ed said, stroking Rick's beard. "It says something about neither snow, nor rain, nor heat, but it doesn't say anything about horny handymen. Can't you make an exception?"

"Don't tempt me." Rick reached for his mailbag.

"Well, do you suppose you could come back tonight? For dinner? I'll even cook. I've got some spaghetti."

"Hmm, spaghetti. What's for dessert?"

"You have to ask?" Ed laughed.

"Let's see. If I get right back to this mail, I should be home in time for some serious Uncle Rick time with the kids. If I can keep them busy so Claire has a chance to rest, then get started with something to eat for them, yeah, I think I could swing dinner and dessert with my handyman."

Ed was pleased. He knew it was a hassle for Rick to spend an evening with him during the week, so he appreciated any effort Rick was willing to make. "Six-thirty, you think?"

"No sweat," Rick said, grabbing Ed for one last quick kiss. "Now I am definitely going back to work before I get us both in trouble."

Ed watched Rick take off down the walk with his easy mailman's stride. Ed shivered from the chilly air coming through his screen door and was glad Rick was clad in cold-weather gear.

"No doubt about it," he muttered, looking at the door. "It's time you stopped being a screen door and became a storm door."

He had to admit that he'd been so caught up in the whole distracting process of falling in love, he'd been neglecting the handyman duties around his own house.

He tried to put his mind on winterizing chores, but thoughts of Rick kept slipping through. He was certain the two of them were settling in for the long haul, relationshipwise, but having a man, no, having *Rick* in his life was still too new, too extraordinary for him to be blasé about it. Oh, he knew that day would come, but until then, he wanted to enjoy the wide-awake version of the best dream he'd ever had.

⋖⋗●⋖⋗

That evening they were seated at Ed's kitchen table enjoying spaghetti and garlic bread. Ed, who usually burned the garlic bread, had managed to get it out of the broiler just in time that night and was feeling quite proud of himself. He reached for another piece, glanced at Rick, and giggled.

"What?" Rick looked up.

"You've got spaghetti sauce on your beard." Ed giggled again.

"Oh, shit, or aw, crud, as you'd say," Rick said, reaching for his napkin.

"Hey, wait." Ed got up and rushed around the table. "That's my job," he said, licking the sauce off Rick's beard.

"Mmm." Rick pulled Ed's mouth onto his. "Is it time for dessert already? Stupid beard."

"Don't you even think about shaving it off." Ed grabbed the last bit of the red stuff with his tongue.

"As long as it keeps you mad with desire for me, it stays."

"Oh, it does, it does," Ed assured him. "Along with the rest of you."

Ed returned to his own side of the table. Desire or not, it had been a long day, and he was hungry for the pile of pasta and sauce on his own plate. He was about to ask Rick about his day when Rick abruptly asked, "Baby, what's your favorite movie?"

Ed, surprised at the question, sat and thought about it, then shrugged. "I don't know. I like a lot of movies, but I don't know if I have a favorite. Why?"

Rick reached into his pants pocket and pulled out a newspaper clipping. "Well, I do have a favorite movie, and it's showing this weekend. Have you ever seen *Harold and Maude*?"

Ed shook his head.

"They're showing it Friday night at the college in Crestland. It's part of a film series they're doing. I'd love to see it again. Want to go with me?"

"Of course."

"Good. I know you'll love it, or at least I think you will. I thought, if you weren't busy late in the day, I'd come over as soon as Claire gets home from work. We can grab something to eat on the way to Crestland and catch the first showing, since I have to work Saturday morning."

"It's a date. We've never been to the movies together before, so this should be fun. Why's it your favorite movie?"

Rick grinned mysteriously. "Oh, you need to see it first, then I think you'll understand." He consulted the clipping. "I'm not really sure where Crestland College is, so can you drive?"

"Oh, sure. I know Crestland like the back of my hand. Uncle Chester and Aunt Eleanor live there."

"Wanna stop by and see them?" Rick's eyes twinkled.

Ed shuddered. "I'll have to see them at Christmas. That's soon enough. Oh," he said apologetically, "they're okay, but I'm still not in the mood to share you any more than I have to."

The phone rang. Ed stood up, groaning. "If that's the Hausers telling me something's backed up, I'm gonna kill myself." He walked to the living room and picked up the receiver. "Hello?"

"Ed? It's your mother. Are you coming over tomorrow morning to help me move furniture? Those carpet cleaning people are due here at nine. I know they'll be late. That type always is. But I want to be ready for them."

Ed sighed. "Mom, I already told you earlier, when you called to tell me what an ungrateful daughter you have, that I would be there at eight. What could have changed since then?"

"I ran into Gwen Hauser at the store. She told me about that plumbing of hers. I could just see her calling you, talking you into going back over there in the morning and abandoning your mother. You wouldn't believe the things she used to do when we were school room mothers together." Norma took a breath and was obviously getting ready to recite Gwen Hauser's sins, but Ed jumped in.

"Mom, I'm eating, and I've got company. I promise I'll be over tomorrow, okay?"

"Company? Who on earth would you be having over for supper?"

"A friend. Rick Benton. I told you about him a couple of weeks ago."

"You two certainly seem to be spending a lot of time together," she said suspiciously.

Since that was true, Ed couldn't think of a reply, so he tried to change the subject. "Hey, Mom, my spaghetti's getting cold. Can I talk to you tomorrow?"

"Spaghetti? With canned sauce, I suppose," she said with a sneer in her voice.

"No, Mom. I used your recipe. Everybody knows you make the best spaghetti sauce in Porterfield." Ed hoped that would shut her up.

"Well, your father always thought so," Norma said. "Now about this Rick character—"

"Can we talk about it tomorrow?" Ed interrupted. "I'd really like to finish eating. I absolutely promise to be there by eight."

"Oh, all right," she huffed. "I'll see you in the morning."

Ed instinctively moved the phone away from his ear before Norma's usual abrupt "good-bye" and phone slam. Ed, shaking his head, walked back to the table. Rick was watching him with a big smile on his face.

"Okay," Ed said. "So what's *your* mother like?"

Rick shrugged. "I think she may be a little, oh, *quieter* than your mom." He chuckled. "Man, I can hardly wait until I meet Norma Stephens face-to-face."

"Yeah, I'll bet," Ed retorted. "You'll probably jump in your car and head back to Indy."

Rick sighed. "You know, baby, it'll have to happen sooner or later. As you well know, I plan to be around here, with you, for a long time. If and when the day comes we start talking about living together, what are you going to do? Pass me off as your boarder?"

Ed poked at his spaghetti. "I know, I know. I'm probably worrying for nothing. I'm good at it, okay?"

"Yes, I know, and I understand why you're upset about it. For the time being, though, there's nothing wrong with two grown men being good friends. By the time she figures it out, I'll have her so charmed she won't care anymore."

"I may think you're the most charming man in the world, but you don't know my mother."

"Never underestimate my abilities," Rick said smugly. "I'll remind you of that when we get to dessert."

⋘•⋙

A few hours later, Ed and Rick lay together in Ed's bed, covers pulled up against the autumn chill. Ed, his eyes closed, was absently running his hand across Rick's furry chest. Even after three weeks, the idea of having a man in his bed was amazing, and the fact that it was Rick made it all that much better. He felt Rick stir and shift positions. Ed opened his eyes and saw Rick looking at the alarm clock.

"I wish you could stay all night," Ed said.

"Well, I can, but you know, Mister I-Set-My-Own-Schedule, that I'll have to crawl out of here at five a.m. to be at work on time."

Ed looked at him, mouth open in surprise. "You can? Really?"

Rick chuckled. "Gotcha, didn't I? Yeah, I came prepared, and I told Claire not to expect me tonight. I know it's only been a few days, but I've been missing my handyman pretty badly. You know I can't make a habit of it, but I figure a weeknight here and there won't hurt anything."

"Well, I'm not worried about you getting up early," Ed said, still surprised, but pleased. "I have to get up early to be at Mom's anyway."

"Okay. Maybe this will hold me until the weekend. I'm hoping I can stay over Saturday night, too."

He reached over and began fumbling with Ed's alarm clock. He glanced at a picture of Ed's niece and nephew on the nightstand.

"Ed," he said, clicking the alarm button into place. "I know Laurie's all cool about us, and that's great, but do you really think your mom is going to be a problem? You don't think she already suspects?"

"What my mom thinks," Ed said with a sigh, "is anybody's guess."

"Well, what was your dad like?" Rick shifted positions again so he could rub Ed's back. "You haven't really talked about him all that much."

"Oh, that feels good. Dad? Oh, he was a nice guy. Everybody liked him. Pretty quiet, I guess." Ed chuckled. "He about had to be, living with Mom." Ed paused, remembering. "I think I had a good relationship with him. He's been gone two years now, and I still miss him sometimes. I could never get into all the sports stuff he liked, but he was really good with his hands, and I loved hanging out in his basement workshop. Everybody says I get my talent for fixing things from him. We had a lot of fun together with that stuff.

"It's funny. I always thought that when I got the nerve to tell my parents that I was gay, I thought I'd go to Dad first. I always felt maybe he'd understand, 'cause we always did seem to understand each other. Well, I think he would have been disappointed, but I think he would have been okay with it. He was always behind anything Laurie and I did, one hundred percent. I guess this is a little different, though."

"Yeah, it is." Rick kneaded the muscles in Ed's back. "But if the look on your face when you talk about him is any indication, he really was a nice guy, and I think he would have supported you on this, and hopefully your mom will, too."

"Mmm, if I was a cat, I'd be purring right now," Ed said, thoroughly enjoying Rick's back rub.

"Just an extra midweek delivery from the mailman to the handyman he loves."

"Thanks, darlin'," Ed murmured drowsily. "I know one thing. If my mom doesn't like you, she's got more screws loose than I think she does."

⇜●⇝

Ed halfheartedly cleaned house Friday afternoon, stereo blasting away. He was dancing more than dusting, singing in his usual awful way, with

Dusty Springfield's "I Only Want to Be with You." He wondered how many times over the years he had sang along with that record, wishing he had someone real to think about. He thought about stepping into Rick's open arms. *I didn't stand a chance, all right.*

He gave the record cabinet a swipe with his dustrag, then used it to jack the volume higher. He winced a bit at the distortion from the scratchy record, suspecting if he had known when he bought it in 1964 that Rick was on the horizon, the record would be completely worn out by now.

The phone rang, and Ed, throwing down his dustrag, ran to answer it. "Hello," he said happily, assuming it was Rick.

"Ed? It's your mother."

Aw, crud, he thought. "Hi, Mom. What's up?"

"The volume on that awful stereo. Turn that noise down. Didn't I get enough of that when you were living here?"

"This is my house, Mom," he shouted over Dusty. "I can listen to it as loud as I want."

"Not while you're on the phone with your mother, you can't."

Feeling abused, Ed slowly cranked the volume back. "Is that better?"

"It'll do. Honestly! It's a wonder you have any hearing left. Anyway, the IGA was having a good sale on pork chops, and I bought enough for an army. I want you to come over for dinner tonight."

"Does it have to be tonight? I kinda have plans."

"Plans! What sort of plans?"

"Well, Mom, it's Friday. People often go out and have fun on Friday night."

"Well, for Pete's sake. Your social life is just growing all the time. And just who do you have these plans with?"

Ed sighed, feeling rather trapped. "I'm supposed to go to the movies with Rick and see *Harold and Maude*."

"Harold and who? Who on earth are they? And why are you going to the movies with them?"

"No," Ed said patiently. "That's the name of the movie."

"Well, I never heard of it."

"It's an old movie, from the early seventies. It's Rick's favorite, and he wants to see it again. They're showing it at Crestland College."

"Humph." Norma was silent for a moment, a rare occurrence indeed. "Well, there's plenty of food for three. You just bring him along with you, then you can do whatever you want. I'm beginning to think I need to get a look at this new friend of yours."

"Oh, Mom," he started.

"Edward, are you ashamed of your mother?"

Well, yes, he thought.

"If he's such a good friend, there's no reason why he can't come over and enjoy a good, home-cooked meal. Why, I used to feed your high school buddies all the time. Even that fat Ted Gillis, and you know what a struggle it was filling him up. I couldn't keep cookies in the house with him around. I always did wonder if they fed him at home. Whatever happened to him, anyway?" She didn't wait for an answer. "You just pick up this Rick Benton character and be here at six. And if he wants anything other than water or coffee to drink, tell him to bring his own."

"But, Mom—"

"Don't 'but Mom' me! Just be here at six. Honestly, to even think of letting good food go to waste. Edward Stephens, I sometimes wonder how I even gave birth to you."

Ed occasionally wondered the same thing. He could only imagine the hell she put Dr. Weisberg, their family doctor, and his delivery room staff through that night.

"Mom, they're only showing the movie tonight. It's part of a film series they're doing. Rick's been looking forward to it all week, and I'm not about to tell him he can't go because my mother insists on feeding him pork chops."

"Oh, for Pete's sake. Well then, come over tomorrow night. Those pork chops will keep. *Dallas* is on tonight anyway. There's nothing on tomorrow night but that silly *Love Boat* and that awful island with the midget. Be here at six *tomorrow* night, then."

"Okay," he said, surrendering. He knew if he worked any harder to get out of it, he would never hear the end of it.

"All right. Say hello to Harold and Mona for me, and I'll see you tomorrow night."

"*Harold and* Maude, Mom."

"Oh, whoever. Bring them for dinner, too. There'll be plenty." Norma laughed, enjoying her own joke.

"I'll tell them when I see them." Ed rolled his eyes at the phone.

Aw, yucky, shitty crud, he thought, hanging up the phone. *How am I going to tell Rick that after a long week at work he has to give up our quiet Saturday night for dinner with my mother?*

He turned the volume up on the stereo. "I Only Want to Be with You" had ended, and the record currently playing was the Zombies and "She's Not There."

"Geez, I wish I had that problem," he grumbled. "Mom's there all right. Boy, is she there."

The back door opened, and Rick bounced in. "Hey, baby. Ready for some fun?"

"Ri-i-i-ick," he began in a much higher than normal voice. A quick look at Rick's smiling, bearded face brought another worry into his head. Unlike her son, Norma always claimed to distrust bearded men. "I sure hope you didn't make any plans for us tomorrow night."

⋙•⋘

"You know, at one time I used to break into pet shops to liberate the canaries," Maude said to Harold on the movie screen, "but I decided that was an idea *way* before its time. Zoos are full, prisons are overflowing . . . ah, my, how the world still dearly loves a cage."

Ed snickered in delight, completely fascinated with the movie unspooling before him.

"Enjoying it, baby?" Rick whispered.

"Oh, yes."

Rick took Ed's hand and squeezed it. Ed's attention was diverted from the screen long enough to note that having his boyfriend hold his hand in a movie theater was a new and satisfying experience.

When the lights came up, Ed remained seated, embarrassingly wiping away a few tears.

"That's one of the best movies I ever saw," he said, watching the crowd file out of the theater.

Rick's smile, "the warm and tender special," as Ed had begun to think of it, shone on his face. "I'm glad. I was hoping you'd get it."

"Oh, I don't know if I got it." Ed reached for his jacket. "I just know I can't remember the last time I laughed that hard."

"Cried a little, too, I see. I'm glad I've got me a man who isn't afraid to cry at the movies."

"Well, that ending. I mean, it's sad and happy at the same time. I almost wish we could stay for the second showing. I used to do that when I was kid, going to the movies at the Strand in Porterfield. We'd hide in the bathroom, then sit through it again."

"Much as I would like that, baby, I have to get home and get to bed," Rick said regretfully, as they slowly followed the crowd into the lobby.

They paused outside the little college theater, zipping up their jackets against the cold November night.

"Did you get the lesson from the movie?" Rick asked.

"Darlin', there were a lot of lessons in that movie. Which one do you mean?"

"Oh, the one that always hits me so hard, whenever I see it again," Rick said, as they slowly made their way to Ed's truck. "The one with the daisies."

"You mean being your own self instead of being one of the crowd?"

"Yeah. I love that. I first saw this movie back when I was really struggling with the gay thing. I remember sitting there, in that movie theater, suddenly knowing that it didn't matter if I was gay or purple or whatever, as long as I was true to myself and I didn't try to be like everyone else."

Ed paused by the truck, looking at Rick. "I know what you mean. I wish I'd seen this back then, too. I loved it, too, when they all freaked out about them being together. I want to remember that when someone gives us shit for being together."

Rick sighed. "I really think that movie helped me survive. Remember that Isley Brothers song, 'It's Your Thing'?"

"Sure."

"Well, I remember thinking it was a great song but a big lie. Everybody back then was running around saying, 'Do your own thing, man,' but when you did something different than they did, they ridiculed you for it. That drove me crazy for years, but then when I saw Harold and Maude kinda flipping the bird to society in general, I decided if they could do it, so could I. I could be whatever I wanted to be. Hell, I even thought about buying a hearse."

Ed laughed, unlocking the door. "I'll bet a lot people thought about buying a hearse after seeing that movie. Will my uncool, beat-up pickup truck do the job for tonight?"

Rick hauled himself onto the seat. "It'll do just fine, but don't drive like Maude. I wanna get home in one piece."

"Well, from something as great as that, to dinner at my mother's," Ed said in disgust, as he turned south onto Highway 107. "Talk about letdowns."

"Oh, baby, don't worry about it. I'm not. She just wants to see what kind of company you're keeping these days. And besides, I love pork chops."

"If you get to eat any," Ed said, passing a badly rusting Pinto. "She'll probably slam you with so many questions, you'll never get one bite to your mouth."

"Man, Ed, give it a rest already. I have excellent table manners, thanks to *my* mom, and despite the fact that I was a twerp in high school, I've learned how to hold a dignified conversation with other adults, even my boyfriend's mother. I swear to God I won't chew with my mouth open either."

"'I suppose you think that's very funny, Harold,'" Ed said, quoting from the movie.

Rick snickered. "Well, yes, as a matter of fact. I do."

"Well, hang on to that attitude, then," Ed grumbled, signaling his way back into the right lane. "'Cause you're gonna need it, darlin'."

Ed moped around the house all day Saturday, feeling as though he were facing an execution. He knew his mother well enough to know that she was suspicious about his sudden friendship with Rick, and this dinner was her way of getting to the bottom of whatever was going on between them. He honestly didn't know if she suspected the truth, but he was well aware of the fact that her badgering might force him to admit it. After that, he simply had no idea what she might say or do.

He thought of the movie the night before, and the things Harold's mother had said when he told her he planned to marry Maude.

"I wonder if Mom would be happier if I showed up for dinner with an eighty-year-old woman instead of Rick?" he said to himself, shuffling through his old records, looking for something to give him courage. He turned over "Give Us Your Blessings" by the Shangri-Las. His hand moved toward the turntable, then he remembered the song ended with the teenage couple dead in a car wreck after they ran off to get married against their parents' wishes. "That's not quite what I had in mind." He shoved it back in the cabinet.

Rick arrived, appropriately dressed for the occasion, and soon they were back in Ed's truck, heading to his childhood home on East Walnut Street.

"I've been dealing with cranky postal customers for almost ten years," Rick said, turning the radio volume down. "And there's no reason for her to think there's anything weird about our friendship. We're just a couple of guys hanging out together. What's wrong with that?"

Ed was pretty sure Norma would come up with something. He turned the volume back up. Stephanie Mills was singing "Never Knew Love Like This Before."

"Don't turn this one down. It reminds me of us."

Rick reached for Ed's hand, shaking his head. "Oh, baby, you're so queer. And I truly do love you for it."

They both laughed, and Ed was pleased to relieve some of his tension. "Did you wear your bulletproof vest?"

"Oh, Ed," Rick scolded him. "If your old lady was really the battle-ax you make her out to be, I don't think you'd have turned out so good. Calm down already."

Ed pulled up in front of the house and parked. Rick looked at the comfortable, old two-story house with interest.

"Now remember," Ed told him. "Don't mention the election. She's still pissed as hell that Reagan won. And if it does come up, for God's sake, don't tell her you decided to vote for John Anderson instead of Jimmy Carter."

"Yeah, yeah," Rick said as they made their way up the front walk. "You gonna show me your room? Maybe we can sneak upstairs and make out while she's washing the dishes. Just kidding," he said, seeing the look on Ed's face. "Shit! I'll behave, I promise."

Ed pulled open the storm door and reached for the knob on the inside door. "Mom?"

"Oh, come on in," she hollered from the kitchen. "Don't just stand there, letting all the heat out."

Ed rolled his eyes at Rick, who smirked at him. They walked to the kitchen, toward the sound of her voice. Ed noticed, as they passed through the dining room, that the table was laid with the good china.

Norma was at the stove, stirring a steaming pot. Her Merle Norman makeup was perfectly applied, and she was wearing her company apron. Ed's eyebrows rose, surprised that she seemed to be turning the meal into an occasion.

She looked up. "Well! This must the Rick I keep hearing about." She slammed a pot lid and turned to face them.

"It's nice to meet you, Mrs. Stephens." Rick smiled at her.

"Oh, just plain Norma will do. Don't even try any of that Eddie Haskell nonsense on me. I always hated that kid. 'How lovely you look today, Mrs. Cleaver.' June didn't fall for it and neither do I." She narrowed her eyes, looking Rick over. "So. Ed tells me you're a mailman. Probably been on your feet all day. Go sit down. This'll be a while. Ed, get him something to drink. I'm too busy." She looked at Ed's empty hands. "Didn't you bring anything? What did I tell you? Well, that's that. You're stuck with water. Ed, get the man a glass of water. Pour yourself one, too. Honestly."

Rick retreated to the living room. Ed moved over to the refrigerator.

"Edward," Norma whispered, catching his arm. "He has a *beard*."

Ed sighed. It was going to be a long night.

⁂

Once they were seated at the dining room table, Ed reflected on how many meals he had eaten at that very table in his life, Laurie sitting across from him, his father at the head of the table, his mother at the foot. Now he sat in his usual chair, and Rick sat across from him in Laurie's old place. After Tim Stephens had died, Norma had moved herself to the head of the table, which was only appropriate, as she'd always considered herself the head of the family anyway.

Norma was giving Rick the third degree, and Rick was performing beautifully, giving pleasant and polite answers to her questions. He was even eating the lima beans, and Ed happened to know that Rick hated lima beans.

"So, Rick," she said, spooning more mashed potatoes for herself. "What do you think of Reagan winning the election?"

It was a trap, Ed thought, glad he had warned Rick.

"It's a damned shame, Norma. God only knows where we'll be in four years."

"Well, if that isn't the truth." Norma snorted. "Probably halfway to hell in a handcart."

"I understand you're a big *Dallas* fan," Rick said, pushing lima beans around on his plate. "Ed told me you predicted it was Kristin who shot J. R. That's pretty good. I thought it was Alan."

"Any fool would have figured that out," Norma huffed. Her eyes narrowed at Rick. "Why on earth do you have all that hair on your face? Gillette invented razors for a reason, you know."

Ed almost choked on his pork chop. Rick blushed.

"Well, I like it," Rick mumbled, then regained his composure. "Actually *my* mother likes it, too."

"Oh, she does not. She's just saying that to spare your feelings and her own embarrassment. No mother wants to see a beard on her son. Why, that mustache of Ed's is bad enough. If he grew a beard, I'd cut him out of the will."

"Mom," Ed said. "A lot of men have been growing facial hair in the last ten years or so. There's not a thing wrong with it."

"Fools, all of them." Norma shook her head. She looked at Rick and changed the subject. Again. "So, Rick, I understand you're in Porterfield with your sister. She married that worthless Hank Romanowski? Is that right?"

"Yes," said Rick warily.

"That's a shame, just a shame." She shook her head. "Well, I guess there are those who make those kind of mistakes. I'm sure your sister is a good woman in spite of it. I just feel bad for those poor kids. I just hope we don't see their faces on 'wanted' posters in that post office of yours someday."

Rick put his fork down, color once again rising in his cheeks. Ed held his breath. He suspected Norma had really stepped on a landmine this time.

"Now look here," Rick said calmly. "If you are trying to imply that my nieces and nephew are going to turn out to be criminals because their worthless, son of a bitch of a father ran out on them, you've got another think coming, lady." He glared at her. "My sister is doing her best in a bad situation, and I'm doing my best to help her raise three good kids. And they're going to turn out just fine, if I have anything to say about it."

Norma drew back a bit. "Well, you don't have to get so huffy about it."

"I think maybe I do," Rick said, calm voice restored. "I've been doing my best to be nice, avoiding the potshots you've been taking at me all evening." He looked at his plate. "I'm even eating these damned lima beans. And I hate 'em!"

Rick glared at Norma, and she glared back at him. Finally a smile twitched at Norma's lips. "Well," she said. "Nothing wrong with a man standing up for his family." She smiled full-out at Rick. "Oh, scrape those beans off your plate, Rick. For Pete's sake, you don't have to eat them on my account. Do you want some more potatoes?" She offered the bowl to him.

Rick looked at her in surprise. Then he smiled as well. "Thanks. Yes, I'd like some more."

Ed stared at them both. *I don't believe it,* he thought. *I just don't believe it.* "Well," he finally said, wracking his brain for something to say. "Think it'll snow before Thanksgiving?"

"Oh, Ed," his mother scolded. "Calm down. There's nothing wrong over here—is there, Rick?"

"Not a thing," Rick said, smiling back at her.

Ed noticed the respect growing between them, and perhaps even a friendship as well.

"Eat up, boys," Norma commanded. "There's certainly plenty. I like to see a man with a healthy appetite, except for that Ted Gillis who used to hang around here. That boy had a little too much appetite. What ever did happen to him? Oh, who cares. I never liked him anyway. So, you two. I suppose Rick will be moving into that house of yours, Ed. Do I need to put him on my Christmas list?"

This time they both choked on their pork chops.

"Mom!" Ed sputtered. "Whatever makes you say a thing like that? Geez."

Norma Stephens rose from the table. Hands on hips, she looked right at Ed. "Edward Stephens. You're twenty-eight years old. You haven't had a girlfriend since high school. I may be a big pain in your bee-hind, but I'm not stupid." Another smile twitched her face. "Now. Who wants coffee?" she asked as she headed for the kitchen.

Ed and Rick stared at each other across the table, open-mouthed.

"How 'bout that," Rick finally said, taking a sip of water. "She may be a big pain in your bee-hind, but she's certainly full of surprises."

"I said, *who wants coffee?*" Norma barked from the kitchen.

"I do," Rick called back. He looked at Ed, gesturing for him to go to the kitchen.

Ed slowly got to his feet. Feeling empty-handed, he grabbed the lima bean bowl and carried it to the kitchen.

"I don't want any. You know I don't drink coffee, Mom."

Norma, her back to him, was plugging in her old coffeepot. "It's about time you did," she grumbled. "It's time you grew up and drank what adults drink."

"Okay then. Pour a cup for me, too," he said, clutching the lima bean bowl.

She turned to look at him. "Oh, honestly. Put that bowl down somewhere before you break it."

Ed placed it on the counter. "I'm sorry."

"I know," she said, her back to him once again.

"You mean you know I'm sorry about the lima beans, or I'm sorry about—"

"I know what you're sorry about, Ed. Don't waste your time." She turned around to face him, a scowl on her face. "I knew this day was coming, so there's no reason for you to get all upset."

Ed put one hand on the counter for support. "How'd you know, Mom?"

Norma sighed, the scowl disappearing, replaced with a look of sadness. She put the lid back on the coffee jar, twisting it tight with great care.

"Eddie," she said, using his father's name for him, "your father and I had a talk about you not long before he died. I kept wondering when you were going to find a girl and get married, and your father finally told me he didn't think you would ever get married. I didn't know what he meant, then he told me what he'd begun to think about you. I was furious with him for even suggesting such a thing, but he reminded me, as he always did with you kids, that it wasn't our place to judge, but our job to stand behind you."

Ed clutched the counter. He felt unable to move. "You mean, Dad *knew*?"

"He *suspected*. After I calmed down, I began to think about it, and what he also said around that time, that he didn't care if we had any more grandchildren, as long as you were happy. He said that if you were . . . were different, his only hope was that you'd find someone who would make you happy and take care of you, so he wouldn't have to worry about you being alone."

Ed felt tears come to his eyes. "Dad really said that?"

"Yes, he did. After he died so sudden, I knew it would be up to me to face whatever happened with you." She paused, looking at the coffee jar. "I don't know, Ed. I was raised to believe this isn't right, but then I look at some of the so-called righteous in this town, sinning left and right, and I remember what your father said. It's not up to me to judge. I just need to be your mother and support you. That's what your father would do if he was here. And I've no doubt that he would like Rick. A part of me wants to throw him out of the house, but another part of me wants to thank him, because it looks like he's making you happy."

"He is, Mom," Ed whispered.

Norma opened a cabinet door to put away the coffee jar. "I'm still not quite comfortable with this, you know. I can only imagine what some people in this town would say, but I guess they don't have to know what's what. But I'm your mother, and you're my son. Despite what I might say, you're a good son, and you always have been. If this is what you want, I'll stand by you.

"That Rick better watch his step, though," she added, sounding more like herself. "I'll be watching him!"

Ed felt relieved laughter bubbling up in his chest. "Oh, I think he knows that, Mom, believe me."

"Oh, for Pete's sake, get out my kitchen," she barked. "You know I can't stand to see a grown man cry. Go tell Rick his coffee will be ready in a minute. And, Ed, you don't have to drink any if you don't want to."

"Thanks, Mom," he said, looking at her through blurry eyes.

⋘•⋙

Norma walked them both to the door an hour later. "Shoo, shoo." She waved her hands toward the door. "I might as well turn on the TV and see who's on that fool love boat this week."

Rick paused in putting on his jacket. "Thanks again, Norma. I really enjoyed it, even the lima beans." He laughed, but then added solemnly, "I want you to know I care about your son very much, and I'll do whatever I need to make sure he, and you, both know that."

Ed blushed bright red, wondering how Norma would react to that. "Aw, Rick."

"Oh, hush up, Ed," Norma commanded. "He's just saying what any good potential son-in-law would say." She shook her head. "Another son-in-law. And with a beard, too! Your father may not be turning in his grave, but the ground where mine'll be is churning. Oh, well. At least I've got someone else to cook for now."

"You can cook for me anytime, Norma," Rick said, his "warm and tender special" on his face.

Ed looked at them both, wondering just who was in charge of miracles and why they'd screwed up and given him two in such a short period of time. Whoever it was, he thought, he owed them one hell of a thank-you note.

Chapter Ten

Ed was riding the Ferris wheel at the Stratton County fair, although the fair seemed to be taking place in his backyard instead of the fairgrounds. A cotton candy stand was near the garage, and his oak tree had been replaced by the Rock-o-Planes. He thought about going on the Rock-o-Planes, but it appeared people were falling out when the egg-shaped cars flipped upside down. He thought he saw his mother pitching hoops at the cigarette game, and his dad was eating a foot-long hotdog, talking with Don Hoffmeyer, the Porterfield postmaster.

He looked for Rick, but didn't see him. Suddenly his dad appeared on the Ferris wheel, in the seat above him, shouting to get his attention. He told Ed he had been talking to Don, and Don had told him Rick was going to Bulgaria as part of a postal exchange program behind the Iron Curtain.

"Does that mean I get a Bulgarian boyfriend?" Ed hollered up at him, but his dad opened his seat's safety bar, then climbed down the side of the wheel to finish his conversation with Don.

Ed shouted at the ride operator that he wanted to get off, but the ride guy said he couldn't find Ed's ticket. The wheel began to revolve, and Ed thought he saw Rick standing in line for the Octopus, but it turned out to be Kenny Rogers singing "Lady." Ed, blinking in surprise, suddenly found himself in his bedroom, looking at his chest of drawers, while Kenny Rogers blared from the clock radio.

"Geez," Ed muttered, reaching out to silence Kenny. He shook his head, trying to shake the remnants of the dream out of his head. "Dr. Freud, wherever you are, don't tell me. I don't want to know what that was all about."

He yawned, scratching his head. "What a way to start the day." He pushed back the covers. "Kenny Rogers instead of Rick. Yuck."

It was the Tuesday after Thanksgiving, and he had set the alarm to remind himself to stop by Hilda Penfield's before his usual Tuesday morning with Mrs. Heston. Mrs. Penfield had called late the night before, apologizing for bothering him, but she had a bit of a problem with her refrigerator, and could he come take a look at it?

Ed sighed his way through breakfast, groaned and cussed in the shower, and scowled at his face while shaving. He was in a piss-poor mood and wanted to get the worst of it out before he saw anyone. He knew what the trouble was. He was going through Rick withdrawal.

He had intended to spend Thanksgiving being properly grateful for his recent blessings, but the Fates that had been so kind recently seemed to withdraw their support. While Rick had spent the holiday in Indianapolis with his parents, Claire, and her children, Ed passed a dull and rather uncomfortable afternoon at Laurie's, keeping an eye on his mother and making feeble attempts at conversation with Todd's parents and younger brother. Norma had little use for Eunice Ames, Todd's mother, who had subtly inferred on past occasions that she felt her son had married beneath his social station. Ed didn't much like her either, but at Laurie's anxious request, he'd done his best to run interference between the two women while the other men watched football.

The rest of the weekend had been equally uninspiring. Rick, with no seniority at the post office, had to work Friday and Saturday, and the time they could have spent together was preempted by plans made before they met each other, including another round trip to Indianapolis for Rick to attend a holiday party with his parents, and Ed's job to act as chauffeur for Mrs. Heston, who was visiting family in South Bend. When Rick was available, he was tired from work and driving and wanted little more than uninterrupted sleep. Ed had understood, but pessimistically wondered if a pattern was being set for the holidays to come.

It was sprinkling as he set out for Mrs. Penfield's, and officially raining as he pulled into her driveway.

"Oh, great," he said, slamming the truck door. "I get to haul groceries in the rain today."

He trotted to the back door, trying to dodge the cold drops. Mrs. Penfield immediately answered his impatient knock.

"Weather got you down, Ed?" she asked archly, always an expert at discerning his moods.

"Yeah," Ed muttered, inspecting the refrigerator. He quickly found the problem, an evaporation motor gone bad. "I'll stop by Ripley's Appliance when I'm through with Mrs. Heston. They're pretty good about letting me raid their parts department. I'm sure they'll have a replacement motor. I'll try to get it installed before lunch. Don't worry about your food. I know it's not very cold in there, but it'll keep for a few more hours."

Mrs. Penfield beamed at him. "I don't know what I'd do without you, Ed. Thanks so much for taking care of this for me."

Ed felt his first smile of the day creep onto his face. It was good to be appreciated.

"How is your Rick these days?" she asked, handing him a mug of tea. Ed, who disliked coffee, found tea an acceptable substitution.

"Your guess is as good as mine." He sipped the comfortingly hot beverage. "I haven't seen much of him. I s'pose this is one of those times when I have to be strong, like you said. Between families and jobs, we can't seem to connect these days."

Mrs. Penfield slowly lowered herself to a kitchen chair. "Don't worry about it too much. You're still at the beginning, and it takes a while to establish patterns for the holidays. Also," she said with a twinkle in her eye, "you're still in the wonderful phase of feeling that every separation is an eternity. That will pass soon enough, so enjoy the feeling while it lasts."

Ed sighed. "I know. I've told myself that. Actually, I was invited to Indianapolis for Thanksgiving, but I decided Mom's orbit had been rocked enough already without me leaving town over a family holiday."

"Ah, so she's aware of your relationship with Rick," Mrs. Penfield said, obviously pleased. "I'm glad. That's one less burden for you."

"Yeah. She's being pretty cool about it, considering," Ed said gratefully, "but I didn't want to make a big deal over Thanksgiving while she's still getting used to the whole thing. Besides, Laurie would have killed me. I had to spend the day sending Mom and Mrs. Ames to their corners. Mom's hated her since she told a few of her snob friends that she thought Todd and Laurie's wedding was tacky."

Mrs. Penfield rolled her eyes heavenward. "Eunice Ames. Such a dreadful social climber. The years she spent on the school board were among my most difficult at Porterfield High. I sympathize completely with Norma. We won't even discuss the grief she routinely gave George about legal matters," she said, referring to her late husband's law practice. "I'm just glad to see you don't seem to be incurring any in-law problems."

"Oh, no. As I said, Mom's being great for Mom, and the Bentons want to meet me. They're teachers, too, by the way. Oh," Ed said, putting down his mug. "I forgot. Rick wanted me to thank you for those books. He'd like to meet you sometime."

"I'd like that," Mrs. Penfield said with a smile. "I understand this is a busy time of the year, but if the two of you can spare some time, do stop by before Christmas."

"I'll try." Ed looked at his watch. "Right now, though, I have a date with Mrs. Heston and a grocery list."

Mrs. Heston's grocery list for the week was thankfully short, and she spent their time together repeatedly thanking Ed for his chauffeuring duties over the weekend, which went far in relieving his bad mood. He managed to install Mrs. Penfield's new refrigerator motor before lunch and was home in time to meet Rick as usual.

"Oh, I needed that," Rick whispered after an extended kiss just inside Ed's front door. "Although I sometimes wonder if the people who live east of you on Coleman Street wonder why their mail seems to be arriving later than it used to."

"Let 'em wait," Ed said heartlessly. "I don't get to see nearly enough of you."

"Hell," Rick said, chuckling. "I don't even have any mail for you today."

Ed was so pleased to be this close to Rick, he found himself acting a bit more aggressively than he usually allowed himself to be at that time of day.

Rick moaned happily in response, but said, "Aw, c'mon, baby. Cut that out. I love it, but I don't want to finish my route with a hard-on."

"Well, let me finish what I started, and believe me, that hard-on will be gone before you leave the house."

Rick sighed. "I wish."

Ed reluctantly let Rick go. "Ah, don't worry about it. Just come back tonight and we can do whatever we want. Think of it as a coming attraction."

Rick looked troubled. "Uh, baby . . . I can't come over tonight. I promised Claire I'd stay with the kids while she goes to a birthday party for the other dental hygienist at the office." He pulled Ed back to him. "Tomorrow night?"

"Absolutely," Ed said, trying hard not to look disappointed.

Rick adjusted the bag on his shoulder. "I'll call you tonight after the kids are in bed. We'll make some plans for tomorrow, okay?"

Ed nodded. Rick turned to leave, then stopped and turned back to Ed, kissing him. "I love you, baby."

Ed kissed him back. "I love you, too." He slapped Rick's ass. "Now go back to work before I do something we'll both regret."

Ed paused at the door as he did most every day, watching Rick resume his mail route, shoulders hunched a bit in the drizzle. Ed knew he was being childish, but he found himself resenting three children across town. He suspected that his gratitude at having Rick in his life was becoming tinged with greed. Now that he and Rick were established, he wanted Rick all to himself.

The past month had been among the finest in his life, but he couldn't help wanting more than Rick could offer at this time. Ed stopped that train of thought and began to mentally count his blessings. He had found the man of his dreams, not in San Francisco or New York or some other glamorous city, but right here in Porterfield, Indiana, population nine thousand, and literally right on his doorstep. Not only was the man of his dreams as crazy about Ed as Ed was about him, but Rick was warm, kind, funny, and smart, not to mention a handsome man, a great kisser, and an even better lover. Rick took his job responsibilities seriously, and was equally responsible when it came to his sister and her three children. Ed did not need to be told how rare that was in any man, let alone a gay one.

Ed sighed, the lyrics of Chicago's melancholy "Wishing You Were Here" going through his mind. He imagined Rick instead of Peter Cetera singing about being away from home because of a job he had to do.

"I'm a pig," Ed whispered to himself. "I've been handed the biggest dream I've ever had, and I still want more. I oughta be ashamed."

He was ashamed, and vowed to be more understanding of Rick's commitments, no matter how much he wanted to feel otherwise.

⋘•⋙

Rick came over the next night, and Ed did indeed finish what he had started the day before. He had Rick undressed and in bed minutes after he had arrived. A noisy, passionate lovemaking session followed, and when all their itches had been thoroughly scratched, they lay next to each, quietly enjoying the afterglow.

"Damn," Rick said, reaching for Ed's hand. "What's that old Foreigner song? 'Feels Like the First Time'? It still does, baby, with you."

"Well, I'm glad to know that you haven't gotten tired of me after a little more than a month."

Rick stretched expansively, pulling Ed closer to him. "I don't think that's gonna happen for quite a while. I tell you, though, I almost wished I smoked after something like that."

"How about something to drink?" Ed asked, rolling toward the side of the bed.

"Not now." Rick pulled him back. "It can wait. I don't think I'm done with you yet," he teased, giving Ed a kiss.

Ed curled up next to him. "This is so nice."

Rick stared at the ceiling, his brow creased in thought. "Yes, it is." He turned to Ed. "About last night—"

Ed put his hand over Rick's mouth. "Don't even worry about it."

"But I *do* worry about it," Rick said, pushing Ed's hand away. "It's not fair. I mean, if I spend all the time with you that I want, I feel like I'm neglecting the kids. And vice versa. And believe me, the last thing I ever want you to feel is neglected."

"Darlin', the last thing I feel right now is neglected. I didn't feel neglected last night either. I'm just so grateful to have found you. Why, just think, what we have is probably more than some guys ever get."

"Still, I wish there was some way I could, you know, kinda *incorporate* my life a little more. Although Claire tells me not to worry about it, I guess I've been reluctant for the kids to see the two of us together a lot. Claire says that stupid, that there's nothing wrong with them being exposed to a healthy, happy relationship. I guess she's right, but this town and all . . . well, you know."

"Oh, yes. I know this town even better than you do. I grew up here, remember? Still, considering the way Mom is doing her best to accept the situation, there may be hope for Porterfield yet."

"Claire says she'd really like to get to know you better, and she'd like the kids to get to know you, too. She says she's impressed with what she's seen of you, so far."

"Really?"

Ed had met Claire and the kids several times before, usually when he stopped by to pick up Rick for an evening out. He had immediately liked Claire, who was a few years older than her brother and seemed to share most of his best qualities. The kids seemed okay, too.

Rick laughed. "Yeah, she said you've given me an excuse to stay here in Porterfield, better than anything she could think up." He kissed Ed. "Ah, and what an excuse you are. So what do you think? I survived dinner with your mother. Do you think you could put on your Uncle Ed face and spend some time with my family?"

"I don't see why not," Ed said, thinking of his own niece and nephew. "It's not like I haven't had any experience." He smiled at Rick. "What the hell. If it means I get to spend more time with you, I'm all for it."

⋘•⋙

Rick looked triumphant when he stopped to see Ed the next afternoon. "Guess what? The perfect excuse has come up for you to spend some time at my place. You can be the handyman and Uncle Ed at the same time. How are you with doorknobs and locks?"

Ed smiled at Rick's eagerness. "Depends. What's going on?"

"Well, the front door lock at that house has never been quite right. And this morning the doorknob came off in my hand." Rick rolled his eyes. "You know, a nice little suburban house with everything guaranteed to fall apart. Anyway, do you think you could install a new doorknob and a new lock?"

"I'm seeing you standing there, holding on to that doorknob," Ed said, and laughed. "I would have loved to have seen the look on your face."

"And heard what I said, or would have said, if the kids weren't around." Rick laughed with him. "Can you do it?"

"Oh, sure. That shouldn't be any problem. I've done it before. I'll just have to look at it, then go over to the lumberyard for some new hardware. Easy stuff," he bragged.

"My man, the handyman. He's good at all kinds of things." Rick grabbed him and sighed happily. "Here's Claire's idea. She thought you could come over Saturday in the afternoon and fix the door, then stay to supper. What do you think?"

"I can do that, on one condition."

"Oh?"

"Yeah, I'll fix your door, and play with the kids, and be nice to your sister, and everything else, if, sometime later, Uncle Ed gets to spend some alone time with Uncle Rick."

"No sweat, baby," Rick said, kissing him. "No sweat."

And so the plans for Saturday were set, at least until Rick called him later that day.

"Claire's come up with another brainstorm," he said with a good deal less enthusiasm than he had shown earlier. "She really wants to go to Fort Wayne and do some Christmas shopping for the kids. She was hoping I'd go with her, and you could stay and keep an eye on the kids while you fix the door. Then, when we get back to town, we'd stop at Gino's and pick up pizza for all of us."

"She wants me to *babysit* her kids?" Ed asked, surprised. "Boy, she really does trust me, doesn't she?"

"Yeah. I told her I thought it was an awful lot to ask, but I promised to ask you anyway. It shouldn't be too bad, though. Judy's going to visit a friend down the street, so that just leaves Josh and Jane. And they'll probably be happy with TV. Well," he conceded, "Jane may drag out Candy Land, but I think you can handle that. But listen, baby, if you don't want to do it, it's okay."

Ed thought for a moment. "Well, the door won't take too long. I can certainly keep an eye on two kids watching the tube. And I do love those ice cream floats in Candy Land."

Rick laughed. "Okay. You're committed now. And have I told you yet today how much I love you?"

"Oh, I think you may have mentioned it." Ed smiled into the phone. "But you can tell me again on Saturday. Hell, *show* me again after that pizza."

"Mmm," Rick moaned. "Pizza and Ed. What a combo! Who knows? I just may pick up an extra Christmas present for you, too."

⋘•⋙

Saturday afternoon, Ed drove across town to Claire's little ranch house in the Westside Hills subdivision. Ed, an east-side-of-town boy, had never spent much time on the far west edge of Porterfield, and he had to admit he much preferred the eastern section of town with its old, solid, established houses and full-grown trees. He suspected that Rick felt the same way, and allowed himself a brief dream of the two of them living in a graceful old home, not unlike Mrs. Penfield's.

He quickly checked out Claire's front door, and as he thought, it would be an easy fix. He drove over to the lumberyard/home-improvement store where he bought most of his supplies, thinking about his babysitting chore ahead of him.

Eleven-year-old Judy appeared to be an average sort of girl on the verge of adolescence. Eight-year-old Josh bore a striking resemblance to his Uncle Rick and clearly doted on him. Josh loved to read, Rick had said, and one of Rick's favorite things to do was take Josh to the Porterfield library. Jane, at five, seemed to be more of a handful, and Ed hoped it wouldn't take much more than a good rousing game of Candy Land to endear him to her.

Back at the house, Ed carried the new hardware and his toolbox in through the attached garage to the back door. Claire was in the kitchen, washing the lunch dishes. She smiled warmly at Ed as he walked in. Claire was several inches shorter than her brother, but their resemblance, from dark hair to identical warm smiles, was remarkable. Claire's face seemed a bit worn from her troubled marriage, and her body had thickened considerably after three children. Still, Ed could see in her the pretty high school girl Rick had mentioned.

"This is so nice of you," she said. "Between fixing the door and watching my monsters all afternoon, I feel like I should be giving you a lot more than some pizza."

Ed smiled back. "Don't worry about it. You know, I'd do just about anything for your brother."

Claire hung up her dish towel to dry. "Yeah, I'm kinda aware of that, and I couldn't be happier. Really. I can't tell you how glad I am the two of you met and that things are going so well. It takes a lot of guilt off me, knowing that Rick is happy, after I practically dragged him here from Indianapolis.'

"You didn't have to drag me," Rick said, entering the kitchen. "Well, maybe a little bit, but it has definitely paid off." He gave Ed a quick kiss. "Who knew Porterfield had such a cute handyman, hmm?"

"Oh, for . . . ," Ed mumbled, blushing.

Claire, grinning, shook her head at her brother. "We sure don't have to stop and see Santa at the mall. He already knows what you want for Christmas. Let me get my coat. And my gloves. It's cold out. They're talking about snow, did you hear?" she said as she walked out.

"Hey, kids," Rick hollered. "Come say hi to Ed."

All three of them straggled into the kitchen, murmured greetings, and listened patiently as Rick told them to behave themselves. Ed noticed that Josh and little Jane were obviously in the midst of some all-day-type sibling feud, but they had managed somehow to unite against Judy, the oldest, who seemed disgusted with both of them. Rick seemed oblivious to it in the way an insider is used to the serial dramas of kids, but Ed wondered what was brewing between them. He didn't ask for details, figuring, at least for the moment, that what he didn't know wouldn't hurt him.

After Claire and Rick left, Judy immediately went to the bedroom she shared with Jane, practically slamming the door behind her. Josh and Jane went to the living room, Jane crawling up on the sofa to return to her television show, Josh to an easy chair to pick up the *Highlights* magazine he had left there. Ed hauled his stuff over to the front door. Music blared out of Judy's room, Pink Floyd's "Another Brick in the Wall." *Well, at least she's got good taste,* Ed thought as he opened his toolbox, nervous though at the thought that the lyrics could incite open rebellion among the children.

"She thinks she's so smart," Josh muttered to Jane, glancing down the hall toward the bedrooms.

"I'm not talking to you," Jane replied, eyes never leaving the TV screen.

Ed smiled, remembering his childhood battles with his sister. He just hoped open warfare would be avoided until after Claire and Rick returned.

The music stopped abruptly with the sound of a phonograph needle being yanked off a record. Ed winced. Judy appeared shortly after that.

"I'm leaving," she said.

"Good," said Josh and Jane together.

"I'm going down the street to my friend Angie's house," Judy said to Ed. "Mom said it was okay."

"I know. Have a good time."

"We're going to make Christmas cookies," Judy said, pulling her coat from the closet.

"Mmm, that sounds good. Think you'll be able to spare some for a hungry handyman?" Ed asked with a grin.

"Oh, sure," she said, buttoning her coat. "Which do you like best, the Santas or the Christmas trees? Or maybe wreaths. I think they have a wreath cookie cutter, too."

"Christmas trees," Ed replied, "with lots of green icing."

"Yeah, me too."

Judy searched her pockets for something. Mittens, it turned out. She pulled them on, then stood silently, staring at Ed. He looked back at her. He noticed, with empathy, her preteen awkwardness, but had no doubt she would be as popular as her mother had been when she hit high school.

"Ready to go?" he asked, made uneasy by her stare.

She blinked once, studying him further, a thoughtful frown on her face. "Uncle Rick spends a lot of time at your house, doesn't he?" she finally asked.

"Uh, yeah," Ed mumbled, searching his toolbox for another screwdriver.

"You don't have any kids, do you?"

"No," Ed admitted.

"Well, then." She looked back at her brother and sister. "I don't blame him. A bit," she hollered in their direction. "I'll see you later," she said politely to Ed. "Bye."

Judy left through the open door, as Ed breathed a small sigh of relief.

"Big turd," Josh muttered.

"Shut up," Jane said.

Ed went back to work, hoping to stay out of the crossfire. He examined the old doorknob. He agreed with Rick. Whoever had installed it had definitely done it on the cheap. The knob fell out and hit his knee.

"Aw, crud."

Josh looked up from his magazine. "Can I help?" he asked, walking over to Ed.

Jane ignored him, still engrossed with Kukla, Fran, and Ollie, and the *CBS Children's Film Festival.*

"Sure. You can hand me stuff when I need it. Here," he said, giving Josh a screwdriver.

"Neat," said Josh, his face lighting up.

Ed grinned at him. He felt as though he were dealing with a miniature Rick.

The two worked together, Josh eagerly handing Ed his tools, while Ed explained what he was doing. Josh leaned over and picked up the keys Ed had bought for the new lock.

"Can I hold these?"

"Well, okay," Ed said. "But be really careful. We can't lose them."

"I will be." Josh turned the keys over in his hand. "I like those colored keys they have better."

"Sorry," said Ed. "This was all they had at the lumberyard. Let's just hope they work okay."

It didn't take too long for Ed to install the new knob and lock. He pushed the door shut and opened it, testing the knob, then locked and unlocked the door.

"Not bad," he said, pleased with his work.

"Are we done already?" Josh asked.

"Nope." Ed opened the door and walked outside. Josh followed him. "Now we need to see if the lock works okay from the outside." He pulled the door shut. "Okay, Josh, hand me a key. Let's see if it works."

Josh got a stricken look on his face.

"Josh, I told you to be careful with those keys," Ed said, twisting the knob. "Don't you still have them?"

"No," Josh whispered. "I knew you wanted me to be careful with them, so I put them on the table so I wouldn't lose them."

Ed tried the door again. Yep, it was locked all right.

Ed looked at Josh. Josh looked back at Ed.

"Aw, crud," said Josh.

"It's not the end of the world." Ed peered through the glass to make sure Jane was still watching TV. "We'll just go around through the garage and—"

Josh was shaking his head. "Mom always locks the kitchen door when she leaves the house."

"Maybe this time she didn't. You wait here."

Ed walked around the house, through the garage, and tried the door to the kitchen. Damn, the kid was right. He walked back to the front steps, where Josh was banging on the door, hollering, "Let us in!"

"No," Jane shouted back. "I'm still mad at you."

Ed wished he had asked earlier what was going on with them. "Okay, what'd you do to her?"

"Nothing," said Josh, sitting down on the steps.

"Come on, Josh." Ed sat next to him. "I was mean to my sister all the time when I was your age. You can tell me. Maybe I can get her to unlock the door for us."

Josh sighed. He looked up at Ed. "Promise not to tell?"

"Cross my heart." Ed did just that.

"Well . . . she took some of the comic books Uncle Rick gave me this morning, just when I wanted to look at them. So I hid her teddy bear."

Ed would have been amused if he wasn't beginning to get cold. "Well, that's no problem. Just tell her where you hid it. Then she'll unlock the door for us."

"I can't," Josh said, looking away.

"Why not?"

"'Cause I don't remember where I hid it," he admitted, rubbing his arms.

It was Ed's turn to sigh. He noticed that Josh was wearing only a T-shirt with his jeans. The temperature couldn't have been much above thirty degrees outside. *It would be just great if the kid gets hypothermia while I'm in charge.*

"C'mon," he said, leading Josh over to his truck in the driveway.

He opened the passenger door and boosted Josh up to the seat. Then he went around to the other side and got in. Fortunately his own keys were in his pocket. He started the truck and jacked up the heater.

"We'll just sit here a minute while I figure out what to do."

"Can we go someplace?" Josh asked, apparently unconcerned about his sister in the house. "I don't think I've ever ridden in a pickup truck before."

"Maybe later," Ed said, hoping to shut him up.

He turned the radio on. Barbra Streisand wailed through the speakers, telling them that she was a "Woman in Love."

"Do tell, Babs," Ed muttered.

He tried to think. Josh was happily exploring the glove compartment. He pulled out an Indiana highway map and promptly unfolded it. Ed glanced at him, wondering if the kid was any better at map folding than he was. He was pretty sure all the windows in the house would be shut and locked. These big-city types, he thought. No one else in Porterfield ever bothered to lock anything. He knew the storm windows were on, too, because Rick had told him about putting them on several weeks ago. He thought about trying to reason with Jane, but rejected it. He remembered that no amount of reasoning had appealed to Laurie at that age. He could break a window and crawl in, but wasn't too thrilled about the idea of explaining to Claire why she had a broken window on a cold day. Ed would replace it, of course, but still . .

He suddenly felt his back pocket to see if his wallet was there. Yes, it was. He opened it and took out his Shell credit card, remembering something he'd once seen on television. He looked over at Josh, who, it turned out, was no better at map folding than Ed was.

"Josh, I want you to wait here for a minute. I'm going to go check on Jane."

"Okay," he muttered, messing with the map.

Ed walked over to the front door and looked in. Jane was still on the sofa, but she was ignoring the TV in favor of the purloined comic books. He hurried into the garage, glancing over his shoulder to make sure Josh was still in the truck. He studied the door to the kitchen. Sure enough, it was relatively flimsy, with a simple, inside door lock on it. He squatted so the knob was at eye level. Looking around to make sure no one was watching, he slid his credit card between the door and the doorjamb, wiggling it against the lock. It had worked on TV, so maybe it would work for him.

"Are you gonna break the door down?" Josh suddenly asked from behind. Ed, startled, fell over, dropping the credit card.

"I thought I told you to wait in the truck," he snapped.

"I wanna see what you're doing." Josh picked up the credit card. "What's that?"

Ed looked at the boy for a moment. "It's a supersecret handyman's tool," he finally said. "It's so supersecret that only handymen are allowed to have them and to use them." Okay, so someday the kid would find out he lied. He'd worry about that later. "I'm going to use it to open the door."

"Neat," said Josh, his eyes open wide.

Ed slid the card back in. It took some work and some silent cursing, but he finally managed to open the door. His Shell card was rather mangled, and he figured he'd catch hell the next time he tried to use it. "Whew," he sighed, walking into the kitchen, Josh behind him. He sat down on a kitchen chair in relief while Josh ran into the living room.

"Hey, gimme back those comic books."

"Not until you give me my bear!"

"Ed, make her give me my comic books."

Ed closed his eyes, suddenly remembering that his truck was still running. Making sure the door was wide open, he ran outside and shut it off. He came back to find Jane hitting Josh with one of the comic books.

"Hey!" Ed clapped his hands. "Who's up for a game of Candy Land?"

⊰≻●≺⊱

Claire and Rick came home several hours later to find Josh on the sofa reading his comic books, while Ed, Jane, and her bear were sprawled on the floor, involved with their sixth game of Candy Land. Ed was once again stuck in the Molasses Swamp, much to Jane's delight. Jane, at Ed's insistence, had given the comic books back to Josh when Josh remembered that he had hidden her bear in the dryer.

"Well," Rick said, taking in the scene. "Looks like it's been a quiet afternoon around here."

Josh ran over to him. "Ed locked us out of the house, and I got to sit in his truck, and then he broke open the kitchen door. Boy, he's neat!"

"Hmm," said Rick, "would that have anything to do with *this*?" He held up Ed's battered Shell credit card. "I found this on the kitchen floor."

Ed was about to defend himself when Jane socked him on the arm. "Your turn."

Ed drew a card, a yellow one.

"Ha! Still stuck," she gloated.

"So you like Uncle Ed, huh?" Rick picked Josh up and swung him around. Claire snuck by with several bags she was obviously going to hide. "Teaching my nephew how to break and enter," Rick said to Ed, grinning mischievously. "Some babysitter you are."

Ed tried to glare back at him, but ended up grinning as well. "So did you bring the pizza or what? We're all hungry."

Judy arrived shortly thereafter with two covered plates of cookies, one for her family and one for Ed, whose plate consisted entirely of heavily iced Christmas trees. At the sight of pizza, the children suspended all earlier fights to happily devour their share of a Gino's extra pepperoni special.

Watching Rick with the kids, Ed felt his shame from earlier in the week return. Rick was wonderful with them and would make a terrific father, Ed thought rather wistfully. Ed had never given the idea of fatherhood much thought, but seeing Rick gently encourage Jane to finish her pizza slice before she attacked the cookies, he wondered what it would be like to have a little Rick or a little Ed running around. The idea of two men having a child was rather radical, so he reluctantly dismissed it from his mind. Rick caught his eye across the table and grinned. Ed couldn't help but wonder if he was thinking the same thing.

"Ed, I hope you'll take some of the leftovers home with you," Claire said, carrying plates to the sink.

"Oh, sure," he said. "I'm the king of leftovers. Just ask my mom."

"We can have it for lunch tomorrow," Rick said, smiling at Ed, who was pleased to know Rick planned on returning home with him for the night.

"Are you staying over at Ed's house again?" Josh asked, wiping away a milk mustache.

"Yeah. I'm trying to think of a way to steal all of his records," Rick whispered to Josh, mischievous grin in place.

Judy looked up at this information. "Do you have a lot of records?" she asked Ed, bright-eyed.

"I sure do. Some of them are kinda old, but if you want, you can come over sometime and see if there are any you like. We'll have a record party, like we used to do in school."

"Cool," Judy said. "Can I bring mine over, too?"

"Sure. That's what a record party is all about." A thought occurred to Ed, and he turned to Josh. "Hey, Josh, does it bother you when Uncle Rick spends the night away from your room?"

"No," Josh answered, flipping a pepperoni at Jane, who promptly flipped it back. "He snores a lot."

"Really?" Ed marveled, looking at though he was learning something new.

"Yeah. It's okay when I fall asleep first, but some nights I have to hit him with my pillow so he'll stop."

Ed chuckled as Rick sighed in disgust.

"Well, I'd change it, if I could," Rick said, looking into Ed's eyes.

Ed sensed the double meaning behind Rick's words. "Well," he said, as Jane crawled into his lap, demanding a Candy Land rematch, "if all we have to worry about is a little snoring, then I guess we're all pretty lucky."

As Ed allowed Jane to drag him back to the Candy Land board, he looked back at Rick, who mouthed "I love you" to him. Ed smiled at Rick, thinking he was luckier than any of them knew.

Chapter Eleven

Rick was making his usual early afternoon rest stop at Ed's house. Unusually, though, they weren't kissing, fondling, or teasing. They were just standing, arms around each other, listening to the stereo as Ed's scratchy 45 of "Ticket to Ride" played. It was December 9, 1980, and like millions around the world, Ed and Rick were in shock after hearing the news that John Lennon had been murdered the night before.

"It's so sad," Ed said quietly, holding on to Rick. "I mean, I was never a huge Beatles fan or anything, not like some of the kids I knew back then. But I always liked them, always thought John was cool, especially all the peace stuff he did. I just can't believe some nutcase would shoot him."

Rick nodded silently. Suddenly he smiled. "Remember seeing them on *Ed Sullivan* for the first time?"

Ed chuckled. "Oh, yes. You should have heard what my mom had to say that night."

The record changer clicked and another 45 dropped into place. "Revolution" began to play.

Rick's smiled dimmed. "All that talk. All that protesting. I don't think this damned world has changed a bit. It's still fucked." He sighed, hugging Ed to him. "Oh, well. At least one thing is going right. I happen to be in love with the cutest handyman in Porterfield, Indiana, and he's in love with me. Or at least I think he is." Rick looked at Ed, almost grinning.

Ed kissed him. "He is. Crazy mixed-up in love."

They both fell silent. The tragedy had taken all the fun out of their daily banter.

"Well," Rick finally said, sighing. "Back to work. You busy this afternoon?"

"Yeah." Ed reluctantly let go of Rick. "I'm installing the Rinkenbergers' new water heater, something I've never done before. If you hear an explosion coming from Oak Street, it's probably me."

"Be *careful*. I don't want you blown to bits now that I have you." Rick lifted his mailbag from the floor. He groaned, pulling the bag over his shoulder. "Damned Christmas mail. And it's only the ninth."

"Well, then, you be careful, too. I may need you for some cheering up later."

"Okay, okay," Rick said, adjusting the heavy bag. "I'll call you later. Maybe we can get together, have a toast to John, play some more Beatles records, and . . ." He trailed off and appeared to think for a moment. "I know. Then we can make love, not war, in honor of John. How do you like that?"

Ed smiled. "I like that *very* much."

"Good. It's a date." With one last kiss for Ed, Rick was on his way.

⋄•⋄

That evening, Ed relaxed with a beer on the sofa, while his old Beatles 45s played once again. He congratulated himself on his successful installation of the water heater, and mentally reviewed all the jobs he had lined up before Christmas. He was pleased to realize he'd have enough extra cash to buy something really nice for Rick. He didn't want to go overboard—it hadn't been two months yet—but he did want to get something to show how happy he was these days. He was contemplating and rejecting various ideas when the phone rang. He reached for it, assuming it would be Rick.

"Ed? It's Claire. We've got a bit of a problem. Rick threw his back out on his route today. He's been to my family doctor, who gave him some medication and told him to get several days' bed rest."

"Oh, no! Is he in a lot of pain?"

"Well, enough to make him a handful, if you know what I mean. He's always been a big baby when he's sick," she said—rather impatiently, Ed thought. "The thing is, between my job, the kids, and all their Christmas stuff starting, I can't really do much for him right now. And you know he shares that tiny bedroom with Josh. I was wondering if you would be willing to put him up at your place for a few days. I think"—Ed could hear a smile in her voice—"that he might get the attention he wants with you."

Wow! A chance to have Rick all to himself. Of course, he wasn't in very good shape, but still . . .

"Sure, I'll take care of him. Do you want me to come over and get him?"

"Oh, would you?" Claire said, sounding relieved. "I'll pack a bag with some of his stuff. Ed, I really appreciate this. First you babysit my kids, now my brother. I'm going to make sure Santa Claus knows about you."

"It's no problem, really. I'll come over after I've grabbed something to eat. Has he had his supper yet?"

"Yes. All *four* of my kids have been fed. Oh, and, Ed, one tip from someone who's been there. I'd suggest you stop off at the IGA on your way over here for some butter pecan ice cream. He always asks for it when he's sick in bed. I blame our mother. She always gave it to us when we were kids."

"Butter pecan ice cream," Ed repeated. "Hmm. Okay. I can do that. I'll be over in, say, forty-five minutes."

He hung up with Claire, excited by the change of events. He and Rick were actually going to be living together. Even though this was only temporary, Ed hoped it might give him an idea of what living with Rick would be like. They hadn't discussed it very much. Both being rather practical, they had more or less agreed that any talk of cohabitation would wait until they had known each other a good deal longer. Still, Ed thought, there's nothing wrong with a trial run.

Ed made and ate a sandwich, then inspected his house, imagining that both he and Rick were living in it together. Ed had bought the small forties-era bungalow for a good price several years earlier. He was no decorator, but he'd been able to create a warm, cozy environment with things he'd acquired over the years.

He climbed the stairs to the second floor, remembering his grand plans for running the plumbing upstairs someday and creating a master bedroom suite. He'd pretty much given up on the idea until Rick appeared in his life, but he was beginning to think about it again, along with even grander plans for a bigger house of their own. He stood, hands on hips, looking the place over, letting his imagination run wild. The phone rang, and Ed, shaking himself back to reality, ran down to answer it.

"Ed? It's your mother." Norma barked her usual greeting.

"Hey, Mom." He wondered how his mother always managed to time her calls for when he had something better to do.

"Ed, you've got to talk to that sister of yours. She seems to think we should have Christmas dinner at her place this year. She seems to think that the children would have more fun there, with all of their Christmas things. Why, what does she think? That I won't have presents for them under my tree? And I hate to mention it, but you know she just can't roast a turkey as good as me. I don't want to bring up Thanksgiving, but—"

"Mom," Ed interrupted. "I'd love to talk Christmas, and I promise to talk to Laurie, but I really need to get going. I promised Claire I'd come over and help out with Rick. He hurt his back at work today."

"What? Hurt his back! After all these years of carrying mail, doesn't he know how to take care of himself? Honestly."

"Well, he did. It was probably all that Christmas mail. Anyway, I'm going to bring him over here so he can rest for a few days."

"Ed Stephens," Norma hollered over the phone. "Have you lost your mind? You call that sister of his right back and tell her you've changed your mind."

"Mom, why would I want to do that?"

"The very idea, taking care of a man with a bad back. Why, my father had a bad back, and I swear it took five years off your grandmother's life! Oh, he was just awful, I tell you. Whining. Complaining. Ordering her around. I'm surprised she didn't go after him with her iron skillet. You know, the one I use for fried chicken? Oh, I could just see her walloping him upside the head with that thing, visions of myself being an orphan when they hauled her off to prison. You just call Claire Romanowski right back and say you realize you're coming down with the flu and you can't take care of him."

"Mom, I can't lie. And besides, I'm looking forward to it."

"Oh, I have raised a fool," Norma moaned. "Here I thought I was going to get you married off so I didn't have to worry about you anymore, and you do this. After a few days of his carrying on you'll never want to see him again. Ed, stick him in a nursing home for a week."

"Mom-m-m-m, I can't do that. A nursing home? Are you crazy?"

"Not as crazy as you are. You mark my words, young man. A man with a bad back is the devil himself."

"I can't imagine Rick being like that."

"They're all like that," Norma said darkly.

"Well, I'll just have to find out for myself."

"You certainly will. Don't come running to me, asking to borrow that skillet either. Get your own."

"Mom, I really should get going. They're waiting on me," Ed said, glancing at his watch.

"Oh, go then. You'll see. Neither you nor your sister ever listen to me. Honestly, why do I bother? Humph. Well, I'd better be going, too. I might as well go out and return Rick's Christmas present. I won't have any use for it after this week is through. You two won't be speaking to each other."

Ed hung up the phone, shaking his head. His mother exaggerated everything, he thought. He didn't expect Rick to be his usual sunny self, of course, but he couldn't picture Rick being the monster Norma predicted either. He grabbed his coat and keys. *First stop, the store,* he thought. *I hope to hell they have some butter pecan.*

⋘•⋙

Ed entered Claire's house through the front door, noticing that the doorknob he'd installed that past Saturday was working fine. Rick was stretched out on the sofa under a blanket, while Judy was sitting in front of the TV, engrossed in *The Newlywed Game.* The rest of the family was nowhere to be seen.

"Hey, there," Ed said softly to Rick.

"Hey," said Rick, weakly smiling at Ed.

"These people are so dumb," Judy remarked, glancing up at Ed. "I wouldn't go on this show until I made sure I knew *everything* about my husband."

"That's the point, Judy," Rick said impatiently. "They're *newlyweds.* They haven't had time to learn everything about their spouses."

Judy shrugged. "Well, I still say it's not worth looking dumb on TV just for a washer and dryer."

Rick sighed and rolled his eyes at Ed. "I hate this show."

Ed, who'd always enjoyed it, didn't respond. Claire appeared from the kitchen, Josh and Jane in tow.

"Hi, Ed," she said. "The Red Cross has come to the rescue. I've got Rick's bag packed. Now all we have to do is get him into his coat and out to your truck."

"How long is Uncle Rick going to be at your house?" Josh asked Ed.

"I'm not sure," Ed said to him. "I guess it depends on how long it takes for his back to feel better. But don't worry. I'll take good care of him."

"Oh, I'm not worried about that. I just wondered." Josh looked up at Ed seriously. "And I just wanted to remind you that he snores. A lot."

Ed was beginning to wonder if Josh was more insightful than the grown-ups gave him credit for. As Ed reached to pick up the overnight bag, Jane came over and grabbed his arm.

"Let's play Candy Land again."

"Not tonight, Jane," Claire said, helping Rick to a sitting position. "Ed needs to take Uncle Rick over to his nice, quiet house for some rest. And you have to get ready for bed."

"Humph," Jane snorted, marching down the hall toward the room she shared with Judy.

With some help from Ed, Claire put Rick's slippers on his feet, then pulled his coat over an old flannel shirt. Ed looked doubtfully at the pajama bottoms Rick was wearing.

"Don't you think you might get a little cold?"

"I'll live," he grumbled. "We're just going across town, not to Siberia. Don't you have the heat on in the truck?"

"Of course," Ed said, stooping to pick up the overnight bag.

"Well, then, I'll be fine!"

Claire and Ed led Rick down the front steps and over to the truck in the driveway. Ed stowed the bag next to the toolbox behind his seat, while Claire helped Rick into the truck.

"Now, you behave," she warned Rick, slamming the door.

With some effort, Rick rolled the window down partway. "Oh, for God's sake. Okay, I'm a little cranky. You would be, too, if your back hurt this much, but I'm not gonna take it out on Ed."

"See that you don't," she said, giving him a level-eyed stare.

Ed started the truck, leaned over Rick, and called out the window, "I'm sure we'll be just fine. A little TLC, and we'll have our boy back handing out Christmas cards again in no time."

Claire looked rather doubtful, but managed a smile. "Okay. Thanks again, Ed. Call me if you need anything."

"Bye," Ed called, as he backed out of the driveway.

Once they were on their way, Rick leaned his head back and heaved a big sigh. "Thanks, baby, for all of this. I love those kids, but they were about to drive me crazy. Claire too. She means well, but she treats me like one of the kids when something like this happens." He glanced at Ed. "I'd much rather be with you."

Ed reached for Rick's hand. "I don't know how good of a nurse I am, but I'll do my best."

Rick squeezed Ed's hand. "I'm sure your best is probably better than I deserve. But could we make a stop on the way? I'd just about kill for some butter pecan ice cream."

Ed smiled. "That's already been taken care of."

⋘•⋙

"How'd you do this, anyway?" Ed asked once he had Rick settled comfortably in his bed.

"Oh, it was so stupid," Rick muttered. "I was at the Johnson house, near the end of my route on Nash Street. I bent over to pick up their newspaper, to put it in their box with the mail, and something just went *ping* in my lower back. I tell you, the pain took my breath away. I stood there, bent over their front steps for the longest time. Mrs. Johnson finally came out and helped me into the house to sit down, which was about the worse thing I could've done, because it took me forever to get back up. I managed to finish my route, but it was a nightmare."

"Poor baby." Ed stroked his hair.

"Then Claire came home and hauled me off to the emergency room at Porterfield General. That quack of a doctor she sees just happened to be there, so he looked me over. Like he could do anything. But he did give me prescriptions for painkillers and muscle relaxers, so it wasn't a total waste of time. He also suggested I go see a Dr. Quigley, some chiropractor here in town. Probably another quack."

"Oh, I don't know. Actually I've heard he's pretty good. It can't hurt. Do you want me to make an appointment for you in the morning?"

Rick shrugged. "Okay. If you want to." He looked up at Ed. "It hurts like hell, but I feel better already, just being here with you. Maybe love is the best medicine."

Ed kissed him. "Let's hope so." He picked up Rick's empty ice cream bowl. "Do you want some more of this?"

"No. Actually, these pills are making me a little sleepy. After all that's happened today, from John Lennon to this, I'd like to just go to sleep. Or at least try to."

"Okay." Ed got up from the bed. "I'll hang out in the living room until bedtime. I promise to be quiet, and I'll try not to wake you up when I come to bed."

"You're going to sleep *here*?"

Ed stopped, halfway to the door, and turned around. "Well, of course. It's my bed, ya know."

"I'm well aware of that," Rick said patiently. "But I'm also aware of how you toss and turn in your sleep. That's about the last thing I need tonight."

"Oh," said Ed, taken aback. "Well, okay. I guess I can sleep on the couch."

"Would you, baby?" Rick turned a pathetic face to Ed. "The doctor said I really need to get as much rest as possible."

The one you said was a quack? Ed wanted to ask, but didn't. "I'll take care of it. Don't worry. Call me if you need anything." He carried the ice cream bowl to the kitchen, wondering if having Rick around was going to be so great after all.

⋖⋗●⋖⋗

By midmorning of the next day, Ed felt more bossed around and abused by Rick than he did from even his most annoying clients. Ed had managed to make an appointment with Dr. Quigley for early afternoon, and Rick had grumbled about having to get dressed to leave the house. He had turned his nose up at the eggs and toast Ed had thoughtfully prepared, saying he only wanted some more ice cream. Then Rick had insisted that a hot shower would help his back, and bitched when Ed tried to help him into the bathroom, saying he could do it himself. Rick had then proceeded to use up so much hot water that Ed's own shower had been rather chilly. Shivering a bit, he got dressed, silently thankful that he was due at elderly Mrs. West's house to help her put up her artificial Christmas tree.

"Is there anything else you need before I leave?" he asked Rick, a little less than pleasantly.

Rick gave an impatient shrug that was beginning to get on Ed's nerves. "I guess not. I sure wish I could watch TV, though."

"I can set you up on the couch. I think it's time for *The Price Is Right*."

"Shit," Rick moaned. "Isn't there anything better than that on?"

"*Hollywood Squares*?"

Rick snorted in disgust.

"What is it with you and game shows?" Ed asked irritably. "I like them."

Rick just rolled his eyes and shook his head. "Well, don't bother then. I sure wish I had that mystery book I've been reading. I can't believe Claire didn't stick it in the bag."

Ed sighed. "I'll stop and pick it up later, after Claire gets home from work. Until then," Ed said, looking at the pile of magazines and some of his own books he'd stacked on the nightstand, "that should keep you busy."

"I don't know." Rick looked at them with little interest. "Maybe I'll just take a nap."

"You do that," Ed said, thinking that a sleeping Rick was not a bitching Rick. "I really need to get over to Mrs. West's. She gets all excited when I'm late."

"Why the hell do you have to put up her Christmas tree? Since when do handymen put up Christmas trees?"

Ed resisted the urge to snap back at him and instead said, with as much patience as he could muster, "You know a lot of my clients are old. They have a hard time doing physical things for themselves. You also know I help Mrs. Heston every Tuesday with her grocery shopping and stuff. I like doing things for them, and the money they pay me helps to pay for this house and that bed you're lying in!"

"Well," said Rick, all offended. "You don't have to get so touchy. I was just *asking*."

"Yeah, you were. And I told you. So now I'm going to go put up an old lady's Christmas tree. Okay?" Ed turned and stomped into the living room.

"Well, don't break any ornaments," Rick hollered as Ed left the house.

Only over your head, darlin', he thought as slammed the door.

Mrs. West was properly grateful for Ed's help, and Ed enjoyed hearing her stories about her ornaments as he helped her hang them. His good nature was completely restored by the time he headed home for lunch. Still, he braced himself before he entered the house. All was quiet as he walked to the bedroom. Rick was in bed, flipping through a *Mandate* magazine.

Rick looked up at Ed's entrance and smiled. "You know, a magazine with pictures of naked guys was probably not the best thing to leave for a man who's having a hard time getting around." He put the magazine aside. "I'm sorry for being so bitchy this morning, baby. I'm just not used to lying around with nothing to do." He held out his hand to Ed.

"Hmm," Ed murmured as he sat next to Rick on the bed, resentment fading. "I think I can forgive you. This time anyway." He went to put his arm around Rick and noticed the rise of blankets over Rick's midsection. "Well, look at that. You are a little excited. I think," Ed said seductively, putting his hand gently on top of the rise, "that I can take care of that without inducing too much pain."

"Oh, baby," Rick whispered, lying back. "That is not what the doctor ordered, but I think it might do wonders for me."

Later that afternoon Ed sat in Dr. Quigley's waiting room, thinking that although he hated to admit it, perhaps for once in her life Norma had been right. Not long after their careful lovemaking session, Rick had returned to his former cranky self and complained all through lunch and all the way to Dr. Quigley's office. Ed wasn't ready to clobber him with a skillet, at least not yet, but he was tempted to help himself to some of Rick's pills.

Ed looked up as Rick and Dr. Quigley walked out of his office. "Now, I want to look at those X-rays I took, and I want you back here on Friday. We'll do a little more work on loosening up that disc. You did yourself quite a mischief there, Rick. Go ahead and make an appointment, and I'll see you on Friday."

Dr. Quigley went back into his office while Rick stiffly walked to the receptionist's desk. Ed caught a glimpse of Rick's face and prepared himself for some more Mr. Hyde behavior. After they were back in the truck, Ed asked him how it had gone.

"I hurt more now than when I went in there," Rick grumbled.

"Well, he's probably just working out the kinks, getting things back where they belong," said Ed, who didn't really know much about it.

"Oh, for God's sake. I know that."

"Then what are you bitchin' about?" Ed demanded, slamming the truck in reverse.

"I am in pain," Rick said through clenched teeth.

"Thanks for the update. I'll be sure and call Walter Cronkite. He'll want to lead with it tonight!"

Ed yanked the truck into drive and roared off onto Main Street, a good ten miles per hour over the speed limit. Shortly past Dr. Quigley's office he approached the Norfolk & Southern tracks without bothering to slow down, hoping in his most evil heart of hearts that Rick would get good and jarred. He hit the worst part of the crossing at full speed, and the truck bounced so hard their heads almost hit the roof of the cab.

"Jesus Christ," Rick yelled. "Don't you have any shocks on this thing?"

"Oh, yeah," Ed said in a sweet-as-honey voice. "Thanks for reminding me. I need to have that looked at."

They glared at each other. The drive to Ed's house was completed in silence.

⁂

Ed stopped by Claire's after his last job of the day. He wasn't feeling terribly inclined to do Rick any favors, but hoped if Rick had his book to read it might keep him quiet. Claire met him at the door, book in hand.

"So how's it going?" she asked.

Ed debated a moment about how truthful he should be. "Oh, not too bad," he finally lied. "We're getting through it."

Claire smirked at him. Ed saw a twinkle in her eye. "You, you," he sputtered. "You set me up."

"Who, me?" she giggled.

Ed grabbed the book from her, resisting the urge to hit her with it. "I will get you for this someday."

Claire's giggles broke into laughter as she closed the door. "Thanks again, Ed. Bring him home when he's human."

Ed stormed back to his truck and threw the book on the seat. *How do you like that. That crafty broad sure knew what she was doing when she dumped Uncle Rotten on me.*

He headed back across town, and his anger began to fade. Despite the current hostilities with Rick, Ed still loved him. In some weird way he thought he loved him even more, now that he knew Rick was just as capable of being a jerk as anyone else, including himself. Ed had been around long enough to know that you really don't get to know a person until you've seen him at his worst. *I hope,* he thought, entering his own driveway, *this is the worst Rick gets.*

Ed went in the house and pulled some hamburger out of the refrigerator for dinner. Then he walked back to the bedroom to give Rick his book. Rick looked up apprehensively. Ed handed him the book.

"Thank you, baby," Rick said softly.

Ed found himself smiling back at the jackass. "You're welcome. I'm going to make some hamburgers for dinner. And a big salad, I think. Do you want some fries? I think I have some in the freezer."

"Whatever you want to do is fine, but do you think you could help me out to the couch? I sure could use a change of scenery."

Ed helped Rick off the bed and into the living room. On his way back to the kitchen he turned on the stereo and restacked his Beatles records. He was tearing lettuce for the salad, happily humming along with "Help!" when Rick called to him from the living room. Ed walked back to see Rick staring with annoyance at the stereo.

"Hey, do you suppose we could hear something else for a while? I mean, enough with the John Lennon tribute already."

"What do you want to hear?" Ed snapped, his good mood crashing and burning once again.

"How 'bout 'The Sounds of Silence,'" Rick retorted.

"Aw, crud." Ed took the needle off the record just as he heard a knock at the back door.

"Yoo-hoo, anybody home?" Norma called.

Ed groaned. *Oh, this is just what I need.* He turned to Rick. "So help me God, if you give her any ammunition, I will flush your pills down the crapper."

Norma came in through the kitchen. "Well, there you are. Looks like you've got supper going so I won't stay. Rick, how are you doing? That back giving you fits?" She barreled on without waiting for a reply. "My father had a bad back so I know how you feel. Oh, he had terrible pain. We all suffered with him, believe me." She turned to Ed. "Everything okay here? I just brought over some cookies I baked for poor Rick here." She handed Rick a paper bag.

Ed narrowed his eyes at his mother. Cookies, maybe, but the real reason she was here was to gloat. He was sure of that.

"We're doing just fine, Mom," he said smiling at her.

Norma narrowed her eyes right back at Ed, telling him she knew better. "That's good to know. Well, Rick, I hope you feel better. Enjoy the cookies. Oh, don't bother to thank me. It wasn't any bother. Chocolate chip. Ed's favorite, you know, so make sure he gets some. I'm sure you'll be back on the mail route in no time."

Rick looked inside the bag and grinned. "I'll thank you anyway, Norma. That was very nice of you. Probably nicer than I deserve. I've been a bit of a creep today, as I'm sure Ed will tell you."

Norma looked surprised. "Oh, now, Rick, I'm sure that's just not so. You misbehaving? I'm sure you're handling this much better than that. I'm sure you're handling it much better than my father did. In fact, I told Ed that very thing when he said you'd be staying with him. 'Take good care of that Rick,' I told him. I just hope he's doing a good job."

Ed glared at her, his mouth open to respond, but Rick beat him to it.

"Ed's doing a wonderful job. I'm very grateful to him."

"Is that so? Well, I like to think I raised him right. You take care now, Rick. I'm just going to run along." She walked back in the kitchen, with Ed on her heels.

"You're a real piece of work, you know that, Mom?" he said, grabbing her arm by the door.

Norma looked at her son innocently. "Maybe next time you'll listen to your mother." She glanced at the stove, where Ed had the skillet ready for the hamburgers. She shook her head. "I knew it."

"Oh, now, Mom, I—"

Norma cut him off. "Don't bother explaining to me. I know all about it. Just don't do something you'll regret later. I'll call you tomorrow to make sure you're both still alive. Good night," she called, letting herself out the back door.

"Mothers," Ed muttered. He looked in the living room, where Rick was stuffing himself with cookies, and right before dinner. "Boyfriends," he snorted. "I give up. I just give up."

⊰❖⊱

Ed bedded down on the sofa for the second night in a row and waited apprehensively for a command from His Royal Highness in the bedroom, but apparently Rick's pills had once again knocked him out.

Ed shifted around, trying to find a comfortable position on the lumpy sofa. He looked at the ceiling and sighed, strangely grateful for the discomfort. He reminded himself that he was learning a good lesson in cohabitation, and how lucky he was to get a look at Rick's darker side before they considered more permanent living arrangements. He thought of his own Mr. Hyde behavior during past sick spells and winced. The marriage vow "in sickness and in health" took on an all new meaning.

Ed got up and walked to the bedroom. Rick was flat on his back, asleep and snoring. A great wave of love and tenderness swept over Ed. He remembered Hilda Penfield's words about compassion, and how they would need more than their share of it to overcome adversity. He made a promise to himself to love Rick even more through this bad spell, even if it meant putting up with a lot of whiny bitching.

Still, he thought as he went back to the sofa. *I have no problem with bouncing him over another railroad track if I need to shut him up again.*

⋖⋟•⋞⋗

They had a few more tense moments, but by the end of the week Rick's pain was lessening, and he was slowly returning to his usual amiable self. By Friday night his apologies were beginning to get on Ed's nerves as much as his bitching had. Ed played "The Sounds of Silence" over and over on the stereo, until Rick finally agreed to cease with the I'm-sorrys.

"I mean, if nothing else, at least we know each other a little better now," Ed said, settling next to Rick on the sofa. "And you haven't seen me sick yet, so I'd really better watch what I say."

Rick grinned at him, then grunted painfully as he tried to put his arm around Ed. "You know something? I am really, really missing my hunky handyman at night. Do you think you might want to crawl back into bed with me tonight?"

"Okay, if you think my tossing and turning won't hurt your back," Ed teased him.

Rick pulled him closer. "Well, I guess we've had a serious lesson in taking the bad with the good. I think I could put up with some serious bad if it means keeping you close to me."

Ed sighed happily. "Me too, darlin', me too. But I'll warn ya, the next time your back goes out, I'm putting you in a nursing home."

Chapter Twelve

Ed woke up Saturday morning to delicious odors from the kitchen. He reached for Rick, but the other side of the bed was empty. Ed stumbled into the kitchen to find Rick standing stiffly at the stove, frying bacon.

"Consider it a peace offering," Rick said, taking in Ed's sleepy, surprised face.

"Darlin', you didn't have to cook," Ed protested, but Rick waved it away with a spatula.

"I know I didn't, but after a week of lying around, I needed some physical activity. Don't worry, I'm fine. Oh, it still hurts, but nothing like the other day. Now, go put on some clothes, and we'll have some breakfast in a few minutes, okay? The sight of my handyman naked is making me think of something other than food."

"Oh," Ed exclaimed, realizing he hadn't bothered to grab his bathrobe as he usually did. To the sound of Rick's chuckling, he fled back to the bedroom.

Dressed in his usual Saturday attire of jeans and sweatshirt, Ed joined Rick at the table, eager to dive into the bacon and eggs Rick put before him.

"It's so weird to have you here on a Saturday morning."

"'Come Saturday morning,'" Rick sang, slowly sinking into his chair. "What comes after that? Where are the Sandpipers when you need them?"

"I think I have that record. I'll look after breakfast."

"You mean *I'll* look, while *you* clean up the kitchen."

"Yes, dear."

Ed enjoyed the easy morning banter and Rick's cheerful presence. Rick seemed to have truly returned to his old self, and Ed relaxed in the knowledge that Rick would be staying through the weekend, the first entire weekend they had ever spent together.

"Can you believe it? A whole weekend, and just the two of us. No jobs, no kids, no nothing."

"Umm-hmm," Rick agreed, his warm and tender special on his face. "I was thinking that myself. I wish I felt up to something big, but I think I'd better take it easy. Still, we'll be together, and that's pretty big in itself."

"I was thinking, if you're up to it, today would be a good day to visit Mrs. Penfield."

Rick's eyes lit up. "That's a great idea. I've been wanting to meet her, and once I go back to the routine, God only knows when I'd get the chance."

Ed nodded. "I'll call her after breakfast."

"After you clean up."

"Yeah, yeah."

Once Ed was busy at the sink, Rick slowly settled himself on the floor in front of Ed's record cabinet.

"You're dad's workshop must have really been something," he called to Ed. "This cabinet is great."

"Dad had a real feeling for wood," Ed said over the sound of running water in the sink. "I always thought he could have made a living at it. I mentioned it once, and he said he didn't think he was good enough at it to support a wife and two kids. I think he was wrong, though."

"You ever think about doing this kind of stuff, baby?"

"Oh, sometimes. I really don't have the patience he had with it. It would be fun, though, to have a place in the basement to fool around. I haven't really thought about it since he died, and considering how wet the basement in this place is, I wouldn't even bother. Mom put most of Dad's tools in storage, so I suppose they're over there, waiting for me to use them someday."

Rick pulled a stack of records out of the cabinet. "Maybe someday we'll have a place where you could do that."

Ed dreamily washed a plate, enjoying that idea. "Yeah, someday. Do you really think we'll have a place together someday?"

"I hope so, baby. I'd love to have a place all our own, when the time is right."

They both fell silent. Ed was so lost in the idea of being with his Dream Man in a Dream House that he put a plate still sticky with bacon grease in the drainer. He looked closer, then put it back in the dishwater, shaking his head back to reality.

"You know, baby," Rick called to him. "I think this is the first time I've really gone through these records. You've got some cool stuff here. Did you ever spend your allowance on anything other than records?"

Ed laughed. "Well, don't tell Mom, but Dad used to slip me extra money for them. We'd go on errands—on Saturday mornings, come to think of it. Somehow we always seemed to end up at Woolworth's. Dad would say, 'Well, Eddie, what's the big hit this week?' Then he'd usually buy it for me, telling me not to tell Mom. Dad liked a lot of them—the Beach Boys, the Mamas and the Papas, and some of the girl groups. He said the Mamas and the Papas had better harmony than some of the groups he liked when he was young."

"Speak of the devil." Rick laughed, as "Monday, Monday" began to play. "He was right, though."

Ed paused in his dishwashing for the moment, enjoying the song and the memories. "I still get chills from Denny Doherty's voice on this one. There's just something wrong with anyone who doesn't like the Mamas and the Papas."

"Agreed. I sure wish I could have known your dad. He sounds like such a cool guy. Hey, I found it," he shouted, waving a record where Ed could see it. "'Come Saturday Morning.'"

Rick put it on when "Monday, Monday" ended. Ed walked into the living room and they both listened—smiles on their faces—to the gentle tune.

"My senior year in high school," Ed said. "Oh, I would have killed to have you with me back then. Remember the movie this song was in, *The Sterile Cuckoo*?"

"Yeah. I loved that one."

"Me too. I loved those scenes with Liza Minnelli and Wendell Burton, spending all those Saturdays together. I almost cried every time I heard this song on the radio, wishing I had someone to do that with."

"I'm here now, baby," Rick said, pulling Ed to the floor. "Will you be my Saturday friend?"

Ed kissed him. "I'd love to have you for my Saturday friend. I'll take you the other six days of the week, too."

One kiss followed another as the song ended, then repeated.

"I love you so much, baby. Thanks for taking care of me this week. Someday it will be my turn, and I promise to do just as good a job as you did."

"I love you too, darlin'. And I'm gonna hold you to that."

After Ed made it back to the kitchen to finish the dishes, he called Mrs. Penfield.

"Why, I'd be delighted to have you over today," she exclaimed over the phone. "Tell you what, Ed, you both come over late this afternoon, and we'll have an old-fashioned high tea. Effie Maude is here," she said, referring to her housekeeper, "and she'll help me with everything. Can you be here around four?"

"Sure, we'd love to. We'll see you then." Ed hung up the phone, then grinned at Rick. "We are invited for high tea at four o'clock." He frowned. "What's high tea?"

"High tea," Rick explained, pulling Ed back to the floor, "means it's high time we had something to eat. If we stuff ourselves enough, we won't have to get all worked up about a big dinner." Rick frowned, though. "You said she has bad arthritis. Is she up to this?" he asked.

"Oh, sure," Ed replied. "Effie Maude is in for the day, so she'll do most of the work."

"*Effie Maude?*" Rick asked in astonishment.

Ed laughed. "The housekeeper. Wait till you see her. She's a real trip, believe me. So what are we going to do until four?"

Rick slid a hand under Ed's sweatshirt. "Well, I can think of a thing or two."

"Or three or four," Ed said, kissing him.

"Did you ever imagine your Saturday friend doing something like this?" Rick asked, his hand sliding lower.

"This and a whole more, darlin'."

⋖●⋗

Ed's truck rolled to a stop in front of Mrs. Penfield's house at the corner of Spruce and Race Streets at ten minutes before four. Rick whistled. "Some place."

"Isn't it? Of all the houses I work in, this is my favorite," Ed said, getting out of the truck. He went around to the other side and gently helped Rick to the sidewalk.

They paused for a moment, admiring the house. It was a three-story brick Second Empire style, right out of the late nineteenth century. A huge porch ran from the front along the west side, and the late afternoon sun reflected off numerous stained glass windows. Oak trees in the front yard, now bare, promised plentiful shade on hot summer days. A tall blue spruce protected the house on the east side by Race Street, and a line of pines grew between this house and the one to the west.

"What do you think, baby?" Rick whispered in awe. "You want a place like this someday?"

"Only if Effie Maude sticks around to clean it," Ed said, knowing the dust battle she routinely fought in the big, old place.

Mrs. Penfield greeted them at the door and ushered them through the front and back parlors to the dining room. The table was indeed set for tea, with plates of finger sandwiches, cakes, and muffins.

"Gosh," Ed exclaimed, taking it all in.

Rick chuckled at his reaction. "Mrs. Penfield, this looks wonderful, but you shouldn't have gone to so much trouble."

"Good heavens," she replied. "Trouble? Not at all. I'd much rather go to the effort for you young gentlemen than for my stuffy book club. Let's sit down, shall we?"

Effie Maude, a large, gray-haired woman, brought in the tea tray. "Will this do ya for the time bein'?" she asked in her raspy voice.

Mrs. Penfield nodded.

"Good enough. I'll go get to that washin' then, since I won't be here Monday." Effie Maude ducked through the swinging door to the kitchen.

Rick watched her go, a look of incredulity on his face. "Great shades of Marjorie Main," he muttered under his breath.

Mrs. Penfield nodded, chuckling, but Ed looked puzzled. "Who?" he asked.

"Oh, Ed, you remember Ma Kettle . . . those Ma and Pa Kettle movies?"

"Oh," Ed said, comprehending, then added his chuckle to theirs.

"She's been working here, with an English teacher in the house, for almost forty years, and her grammar is still as dreadful as it was the first day, God bless her," Mrs. Penfield said, reaching for the teapot.

Mrs. Penfield then instructed her two novices on the proper rituals and decorum for afternoon tea. Ed felt a bit foolish and faggier than usual, but enjoyed the strong tea and the dainty cakes prepared by Effie Maude.

"You have a beautiful home, Mrs. Penfield," Rick said, nibbling on a sandwich. "I'd love to see more of it, if it's possible."

"Of course," Mrs. Penfield said. "I'm not sure I'm up to the tour today, but Ed knows it well enough to take you through it. Ed? After tea?"

He nodded. "I've repaired something in practically every room in this place," he bragged to Rick.

"That he has." Mrs. Penfield shook her head. "Oh, it takes a lot of work to keep a place such as this together, but Ed and I have done hearty battle with it over the years. I don't know what I'd do without him, Rick. He's been a godsend."

Ed blushed. "It's the least I can do for the only English teacher I ever had who gave me straight A's."

"You earned them, both you and your sister. I often wished the two of you would have gone on to a good, four-year college, but you've both done well with your gifts. Laurie's a blessing at the office, and you've found your niche as well, Ed."

"Office?" Rick asked.

"Laurie works for the law firm of Mason and Schultz, which was formerly Penfield, Penfield, and Mason," Mrs. Penfield told him. "My father-in-law started the firm, then partnered with my husband. Mr. Mason came along sometime later. When George died, he partnered with Mr. Schultz."

"Lawyers," Rick said, and nodded. "That explains this place."

Mrs. Penfield smiled. "Oh, yes, my father-in-law had rather grand notions. He had this house built in 1898, when Spruce Street had more vacant lots than houses. He felt the need of a house befitting the town's most important lawyer, which he felt he was, of course. He also had a carriage house built on the alley, which has since been converted into a garage. He felt this location, on what was then the south edge of Porterfield, was a good, brisk walk away from his office on East Commerce Street. I think he would be surprised to see how Porterfield has grown up around this house, and to the south and west."

"When did you move here, Mrs. Penfield?" Rick asked.

"I came to this house as a bride in 1931, during the height of the Depression. Much of the house was closed off, and my father-in-law, who'd lost a good deal of money in the stock market crash, would have sold it, but his pride and a lack of buyers kept him from it. It was a good thing I was already teaching, as that income kept us going through those lean years. We also took in boarders, other teachers from the town's schools. The law practice was struggling, mostly from a lack of paying clients. George refused to turn anyone in need away, and took whatever was offered in payment. Sometimes a chicken or a basket of fresh vegetables meant more than cash itself."

"Wow," Rick murmured. "My dad's a history teacher, so I've never had a lack of it in my life, but it means more when you're right on the spot, so to speak. Did you have any children, though, Mrs. Penfield? I can't imagine this big house without children."

"Yes, we had a son, George Junior. He was killed in Korea."

"Oh, I'm sorry," Rick said in embarrassment.

"There's no need," she said gently. "Although I miss both my Georges to this day, I was blessed to have many other children during my teaching years." She glanced at Ed. "I tried not to, but Ed can tell you I occasionally played favorites. I can honestly admit to that now, and to the fact that the Stephenses were among them—Ed, Laurie, *and* their father."

"Aw," Ed muttered, blushing once again.

"I was just telling Ed today how much I wish I could have met his father," Rick said, grinning at Ed. "What was he like in class?"

"Tim Stephens? Oh, much like his children, bright and inquisitive. Rather shy, as Ed was in his sophomore year. Tim did, however, associate with quite a bunch of rascals, and I had to pull him into line more than once. I had the same struggle with Laurie occasionally, but Ed, of course, was never any problem."

Ed rolled his eyes. "You just didn't know what Ted Gillis, Greg Donovan, Steve Kiley, and I were up to outside of class."

"No, I didn't, and I'm glad of that," she said, giving him a reproving look. "It might forever tarnish the image I have of you as a perfect young gentleman."

They all laughed. Rick looked through the dining room entrance into the parlors and the hall. "Is there really an upstairs room made over into a library?" he asked eagerly.

"Yes. George had a study on the first floor, on the other side of the stairs. What law and reference books he didn't have in his office downtown, he kept here. We began to amass such a collection of books—books of all kinds—that I suggested we convert one of the unused bedrooms into a library. It's rather empty now, thanks to Ed's recent help."

Rick sighed. "I've always wanted a room just for books. I've moved around so much in the past few years that most of mine are in boxes."

"Ed told me your reasons for being in Porterfield. Do you think you'll be staying when your sister is back on her feet?"

Rick looked at Ed. "Definitely," he said, smiling.

Mrs. Penfield beamed at them both. "That's good news. I'm sure Ed has told you of my concerns for the two of you, but I have great faith that you'll both overcome any difficulties you may encounter. Now, Ed, Why don't you take Rick on a tour of the house? I fear his curiosity is interfering with his appetite."

She watched them both rise to their feet, Rick a good deal slower than Ed. "Ah, Rick," she sighed. "I can only hope your injuries are temporary. I wouldn't bless this affliction of mine on my worst enemy."

"Even Eunice Ames?" Ed teased.

"Don't tempt me," Mrs. Penfield retorted with a laugh.

Ed took Rick through the downstairs rooms—front and back parlors, sitting room, study, dining room, and kitchen. They trooped upstairs and peered into the master bedroom suite across the front of the house and into the smaller bedrooms, ending with the library, which looked forlorn and empty, denuded of books.

"This place is really something else," Rick whispered to Ed, looking out a window into the small but attractive backyard. "But I'll bet the upkeep is incredible as well."

Ed lowered his voice, too. "Yes, it is. It needs a lot of work, projects bigger than I could ever handle on my own. I've managed to keep it up just enough to keep her comfortable. I worry, though, about her arthritis. I wonder how long she'll be able to stay here, with just Effie Maude for help. You know, she doesn't have any family left, not that I know of anyway. I'd hate for her to have to sell this place and go to a nursing home."

"That would be a shame," Rick agreed, turning back to Ed. He suddenly smiled and leaned over for a quick kiss. "Oh, well, baby. It may be a little more than we need, a house like this, but it sure is fun to dream, isn't it?"

They returned to Mrs. Penfield and the rest of the tea. She inquired as to Rick's background and education and seemed pleased to hear of his two years at Indiana University as an English major.

"I know my parents wish I would finish my degree. Maybe I will someday."

"When you feel the need for the enrichment, you will," Mrs. Penfield promised. "I would be the first to admit that a liberal arts degree is not worth much in today's work world, but for one's own personal growth, it's invaluable. I'm so glad you're encouraging Ed to read again. Perhaps we'll steer him toward some ivy-covered buildings one day."

Mrs. Penfield and Rick laughed as Ed smirked at them. "I wouldn't count on it. I'm perfectly happy being a simple handyman."

"Handyman, yes, Ed," Mrs. Penfield said, still chuckling. "But simple? Never. It takes an intelligent man to tackle some of the problems I hand you on occasion. More tea, gentlemen?" She encouraged them to eat their fill and insisted on Effie Maude wrapping the leftovers for them. "It'll just go to waste here," she said, waving a hand at their objections.

When it was time to go, she walked them to the door, leaning heavily on her cane. "I've always enjoyed the starkness of our Indiana winters," she said, "but I must admit my joints are longing for sunny Florida. Now, don't be strangers, you two. I can't tell you how much I've enjoyed our visit. Please come again, Rick. It's been a pleasure to meet you, and might I add, I'm very pleased you're in Ed's life."

"Oh, no one's happier about that than me," he assured her, smiling. "It's been a pleasure for me as well, Mrs. Penfield. I look forward to seeing you again."

The drive back to Ed's in the early twilight was silent. Rick sighed as the truck pulled into Ed's driveway.

"What an amazing woman," he said softly. "We didn't even scratch the surface of the stories she can tell. I'd really like to go back sometime, baby. Her honest . . *joy* in our relationship just blows me away."

"Mr. Penfield was the same way," Ed said. "Just nice and honest. With his position they could have been snobs, like Todd's mother, but they never acted like that. They both did a lot of good for this town." Ed shook his head. "I wonder if they make 'em like that anymore."

"Yes, they do," Rick said, looking at Ed. "I know, because I'm sitting next to one of them. You do a lot of good for this town, too, in your own way. That's why I sometimes wonder, if everyone did know the truth about you, or about us, if they'd really care all that much. You know, some of your clients are on my mail route. I can tell you honestly, baby, that they think the world of you."

"Don't make me blush again," Ed protested. "Anyway, that may be so, but I don't think we should push it. I can just see what someone like Eunice Ames or some of those snotty bitches she hangs out with would say about us."

"I don't know, baby," Rick said, straining somewhat to open his door. "Maybe our future is in Porterfield, maybe it isn't. I don't really care right now, as long as we're together."

Ed watched Rick's face tighten. "Oh, let me do that." He hopped out and ran to the other side of the truck. He helped Rick to the pavement, put his arm around him, and walked him to the house.

"Aren't you afraid someone will see you being so affectionate with me?" Rick teased.

"Fuck 'em. I love taking care of you, and if they can't handle that, tough shit."

"And I love being taken care of by you," Rick said softly as they reached the back door.

⋘●⋙

In the fading hours of that Saturday, Rick sat on the floor, his back propped against the sofa. Ed was stretched out on the floor, his head in Rick's lap.

"You know, baby," Rick said, stroking Ed's hair. "What this room needs is a Christmas tree."

"I know. I've been thinking about it all week. I was just waiting for your back to feel better. Some night this next week, let's go out to the tree lot and buy one. I mean, you're going to help me decorate it, aren't you?"

"Of course! After the grief I gave you the other day, do you think I'd let you do it alone?"

Ed smiled. "Our first Christmas tree."

"Only the first," Rick said. He glanced at the stereo, where "Come Saturday Morning" was playing again. "So, baby, was this a Saturday you'll always remember? We really painted the town."

"Yes," Ed said definitely. "I will always remember this Saturday, because it was the first one we spent together from start to finish. What we did wasn't important. All I wanted was to spend it with you, Saturday friend."

Rick sighed. "Companionship. Not just a lover, but a friend. Do you have any idea how long I have hoped for that?"

"As long as I have, probably."

"This won't be our last Saturday like this. Oh, with my job, Saturday's are kinda shaky, but eventually I'll have been at the post office long enough to earn some vacation time. We'll go away together, over a weekend. We'll go someplace neither one of us has ever been, and we'll play, and run, and be just as free, if only for a Saturday, like the couple in that movie."

"Mmm," Ed murmured drowsily. "Yes."

"Then, some day, we'll take an even bigger vacation. Any place you've always dreamed of seeing, baby?"

"Lots of them."

"Good. Then we have lots to choose from." Rick, his eyes closed, allowed his imagination to go even farther. "And someday, we'll have a big, old house, maybe not as grand as Mrs. Penfield's, but a place all our own, where you can have a basement workshop, and you can make cabinets as good—no, better—than your dad made."

"Yeah?"

"Yeah. They'll be so good, in fact, that I'll quit my job and sell them for outrageous prices. Everyone will be clamoring for an Ed Stephens original. We'll get rich, and we'll be able to go anywhere we want to."

"The moon?" Ed teased.

"Why not? If NASA gets that space shuttle program started, who knows? Maybe people will take vacations on the moon in the twenty-first century."

"I'd settle for California. I've wanted to go there since the first time I heard 'California Dreamin''"

"What do you want to see in California, baby?"

"The redwoods. I don't care about LA, or San Francisco. I want to go someplace green, where the trees are bigger than I can even imagine."

"Just don't get any ideas about cutting them down for those cabinets you're gonna make."

"*You* said I was gonna make."

Rick chuckled. "Okay. Whatever we end up doing, as long as we're together and enjoying it, I don't care. Now. How about sitting up so I can kiss you? My back won't let bend over that far."

Ed pulled himself up. He put his arms around Rick and kissed him.

"Dreams," Ed said, sighing. "I've been dreaming my whole life, but I think you're the first one that really came true."

"Well, as Blondie sang, 'dreaming is free.' Maybe some Saturday we'll look back and remember what we talked about, amazed that more of them came true. Maybe that's what Saturdays like this are for—dreaming dreams for another Saturday to come." Rick pulled Ed closer. "I love you, baby. I can't think of anyone else I'd rather do some dreamin' with."

Ed kissed him again. "Me too, darlin', me too."

Chapter Thirteen

Ed drove slowly over the slippery streets of Porterfield, heading home for lunch. A light snowfall had left the streets just slick enough to require careful driving. The trees and houses Ed passed were frosted with white, and he had to admit to himself that if it didn't feel like Christmas, at least it looked like Christmas.

Karen Carpenter came on the radio, singing "Merry Christmas, Darling." Ed reached over and snapped the radio off, growling, "Oh, shut up already." Ed had always loved the song until this Christmas when, unfortunately, the lyrics hit a little too close to home. Like the lovers in Karen's song, Ed and Rick would be apart for Christmas.

They had talked about it, and simply saw no way around it. They both had family obligations to meet, plans that had already been in motion before their relationship had progressed to a point where Christmas apart seemed unthinkable. Ed, as usual, would spend Christmas Eve driving his mother to nearby Crestland to spend the evening with his aunt and uncle and their family, and Christmas Day would be spent with his mother, Laurie, and her family. Rick's plans were even more involved, including a road trip to Indianapolis with his sister and her children to spend the holiday with his parents. Ed was trying his best to be adult and dignified about the situation, but deep inside he felt cheated. He suspected that Rick felt the same way.

Ed pulled into his driveway and sighed. He wouldn't even have his usual after-lunch meeting with Rick at the front door. When Rick returned to work after his back problems, not entirely healed, he'd been pulled off his mail route and stuck in the back room of the post office, sorting Christmas cards instead of delivering them. The only immediate bright spot in Ed's future was their plan to get together that night. They were going to buy a

Christmas tree from the lot by the IGA, bring it back to Ed's, and then trim it together.

Ed ate a hasty lunch, then trudged up his stairs to see if he still had a box of tree trimmings stashed away. Digging through his storage closet he almost tripped over a box he'd put there recently. He smiled. The box held Rick's Christmas present, a denim jacket Ed had seen in the window of Gibson's Men's Clothing in downtown Porterfield. He thought the coat looked as though it was made for Rick, and Ed, who usually had no confidence in his abilities to pick out Christmas gifts, was sure Rick would like it. He just wished he could give it to Rick on Christmas morning instead of the day after, when they had agreed to exchange their gifts.

The phone rang. Hoping it was Rick calling on his lunch break, he ran downstairs to answer it.

"Well, if it isn't my son the traitor," Norma barked into the phone.

"Oh, Mom," he groaned. "If this about Christmas at Laurie's, I—"

"It most certainly is," she interrupted him. "We've always had Christmas dinner right here in the house where the two of you grew up. Christmas is about tradition, you know. Honestly. Why your sister suddenly thinks we should change things and have dinner at her house. Your father would have a fit."

"Mom, you know that's not true," Ed said patiently. "Dad wouldn't mind at all. In fact, he'd see Laurie's side, which is exactly why I'm siding with her. She has a good point. Lesley and Bobby would be a lot happier, and a lot less trouble, if they can spend the day playing with the stuff Santa Claus brings them. That isn't going to take away from anything you, or I, give them. You know how kids are. Don't you remember how Laurie and I acted? Kids are greedy at Christmas. They forget to say thank you, and by the end of the day they're cranky and tired. Wouldn't it be a whole lot easier for Laurie to deal with that on her home turf instead of at your house?"

"Humph," Norma snorted. "Imagine, my own children ganging up on me. Who thought I'd live to see the day. Well, I'll tell you one thing. I'm not eating any turkey that sister of yours makes after what happened on Thanksgiving. I'll do it here myself, and you can just help me carry it over there."

"Fine, Mom," he sighed.

"What about Rick? Should I tell your sister to set another place? All the time you two spend together, don't you think it's about time he spent some time with the rest of the family?"

"He won't be here," Ed said quietly. "They're all going to Indianapolis to spend Christmas with his parents."

"Oh." Norma fell silent, an unusual occurrence for her. "Well," she finally said, "that's too bad. I was looking forward to seeing him. You make sure he stops by here sometime. I have a gift for him, you know."

Ed found himself smiling. "You really like him, don't you, Mom? Admit it."

"Humph! Yes, I like him. He's better than you deserve, though. And I'll tell you, I still haven't figured out how to tell them at the garden club that my son has a boyfriend instead of a girlfriend, but, yes, I like him. He's a good man. I have a lot of respect for the way he's helping out his sister. And, Ed," she continued in what was for Norma a soft tone of voice, "although it takes a mother some getting used to, I'm glad he's there for you. You've been a lot happier lately, and that's good to see."

"Thanks, Mom. I really appreciate that."

"See that you do," she said in her normal tone of voice. "Honestly. Some mothers would cut their children right out of the will for something less. I'm a good mother, and don't you forget it, Ed Stephens."

"I won't, Mom," he said, laughing. "You'll never let me."

⋦⋗●⋦⋗

That night, while Ed and Rick were stringing lights on the tree they had bought, Ed repeated the phone conversation. Rick chuckled.

"Oh, Norma's a good old gal. I'm really touched that she went out and got me a gift. Actually, I have one for her, too."

"A muzzle?" Ed asked hopefully.

Rick playfully slapped Ed's ass. "No! A new mailbox. That one by her front door is awful. Mailmen notice things like that."

Ed grabbed for Rick, almost tipping over the tree. "My man, the mailman. Always responsible. Always thinking business. Don't you ever put that bag down?"

"I do when I'm with you," Rick said, giving Ed a kiss. "The entire United States Postal Service could grind to a halt right now and I wouldn't care. Now, untangle those damned lights. We've still got half this tree to cover."

They happily worked together, placing and rearranging the lights until they were both convinced it looked just right. Ed reached for the box with the ornaments, but Rick put out a hand to stop him.

"There's something I have to get first. It's in the car. Hold on a minute."

Rick took off out the back door, then returned moments later with a bag from one of the city department stores.

"I picked this up the day I was in Fort Wayne, shopping with Claire. I saw it and liked it, and just thought . . . well, I thought it would be nice to put on your tree."

He handed the bag to Ed, who opened it and took out a white box. Inside was a glass snowman ornament. The snowman was round and jolly, wearing a bowler hat and holding on to a broom.

"I don't know," Rick said, looking embarrassed. "I just heard 'Frosty the Snowman' in my head when I saw him, and I thought it would be nice to have an ornament to remember what I hope is just our first Christmas together."

Ed was so touched he was afraid he might break down and cry. "I love it," he whispered, looking at the snowman, then at Rick. "I love it almost as much as I love you." Carefully holding the ornament, he reached out and pulled Rick to him for a kiss.

"I love you, too, baby. And I meant what I said. I really hope this is just the first Christmas for us."

"Me too." Ed held the snowman up where they could both admire it. "I think I have an old album with the Ronettes singing 'Frosty.' Let me see."

He handed the snowman to Rick, then went charging upstairs. After shuffling through some LPs, Ed pulled out a record and returned to the living room. Soon Ronnie Spector was singing the story of "Frosty the Snowman."

"Now," Ed said, smiling happily at Rick, "we can hang him on the tree. Where do you think he should go?"

They studied the tree, then finally agreed that halfway up the front side would be perfect for Frosty. Rick carefully hung the snowman, then they stood back to admire him again.

"Maybe we'll get a Santa Claus next year," Rick mused.

"I don't care," Ed said, "as long as you're here to put it on the tree."

"That's a promise, baby." Rick smiled at the snowman. "I just wish . . ." He sighed.

"Don't say it. We already agreed. Christmas for Ed and Rick is December twenty-sixth. Maybe next year things will be different."

"They'd better be," Rick grumbled. "C'mon. Let's put the rest of this stuff on the tree." He reached for the ornament box, then stopped. "I can't help it. I feel like I've been naughty and Santa Claus won't bring me what I really want."

"Me too," Ed said wistfully. "But family is important. You haven't seen your folks since Thanksgiving, and the kids would be really disappointed if you weren't there."

"*You're* important." Rick hugged him. "Don't you ever forget that."

"I won't. And you know? That's really the best Christmas present I could hope for. When you think about it, Christmas came in October this year, when we first got together. Santa was really working overtime, getting you on my doorstep two months early."

"Ah, you've been a good boy this year, Ed Stephens," Rick said, finally smiling again. "And believe me, I've got presents for you that Santa would never think to give you."

⋘•⋙

That night turned out to be one of the last relaxing evenings Ed and Rick were able to spend together as Christmas approached. Rick was rushed and exhausted from his long hours at the post office, and his evenings were spent helping Claire prepare Christmas for the children and prepare for their trip to Indianapolis.

Ed was busy, too. One of his clients, Ruth Dorsey, suddenly decided that her kitchen and dining room needed to be painted before her family Christmas party. Ed was annoyed at her last-minute decision, but was grateful for the extra money and the distraction. He came home in the evenings, paint splattered and tired, and headed directly for the Christmas tree to turn on the lights. He'd stand and stare at Frosty, thinking how lucky he was to have Rick.

Finally, on December 23, they managed to schedule an evening together. Rick picked up Ed in his battered, old Monte Carlo, and they drove out to the Wood Haven restaurant on North Main Street for what they hoped would be a quiet meal together.

"Those kids," Rick said, shaking his head as they slid into a booth. "I wish I had some of those pills left from when my back was out. I'd grind them up and put them in their Kool-Aid. They're so excited about Christmas and Santa Claus and seeing Grandma and Grandpa, they are about to drive me crazy."

Ed laughed. "Laurie called today. She pretty much said the same thing about Lesley and Bobby. Poor Laurie. She wanted to make sure I'd keep an eye on Mom, in case she has some sneaky plot to switch dinner to her house."

Rick laughed with him. "That Norma. I can't wait to hear how she behaves through all of it."

"You know what, though? This was really cool. Laurie said she really wished you would be joining us. She told me she was disappointed, and had been counting on your support where Mom was concerned."

"How 'bout that. Isn't it something, our families? Most guys have to go through hell when it comes to stuff like that, and here both your family and my family are okay with it. My mom has dropped some hints that she would like to meet you. We may have to take a road trip to Indianapolis together after the holidays so she can get a good look at you."

"Talk about Christmas miracles," Ed commented, opening his menu. "How *did* we get so lucky with this stuff?"

Rick shrugged. "Beats me. I guess sometimes you just get lucky."

⋄•⋄

Later that evening, Rick had his coat on, keys in hand, reluctant to leave Ed's place.

"I can't believe I'm not going to see you for three whole days," he said, holding Ed close to him. "I'm going to call you the minute I get back on Friday. I won't even take my coat off. I'm running straight to that phone and calling you and telling you how much I love you."

"Screw the phone call. Just come over here and tell me."

"I'll do that. I'll push Claire, the kids, and all their presents out in the driveway and come right over here. I can't wait for you to see what I got you."

"Me too." Ed glanced at the gift-wrapped box containing Rick's present under the tree. Rick had been trying to grab it and shake it for the past two hours, but Ed had managed to keep him away from it. "Merry Christmas," he whispered, stroking Rick's beard. "Come back to me, okay?"

"Merry Christmas," Rick whispered back. He kissed Ed, a long kiss filled with love and happiness, but also with longing and regret. "I promise, baby. The minute I get back."

After an extratight bear hug, Rick let Ed go and walked to the door.

"Be careful. I want you back here in one piece, ya know."

"I will be," Rick answered.

He hurried out the back door. A few moments later Ed heard his car start, then pull out of the driveway.

Ed stood motionless, listening to the silence. "Aw, crud," he muttered. He walked into the living room and looked at Frosty on the tree. "It'll be okay. Somehow it'll all be okay."

⋄•⋄

On Christmas Eve, Ed sat glumly in front of the TV, dressed for the trip to Crestland with his mother, killing time until he needed to leave. He was watching a rerun of *The Mary Tyler Moore Show*. It was a Christmas episode, and he couldn't say it was doing much for his mood. First Mary was told she had to work on Christmas Day, ruining her plans to spend the day with her parents. Then, after making plans to spend Christmas Eve with Rhoda, a co-worker conned her into working his Christmas Eve shift, meaning she had to cancel her plans with Rhoda and spend the evening alone in the newsroom.

"Terrific! Wonderful!" Rhoda hollered. "You get me all hyped up for Christmas Eve and then you run out like this. What am I supposed to do, stand out in the snow and light matches?"

"I hear ya, Rhoda," Ed said to the TV.

"Rhoda, will ya please?" Mary pleaded. "This has been a rough week, and the worst part is just about to begin."

"I'm with ya, Mary," Ed said.

The fade-out was on Mary, standing alone in her kitchen, surrounded by her Christmas decorations, eating a peanut butter sandwich. The commercial came on, and Ed suddenly realized he had tears running down his face.

"Aw, crud," he whispered, wiping them away. He glanced over at the Christmas tree. There was Frosty, smiling at him as usual.

The episode resumed, ending happily with Lou, Murray, and Ted surprising Mary in the newsroom, rescuing her from a Christmas Eve alone.

"Boy, I wish," Ed muttered.

Suddenly he stood up, looking at the tree. He walked over and gently placed his hand around Frosty.

"I know this is stupid. But, Frosty? Bring him back to me, okay? I lied. Just knowing he loves me and wants to be with me next Christmas isn't enough. I really need him here tonight."

The phone rang, and Ed was so startled he almost pulled Frosty off the tree. His heart beating a little faster, he went to answer it.

"Ed?" Norma barked. "Where are you? It's time to go. You know how your aunt Eleanor will act if we're late to dinner."

"I'm coming right over, Mom," he said, sighing.

He clicked off the TV, then turned off the Christmas tree lights. Pulling on his coat, he looked around the dark, quiet room.

"Well. So much for wishes."

⋘•⋙

Ed returned late that evening, now grateful for the quiet house after an evening spent with family. His aunt Eleanor was the only person he knew who could outtalk his mother. Still, it hadn't been a bad evening, and except for one painful moment on the way home, when "Merry Christmas, Darling" came on the radio, Ed felt much more at peace and had finally accepted the fact that Rick was over a hundred miles away on Christmas Eve.

He crawled into bed, hoping that sleep would come to his immediate rescue. Ed was about to drift off when his eyes suddenly flew open. *What was that sound?* "Santa Claus?" he whispered. He sat up, listening intently. Yes, there it was again, a light tapping. It sounded like someone was knocking on the back door.

He flashed on Mary Richards, alone in the newsroom, thinking she was on the verge of being murdered when she heard the elevator roar to life.

"Don't tell me Lou and Murray have come to visit," he muttered as he got out bed.

He pulled on his robe and walked through the living room, where the Christmas tree ornaments were shining in the dim street light coming through the windows. He cautiously approached the back door, wishing it had a window. He fumbled with the knob, then slowly opened the door.

Rick stood on the walk.

Ed blinked. Then blinked again. Yes, it really was Rick, his arms around a big, gift-wrapped box, grinning at Ed like an idiot.

"Surprise," Rick called out softly.

Ed fumbled the storm door open and threw himself at Rick, somehow managing to get his arms around Rick and the box he was holding. He felt the stinging cold of the cement walk on his bare feet, but he didn't care.

"What are you doing here?" he exclaimed, his face against Rick's beard.

"December twenty-sixth just wasn't good enough, baby." He gently pushed Ed's face away from his and looked right into Ed's eyes. "Merry First Christmas," he said.

⁂

A few minutes later they were sitting on the sofa. Ed had let go of Rick only long enough to plug in the Christmas tree lights, and for Rick to take off his coat and deposit the box he was carrying under the tree.

"How did you know?" Ed said, practically pulling Rick into his lap. "How did you know that all I wanted tonight was to be with you?"

"Simple," Rick answered, that idiot's grin still on his face. "Because it was the only thing I really wanted. All the way to Indy I kept wanting to turn back. The kids were fighting in the backseat, and Claire kept messing with the radio. I think I heard 'White Christmas' about forty-seven times. And all I could do was wish I was back here, spending Christmas with the cutest handyman in Porterfield, Indiana.

"Well," he continued, stroking Ed's hair, "we had been at Mom and Dad's for a couple of hours when Mom dragged me off to the kitchen. She wanted to know what was the matter with me. I lied and said that nothing was wrong, I was just tired, but she didn't believe me. She finally got me to admit that I was missing you, that I wanted to spend at least part of Christmas with you. Then she let me have it. She said that I should have said something weeks ago, and that I took family responsibility too far sometimes. Next thing I know, she was all but marching me out to the car, telling me to come back late tomorrow afternoon to pick up Claire and the kids, and to drive safely, and not break any speed limits."

"Did you? Break speed limits, I mean?"

"Well, maybe one or two. Mom also insisted that I bring you down to Indy on my next day off. She wants to see the man who's got me so stirred up."

"Are you, darlin', stirred up?"

"Like a very bad martini." Rick laughed. "Oh, but I feel better now. I don't think I've ever felt better in my whole life than I do right now."

"I just can't believe it," Ed said. "Hey! I'll have to call Laurie in the morning and tell her to set another place at the table. Man, won't *they* be surprised." He shook his head. "But no way, *no way,* as surprised as I am. And happy. Darlin', I am so happy right now I could . . . I could . . . hell, I don't know," he ended helplessly.

"For starters, how 'bout a kiss for Santa Rick?"

"No problem," Ed said, reaching for him. "No problem."

Even for Ed and Rick it was a long kiss. Neither one of them seemed quite ready to let go, but finally Rick pulled away.

"Hey, enough of this. Don't you want to see what Santa brought you?"

"Besides you?" Ed laughed. "What else do I need?"

"That big box under the tree is for you, you goof. C'mon, I'm dying for you to open it."

Ed got up and went to tree. He paused for a moment, smiling at Frosty.

"Thanks," he whispered.

"What?" Rick asked from the sofa.

"Oh, nothing."

Ed thought that maybe he'd wait until next year to tell Rick about his wish with Frosty. He got down on his knees, but instead of picking up his gift, he pulled out the box containing Rick's present.

"Here. Open yours first, okay?"

Rick frowned at him, taking the box. "After all that shit about how I couldn't shake it or anything, you're gonna let me go first? Okay, okay."

He tore the paper from the gift. He opened the box and pulled out the denim jacket.

"Oh, wow," he softly exclaimed, getting up to try it on. "I love it, baby. I just love it."

"Well," said Ed, admiring Rick in the jacket, "you can't really wear it too much for a few months."

"Who cares? I'll wear it anyway. The hell with the cold!. I'll look too great to care."

Rick buttoned up the jacket, then headed for the bedroom to see himself in the mirror.

"It's great," he said, walking back into the living room. "Thanks, baby. I really love it. But now it's your turn."

He stooped by the tree and shoved the box he'd brought with him over to Ed.

Ed slowly unwrapped the box, trying to make the suspense last as long as possible. He uncovered a box so tightly sealed he had to get the scissors to open it. Once he had it open, he pulled out a deluxe toolbox, just the kind he wanted, but hadn't allowed himself to buy.

"What do you think, baby?" Rick asked softly.

"It's . . . it's wonderful." Ed looked at the toolbox in his lap. "Green too. My favorite color."

"Hey, you think that was some kinda coincidence?" Rick hugged him. "But you need to open it. See what's inside."

Ed frowned, shaking the toolbox. It sure seemed empty to him. But he unfastened the lid anyway. It *was* empty. He looked up at Rick questioningly.

"Look inside the lid," Rick commanded with a smile.

Ed did, and his mouth fell open in surprise. Attached to the inside of the lid was a gold plate, the sort used on trophies. It read:

FOR THE CUTEST HANDYMAN
IN PORTERFIELD, INDIANA
LOVE, RICK

Ed looked up at Rick. "Thank you," he whispered.

Rick wiped a few tears away from Ed's eyes. "You don't have to cry about it," he said softly, stroking Ed's face. "But"—Ed heard a catch in Rick's voice—"I just might join you."

Ed reached out to Rick's face and wiped away a few tears himself. "Hell, if we're so happy, why are we crying?"

"I don't know, baby. I don't know." Rick gathered Ed in his arms, and they sat quietly for a moment, enjoying their first Christmas together.

"How'd I get so lucky?" asked Ed, his gaze moving from Frosty on the tree to Rick. "How did *we* get so lucky?"

Rick was quiet for a long time, then he smiled. "Beats me. I guess sometimes you just *get* lucky."

Chapter Fourteen

Ed, finishing the dinner dishes, lip-synched to "Lady Willpower," which was blasting from the stereo in the living room. Using a spatula as a microphone, he silently belted the lyrics to the kitchen window, wishing for the millionth time that he had Gary Puckett's voice. As the song faded out he hollered into the living room, "Hey, play that one again."

"No," Rick yelled back. "I'm making a tape, remember?"

"Aw, crud. I swear for a moment there I really was Gary Puckett."

Ed walked into the living room. He looked at Rick, who was fiddling with the cassette player/recorder on Ed's stereo, then at the mess on the floor.

"Geez, it looks like a record store exploded in here."

Almost all of his 45s, it seemed, were scattered across the carpet. Rick was recording the ones he liked best onto a cassette for an Indianapolis road trip they had planned for the next day.

When Rick returned on Christmas Eve with the message that his mother wanted to meet the man who had stolen her son's heart, Ed had known they'd be making the drive soon. With Norma for a mother, Ed was used to obeying a mother's commands, so on this Sunday between Christmas and New Year's, they were preparing for the visit, Rick's third round trip to Indianapolis in less than a week.

"After this one, I think I'll be able to drive I-69 blindfolded," Rick had said.

Normally Ed would be thrilled with the idea of a spending an entire day with Rick, and the idea of getting out of town for a day had its own appeal. However, Ed had to admit he felt more dread than anticipation about this trip.

"They're going to love you, maybe not as much as I do, but it's going to be fine. I *promise*," Rick had reassured him over and over, but Ed was nervous, and knew he would be until it was over.

Trying to shove the impending trip from his mind, Ed bent over and began stacking the records.

"Okay, if I can't hear Gary Puckett and the Union Gap again, what are you going to play?" he asked.

"Ah," Rick said, settling a record on the turntable. "Perfect." He clicked the recorder on just before the song began to play. "And this one," he said, turning to Ed, "is dedicated to you, from me."

Ed recognized the opening chords of "This Guy's in Love with You" by Herb Alpert.

"May I have this dance, sir?" Rick asked, standing up and opening his arms.

Ed stepped into Rick's arms. Moving away from the records on the floor, they swayed slowly to the rhythm of the song, holding each other close.

"I haven't heard this song in years," Rick murmured into Ed's ear. "It sure says what I feel about you, though."

Rick began singing along with Herb, and Ed had to admit that Rick couldn't sing any better than Ed himself could. Still, having the man he loved sing a mushy song into his ear, off-key or not, was something he'd only dreamed about until Rick came along.

"Why don't they play this stuff on the radio anymore?" Rick whispered.

"Probably 'cause we're the only ones who want to hear them," Ed answered, giggling.

"We just have better taste than the average radio listener. That's why I'm making a tape for this trip. I am going to drive triumphantly into Indianapolis, with the cutest handyman in Porterfield, Indiana, by my side, and the music I heard when I dreamed about finding someone like him will be playing. Loudly. I may even blow the speakers in my car. I want everybody on East Fifty-seventh Street to know the kid with the zits finally got lucky."

"So are we at the senior prom right now?" Ed asked, imagining Rick and himself dancing across the Porterfield High gym floor.

"Sure! Let's pretend there's a mirror ball right over us."

"The Christmas tree lights help."

"Yeah, they do. We need crepe paper streamers across the ceiling, though."

The song ended, and Ed regretfully let Rick go to pause the recorder.

"I remember hearing that song on the radio back then, summer of '68, right before my senior year," Rick said, taking the record off the turntable.

"And, oh, I didn't want to admit it, but I didn't think about singing it to some girl. I wanted some guy to sing it to me." Rick sighed, a faraway look in his eyes. "I wish someone could have told that gawky, pimply-faced kid that twelve years later he'd meet this incredible guy in Porterfield, Indiana, and he'd get to dance with him to that song."

"I know what you mean," Ed said, reaching for Rick's hand. "I remember the senior prom and dancing with Cathy Carroll. The prom committee had hired this awful band from Marion, and they were playing the worst rendition of 'Something' I've ever heard. Cathy was looking over my shoulder at Troy Williams, and I was looking over *her* shoulder at some guy Debbie Crocker was dating from Fort Wayne. I couldn't get over how cute he was, and all of a sudden, all those thoughts I'd been trying to avoid about liking boys instead of girls came crashing down on me. I even got a hard-on. I all but dumped Cathy on the dance floor, then ran to the restroom. I hid in there till I thought I could face everyone again, but I knew, right then and there, that I'd never date another girl, even if it meant being alone for the rest of my life."

Rick squeezed Ed's hand. "I didn't even go to my senior prom."

"You're kidding."

"Nope. I had dated a few girls in high school, but by the end of senior year I'd pretty much given up on the whole thing. When I told my mom I wasn't going, she threw a fit, saying I'd regret it all my life if I missed my prom.

"So I lied about it. Rented a tux and told her I had a date with a girl named Paula, who was a friend of a friend and lived across town. I left home, all dressed up, corsage box in hand, and spent the evening driving around town in my beat-up Ford Falcon. I finally ended up in some all-night coffee shop near downtown, drinking coffee and talking with this waitress, who told me not to worry about it, that I'd be so handsome in a few years I'd be beating the girls off with a stick. I was tempted to tell her I didn't care about the girls, but hoped the boys would feel that way about me. I gave her the corsage, and she wore it through her whole shift.

"I finally drove home about five in the morning, totally wired on coffee, wishing so bad that there was a guy in the car with me. I think that's the first time I heard 'Baby, I Love You' on the radio. Remember when I sang that song to you?"

"I'll never forget that as long as live," Ed promised, his arms around Rick.

"When I saw that record I remembered that night and how alone I felt, wondering if I'd ever get to fall in love like other people. Being able to tell you I loved you, and with that song . . I don't know . . . it healed something in me, I guess." Rick shrugged. "High school really sucked, no two ways about it."

Ed nodded, remembering other high school horrors. "Isn't it funny, though, how good these songs sound now? You'd think we'd just hate 'em, thinking back on those days, but I like them even more now."

Rick thought about that. "That is strange, isn't it? I don't know. Maybe it's 'cause we survived all that, and listening to them is . . . healing, like I said." He shrugged helplessly, looking up at Ed. "You got me. All I know is I love hearing them again, especially with you."

Ed got on the floor next to Rick and began pawing through the scattered 45s.

"Here," he said, handing one to Rick. "Now *this* is a song I always wished I could dance to with another man."

Rick looked at it and smiled. He put it on the turntable, and soon the sounds of the Association's "Everything That Touches You" were coming out of the speakers.

"The hell with that tape for right now," he said, grabbing Ed. "Let's just dance."

Holding each other close once again, they moved together, the romantic lyrics of the song weaving a spell that turned two lonely, unhappy teenage boys into two grown men who had finally found the love they had dreamed about.

"I love you so much, baby. Thanks for coming into my life. These old songs, thinking about going home tomorrow, well, I'm just so glad you're going with me."

"Do me a favor. Tell that gawky kid with the zits that he became the handsomest man in the world, and that I'm very, very much in love with him."

"He knows, baby," Rick said, pulling Ed closer. "And he's very, very grateful."

⋘●⋙

Rick was still stacking 45s on the turntable the next morning while they prepared to leave for Indianapolis. Half-dressed, he was bouncing around the living room, playing air guitar to Deep Purple's "Hush."

"Nope," he said, bounding toward the bathroom, where Ed was shaving. "I never wanted to play basketball, like everyone thought I should. I wanted to be Jimi Hendrix, or maybe Eric Clapton."

Ed glanced at him. "The way you're hangin' out there, darlin', you remind me more of Jim Morrison."

"Oh, God," Rick moaned. "I wanted him so bad. Shit, I think that's when I knew I liked boys."

"Yeah? Well, you can light my fire anytime."

Rick laughed as he headed to the bedroom to finish dressing. "Who'd you wanna be, baby?" he called out.

Ed wiped the lather off his face. "Oh, I don't know. I guess I was more queeny than you. I used to lock the door to my room and lip-synch with all my Supremes records. I thought Diana Ross was the greatest. Still do, for that matter."

"Oh, hell," said Rick, pulling up his pants. "I did that, too: The Shangri-Las, Lesley Gore, Dusty Springfield. God, I loved 'Son-of-a Preacher Man.' It's no wonder we both turned out queer."

"Actually," Ed said, joining Rick in the bedroom, "I wanted to be Neil Armstrong. I thought the moon landing was so cool. But when I found out how hard it was to become an astronaut, I gave up that idea in a hurry."

"Hmm. From astronaut to handyman. Oh, well. I'd say you turned out okay."

"Yeah. And Jimi Hendrix and Jim Morrison are dead. I guess you turned out okay, too," Ed said, trying to decide what shirt to wear. He frowned, pushing clothes back and forth in the closet.

Rick came up behind. "Are you worrying about what to wear? Shit, don't make this into a bigger deal than it is. Here." He pulled a shirt off a hanger. "I like this one. Now, get dressed already. We need to hit the road."

The record changer clicked in the living room, and the Guess Who's "Undun" began to play. Ed sighed. He couldn't help it. He was feeling a little undone himself at the moment. He so wanted to make a good impression on Rick's parents, but as usual, he didn't have enough confidence in himself to think he could pull it off.

"You'd better strap my seat belt on me," he said to Rick, who was putting on his shoes. "Just in case I try to bail out of the car halfway there."

Rick rolled his eyes at him. "If it wasn't seven-thirty in the morning, I'd probably throw a couple shots of vodka down your throat. Maybe that would calm you down." He got up from the bed and put his arms around Ed. "I told you. They're just a couple of nice, middle-aged, middle-class, liberal teacher types who want to see the man their son is so crazy about. Hell, for all I know, they're nervous, too. They survived Jack," he said, referring to his ex-lover, "and he survived them with no problem. Considering that you're twice, no, three times the man he is, I know they're going to like you."

The mere mention of the name of Rick's ex sent a pain through Ed. He knew the guy was still somewhere in Indianapolis, and in his gloomier moments he pictured this Jack guy swooping down out of the sky to reclaim Rick.

"Did they like Jack?" Ed asked.

Rick looked undecided about what to say. "Well," he said hesitantly. "They did and they didn't. Jack was handsome and charming, and he knew how to behave around someone's parents, but I don't think Mom ever really trusted him." His mouth hardened. "Turned out she was right."

"Oh, great," Ed wailed. "Your mom's gonna hate me, then you'll think I'm a creep like your ex."

"I knew I shouldn't have told you that," Rick said with disgust. "It just upset you. Now look, Jack *was* a creep. So, okay, I didn't see it until it was too late. I was young and stupid, and I thought he loved me. Turned out he couldn't love me without loving half the other men in Indy. And he couldn't keep a job, and he totaled my damned car one night and lied about it. I could go on, believe me, but does that sound like you for even one minute?"

Ed buried his face in Rick's neck. "No."

"Well, then," Rick said, stroking Ed's back. "Sometimes I just wanna paddle you. Just once I wish you'd realize what an incredible guy you are. Everybody likes you. And your clients? I was telling you just a few weeks ago how great *they* think you are. If you can handle a bunch of cranky old folks, my parents are not going to be a problem." He gave Ed's ass a good whack. "Now, do I go get that vodka, or what?"

Ed sighed again. "No. I don't think I'd make too good of an impression with booze on my breath. But how about a Pepsi for the road, huh? I probably don't need the caffeine, but it sure would taste good."

Rick let Ed go with a shake. "Okay. I'll get us both one. I just wish I had a Valium to put in yours."

⋘●⋙

Once they were on the interstate, heading south, Rick put on the cruise control and settled more comfortably in his seat.

"Getting tired of this drive, darlin'?" Ed asked, watching the scenery with interest. He hadn't been south of Porterfield in quite a while.

Rick shook his head. "Oh, not really. I'm just so glad to be away from work today, on the open road with you, that I don't really care where we're going."

"How's your back?"

Rick shifted from side to side, as though testing it. "It's not bad at all. A twinge now and then, but that's it. I wish I could go back to walking a route, but Don insists on me waiting at least a month. I don't know why," he grumbled. "The mail is lighter now, and I'll certainly be a lot more careful. I hate being cooped up all day."

Ed turned his gaze from the gray December landscape to Rick. This was the first time he'd ever heard Rick come close to complaining about his job.

"Is it that bad, working in the back of the post office? I suppose they could put you at the counter, selling stamps or something."

Rick sighed, steering the car into the left lane to pass a truck. "I'm just not used to being around people all day. Every time my mind drifts off to something pleasant to think about, someone calls my name or starts a conversation. Let's face it, I don't have a lot in common with most of those guys. I can't tell you who's playing in the Rose Bowl this week, and care even less. Some of them think that's a little weird."

"Reminds me of the factory," Ed said.

"I'll bet. Plus, I'm still the new guy around there. I haven't really spent enough time around them to have been . . . *initiated* into their little fraternity. Most of them are okay, really, but there are a few I could do without. You know, the kind who gives you a look like you're trespassing until you've been there for ten years."

"There were guys like that at Marsden," Ed said, grateful for his self-employment. "They were the ones who gave me even more shit because my dad was a manager. They always seemed to know just how far they could push before they got in trouble."

"Yeah," Rick grumbled. "I heard that. Oh, well. Don's the boss, and he's happy with me. I know, because he told me I'm the best hire he's made in a long time. As long as he's satisfied with my work there isn't much anyone can do. And it's temporary. I'll be back on the street in a few weeks. There's a rest stop coming up, baby," he said, abruptly changing the subject. "You need a pee break?"

"Uh, yeah," Ed said, trying to shift mental gears. "I don't want to have to pee the minute I see your folks."

"Don't worry, baby," Rick said absentmindedly, rolling back into the right lane. He gave Ed's leg a quick pat, then turned up the volume on the tape player.

Ed turned his attention back to the bare fields they were passing and listened with half an ear to Spanky and Our Gang's "Like to Get to Know You." He felt an uneasiness in his stomach, suspecting Rick's complaints about work had more substance than he was willing to admit. He looked at Rick. He was singing softly and tapping the steering wheel with his fingers. He had his sunglasses on, so Ed couldn't see his eyes, but something in his face troubled Ed. He considered pursuing the subject, but decided against it. He didn't want to upset Rick in any way before seeing his parents.

He searched his brain for a non-work-related topic. "Living in Indy, did you ever get to see any of these groups in concert?" he asked, surprised, actually, that he'd never thought to ask before.

Rick smiled. "I saw Spanky and Our Gang once, heard them do this one live."

"Cool," Ed exclaimed. "Tell me about it."

Rick went into an anecdote about that particular show, then told several others. Ed watched the tense look disappear from Rick's face, happy to have distracted him. Still, Ed found himself, for the first time since meeting Rick, a little worried about his mailman.

When they were a few miles north of the city, Rick refreshed Ed's memory on his parents. "Dad's name is John, and he teaches high school history and does some college counseling. Don't let him get started on that. Mom's name is Vera, and she teaches fifth grade, and no, neither Claire, nor I, ever had to deal with them in school. They purposely moved into another district when we were small to avoid that.

"Anyway," Rick continued, "as you know, they're quite liberal, bleeding-heart liberals, actually. They support about every cause you can imagine, and even went to Washington in late '69 for that big peace march against the war. I mean, there I was, a freshman in college, and my parents were more radical than the guys in my dorm. That was weird, let me tell you.

"I came out to them when I was working out of the Nora post office in northeast Indy. I had gotten my own place, so if they decided to disown me, I wouldn't be on the street. I didn't think they would, but you never know, right? They took it pretty well, but I could tell they were disappointed, and things were, well . . . a little rocky for a while. I realize now that was my fault. I was so off on my *Harold and Maude* trip, so concerned with being true to myself, that I was kind of belligerent about the whole thing. Once I realized I was being a real asshole, things got better.

"I also happen to know," Rick said, his warm and tender special in place as he glanced at Ed, "that Claire and the kids spent part of Christmas Day raving about how wonderful you are. So don't worry. Your politics match theirs, and you're a kind, generous, intelligent man. I would add that you're also the most handsome man in the world, but I don't think that will impress them the way it does me."

Ed sighed, still nervous. "Yeah, a kind and generous man with nothing more than a high school education, who will probably spend the winter shoveling snow for old people. That'll impress 'em."

Rick frowned at him. "Does Mrs. Penfield look down on you for that?"

"No," Ed admitted.

"Well, then. They won't either. Not all smart people go to college. Sometimes I think the smartest ones avoid it. There's something to be said for learning what there is to learn from life, as opposed to sitting in some lecture hall, letting someone just tell you about it. That's kind of the way I've felt these past few years, anyway," Rick added, as he turned off the cassette player.

"Why'd you do that?"

Rick smiled. "'Cause the next song on the tape is the one I want to be playing when I roll into our neighborhood, you by my side, baby."

He piloted his old Monte Carlo confidently off the interstate and onto surface streets unfamiliar to Ed, who'd spent little time in Indiana's capital city. Rick turned onto Keystone Avenue and pointed out the Glendale Mall.

"That's where I bought *my* records, baby," he said with a grin.

Rick turned the tape player on, and Argent's "Hold Your Head Up" was soon blasting from the speakers.

"This song was big around the time I was trying to accept being gay. I think it helped me as much as *Harold and Maude* did," he shouted over the music.

Ed shook his head in amazement, as he had always felt the same way about the song, and still did. Forgetting to be self-conscious about his awful singing voice, he sang along with Rod Argent and Rick.

Rick reached for Ed's hand. "Remember what I said last night about healing? Your love has done more to heal the wounds I have from those years—and those years with Jack—than anything else I could have found. Not only do I love you, baby, but now I really can hold my head up high."

Ed thought back to when he had first heard "Hold Your Head Up" on the radio years before. He'd been a nineteen-year-old factory worker, alone and afraid, wondering how it would feel to be close to—let alone be in love with—a man. Somehow, that song had given him the courage to believe he wasn't the only person struggling with being different.

"I feel the same way," Ed said, and turned down the music. "I think maybe you've healed some of my wounds, too. You know what? I didn't think there was anything you could say to me that would stop my being nervous, but that did. I love you too, darlin'. More than you'll ever know."

Ed put his hand on Rick's leg and left it firmly in place until Rick pulled up in front of an attractive, two-story brick home in a quiet, tree-filled neighborhood.

"Well, this is it," Rick said, shutting off the ignition. "About one-third the size of Mrs. Penfield's brick pile, but it's where I grew up."

"Looks nice."

Ed reluctantly took his hand away from Rick's leg. He wanted to hold Rick's hand as they approached the front door, but was afraid his parents might disapprove.

As they climbed the front steps the door opened, and a tall, slender gray-haired woman appeared, smiling.

"Rick, honey," she cried, reaching out to him for a hug. "And this must be Ed. I'm so glad to finally meet you."

"You too, Mrs. Benton," Ed said, smiling into her warm brown eyes, so much like Rick's. "I guess we've both heard a lot about each other." He had practiced that line to himself all the way to Indianapolis and was pleased now to hear her chuckle.

"Oh, call me Vera, please. I get enough of 'Mrs. Benton' at school. Come in! Come in!" She ushered them into a small entryway, urging them to take off their coats. "I'm so glad it was a clear day for your drive. Do you suppose we'll get much snow this winter? I understand that's something you'll have to deal with, Ed."

Vera continued to chat with Ed in a pleasant manner and soon had them seated in the family room. Ed looked around with appreciation. The room was paneled in pine, with floor-to-ceiling bookshelves lining one wall.

"I don't think Rick ever mentioned what a cozy house you have," Ed murmured, studying a beautiful landscape over the fireplace.

Vera beamed at him. "Cozy—isn't that just the word? I like you already, Ed. That's exactly what I've aimed for all these years."

Rick gave Ed an I-told-you-so look. "Ed's good at cozy, Mom. You should see his place."

The sound of footsteps on the stairs was followed by John Benton's entrance into the room.

"Sorry I wasn't here to meet you at the door, boys," he said, a sheepish grin on his face. "I was taking care of some important business."

"Oh, John," Vera scolded, with a look at her son.

Rick and Ed rose to their feet. John crossed the room to shake hands with Ed.

"Good to meet you, Ed. Sit down, sit down," he said, waving them back to their seats.

Ed looked at John, wondering if he was seeing Rick in twenty-five years. John had the same thick hair, but it had gone from dark brown to gray at some point. He was almost as tall as Rick, but not quite so broad through the shoulders. And—Ed's mother would be horrified—he had a graying beard, similar to Rick's as well. Much to his relief and astonishment, Ed felt immediately at home with him.

Conversation resumed; the usual polite process of people getting to know one another. Vera disappeared for a few minutes, then returned with a coffee tray.

"If you're a tea drinker, Ed, I can put the kettle on."

"Oh, no, thank you. This is fine," Ed said, accepting a cup from her.

Rick frowned at him. "Actually, Mom, Ed isn't a coffee drinker, but he's too polite to say so."

"Rick," Ed groaned, embarrassed.

Vera laughed. "No, I'm glad he said something, Ed. Do you drink tea?"

Ed nodded, blushing as usual.

"Well, I'll just boil some water. Earl Grey?"

Ed nodded again, not entirely sure who Earl was, but assumed it had something to do with tea. He put the coffee cup back on the tray, as Vera returned to the kitchen.

"Don't worry about it, Ed," John said jovially, lighting a pipe. "The extra exercise will do the old girl good, since she talked herself out of doing any cooking today."

"I heard that, John Benton," Vera called from the hall.

The men shared a good laugh. John asked Ed what kind of food he enjoyed.

"Oh, I'm pretty much a Hoosier meat-and-potatoes kind of guy," Ed said. "As Rick can tell you, I don't care much for fish or other seafood, but I'm willing to try about anything else."

"I'd like to give his palate a little more education," Rick said, glancing at Ed fondly. "But can you believe it, Dad? There's not even one Chinese restaurant in Porterfield. The most ethnic thing we have is a pizza place."

"You must be going through withdrawal," John said, still trying to get a good light on his pipe. "Every time we'd go to his old apartment," John said to Ed, "it smelled like Chinese takeout. He told us he did a lot of his own cooking, but I never saw the evidence."

It was Rick's turn to blush, as Ed laughed. "Well, I've seen the evidence. He certainly knows his way around eggs and pancakes. I think I've put on weight, eating his breakfasts. They're great, believe me."

"I was thinking we'd go out for lunch," Vera said, reentering the room. "Would you like to try one our favorite Chinese places, Ed? I know that's terrible, but with all the holiday hubbub, I just didn't get around to any extra shopping."

"Oh, Mom," Rick groaned. "Don't worry about it. She gets nervous, cooking for company," he said to Ed, his mischievous grin on his face. "That's just her cop-out, that she was too busy."

"Richard . . . ," she said with a warning smile.

"Uh-oh. If she calls me Richard, I'm in trouble," Rick said, laughing.

Ed said, "I think that would be great—Chinese, I mean. My mom used to make chow mein for my sister and me when we were kids, but I'm guessing it was a lot more Indiana than China."

John, finally satisfied with the draw on his pipe, turned to Ed once again. "So, Ed, tell us about your job. How did you get to be Porterfield's finest handyman?"

Ed felt himself blushing again. "Well, I don't know about 'finest,' but I do my best."

"He *is* the best," Rick said confidently. "Some of the folks he works for are on my route. They think he's wonderful."

"It's kind of a long story," Ed began. "I didn't want to go to college after high school, because I didn't really have a goal in mind, so I went to work for Marsden Electric. That's a factory in town that makes electric motors for appliances and such. My dad was a plant manager there. Anyway, I just stuck with it, thinking I could work myself up to a job like my dad's, but then the recession hit, and all the people who didn't have seniority were laid off.

"So, I sat around home for a couple of months, getting on my mom's nerves. Then one day a friend of hers called and asked if I could fix a lamp of hers that wasn't working right. I'd always been good with that sort of thing, thanks to watching my dad tinker around with that stuff, so I did. Next thing I knew, I was doing odd jobs for her, then for her mother, who told a friend of hers, and pretty soon every old lady in town was calling me. I decided the heck with waiting to go back to Marsden, and went into business for myself."

"Isn't that interesting?" John marveled.

"You do more than fix things, though, isn't that right?" Vera asked.

"Oh, yes. I shovel walks, as you know, help clean out attics or basements, whatever they need done. I help one woman with her grocery shopping every week. She can only get around with a walker, and she says my help keeps her out of a nursing home. I even"—he glanced at Rick with a grin—"put up Christmas trees. I do quite a bit of painting, too. Whatever. No two days are ever the same, and I really like it. It's constant variety, and it never gets boring. The people, for the most part, are great. Especially the old ones. I really get a kick out of them."

"I think that's wonderful," Vera said, smiling at him. "You're performing quite a service for those elderly folks. There really should be more people doing that."

"I keep telling him he should incorporate and start some kind of a chain," Rick teased.

"Oh, I've got enough to keep me busy as it is. That, plus my mom calls a lot, getting all her work done for free."

"Ed's mom is quite a character, let me tell you," Rick said, shaking his head.

"Rick," his mother said, disapproving.

"Oh, no, she is," Ed said hastily. "But she really likes Rick. Thinks he's better than I deserve. At least that's what she keeps telling me."

They all laughed comfortably.

"You should meet Mrs. Penfield," Rick said. "One of Ed's clients is his high school English teacher. She lives in this incredible Victorian home, and had us over for tea a few weeks ago. So don't worry so much about us, Mom. They *do* have civilized people in Porterfield."

Vera shook her head, lips pursed. "I'm sorry, but I do worry. When Rick first moved there," she said to Ed, "I worried about him being exposed to bigotry and prejudice, but I'll admit it's going better than I thought. My mistake, I think, was judging the town by our son-in-law."

"Oh, Porterfield's not so bad," Ed said. "I think there are a lot more folks like Mrs. Penfield than Hank Romanowski."

"That's good to hear," John said, raising his coffee cup. "However, before we journey down that particular unpleasant road, let's get back to Ed's job. Do you think you could do anything about that fluorescent light in our kitchen? I changed the bulbs, but it still isn't working right."

"Dad! This is Ed's day off," Rick protested.

"That's okay," Ed said, eager to show off his skills. "I'd be happy to take a look at it."

They all trooped into the kitchen. John flipped the light switch. The ceiling light flickered, shone brightly for a moment, then flickered again before one of the bulbs went completely out.

"Hmm," Ed said, stroking his chin. "Something's loose up there, I'll bet. Do you have some tools? And a stepladder? I want to see what's going on."

John fetched his toolbox, while Vera pulled a stepladder out of a kitchen closet. Rick watched Ed climb up the ladder.

"Be careful, okay?" Rick murmured, looking anxious.

"I'm not gonna burn your parents' house down," Ed said, removing the bulbs, feeling totally confident for the first time that day. "I do this sort of stuff all the time."

Ed handed the bulbs down to Rick, then climbed down from the ladder to inspect the tools in the box John had brought up from the basement. Ed wished he had his own toolbox. John's was a jumble of mismatched tools, and Ed prided himself on stocking an efficient toolbox.

"You know, boys," Vera said, turning off the gas under the whistling tea kettle, "I think unless he needs some help, we should all go back to the other room. He might get a little distracted with an audience. All right, Ed?"

"Umm-hmm," he mumbled, already engrossed in the chore.

John, Vera, and Rick left the room, Rick glancing back nervously on his way out. Ed, screwdriver in hand, climbed the ladder again. Soon enough he found the problem. It was a loose connection, as he had suspected. Someone had probably slammed the kitchen door a few too many times, he thought. He easily tightened all of them, then replaced the bulbs.

"Now, how's that for impressing your prospective in-laws," he whispered to himself, smiling. "Didn't even need to flip the circuit breaker. Talk about easy."

He turned to climb down the ladder, but somehow lost his footing. Before he knew what was happening, he somehow managed to kick the ladder out from under his feet. The stepladder skidded across the floor, and Ed went crashing down after it with a muffled yelp. Fortunately, he landed square on his ass, but it was quite a shock.

The other three ran into the kitchen and surveyed the scene in surprise. Ed looked up at them, his earlier confidence swirling down the proverbial drain. *That's what I get for being so cocky,* he thought.

"Light's fixed," he said, grinning in embarrassment.

Vera rushed to help him, while John and Rick began to laugh.

"John! Richard!" she scolded. "It's not funny."

"Yes, it is," Ed said, beginning to chuckle himself. He got to his feet and dusted himself off.

"Are you all right?" Vera asked anxiously.

"I'm fine," he assured her. "Nothing broken but my dignity."

"We've all broken that at one time or another," John said, flipping the light switch on and off. "But you've certainly fixed the light, Ed. Thank you. That flickering's been driving us crazy for weeks. I don't want to offend you by offering you money, but how about some hot and sour soup?"

"Sounds good to me," Ed said, returning the screwdriver to the toolbox. "I never turn down food in exchange for cash."

Ed looked up and saw Rick's eyes upon him, his warm and tender special in place.

"You're something else, you know that, baby?"

John looked at his son, then at his wife. "I don't think you need to worry quite so much, Vera." He grinned. "I get the feeling Rick's in good hands in Porterfield."

After a lunch of hot and sour soup and garlic chicken, which Ed thoroughly enjoyed, they returned to the Benton house for another round of coffee. Ed was beginning to see where Rick had acquired his coffee habit. He relaxed in his chair, tea mug in hand, feeling almost at home as he would with his own parents.

By late afternoon Rick was glancing at his watch and making noises about having to get up early for work the next day. "It's a long drive back, and I'd like to have some downtime before I go to bed."

"We understand," John said, with a glance at his wife. "Not everyone is lucky enough to be teachers with a long Christmas vacation."

"That sucked when we were kids," Rick said to Ed. "With our parents on the same schedule, Claire and I never got away with anything."

"Well, I'm sorry you need to leave, but please come back when you can, both of you," Vera said, rising to her feet.

The other three joined her.

"You need to drive up to Porterfield some weekend," Rick told her, allowing himself to be hugged.

Vera moved over to Ed for a hug as warm as the one she had given her son. "We'll do that. Perhaps for Rick's birthday in March, if not sooner. I hate to make definite plans at this time of year, considering how brutal our past few winters have been." She gave Ed an extra squeeze. "It's been a real pleasure, Ed. Please do come again."

"Oh, I will, thank you." Ed smiled at her in gratitude, as he was pretty sure he had passed inspection.

"You watch that back of yours, Ed, with all that snow shoveling," John said, shaking his hand. "You don't want to end up like Rick here."

Rick sighed. "I'll keep an eye on him, believe me. One bad back in the family is enough." He hugged his father. "Thanks again for the book, Dad." At Rick's request, John had located and loaned to him a book on Victorian architecture. "I've really been curious about this since we visited Mrs. Penfield. I'll give it back the next time I see you."

"No hurry," John assured him.

"You'll call when you get home, won't you?" Vera asked worriedly as they went to the door.

"Oh, Mom," Rick groaned.

Ed gave Rick a mock punch to the arm. "I'll make sure he does," Ed told her.

Vera smiled at him. "Thank you, Ed, for that and everything else."

Good-byes were said, and soon the two were back in the car, headed toward the freeway. Rick began to chuckle.

"Why is it," he said, "that every time you fix something for someone in my family, you end up in trouble?"

Ed punched him for real this time. "I took handyman lessons from the Three Stooges," he retorted. "But, hey! Once again, I fixed it, didn't I?"

"You sure did, baby, you sure did," Rick said, pointing the car north, toward home.

"So how'd I do?"

"What do you think?" Rick scoffed. "They loved you. I knew they would. All that worry for nothing."

"Well, I'm still relieved it's over. I mean, relieved that the first meeting is over, if you know what I mean. I can go back there and know I'm welcome. Besides, I really liked them. It would be fun to visit again."

The warm and tender special was firmly in place on Rick's face. "You don't know how much that means to me, baby. I know you were nervous about them liking you, but I was nervous about you liking them. So you think you can handle them for in-laws?"

"Definitely."

"If I wasn't concentrating on three lanes of traffic, I'd give you a big ole kiss. Remind me to do it when we hit that rest stop, okay?"

"You got it," Ed said, putting his hand possessively on Rick's leg.

Rick reached for the car stereo and slipped his mix tape back in to play. The Spiral Starecase came blasting through the car speakers with "More Today Than Yesterday."

"Ain't that truth," Rick shouted. "Baby, I love you more today than yesterday, and I have a damned good feeling that it's *not* as much as I'm gonna love you tomorrow."

Chapter Fifteen

With one bare foot jammed under the other blue-jean-covered thigh, Ed sat at his kitchen table, hunched over his pocket calculator. He was muddling through one of his least favorite chores: end-of-the-month billing for his regular clients.

He frowned at his scrawled notes, added hours worked, multiplied by dollars per hour, and gave thanks to whoever invented the pocket calculator. Mrs. Penfield may have given him straight A's, but none of his math teachers had ever been inclined to do so.

The phone rang, and Ed heaved a sigh of relief. He didn't care who it was; even his mother would be a welcome change from pages of numbers.

"Happy New Year," Glen shouted when Ed answered. "How'd it go with Rick's folks?"

"Hey, Happy New Year to you too," Ed said. "It went fine, really. I like them, they liked me. No sweat."

"Amazing," Glen snorted. "I haven't met Michael's parents, and frankly, I don't care if I ever do from the way he talks. You guys are, like, charmed or something."

Ed sighed, smiling. "Yeah, we sure are."

"Oh, God. Don't get started. Any minute Barbra Streisand's gonna start singing the love theme from *A Star Is Born.* Listen, though, the reason I called—you remember Greg and Randy?"

Ed frowned at the phone. "Vaguely. Are they the ones who had that Halloween party last year that all the drag queens crashed?"

"Yeah, that's them. Anyway, they're having a New Year's bash tomorrow night. I know it's last minute and all, but they said you and Rick are more than welcome to come."

"Hmm. Well, I could live without another drag queen invasion, thanks just the same. We've already got plans, but tell them thanks for the invitation."

"Plans? Big New Year's plans in Porterfield? What are you gonna do, drink a beer and watch the traffic lights change color?" Glen snickered.

"Oh, you're so funny. If you must know, we are babysitting."

Glen gasped. "Babysitting? On New Year's Eve?"

Ed smiled. He knew that would get him. "Yes, babysitting. Claire's going to Indy overnight to see some old high school friends, so Rick and I are staying at the house with the kids. New Year's just isn't that big a deal to us."

"My God, I can't believe it. It's bad enough he's over there playing daddy, but now you are too. What's next? When are you gonna buy a station wagon and move to the suburbs?"

"Look, Glen, I know it's weird, and I know it's nothing you would do or would want to do, but it's okay with me. The kids are important to Rick, and I don't mind spending time with them. And if Rick and I are not behaving like two gay guys in love should behave, well, tough shit. I don't really give a rat's ass what anyone thinks. We're enjoying ourselves, and that's all I care about."

Glen was silent for a moment. "I'm sorry, Ed. I'm just kinda surprised."

Ed felt bad for getting so indignant with Glen, yet realized that what he had said held a great deal of truth.

"I'm sorry, too. I didn't mean to get so huffy. I guess I'm just realizing what I have with Rick is what I always wanted. No drag queens, no gay bars, no bullshit. I hate to admit it, but I think I'd rather spend New Year's with three kids than a bunch of bitchy queens."

Glen sighed. "Well, you always have been kind of different. If Rick is giving you everything you need, then I'm really happy for you. Not many guys get that lucky, you know."

"I know. Believe me, I know."

"So enjoy it. But don't be a stranger, okay? Give me a call sometime."

"Sure," Ed said, hearing the back door open. "Listen, Rick just showed up with our lunch, and he's got less than an hour to eat and get back to the post office. I'll call you after the holiday, okay?"

"I'll hold you to that," Glen said as he hung up.

Rick put a paper bag of takeout from the Cozy Hearth Café on the table, shoving aside a pile of invoices, envelopes, and stamps. He then reached out for Ed.

"Mmm," Rick moaned, kissing Ed deeply. "Hi, baby. Who was on the phone?"

"Just Glen," Ed said, stealing a quick kiss of his own. "He was inviting us to some party for tomorrow night."

Rick chuckled as he opened the bag. "I'll bet he about shit his pants when you told him what we're doing," he said, handing Ed his sandwich.

Ed grinned. "Of course. I think I took a little too much pleasure in telling him about our hot New Year's plans. Oh, well. We're weird and proud of it, right?"

"Right," Rick said, sitting down. "I don't care where I am when 1981 begins, as long as you're with me, kids or no kids. Now, do I get a cold Pepsi or what?"

"I'm working on it," Ed grumbled, going to the refrigerator. "Be careful with that sandwich, mister. Don't get any mayo on my invoices, you hear?"

Rick smirked at him. "What will happen if I do?"

"You can spend New Year's Eve with Glen and Michael, instead of me."

Rick shuddered. "I'll be careful. I promise."

Ed laughed, handing him a Pepsi. "Don't worry. I love you too much to inflict that kind of punishment on you. Besides, right now I'm just happy to see you. I miss seeing you at lunchtime every day, so this is special. Having you here is even better than the Cozy Hearth roast beef sandwich you brought me, and you know how much I love them."

"Well, eat up, then." Rick gestured at Ed's sandwich. "I even remembered the rye bread. Yeah, even if I can't stay very long, I'm glad to see you, too. Man, I can't wait to get my route back."

"Any word from Don on when you'll be back on the street?"

Rick shrugged. "I hope it's not too much longer," he mumbled through a mouth full of food.

"You want me to put in a good word for you?"

"You know him?" Rick asked, swallowing hard.

"Of course! I told you he used to play cards with my dad every week. Hell, he was one of the pallbearers at Dad's funeral. I've known Don Hoffmeyer my whole life."

"How 'bout that. Influence with my boss." Rick attempted a smile, but failed. "I'm about half-tempted to take you up on that."

There it was again, Ed thought. Something was bothering Rick about his job, and it was something more than missing his mail route. "What's wrong?"

Rick looked uneasy. "I'm just tired of that sorting room, that's all."

"No, there's something else. I can tell. It's been on your mind for days now." Ed put his sandwich down, went around to Rick's side of the table, and put his arms around him. "Darlin', please tell me. That's what I'm here for, the good stuff and the bad. I hate seeing you upset about something, then not sharing it with me."

Rick put his sandwich down, sighing. "Oh, shit. This is so dumb," he said, then paused. He looked up at Ed, obviously reluctant to continue, but Ed stared him down. "Well, there's this guy who's been ragging on me. He's seen us together and has somehow put two and two together. I mean, it's subtle, so far, but I don't want the other guys to pick up on it. I figure once I'm out of there, that'll be the end of it. Plus, Jim's such an asshole that I'm hoping the other guys aren't paying much attention to him."

"Aw, crud." Ed rolled his eyes. "Jim *Murkland*? Oh, God. I forgot he worked there."

"Yeah, that's who it is," Rick said, looking surprised. "Shit, do you know *everyone* at that post office?"

"Pretty much," Ed said. "My dad, through Don, knew most of the older guys. And I went to school with"—Ed closed his eyes to count—"at least three of the younger ones: Gordy Smith, Dave Brown, and Murk the Jerk. God, I hate that guy. Why does it not surprise me to hear that he hasn't changed a bit?"

"He was a jerk in high school, too, huh?" Rick asked.

Ed nodded. "Oh, yes. Good old Jim Murkland, Class of '70 with me. The class wiseass. Only he wasn't particularly funny. He was just mean. Picked on the homely girls, the fat girls. Oh, and he picked on my friend, Ted Gillis, who was overweight. Since I was dorky and shy back then, not that I'm not anymore, he nailed me, too. God, what a creep."

Ed paused for a moment, remembering. "He hung out with a group of guys that were pretty much like him—losers with the girls, not good enough to be on the teams, not tough enough to hang out with the hoods. So their claim to fame was bugging the teachers, picking on the other kids. Jim was kinda the ringleader. I remember"—Ed chuckled—"that of all of the guys in our class, Jim had the lowest lottery number. I don't think I'm the only one who hoped he'd get shipped to 'Nam and get blown to bits."

"Did he? Go, I mean?"

"Well, he was drafted. But I don't think he ever made it out of the States. Things were winding down by that time. I vaguely remember him coming home, acting like a big shot, although I don't think anyone was really impressed. He goofed around for a while, and finally Don hired him at the post office. Why, I don't know. I always gave Don credit for more brains than that. But Jim's been there ever since." Ed shook his head. "And still making trouble. How have you been handling him?"

Rick shrugged. "Saying that you and I are friends, and I don't understand why he's making a big deal about it. Come to think of it, I really don't know why he is. It's not like you and I are a couple of screaming queens, necking in public."

"That's just Jim," Ed responded. "I'm sure he doesn't know anything, but he had to find something to razz you about. He won't leave anyone alone. I'm guessing, too, that you are a hell of a lot better at sorting mail than he is. He couldn't find his ass with both hands and a flashlight. He also gave it to the smart kids, too. He's just a bigmouthed loser."

"That's for sure," Rick mumbled.

"What does Don say about it?"

"Oh, I haven't said anything to him about it. I'm sure he's heard it all before, and I'm a grown man. I can handle Jim. I just wish I didn't have to," Rick said, going back to his sandwich.

"Boy," said Ed dreamily, "I'll tell you, once I grew a couple of inches and got a lot stronger, there was nothing more I wanted to do than beat the livin' shit out of that guy. Here's my excuse."

"You stay out of it," Rick said sharply. "He really doesn't have any evidence that we are anything more than friends, and I'm not going to give it to him. I'll be back on my route eventually, and that'll be the end of it."

"Yeah, but you know? I sure would love to get just one lick in, just one."

"Didn't anyone else ever beat him up?" Rick asked curiously.

"Umm, I don't think so. He knew better than to give any shit to guys who were bigger and tougher than him. He wasn't that dumb. Gordy Smith, for instance, there at the post office. Gordy was a couple years ahead of us, played football and all that. I bet Jim never rags on him."

Rick looked thoughtful. "Come to think of it, you're right. He doesn't mess with Gordy. Oh, well. I'm still the new guy. I suppose that's my crime."

"Well, I know one thing," Ed said. "You ever need backup, you'll get it from Gordy. I can't imagine him putting up with Murkland. And he's always been a pretty cool guy."

"Yes, he is. I like Gordy. I can handle most of the guys there, but this guy is the biggest pain in the ass I've ever worked with."

Ed smiled, trying to cheer him up. "You're right. You'll be out of there soon. Until then, just threaten to rearrange his face, and I bet he'll back down. He's a loser through and through, and I've no doubt you can take him."

Rick looked at him sternly. "I'm not going to start any trouble. I could just see him going to Don. No, I'll just deal with it for now. And you," he said, reaching across the table to give Ed a mock punch, "keep your macho fantasies to yourself."

Ed showed up at the Romanowski house the next evening with a big box full of records, and an overnight bag. Ed spending the night at Rick's was novel, to say to least.

Judy met him at the door. "Oh, cool. You brought your records. Mom said we could use her stereo if we're careful."

Ed grinned at her. "Great! I just hope there are some songs in here you like."

"Ed's here! Ed's here!" Jane chanted, jumping up and down on the sofa. "Look what I got for Christmas, Ed." She pointed at a Chutes and Ladders game on the floor.

Thank God, he thought. He was getting burned out on Candy Land.

"Aw, I want Ed to play Battleship with me," Josh hollered, indicating the game *he'd* gotten for Christmas.

"Ed and I are going to play records," Judy told them both bossily. "Uncle Rick can play with you."

"Geez, I don't know when I've felt so popular," Ed said to Rick, who came in from the kitchen.

"Hey, hey," Rick shouted, as the children fought over who would get ownership of Ed. "There's enough of Ed to go around. Judy, you look through Ed's records while he plays some Chutes and Ladders with Janie. She'll have to go to bed pretty soon anyway. Josh, you and I can play a round of Battleship. Ed can play the winner." Rick winked at Ed, who knew damned well who was going to win that game.

Jane grabbed Ed's hand in triumph, pulling him down to the floor by her game. "I'm *not* going to bed. I'm going to stay up and watch that ball fall down."

"Me too," Josh chimed in.

"Uncle Rick," Judy whined. "Do they get to stay up too?"

Rick winked at Judy this time. "If they want to stay up, they can. Midnight's a long way away, kids. Heck, I might be asleep by then."

They settled in for the evening. Rick turned out to be about the most deliberately inept Battleship player ever, so while Ed faced off against Josh, Rick went to the kitchen to make popcorn. Judy had latched on to Ed's 45 of "Dancing Queen," and both she and Jane swayed and swooped around the room, pretending to be the girls in Abba.

"Do you have any more Abba records?" Judy asked after "Dancing Queen" had played five times.

"F5," Ed said to Josh.

"Missed me."

"Aw, crud. Yeah, Judy, I think 'S.O.S.' is in there. Do you remember that one?"

"Cool," Judy exclaimed, going back to the record box.

Ed made a mental note to get her an Abba greatest hits LP for her upcoming birthday.

Rick returned with the popcorn. "Hey, watch it," he said as Jane grabbed for the bowl. "Be careful. You get any butter on Ed's records you'll be in big trouble."

"J10," Josh said to Ed.

"Double crud! You just sank my sub," Ed said in mock rage.

Josh giggled. "You're not any better at this than Uncle Rick," he said with a yawn.

"I'm not done yet, you little pirate. E7."

"Rats!"

"Ha! I knew it."

"Come on, you two," Rick said. "Don't you want some popcorn?" He grinned over Josh's head at Ed.

Ed grinned back. "Not until I send his lousy fleet to the bottom of the ocean."

Ed fought valiantly, but it was Josh who laid waste to Ed's fleet.

"I'll get you next time, you little creep," Ed said, mussing Josh's hair.

"You'll come over and play again?" Josh asked, sleepily pulling pegs out of the game boards.

"Sure, after I bone up on my strategy."

Rick glanced at Josh, who was yawning again, and at Jane, who was practically asleep in his lap. "I think it's time you two hit the hay, don't you think?"

"No, we wanna stay up for the ball," Josh whined.

"I've got an idea," Ed said. "Let's pretend it's midnight right now. We can do a countdown and everything. Then, anyone who's tired can go to bed, and it'll already be 1981, okay?"

"The official beginning of the eighties," Judy remarked, digging through Ed's record box again.

"Huh?" Ed asked.

"Mr. Hopkins, my teacher, said that the decade really begins with the year that ends with a one. So 1980 was the last year of the seventies, and this is the first official year of the eighties," she said, smiling over several KC and the Sunshine Band records she had found.

"How 'bout that?" Rick said to Ed. "I guess I knew that, but I hadn't really thought about it."

"So we're really starting the eighties tonight," Ed said, thinking how wonderful it was to start a fresh, new decade with the man he loved, even if he had to share him with three kids.

They had their pretend countdown, noisemakers and all, then Rick herded Josh and Jane off to bed. Judy and Ed, with the stereo volume turned down, enjoyed "Get Down Tonight," and "(Shake, Shake, Shake) Shake Your Booty."

"Angie says disco is dead," Judy said, bouncing to the beat, "but I really like these songs. They still play disco records on *Dance Fever* and *Solid Gold.*"

"Disco isn't dead," Ed assured her. "It's just not as popular as it used to be. Some Saturday, when Rick's working, I'll take you downtown to the Record Rack, and we'll look at the albums that have lots of disco songs on them. Then you can listen to dance songs all you want."

"That would be cool," Judy said with a yawn.

Ed wondered if she would make it to midnight herself. He selfishly hoped she'd crash and burn, too, as he was looking forward to an extralong kiss at midnight with Rick.

Wide-eyed and determined, Judy was still hanging in there by eleven-thirty when Rick turned on *Dick Clark's New Year's Rockin' Eve.*

"Doesn't that guy *ever* get older looking?" Rick shook his head.

Ed chuckled. "I love Dick Clark. I used to watch *American Bandstand* after school every day, then every Saturday when they moved to California. My mom still blames him for my record habit."

"He's still on every Saturday," Judy commented.

"I know. But I used to watch him in black-and-white. That's how old I am."

"Well, for an old guy, you have good taste in music," she said kindly.

Ed bowed to her. "Thank you, ma'am."

"What is it about this moment?" Rick asked, watching the bedlam in Times Square. "I can sit here and tell myself it's no big deal, but my heart's beating faster, and I can't wait to see that damned ball drop."

"I don't know," Ed said. "I guess we're just trained to think it's a big deal."

"Okay, folks, let's hold hands and count it down," Rick said, when less than a minute remained. He took Judy's hand, and Judy took hold of Ed's.

"Five, four, three, two, one, *Happy New Year,*" they shouted, as *1981* lit up on the television screen.

"Welcome to the official eighties," Ed exclaimed, kissing Judy's hand.

Judy looked pleased to be sharing what she obviously considered an adult moment. "Happy New Year," she shouted again, giving first Ed, then Rick, a big hug.

"Shhh," Rick hissed, looking toward the bedrooms. "Keep it down, okay? Hey!"

He cocked his head toward the front door. Someone in the neighborhood was shooting off firecrackers.

"Hope that doesn't wake up the kids," he said, worried.

"Oh, they sleep through everything," Judy said with a smirk. She looked at Rick, then turned and stared at Ed for a moment. "Aren't you two gonna kiss for the New Year?"

They looked at each other in surprise.

"Why would we do that, Judy?" Rick asked.

She gave him a disgusted look. "I know what's going on. I'm not dumb, ya know. I watch *Phil Donahue*."

Ed began to snicker. He couldn't help it. "*Phil Donahue*, huh?"

Judy gave him her most superior look. "I know you guys are in love with each other, like those guys he had on his show. Besides, I overheard Mom and Grandma talking about it on the phone. Well, aren't you gonna kiss like you're supposed to at midnight?"

If possible, Rick was outblushing Ed for a change. "Well, okay," he mumbled, reaching over Judy to give Ed a very brief kiss.

"That's better," Judy said, satisfied. "People who are in love are supposed to kiss each other."

"Judy," Rick said, still blushing. "You do understand that what Ed and I feel for each other is, well, a little different, right?"

"You mean you're homosexuals," she said solemnly. "Yeah, I understand all that."

"So, do you also understand that a lot of people don't really approve of it?"

"Yeah, there was this fat lady on the show screaming Bible verses at those guys. I didn't like her. She was stupid. I mean, if you love Ed, instead of a woman, why is it her business?"

Ed looked at Rick. "You know, she's got a point. Why is it that fat lady's business?"

Rick scowled at both of them. "That's *not* the point. Judy, I love Ed very much, and I hope someday we'll be, well, not married, but like married to each other. The thing is, a lot of people don't approve, and they think they have the right to say very mean things to us. They also think they have the right to hurt us for being different. Sometimes these people gang up on guys like Ed and me and beat them up, even kill them. Do you understand what I'm saying?"

Judy's eyes grew big. "You mean someone would try to kill you just for loving Ed?"

Rick sighed. "Yes. Some people think they have the right to do that. Judy, you pay a huge price in this world for being different. You might as well learn that now. So I need to ask you something important. Have you told anyone about Ed and me?"

"No. I could tell by the way Mom was talking to Grandma that it was supposed to be a secret. I know how to keep a secret. I think it's dumb, though. You shouldn't have to keep it a secret. I like Ed a lot."

"Thanks, Judy," Ed said softly. "I like you a lot, too."

"Look, you two," Rick said gently. "I'm glad we all like each other, but the important thing right now is that we keep this to ourselves, okay? So, Judy, that means you can enjoy having another uncle, but you don't have to tell Angie about it."

Judy gave him a scornful look. "Oh, I wouldn't tell her. She can't keep a secret for anything." She looked at Ed. "Does that mean I can call you 'Uncle Ed'?"

Ed smiled at her. "I'd like that, but let's just stick to 'Ed' for now, like Rick says. I'm just your uncle's best friend, really. That's all anyone needs to know."

Judy nodded, a huge yawn escaping her.

"Okay," Rick said, "you made it past midnight, and it's officially the eighties now. Think you can go to bed?"

"Yeah," she said, hugging them both. "Good night, Uncle Rick. Good night, Uncle Ed," she whispered, smiling.

"Good night," Rick whispered, playfully shoving her toward her room.

Judy paused before turning the corner into the hall. "You know what's really dumb? I bet that fat lady and those people who beat up homosexuals would think it'd be better if Dad was still here instead of you, Uncle Rick, but things have been better here than they've ever been since you came and since Ed starting coming over. That's *really* dumb." And with that pronouncement, Judy called it a night.

"Pretty smart for just going on twelve, isn't she?" Ed sighed.

"Smarter than I gave her credit for, I'm ashamed to say," Rick said, putting his arm around Ed. "Okay, now that we're alone, how 'bout a real New Year's kiss?"

Ed was happy to oblige. "Happy New Year, darlin'," he whispered. "I love it that I'm starting the decade with you."

"Me too, baby, me too." Rick gave him another kiss, then one more for good measure. "I gotta go to bed, too. I've been up since five a.m. Look," he said in a low voice. "I'll go into Josh's room and change my clothes. You go down the hall to Claire's room, and I'll met up with you there later. I don't think it will be any big deal, and we can lock the door. All I want to do is sleep anyway, but I'll be damned if I'll sleep in the same house with you but in another room. Tell that to that fat lady."

"Your handyman already checked out that lock," Ed whispered back. "It's solid."

Ten minutes later Rick, clad in flannel pajamas, slipped into Claire's bed next to Ed.

"Your jammies are wonderful." Ed rubbed the soft flannel.

"Well, one of us needs to be dressed in case of an emergency," he grumbled, eyeing Ed in his Jockeys and T-shirt.

"I don't have any jammies," Ed teased him. "This is the best I can do."

"Well," Rick said, pulling him close. "It's better than having a naked handyman running around. I might lose control and get us into all kinds of trouble." He sighed. "You were fantastic tonight, baby. Thanks for spending New Year's with us."

"My pleasure," Ed said, stroking Rick's flannel-covered body. "I really had a good time, believe it or not."

"I believe it. I just can't believe I have a boyfriend who would spend New Year's this way *and* have a good time."

"Well, Glen said I was different."

"Different, and very special, baby," Rick said with a kiss.

Ed yawned. "Rick, what about Hank? If what Judy said is true, I don't think the kids miss him much. Do you think he'll ever come back?"

Rick sighed. "No, they don't miss him much. There wasn't a lot of good for them to miss in that last year or so. And just between us, no, I don't think he'll be back."

"What makes you think so?"

"Look," Rick said. "What I'm about to tell you doesn't go any further, okay?"

Ed nodded.

"Well, when I first moved up here, I did a little snooping around. Seems our buddy Hank was dealing a little dope on the side, in addition to all his other extracurricular activities. If my sources are right, he was about to get fired from his job, and I also think the Porterfield cops were sniffing around, too.

"Here's the thing: I don't think Claire is aware of any of this, and I don't want her to be. She's had enough to worry about. As it is, at some point she can file for divorce on grounds of desertion, and she'll get full custody of the kids. I mean, that'll happen without anyone even having to know about the other, as long as Hank stays gone. My hunch is that he's out somewhere around Las Vegas. That's where his folks moved several years ago. Hopefully he'll just stay out there, and we can all live happily ever after."

"Hmm, I can just imagine what he'd say if he knew you were living here, and that the two of us were in his bed right now." Ed chuckled.

Rick full-out laughed. "Oh, yeah, he'd be pretty hot. He didn't have much use for his fag brother-in-law, and I have to admit that's one of the reasons I agreed to move here. I knew if he found out, he'd be good and pissed. Still though, I don't think we have to worry about it."

Rick turned to Ed. "Hank aside, there's a bigger issue here. Unless Claire gets that divorce, and just happens to meet a guy who's stepfather material, I'm probably going to be involved in the upbringing of these kids for a long time. You know that, don't you, baby?"

"I know."

"And you're okay with that?"

Ed nodded. "Do you remember that night we met at Carlton's? Hell, you told me all about the kids and why you were living here before you even told me your *name*. It was almost like you were telling me, or anyone you might happen to meet, how important this was to you. I understood it then, and I understand it even better now."

"I repeat, you are very special, baby."

Ed shrugged. "Maybe. This is just how the story is playing out for us, and I don't have a problem playing Uncle Ed to three more kids. We'll never have kids of our own, so between my niece and nephew, and your three, we have five we can borrow from time to time."

Rick gazed at him fondly. "I have to admit, there's a part of me that would love to have a little Ed to raise, but I don't suppose that'll ever happen."

"Probably not. But I think we have our hands full already."

"You're right, baby. Five is enough. Let me see, Jane will probably graduate high school in . . . my God, 1993." He shook his head. "I hope I'm out of this house by then."

Ed poked him playfully. "You'd better be. I am not waiting twelve years to go to bed with you every night."

"Oh, we'll be together long before then, baby, I know it. I just need to know you're ready to help me keep an eye on these three wonderful children for as long as it takes."

Ed kissed him. "No problem. No problem at all." He kissed Rick again, a very long kiss, filled with a great deal of love and affection. "Welcome to the official eighties, darlin'. I have a feeling you're gonna be stuck with me for the whole decade, whether you wanna be or not."

Rick's return kiss was as long, loving, and affectionate. "I definitely do not have a problem with that. I love you, baby."

"I love you, too, darlin'."

Ed and Rick moved closer together, and they slowly drifted off to sleep, in each other's arms, on that first official day of the 1980s.

Chapter Sixteen

One Sunday morning, deep in the heart of January, Ed and Rick lay in bed together watching a gentle snow fall over Porterfield. The snow was gradually turning the limbs of the lilac bush outside Ed's bedroom window white, and if either one of them had bothered to stand up by the window and look, they would have seen Rick's burgundy car, sitting in the driveway, turning white as well. Ed's truck was safely parked in his little one-car garage, a fact he always noted with gratitude on snowy mornings. Ed sighed and moved closer to Rick.

"How can something so beautiful be such a pain in the ass?" he murmured, thinking of the walks he'd no doubt be shoveling the next day, if not today.

Rick propped himself on one arm for a better view out the window. "Hey, look at that," he said softly, pointing at a cardinal couple in the lilac bush.

Ed glanced out the window and smiled as well. "Yeah, Mr. and Mrs. Redd, I call them. They live in that hedge between my yard and the Hendricksons'. Mrs. Hendrickson has a bird feeder in their backyard. I gave her some money to help pay for the birdseed last fall, because I enjoy seeing the cardinals as much as they do. Indiana state bird, ya know. Sometimes, around dusk, all the cardinals in the neighborhood will hit their bird feeder for supper. It's really something. Maybe one of these days you'll be here at the right time and see it."

The red birds suddenly flew away, knocking snow off the lilac branch.

"Probably on their way to the Hendricksons' for Sunday brunch," Rick commented. He stretched and groaned. "Oh, I'm hungry, too, but in no mood to leave this warm bed." He put his arm around Ed and sighed with contentment. "It's always so peaceful here. And safe. And warm. Right about now at home the kids would be arguing over the Sunday funnies. God love 'em, but there are times I'm glad I'm just an uncle and not a dad."

"Yeah," Ed said. "New Year's was great, but I don't want to make a habit of it."

Rick chuckled. "Vicarious fatherhood. Yeah, I think we've got the parental thing well covered, probably better than a lot of guys like us."

"Yeah, and despite what Glen said, I have no desire to move to the suburbs and buy a station wagon. I'm content just to have you here with me, just the two of us." Ed kissed Rick to show him just how content he was.

Rick smiled at him with sleepy, Sunday-morning affection. "You do know there are times I wish I was here all the time so I could see things like the cardinals at dusk." He chuckled again. "'Cardinals at Dusk.' Sounds like the name of a painting. But—"

"I know," Ed interrupted him. "It's too soon, and you're not ready to leave Claire alone with the kids. I'm okay with that, remember? Besides, now that the holidays are over and things have calmed down, we've settled into a nice routine. We get to see each other every day at some point, and Claire's been really cool about you staying over here every Saturday night. I just wish," he said thoughtfully, thinking of Rick's car in the driveway, "that I had a bigger garage."

Rick hugged him. "Ah, don't worry about it. As much as I like your place, I keep thinking about a bigger place, a house where we can spread out and have all the things we've always wanted. Hell, I'll just add a two-car garage to the wish list."

"Hmm, a basement workshop for me, a library for you, a two-car garage for both of us . . . what else?"

"Well," Rick said, "I wonder about the location. Sometimes I think about us moving somewhere else, someplace a little more open to guys like us, but I don't really want to move away from the kids until they're a lot older, and I can't imagine you leaving all the old folks that depend on you." He giggled. "At least not until they all die off. But there will be plenty more to take their place. They're all crazy about you, and it would be hard to build up a business like that in a big city. I'm guessing it would, anyway."

"I never even really thought about it until you came along," Ed said. "I guess I just saw myself growing old here as the bachelor, closeted handyman. Oh, I thought about moving away, even moving to Chicago or some other city, where it would be a lot easier to be gay. I've watched some of Glen's friends do that. You know what, though? They always seem to move back after they've had their fun. It makes me wonder if it's really any easier to be a gay man in a big city than it is here. I'll bet even San Francisco has lots of drawbacks that we hicks here in Hoosierland don't know about.

"Still," he continued, "I wonder about us living together here. What some of my clients might say, or the neighbors. I hate to admit it, darlin', but maybe that's one of the reasons I'm willing to put off the thought of your moving in here. I mean, the Hendricksons are great neighbors, but what if, ya know?"

"Yes, I do know." Rick looked troubled for a moment, then smiled. "All this serious talk on a Sunday morning. It's Sunday, it's snowing, and we're here where it's safe and warm." He slapped Ed's ass under the covers. "How 'bout I make the cutest handyman in this little burg some French toast, huh?"

"I'll get the syrup." Ed threw the covers back to get out of bed.

Once they were at the kitchen table, enjoying French toast and sausage, they discussed plans for the rest of the day. Ed was all for driving into the city to see the new comedy hit *9 to 5*.

"The way they keep playing that Dolly Parton song on the radio really makes me want to see it. I was hoping we could go over Christmas, but we were both too busy."

"Oh, baby, do you really want to drive through all this snow?" Rick asked, pouring himself more orange juice. "Why don't we just stay here? I know, let's get out your Monopoly set. I know you have one. I saw it upstairs once."

"Monopoly," Ed groaned. "After all those games I played with the kids on New Year's Eve? Oh, brother. I suppose you're one of those assholes who grab Boardwalk and Park Place and run everyone else out of the game, right?"

Rick laughed, almost spitting juice. "No way. I'm usually lucky if I get Baltic Avenue. Claire's the Monopoly villain in our family. Oh, the fights we had over that when we were kids. Sounds like we're on about the same level then. How 'bout it?"

"Okay," Ed reluctantly agreed. "But you have to be the banker, and I get the racing car."

"You got it," Rick said, taking his plate to the sink. He paused, looking out the window above the sink. The snow was still falling, a bit heavier now. "I sure wish I could go back to my route tomorrow," he said wistfully.

"In this snow?" Ed was disbelieving. "Oh," he said, turning to Rick with an empathic look. "Murk the Jerk still buggin' you?"

Rick sighed. "Murk the Jerk. Man, that's about the nicest thing I can think of to call him. Yeah, he's still being a pain in the ass. But really, baby, I'm coping with it. Don't worry. I just miss being outside, being on my own during the day, even in the snow. That's one of the reasons I've always liked the job. Being cooped up in that sorting room every day . . . I'm sick of it. But Don says I can't until I get a clean bill of health from Dr. Quigley." He reached behind to rub his back. "It feels fine," he grumbled. "I don't know what he's waiting for."

"Well, you see Dr. Quigley again this week, right? Maybe he'll finally declare you healed." Ed joined him at the sink.

"I hope so," Rick said, running water for the dishes.

"Hey, you cooked, I'll clean," Ed said, playfully nudging Rick away from the sink. "Geez, look at that snow. We may be worrying about my back by this time tomorrow. I can't bitch, though. The money will sure come in handy. Things always slow down for me this time of year."

"I promise to come over sometime tomorrow, or tomorrow night, and give my handyman a back rub," Rick promised. "Are you doing okay, though, baby? Moneywise? I'm torn, thinking it's none of my business and thinking it is." Rick chuckled uneasily. "After all, we are talking kind of seriously about a future together."

"I'm fine," Ed assured him. "Things slow down every winter. People start putting off all their repair jobs, except emergencies, until spring. I'm used to it. I'm like a squirrel. I put as many nuts in the bank every fall that I can, and that, plus the regular stuff that I do for people and the snow removal, keeps me warm and well-fed until spring. My dad may have taught me how to fix things, but my mom taught me the value of a dollar and how to save 'em."

"Ah, it's nice to know I'm not in love with a spendthrift." Rick gave him a hug. "We're gonna need all the nuts we can store away to make some of those bigger house dreams come true."

"Now, if Ruth Dorsey would just pay me for all that painting I did right before Christmas," Ed said, clattering dishes into the sink, "I wouldn't worry at all. 'I'll give you a check as soon as Christmas is over, Eddie,'" he said, mimicking her haughty voice. "Eddie, she calls me, like I'm some little boy she's doing a favor for. You know what, though? I've noticed those with the most money are always the slowest to pay."

"One of Porterfield's elite, I take it?"

"Well, she thinks she is. She hangs out with Eunice Ames and that crowd, at least on the outer fringe of it. Her husband's a big shot out at Marsden, though I was never too impressed with him. I don't know, darlin'. As much as I wish we were rich and could do whatever we want, I'd hate for us to end up like that."

Rick hugged him again, from behind. "Baby, I think you could have all the money in the world and you'd still be the shy, down-to-earth man I fell in love with. I'm just glad to know you're taking care of yourself financially. As much as I sometimes envy your self-employment, I must admit I like getting a regular paycheck."

Ed glanced over his shoulder at Rick's face, noticing that slightly troubled look again. "Why are we talking about work and money and that serious stuff? Let's just enjoy the few hours we have left together. Any minute my phone is gonna ring, all people wanting their walks cleared right away. Let's have some fun. Why don't you go dig up that Monopoly game while I wash up?" he said, hastily scrubbing some knives. "All of a sudden I'm feeling lucky."

Rick slapped Ed's ass, smiling. "Ah, I'll have you in jail before you know it."

"Yeah?" Ed retorted, glad to see Rick's smile. "I hear they've got a cute guard. That might not be such a bad thing!"

<∋•∈>

A few days later, Rick stopped by Ed's house for lunch, with a bag of their usual takeout from the Cozy Hearth Café with him.

"Let's eat fast," Rick said with his most devilish look. "Then maybe I'll have time to molest the handyman before I go back to work."

"You're in a good mood today," Ed remarked, unwrapping his roast beef on rye.

"I sure am. Don's letting me go back on my route next week." He laughed. "What with Dr. Quigley's okay and Ralph bitching to him about hauling mail in the snow, he finally saw reason. Baby, I will be out of that stuffy building, and Jim Murkland can go fuck himself."

"That's great, darlin'." Ed beamed at him, sandwich forgotten.

"We need to celebrate," Rick said, raising his Pepsi can in a toast. "I don't suppose you have Rare Earth's 'I Just Want to Celebrate' in that stockpile of yours, do you?"

"No," Ed said regretfully, raising his can as well. "You finally asked for one I don't have. Oh, well. Maybe I'll stop by the Record Rack or Woolworth's and get that new Kool & the Gang song they're playing on the radio, 'Celebration.'"

"You do that." Rick's warm and tender special was glowing on his face. "And let's go to Fort Wayne this weekend and see that movie you want to see, and anything else you want to do. Hell, I'll even spring for a nice dinner out someplace."

"It's a date."

Ed smiled back at him, relieved that Rick was so happy about the change in his job, but Ed was still a bit worried about Jim Murkland. True, Rick would be away from the post office most of the day, but he still had to put in some time there. He couldn't avoid Murkland entirely.

Rick wolfed down his sandwich. "Hurry up with that thing, baby," he said impatiently. "I may not have time to make some serious love with you, but I sure would like to show you how much I love you before I have to go back."

"What'd you have in mind?" Ed teased, stuffing potato chips in his mouth.

Rick grinned mysteriously. "Meet me in the bedroom in about five minutes, and I'll show you."

Ed made it to the bedroom in four, and Rick did indeed show him exactly what he had in his mind, and a few other places as well.

"I'm no big fan of quickies," Rick sighed happily, "but this time I just couldn't wait. You okay, baby?"

"I can't imagine being naked with you and not being okay," Ed whispered, kissing him. "I'm gonna have to take this afterglow on the road, though. I have to reinforce one of the legs on Mrs. Ilinski's couch."

"Reinforce it? Huh?" Rick asked, puzzled.

Ed smirked. "Let's just say there's a lot of Mrs. Ilinski, and sometimes she's not too careful about parking it."

"Oh!" Comprehension flashed in Rick's eyes, above his smile. "Well, I'm taking *my* afterglow back to the Porterfield Post Office. I hope I'm shining so damned bright that it blinds Jim Fucking Murkland." He reached for his pants, then hesitated, turning back to Ed. He pulled Ed to him for another kiss. "How anyone could ever find something ugly in me loving you, Ed Stephens, is beyond me. Loving you is the most beautiful thing that's ever happened to me."

❧•❧

After that, the whole Jim Murkland situation slipped away from Ed's mind as he began dealing with a problem of his own. The heater in his truck was blowing nothing but cold air, which was rather unfortunate, it being the middle of January. After shivering his way from job to job, he finally gave up and called the service department at Wagner's Chevy/Olds on the north edge of town. They told him to bring it in Friday morning.

Ed drove there contemplating the possible expense, not to mention being truck-free for a few days. Fortunately the bulk of his clients were within walking distance of his house, Porterfield not being any sprawling metropolis. However, carrying his new Christmas toolbox on foot from place to place wasn't too appealing.

"Isn't that something," he mumbled to himself as pulled into Wagner's lot. "Rick's back on the street Monday, and I will be, too, swinging a toolbox instead of a mailbag. Go figure."

He toyed with the idea of trying to borrow Rick's car during work hours, or even his mother's, but decided the exercise would do him good. With both Rick and Norma taking turns feeding him these days, he thought his jeans were getting a little tighter than usual. Hoofing it back and forth across Porterfield wouldn't be such a bad thing after all.

The service guys at Wagner's cheerfully took custody of Ed's truck, assuring him it wouldn't take more than a few days to take care of the problem. Ed didn't quite believe them, but decided to take them at their word. He walked south on Main Street, toward downtown Porterfield, grateful that Rick's car was available for their weekend plans in Fort Wayne.

Ed didn't have any jobs scheduled until midafternoon, so he took his time walking through town, stopping occasionally to look in store windows.

He paused in front of the Record Rack, debating whether he should spend any money. He wanted to get Judy's birthday present, and he really did want that Kool & the Gang song, but with truck repairs staring him in the face, he hesitated. Shrugging, he pulled open the door. The records would probably be cheaper at Woolworth's, but that would mean retracing his steps down Main and heading out of his way on West Commerce Street. Not only that, he liked the aging hippie guy who owned the Record Rack, and wanted to help him keep the struggling store open.

Paper bag of record purchases in hand, he waved good-bye to Andy, the owner, and resumed his walk south. Less than a block away from the post office on the corner of Main and Clark, he noticed with surprise Rick standing in the parking lot behind the building, talking with Gordy Smith. Since Jim Murkland was nowhere in sight, he decided to stop and tell Rick about the truck.

As Ed got closer he saw they were both drinking coffee from Styrofoam cups. Gordy sat on the ledge of the stairs at the employees' entrance, smoking as well. They both looked up as Ed approached. They had obviously been sharing a good laugh, as they were both still chuckling, Gordy choking a bit on the cigarette smoke.

"Hey, Ed," Gordy greeted him, still wheezing a bit. "Long time no see. Where's that big bad pickup of yours?"

Gordy, who had to be past thirty now, Ed thought, still had his football player's build, but seemed to be growing a comfortable beer belly. Ed, like any good gay man, noted that Gordy was still blond, blue-eyed, and handsome; the cheerful smile that had driven the girls crazy in high school was as bright as ever.

"Just left it at Wagner's." Ed reached for Gordy's outstretched hand for a good shake. "God only knows when I'll see it again."

"What's up with it?" Gordy asked, taking another drag.

"Heater," Ed said with a rueful grin.

"Aw, man. And in January? That sucks." Gordy chuckled.

"I guess you're driving us to the city for the movies this weekend," Ed said to Rick.

"No sweat." Rick smiled at him.

The three of them continued to talk casually for a few minutes. Ed was about to take off for home when the employees' door banged open and Jim Murkland walked out. He took in the three men at the bottom of the steps, and the nasty grin that Ed remembered so well from high school spread across his face.

"Well, look who's here," Jim said snidely. "If it isn't Benton's boyfriend. What you two gonna do, go buy some new dresses on your lunch hour?"

Gordy rolled his eyes at Jim. "Oh, can it, Murkland."

Rick stared Jim down. "No dresses today. Actually, I'm gonna get you a muzzle."

Gordy snickered. Ed probably would have, too, but just seeing that flat, squinty-eyed face again irritated him so much he felt his hands draw into fists.

"And a leash, too," Ed found himself saying. "Isn't there somewhere around here where dorks like him can be tied up?"

Gordy looked at Ed in approval, while Jim blinked at him. It was probably the first comeback he'd ever gotten from Ed, and Ed was well aware of it. He was no longer a skinny, scared sixteen-year-old, and he wasn't intimidated by the Jim Murklands of the world anymore.

"Save the leash for yourself," Jim said to Ed. "I understand you guys are into all that bondage shit. Which one of you says 'yes, master' anyway?"

"Probably the one who wins the coin toss for beating the shit out of losers like you," Ed fired back at him.

"Ed, cool it," Rick murmured.

"Aw, ithn't that thweet. Ricky's protecting his boyfriend—no, his girlfriend." Jim sneered. "That doesn't surprise me. You never were worth a shit in school, Stephens."

Gordy erupted into laughter. "And you were, Murkland? Shee-it. Why don't you go crawl back in your hole?"

"Because one of these two, or probably both of 'em, would crawl in after me. Watch it, Gord. You aren't safe with these two."

"I can't imagine a gay man in this world wanting anything to do with you," Rick said calmly. "From what I hear around town, the women aren't too crazy about you either."

Rick definitely hit a sore spot. Jim's mouth tightened a moment before it opened for his next assault. "Least I'm not some fuckin' fairy. Like you two. Say, which one of you takes it up the ass anyway?"

Rick and Gordy looked stunned, but Ed's brown eyes were darkening with fury. Images of himself meekly taking Jim's put-downs and insults all through his school years flashed through his mind. There was no way in hell, or at least in Porterfield, that he was going to take it anymore. His father had taught him a thing or two about using his fists, and he suddenly knew the time had come to see if the lessons had stuck.

"Murkland," he said through clenched teeth. "I've had it with you." He put his bag of records against the steps. "Get that ugly mug of yours down here so I can pound it into the parking lot. So help me God, when I'm done it's gonna be even uglier."

Jim snickered. "You? Beat me up? With those limp wrists?" He leaned against the post office wall, sneering at Ed. "I'd like to see you try."

"Well, I don't see you moving, Jim," Gordy said. "You afraid of him? Those wrists don't look very limp to me. In fact, Ed works a lot harder than you do. I'll lay down five bucks says he can put you in Porterfield General without too much effort."

"Me too," Rick said, surprising Ed to no end. "But let's make it ten."

"Hell, twenty," Gordy roared. "Easy money. C'mon, Murky. Let's see whatcha got." Gordy hopped down from his perch on the stairs, flipping away his cigarette. He looked up at Jim. "Ya know, Murkland," he said, suddenly serious, "I'd love nothing more than to shut that trap of yours for good, so what Ed can't finish, I will."

Jim looked back at the three of them, blinking. He couldn't seem to think of anything else to say. Ed was about to start up the steps toward him when the door banged open again and Porterfield postmaster Don Hoffmeyer walked out. Don—graying, paunchy, and granite-faced—surveyed the men in the parking lot, hands on big hips. He turned to look at Jim.

"Everything okay out here, boys?" he asked.

"Aw, hell, Don, we're just enjoying our coffee break," Gordy said cheerfully. "You got your smokes on you? I left mine inside."

"Jim?" Don asked, ignoring Gordy.

"Yeah, everything's fine," Jim muttered.

"Well, then, why don't you get back to work?" Don said to Jim. "I haven't seen too much action out of you today. And I don't see you drinking any coffee. How 'bout it?"

With one last defeated glare at the men standing below him, Jim yanked open the door and vanished inside. Ed, fists still clenched, realized how hard his heart was beating. He was both disappointed and relieved at the same time.

"Hi, there, Ed," Don said, nodding pleasantly. "Good to see you. How's your mother doing?"

"She's just fine, Don," Ed said, finally letting out a breath he didn't realize he was holding. "Same old Mom, bitchin' up a storm about the cold weather."

Don chuckled. "Well, that's about what'd I'd expect from Norma. You tell her I said hello. That oughta get her good and riled up." His eyes traveled from Ed to Rick. "I understand," he said after a moment, "that you two are getting to be pretty good friends."

Ed, wondering if Don was just making conversation, looked him right in the eye. "Yes, Rick and I have gotten close here lately."

Don's eyebrows went up a bit, but otherwise his expression didn't change. He seemed to be weighing his words before he spoke. "I always said Tim Stephens raised a good son," he finally said. "And Rick here is the best thing to happen to this post office full of goldbrickers in a long time." He looked at Gordy pointedly, who just smirked back at him. "You two go on being friends. Nothing wrong with that. But for the sake of my ulcer," he continued, looking back at the door, obviously indicating Jim, "try to keep it away from the office. Okay?"

Rick nodded. "No problem, Don."

"Ed, take care," Don said, nodding at him. "You two, I'll see you inside later." He pulled open the door and walked back in the building.

The three men stared at the closing door, then at each other. Gordy started to laugh.

"I don't think you have to worry about Murkland anymore, Rick. You either, Ed. I've never seen him raise a fist in his life. All blow and no show. What an asshole."

"He can talk, though," Rick said, looking at the ground. "He's not here twenty-four hours a day."

"Hell," Gordy said, shaking his head. "Don't worry about it. Shit, Rick, Ed here can tell you that no one's listened to a word Murk the Jerk's said in years. He wouldn't even be working here if Don didn't have such a soft heart. I think Don just keeps him around as a favor to Jim's dad. They were in the war together. Besides, this may be Porterfield, but no one's gonna mess with Ed Stephens. Or his boyfriend. Hell, I'll see to that."

Ed and Rick glanced at each other uncomfortably.

"Now, Gordy," Rick started.

Gordy held up a hand to silence him. "Don't sweat it. Hell, for once in his worthless life, Murkland was right. I can see that. But shit, Ed," he said, winking, "I wish I'd known before Rick showed up. He would have had some competition."

Ed looked at Gordy in amazement.

"Sure." Gordy's eyes twinkled at them both. "You know, Rick, there are a lot of secrets in this town. Some are just kept better than others." He slapped them both on the back, then bounded up the stairs into the post office.

Ed looked at Rick. Rick looked at Ed.

"How 'bout that?" Rick finally remarked. "This town never ceases to amaze me."

⋖⋅●⋅⋗

That night they sat in Ed's living room, rehashing the events at the post office. Ed was shaking his head, still marveling at Gordy Smith's revelation.

"I've known that guy most of my life, and I never guessed, never suspected. Of course, I sure wasn't looking at him that way. I never had a reason to."

Rick stretched out happily, the week's tension ebbing away. "Well, it just goes to show, we don't all have limp wrists, girlish voices, or funny walks."

"Oh, I don't know, darlin'," Ed teased him. "You were walking pretty funny when your back was out."

Rick began tickling him in revenge. Ed laughed and struggled away from him.

"It's cool, though, about Gordy, isn't it? Maybe we can invite him over sometime. It would be great to have another friend here in town. Glen and I don't seem to have much in common anymore. Well," he conceded with a grin, "not that we ever did, really, but I've always liked Gordy a lot, even if I don't know shit about football."

"We can do something with Gordy as long as he keeps his hands off you," Rick said firmly. "I saw the way he was looking at you today."

"You don't have a thing to worry about," Ed told him. "I'll take a tall, dark, bearded mailman over a blond ex-football player any day."

Rick pulled Ed back to him for a hug. "And I'll take my sandy-haired handyman who's not afraid to defend himself. Or me."

"Really?" Ed looked at him speculatively. "I was afraid you'd get all pissed off at me for threatening Jim like that. I was just so mad. Thing is, though, I was more mad for myself than I was for you."

"I know that. And that's why I wasn't pissed off." Rick kissed him. "I was so proud of you. Proud that you'd stand up for yourself, and even for me if you had to. Don was right. Tim Stephens did raise a good son."

"Speaking of Don," Ed said, basking in Rick's pride, "do you s'pose he figured us out? I couldn't tell."

"Me either. And I don't care. He made it clear he respects my work, and for now, that's all that's important. I think Jimmy Jerk Murkland has a much better chance of losing his job than I do."

"Ah," Ed said, thinking back, "I wish I could have gotten one good punch in."

"Cool it, Muhammad Ali," said Rick, his troubled look returning to his face. "Save it for when you need it. Unfortunately, you may really need it some day. Jim Murkland isn't the only fag-hater in this town. Despite what Gordy said, Jim can talk, and if he wanted to, he could stir up trouble for us."

"I know. But I'll be damned if I'll let him run me out of Porterfield." Ed considered, for a moment, leaving his hometown, his family, and his clients. "I won't go without a fight. I proved to myself today, even if I didn't get to knock Murkland flat, that I'm not afraid to fight if I need to. Remember what you said the other day, about how wrong it was for someone to find something ugly in you loving me? Well, I feel the same way about you. I'll defend my right to love you, even if the Welcome to Porterfield sign is in our rearview while I'm doing it."

Rick's arm around Ed tightened. "I love you so much, baby," he whispered. "You're more of a man than Jim Murkland could ever hope to be. You'd think people would see that, and maybe some of them do. Maybe that's why Don didn't say any more than he did today. I don't know. I guess time will tell if Porterfield will accept or at least tolerate us. I don't want to leave, either. For whatever reason, this goofy town has become home for me. Maybe it's because I found you here, but I can't imagine living anywhere else. I just want you to know, though, that I can live with you, and love you, in Porterfield or anywhere else in the world. You know that, right, baby?"

"I know that. I feel the same way. As long as we're strong, like Mrs. Penfield said, we'll be okay, wherever we are."

Ed kissed Rick, loving him deeply. He didn't know what time would tell them about living in Porterfield, but he knew that time had already proven to him that Rick Benton was the man with whom he wanted to spend the rest of his life. That knowledge, he thought, made him feel stronger than he'd ever felt in his twenty-eight years.

Ed looked at the stereo, where "Celebration" was lying on the turntable. He got up and flipped the switch. The record began to spin, and soon the joyful song was pouring out of the speakers.

"Enough of this fag-hater talk." Ed pulled Rick to his feet. "We are gonna spend this whole weekend celebrating. You have your route back, I almost decked the biggest pest I've ever known, and I think we made a new friend today. Last time I checked too, you didn't have to work tomorrow, which means I get to spend *two* nights with the man I love. If that ain't worth celebrating, I don't know what is."

Rick, laughing, began to follow Ed's shuffling steps to the music.

"You forgot one thing," Rick said, putting his arms on Ed's shoulders. "Every day I spend with you is worth celebrating. Being with you, baby, is a party that never ends."

Chapter Seventeen

Ed rolled his truck to a stop in his snow-covered driveway and wearily took in the unbroken expanse of white surrounding his house. After a day spent removing snow from his clients' walks and drives, he now had to take care of his own.

He drove the truck into the garage and grabbed his shovel from the bed. His fingers were tired and his toes were tingling from the cold. As much as he wanted to clear the four inches of new snow from his walks—just get it over with and call it a day—he knew he had to go inside for a rest and allow his toes to thaw for a while.

Ed dearly loved every season of the year and their individual gifts, but he had to admit he'd had enough of winter's gift of snow. Arctic air had settled over northern Indiana, and a chain of weather disturbances had sent lake-effect snow blowing across Porterfield nonstop for several days. Ed was proud of the fact that he kept his regular clients' walks cleared with just a shovel and his own sturdy back, but he was beginning to think wistful thoughts about the snow blower he'd seen recently at the lumberyard. Groundhog Day wasn't far off, and he hoped that any critters who popped their heads up that morning would have to look damned hard to find a shadow.

Once he'd settled in an easy chair with a cup of hot tea, he began to unwind. The furnace thrummed reassuringly in the basement, and he allowed the warmth of the house to settle upon him. He gave thanks it was Saturday; soon Rick would arrive, cold and tired from his daily struggle of delivering mail through the snow. They would have the rest of the weekend to pamper and care for one another, to renew their energy for another week of battling the elements.

He caught a glimpse of a vehicle turning into his driveway. He stood up to see who it was, as it was too early for Rick. It turned out to be his brother-in-law, Todd, who had borrowed Ed's electric drill the night before.

Ed met Todd at the back door. "You didn't have to drag yourself out in the snow to get this back to me," Ed said by way of greeting.

Todd stamped his snow-covered boots on the already snow-covered mat inside Ed's door. "Call it cabin fever." Todd grinned. "The kids are driving Laurie crazy. They're bored with the snow and their Christmas toys. I would have taken any excuse to get out of the house for a while."

Ed laughed, ushering Todd into the kitchen. "Sit down, sit down." He poured another cup of tea for Todd. "I'm trying to get myself outside to clean my walks, so *I'll* take any excuse to stay inside awhile longer."

Todd gratefully accepted the hot drink. "Thanks again for letting me borrow your drill. I save a fortune in tools, having a brother-in-law who's a handyman."

"No sweat," Ed said, joining him at the table.

They talked amiably for a while about Laurie, the kids, and the weather.

"There's something else I should probably tell you, Ed," Todd said, looking into his tea mug. "I debated all the way over here whether to say anything, but I guess forewarned is forearmed, as the saying goes."

"What's up?"

Todd sighed, sipping his tea. "Well, after my businessmen's basketball league game Wednesday night, I stopped by Buck's Bar downtown with some of the guys. That jackass Jim Murkland was in there. He'd had a few, and he came staggering up to me, wanting to know how I felt about having a faggot for a brother-in-law."

Ed felt a chill that had nothing to do with the weather. "What'd you say to him?"

Todd shrugged. "Told him to shut his face if he didn't want to pick his front teeth out of a snowdrift. What else? Like I'd give a rat's ass what Murk the Jerk says, but I thought you should know."

Ed scowled, looking out the window above Todd's head. "Yeah, I almost beat the crap out of him a couple of weeks ago at the post office. He'd been giving Rick shit about hanging around me. Considering how dumb he is, I don't know how he figured out what's going on with us, but somehow he did. Either that, or I just confirmed his suspicions, threatening him the way I did. I don't know."

"Don't worry about it, Ed. I know that's easy for me to say, especially since I'm the guy who told you about this, but I just wanted you to know what he's saying, and that you can't think of you and Rick as some deep, dark secret. People are beginning to be aware of it. You know Laurie and I don't care, and I was really impressed with Rick when you brought him over on Christmas. Hell, I'd trust the two of you with my kids before I would my own brother. It's just that people in this town talk. They always have and they always will. I oughta know. My mom's one of the best talkers in Porterfield."

Ed thought briefly of Eunice Ames, Todd's mother, and what she might have to say about his relationship with Rick. "Does she know about it?"

"I don't know." Todd looked unconcerned. "But again, I wouldn't worry about it. Homosexuality isn't one of her hang-ups. She gets hot and bothered with how much money someone has and what their social standing is. You know that. Besides, whatever feud she may have with Norma, she's always liked you. I don't think it would faze her all that much."

Ed tapped his fingers on the table in frustration. "So what are you telling me, Todd? Porterfield is talking about Rick and me in shocked whispers or something, and I should ignore it? Or is this when I put a For Sale sign in the front yard and leave town?"

"Ignore it," Todd said flatly. "Don't get all crazy on me here. Look, people talk, like I said. They don't have anything better to do, but they're not gonna *do* anything. They want to feel they're better than you in some way, and let's face it, it makes good conversation at the bar or over a bridge table. Bottom line, nobody in this town is gonna mess with someone named Stephens, anymore than they'd mess with someone named Ames. If anyone notices what Rick and you have got going on, they're also gonna notice that you're still the same Ed Stephens, shoveling walks and repairing lamps and stuff. When they get bored with the topic, they'll move on to someone else, like always.

"Again," Todd stressed, "I just wanted you to *know,* so if some asshole actually has the guts to say something to your face, you're prepared. Okay?"

"Yeah," Ed muttered.

"What's the old song from the sixties, the one about the P.T.A.? You're such a music nut you should remember it."

"'Harper Valley P.T.A.,'" Ed said, a grin actually coming onto his face.

"Yeah, that's the one." Todd grinned back at him. "All small towns are like that, just a bunch of hypocrites talkin' shit while the skeletons fall out of their own closets."

"I know, but I can't help but worry about Rick's job."

"I wouldn't. Don Hoffmeyer was one of your dad's best friends, and he's not stupid. He's not gonna unload a good employee because someone like Murk the Jerk is talkin' trash. And don't get any ideas about leaving town. This is your home, and it's Rick's home, too, now. Your mom needs you, and

Laurie and the kids need you. Hell, I need you, too." Todd laughed. "If you take off, who am I gonna borrow tools from?"

Ed sighed, already wondering if he should tell Rick about this conversation, but knowing he probably would, whether he wanted to or not. "Thanks, Todd. For telling me about this, I guess, but more for being so cool about it. Rick and I are really lucky that our families support us. That's pretty rare, you know."

Todd shrugged that off. "That's what families are for, or they're supposed to be anyway. I suppose I should get home, make sure Laurie hasn't killed one of the monsters yet. Thanks for the tea, and for letting me borrow your drill." He clapped Ed on the shoulder. "You're a good man, Ed. Truth is, they don't come any better. Don't let any of the assholes in this town tell you any different."

Ed watched Todd drive off, Jeannie C. Riley's voice in his head, singing about small-town hypocrites. Todd was right. Ed knew that. Since the night he had abandoned Cathy Carroll on the dance floor at the senior prom, he'd wondered if someday the people of Porterfield would talk about him. He'd been listening to their gossip for years, letting it roll in one ear and out the other, not unlike the soap operas a lot of his clients watched every day.

So Ed Stephens's name had finally entered the gossip mill that was Porterfield. He briefly longed for his days of invisibility, but knew to return to that time meant giving up Rick, something he'd never do. Rick and his love had given Ed's life a meaning it had never had, and to lose that was unthinkable. Janis Ian's song, "At Seventeen," came to his mind, and he tried to remember that one line, something about gaping small-town eyes. *Let 'em gape,* he thought, his tired back straightening. *Let 'em get a good, long look at what real love is.*

Ed, as any good man in love should, felt the love he and Rick shared was bigger, better, and purer than any love the world had ever known. Anyone who saw fit to disparage it was automatically a fool in Ed's eyes. A lesser man might have have poured himself another cup of tea, maybe throwing a shot of whiskey in it. Ed, however, pulled his snow boots back on and went outside to shovel his walks in plain sight of Porterfield.

⋘•⋙

Ed was pulling his boots off again when the phone rang. He clumped, boots unlaced, to answer it.

"Ed? It's Effie Maude Sanders." The voice of Mrs. Penfield's housekeeper rolled into Ed's ears, not unlike the sounds of the scratchy records he'd been playing for months now. "I thought you should know Mrs. P.'s had a bit of an accident. Slipped on some ice on the front porch."

"Oh, no! Is she badly hurt?"

"Naw," Effie Maude said. "Pshaw, she just twisted her ankle. Scared her more 'un anything. Doc Weisberg looked her over and told her to keep her weight off it for a few days. I've got her all set up in the study where she sleeps when that 'ritis of hers keeps her from climmin' steps.

"Anyways," she continued, "I'll stay over here for a few days. No problem, since my brother can tend the stock out to the farm, but I need to be at the church social tonight. Promised I'd take care of things in the kitchen. You think you could come over and sit with her for a spell while I'm gone?"

"Of course. When do you need to leave?"

"Oh, six should be just fine, if you can make it. I want to leave a li'l early, on account of the snow. I'm much obliged to ya, Ed."

"No problem. Rick and I will come over as soon as we've eaten," Ed assured her. "We'll be over there by six."

Ed hung up the phone, just as Rick's car pulled in the driveway.

"Well, this weekend sure isn't turning out the way I had hoped," he said.

He was sorry for Mrs. Penfield's misfortune, but glad of an excuse for them to visit her. Thinking back on his conversation with Todd, he thought a visit with one of their biggest fans might be just what they needed.

⋖⋗•⋖⋗

Ed and Rick jumped out of Ed's truck, their door slams sounding like rifle shots in the cold, still night. They walked from Mrs. Penfield's driveway to her back door along the path Ed had cleared earlier that day. Rick's face was tight and troubled. Over dinner Ed had told him of his conversation with Todd, and nothing Ed had said since would erase the look from Rick's face. Ed hoped Mrs. Penfield might have better luck with easing Rick's mind than he'd had himself.

Effie Maude met them at the back door, dressed for the cold and snow in a huge parka, the hood thrown back to reveal her gray hair pinned tightly into a bun. Her polka-dot, Saturday-night social dress just cleared the tall, heavy rubber boots she wore. Ed was relieved to see the ghost of a grin flit across Rick's face at the sight of her.

"C'mon in, boys," she rasped as usual. "Good to see you. How're the roads out there?"

"Snow-covered," Ed reported. "It's too cold for the road salt to do much good. Be careful, okay?"

"Pshaw, I've been drivin' in snow since before either one of you was born. Only day I didn't make it in to Mrs. P.'s was the blizzard of '78, ya know. I can handle this stuff easy."

"How's Mrs. Penfield?" Rick asked.

"Aw, just fine," Effie Maude said, leading them into the kitchen, showing them where to leave their wet boots. "Doc Weisberg was over here first thing after I called 'im. You know those two go way back and all. Mrs. P.'s probably the only one left in town he'd do a house call for."

"That really is something," Ed said. He hadn't received a house call from Dr. Weisberg since he'd been in grade school.

"Well, ya know I always thought, with Mr. P. gone and the doc's wife gone, that those two would get together, but what with the doc bein' a Jew, and how this town talks, I guess it'll never happen."

"Effie Maude," Ed protested. "What a thing to say."

"Now, Ed, you know well as me how this town is," she said, heading for the door. "Talk, talk, talk. That's all most of 'em are good for. Don't bother me none. Never has. If you live a good life, nothin they say can hurt ya any. Mrs. P. knows that, but maybe she decided she was just too old to take on another man." She shrugged. "Thanks, boys. I'll be back in a few hours." She threw the hood of her parka over her head and slammed the door behind her.

Rick actually laughed at the expression on Ed's face.

"Dr. Weisberg and Mrs. *Penfield*?" Ed asked in surprise. "I think the old girl has more going on than I know."

"Let's go ask her," Rick said, mischievous grin in place. Ed was glad to see it.

Mrs. Penfield was resting in a twin bed she'd had placed in her late husband's study. She was sitting up, a book in her lap, and was very pleased to see her company.

"How nice of you to come see a foolish old woman," she exclaimed, closing her book. "You'd think I would know better, going after the mail in this weather. I should have let Effie Maude do it, but, no, I deliberately went on that porch, slipped, and fell. I'm just glad she was here to help me back inside."

"I'm feeling very guilty." Ed parked himself in a wing chair by the blazing fire. "If I had done a better job of cleaning the snow and ice off the porch, this wouldn't have happened."

"Nonsense. With the constant snow we've had this week, it's impossible to keep that porch perfectly clear."

"Well, if I were your mailman, Mrs. Penfield," Rick said grandly, "I would ring your bell and hand you your mail personally." He glanced at Ed. "That's the service I provide for my very favorite customers."

Mrs. Penfield laughed in delight. "Oh, it's such a joy to see you two. Perhaps I should twist my ankle more often, if it means I would receive such charming company on a Saturday night."

Ed held his hands out to the fire. "You'll probably throw me out after I ask this, but what's up with you and Dr. Weisberg?"

Mrs. Penfield snorted. "Has Effie Maude been talking again? Honestly, that woman is incorrigible. She has fancied a romance between Nathan Weisberg and myself since our respective spouses passed away. While it's true that Nate and I have been dear friends for many years, there simply is no more to the story. I think our Effie has read a few too many romance novels."

Ed and Rick joined her in laughter.

"Oh, it feels good to laugh," Ed said, smiling at them both.

"Is there a reason laughter has been scarce for you today, Ed?" Mrs. Penfield asked. "Are your snow chores getting you down?"

"No," he answered. "Something else."

"Ed, I don't think we should bother Mrs. Penfield with that."

"She's exactly who we should bother, because she would be the first to understand," Ed insisted.

"Perhaps Mrs. Penfield should be allowed to judge for herself," she said. "What seems to be the trouble?"

Ed told her of the incident with Jim Murkland at the post office and repeated his conversation with Todd. "We're doing our best to be strong, as you told me to be," he said in conclusion. "Thing is, all of a sudden I feel as though I'm, *we're*, living in a glass house."

Mrs. Penfield looked from Ed's annoyed face to Rick's troubled one. She nodded. "I see. You're worried, then, that some of the less tolerant residents of Porterfield might take it upon themselves to shatter the walls you've so carefully built, is that it?"

Ed shrugged. Rick jumped up from his seat and began to pace.

"Here's the thing, Mrs. Penfield," Rick said. "I've got my job, my sister, her children, *and* Ed and me to think about. I don't want to do anything that would jeopardize any of that. By the same token, I wouldn't dream of leaving Ed. It wouldn't stop the talk. The damage has already been done, hasn't it? Small towns are new to me. I'm afraid, and I'm not sure how not to be."

Mrs. Penfield's eyes followed Rick's progress around the room. "Rick, dear, do sit down. Just watching you is making me tired."

Rick did as he was told.

"I understand your anxiety, but I'm also relieved to see you've made one excellent decision."

"What's that?"

"Why, not abandoning your relationship with Ed, of course," she exclaimed. "I can see with my own nearsighted eyes how deeply you care for one another. When you get to be my age, you'll understand how rare that kind of devotion really is. Why, that's half the battle right there."

Rick looked puzzled.

"Ed, why don't you see about removing those ice patches from the front porch? I think Rick and I need to have a talk."

"But I don't have my shov—"

"You'll find everything you need in the garage," she interrupted. "Now, run along. Rick has never experienced Hilda Penfield the teacher, and I think it's time he did."

Ed grinned mischievously at the still puzzled Rick. "Her essay tests are murder," he said, leaving the room.

Ed pulled himself back into his boots and winter coat. He located a shovel in the garage and went to work, chipping away at stubborn frozen footprints on the porch and front walk. The night was bitterly cold, no more than a few degrees above zero, but Ed was warmed by the thought of Mrs. Penfield's ability to find comfort in an uneasy situation.

He listened to the traffic on Main Street, just a block away, the only other sound besides his shovel against the hard packed snow. He thought of an old Simon and Garfunkel song, "My Little Town." It had been going through his mind all evening. Ed loved the song, and thought any small town guy who'd grown up feeling different and alienated probably related to its contemptuous lyrics as much as he did.

Ed supposed he had fought his own internal war with Porterfield. He had been annoyed as a teenager when the upheavals of the sixties had barely registered on Porterfield's radar screen. He'd been scornful of the town's obvious prejudice against anyone of color. As a gay man, he'd been both resigned and angry at the town's potential for homophobia. However, Ed's pragmatism would not allow him to see the town from that viewpoint alone. Although the rainbows in Simon and Garfunkel's little town were black from lack of imagination, the rainbows Ed had seen arching over Porterfield had always been full of color and promise.

His thoughts of moving away had always been brief and fleeting. The siren's call of "My Little Town" told him he was a fool to stay, but it simply wasn't compelling enough to make him leave the place in the world he knew best and felt he understood. Despite any negative feelings he may have harbored against the town and its people, Porterfield was his home. It was where his family was, and had been, for many years.

He remembered trips to Fort Wayne with his family as a little boy, returning to Porterfield in the evening, seeing from a distance the illuminated clock tower of the Stratton County courthouse rising tall and proud in the night. As a child, he'd thought the regal, imposing sandstone building, its tower piercing the sky, protected the town and all who lived in it. As a gay man alive and well in 1981, he suspected little justice would be due him inside its walls, but still felt an odd sense of protection from the building itself.

As if to remind him of its presence, the courthouse's clock tolled the hour, seven bell strikes resounding across the cold, crisp air over the town. He turned to the north, but trees obscured the view of the tower.

His concerns about continuing his relationship with Rick in such a town were reasonable ones, but he knew somehow he'd made his peace with it. Stratton County and Porterfield were his birthright, and no one's talk—misguided, hateful, or ignorant—could change that. If Rick chose to leave, Ed would leave with him, and with no second thoughts. Ed knew, though, they didn't have to leave. The strength of their love would see them through any adversity the town might show them. Mrs. Penfield had shared that wisdom with him, and hopefully she was sharing it with Rick at this very moment.

He heard the front door open quietly behind him. He turned and watched Rick walk across the porch and down the steps.

"Hey, baby," Rick said softly.

"Hi."

Rick came to a halt behind Ed on the front walk and lightly placed his arms around him.

"Can we go for a little ride? I'd like to get outside of town, where we can really see the stars. It's a beautiful night for it." He kissed the back of Ed's neck. "Damn, you're cold, baby. Come inside and warm up a bit before we go, okay?"

"What about Mrs. Penfield?"

"She'll be fine. The drive is her idea. We won't be gone all that long."

Ed, puzzled but feeling hopeful, followed Rick into the house. Rick pulled himself into his winter gear, and they walked out the back entrance to Ed's truck.

"Where to?" Ed asked, once he had started the engine.

Rick smiled at him. "Just someplace dark and quiet, where we can see the stars."

"My Little Town" was still in Ed's mind. The line about the dead and dyin' played on his internal stereo and he almost laughed. Instead he smiled back at Rick. "Okay, I can do that."

He promptly drove to the little cemetery where his ancestors were buried.

Rick shook his head while Ed carefully navigated the snow-filled drive to the older part of the cemetery.

"I should have known you'd get me back here someday. You just want my body, don't you? Well, you'll have to wait. We have some talking to do first."

Leaving the truck running, they hopped out, the virgin snow crunching under their boots. Arms around each other's waists, they turned their eyes heavenward, where the skies were ablaze with stars in the clear, cloudless night.

"Isn't it something?" Rick murmured. "We can't see it in town, with all the lights. I'm glad Mrs. Penfield suggested it, although I'm about to freeze to death."

"Why'd she want us to come out here?"

"She said we needed to get outside of the town, look out into the universe, and put it back into perspective. She was right. I feel better already. Porterfield really isn't that important in the bigger scheme of things."

"I don't think I'm following your thoughts, Rick."

Rick chuckled. "That's okay. Let me back up. Mrs. Penfield gave me the lecture she gave you last fall, all about the unique problems we'd face as two men in love, trying to build a relationship. I'd thought it was pretty good, getting it secondhand from you, but it was really something, straight from her mouth, with her words. I needed to hear it.

"She told me a lot of other things, too. She told me how much she loved her husband, and how the loss of their only child could have torn them apart, but it only made them closer. She absolutely blew me away when she told me, in her opinion, that our love was the most sincere and honorable she'd seen in anyone since her husband died. She said we had an obligation—to ourselves and to each other—to see it through, despite the odds against us."

Rick sighed. "She also said that Porterfield did have the power to hurt us, if we let it; that, yes, I could lose my job; that other kids could be cruel to Judy, Josh, and Jane; that people could be just as cruel to Claire, or to anyone in your family. She reminded me that people could indeed try to hurt us physically.

"But," Rick said definitely, "she also reminded me that every single person in this town lives with the same fears and possibilities, but for different or even similar reasons."

"Wow," said Ed, trying to take it all in.

"Yeah. It was quite a lecture, but everything she said was right. And true. Our situation may be unique, but the fear isn't. Everyone's afraid of something. She asked me, would I feel any safer if we packed up us and our families and moved to San Francisco or New York? She reminded me that we might lose our fears about gay prejudice, but we'd be adding a great many fears to our lives that we don't have here in Porterfield."

Even with Rick's arm around his waist, Ed was damned cold, standing in the snow, looking upward at the distant stars.

"So what are you trying to tell me, darlin'?" he asked, shivering.

"I'm trying to tell you that we stay. We fight, if need be. Most importantly, we love. We love our families, and we love our friends. And best of all, I get to keep loving you, and you get to keep loving me. I hate to sound overly dramatic about it, but I'd die if I couldn't keep loving you, baby. I've said it before, and I'll say it again: I don't care where we are, as long as we're together and we love each other. But this town, for all its faults, is our home. I choose to continue loving you right here."

Ed turned to Rick, smiling. "I knew that crafty old broad would get you to see reason."

Rick's loud, happy laugh echoed among the trees and tombstones. "Oh, baby, I guess I always knew you didn't want to leave, and I don't blame you. This is your home. I've never felt that way about Indianapolis. I guess I've always known my home would be wherever my heart is. Right now, and forever I think, it's with you."

Their lips came together. The strength of their love flowed between them, warming them against the frigid night, and protecting them, at least for that moment, against anything in this world that could harm them.

"We're gonna be okay, baby," Rick whispered against Ed's lips. "I know that now. Just standing here, looking at the universe, I know we're gonna make it. Mrs. Penfield said the universe had worked hard to bring us together, so surely it wouldn't make any big effort to tear us apart. I believe her. Do you?"

"Yes," Ed whispered.

"I still think it's too soon for us to move in together and start acting like we're married, but I'm sure it will happen."

"Me too." Ed stroked Rick's beard. "I was thinking maybe in the spring, when the snow's gone. You know, when the grass turns green again and the trees start to bud. Maybe when the earth wakes up, it'll tell us that it's time. Right now, though, all I need is to know you're here and you're loving me as much as I love you."

"I do, baby, I do," Rick whispered, pulling Ed as close to him as he possibly could. "You think, though, that we can get back in the truck now? I'd hate to have this tender moment end in frostbite."

Laughing, they ran for the truck. Once inside, they huddled together, slowly relaxing in the warm air from the newly repaired heater.

"One last thing," Rick said, rubbing his hands together. "Mrs. Penfield says that although we're not ready to make some kind of marriage commitment to each other, we still need to plan for the future. I told her about some of the stuff we had talked about, and she said we should stop dreaming and start planning. She said if we have our own work and our own money, it will be harder for people's attitudes or actions to hurt us. I think she's right, so I'm gonna start thinking that way."

"What way?"

"Oh, think about how we can be self-sufficient. Like, maybe I can find some kind of self-employment, like you, away from the post office. She also wants me to continue to encourage you to pick up your father's woodworking hobby. She thinks, as I do, that you may have a real talent for it. The more we can do for ourselves, the less we'll have to depend on people who might disapprove of us. Get it?"

Ed smiled. "I get it. Not only that, but I like it. I like it very much."

Rick looked at his watch. "We should get back and check on her, before Effie Maude comes home and hollers at us for leaving her alone."

Ed put the truck in gear, then slowly and carefully drove through the snow toward the road.

"Do you suppose we'll ever think of a way to thank her for all she's taught us?" he asked Rick, gently guiding the truck through the drifts.

"I'm guessing," Rick said thoughtfully, "that the only thanks she wants or needs is our success. I don't know about you, baby, but I don't have a problem working toward that kind of thanks."

"Me either."

Once he had the truck safely on the snow-packed road, he slipped the transmission into neutral, turning to Rick. "I love you, darlin'," he whispered.

"I love you, too, baby."

"Do you suppose," Ed asked with one last kiss before he turned his attention back to the road, "that when we get home we could maybe take a really hot shower together? Then maybe you could rub a tired handyman's aching back?"

"I can do that, baby," Rick said softly. "Hell, I'll even make you breakfast in the morning."

"Deal."

Ed put the truck in drive. It slowly moved down the road, toward Porterfield and home.

Chapter Eighteen

Ed, Rick, and Norma were seated at Norma's dining room table, enjoying her pork roast dinner. Ed, reaching for another biscuit, reflected on the fact that in all of his fantasies of the Dream Man, never once had he seen them having a cozy, midweek dinner with his mother. That it was actually happening, and on a regular basis, made the whole thing seem even more dreamlike.

Norma had called Ed one day after Christmas to invite him to dinner as she always did, but had surprised him by adding, "You bring Rick along with you. I don't suppose he's leaving the picture anytime soon, so I might as well get used to having another son-in-law." Now, in early February, Rick was automatically included in her weekly dinner invitations, and he always made it a point to show up with Ed, unless he had a conflict.

"Norma," Rick was saying as he helped himself to seconds, "you make the best pork roast I've ever tasted. I'm glad, though, that I don't eat here every day, or I'd have an even bigger weight problem than I already have."

"Oh, for Pete's sake," Norma said, obviously pleased by his words. "You look fine, Rick. I never had any use for skinny men. They're always puny and weak-minded. Eat all you want and don't worry about it. You get plenty of exercise. Leave room for dessert, though. I made a chocolate cake today."

"Oh, no," Rick moaned. He looked at Ed. "How come you're not overweight, growing up in this house?"

Ed chuckled. "Sheer willpower. But I'll take all the cake Rick doesn't eat, Mom. I'll burn it off shoveling snow."

"Oh, I hope we've seen the last of this snow. I've had enough. Spring can't come soon enough for me," Norma stated, slapping the table for emphasis. "It's almost Valentine's Day, though, so spring can't be too far behind. Speaking of Valentine's Day, did I tell you what that lazy sister of yours talked me into? I'm baking my heart cookies for Lesley's kindergarten class. Now, what kind of mother doesn't do that herself?"

Ed rolled his eyes at her. "Oh, Mom, give it a rest. Laurie asked you to do it because she knew you'd enjoy it, and that you probably miss making them for Dad like you always did."

"Humph. That may be, but a bunch of ungrateful kindergartners are a poor substitute for your father. Still, I'll make some for you and Rick, too. I'll drop them off on my way to the school on Friday. Even if your father isn't here, we might as well keep the tradition going."

Rick looked puzzled. "What tradition?"

"That's how Dad met Mom," Ed told him. "It was all because of her Valentine's cookies. Mom, tell Rick the story. Laurie and I loved hearing it every Valentine's Day, when we were kids."

"Oh, he doesn't want to hear that old nonsense," Norma scolded, smiling just the same.

"Yes, I do," Rick said, encouraging her. "C'mon, Norma, give."

Norma, still smiling, gazed off into space. "It was Valentine's Day, 1947," she remembered. "My mother and father had all but kicked me off the farm the summer before, telling me I'd never find a man out in the sticks. By that time all the men were home from the war, and they thought I'd catch a husband if I was working in town. They didn't believe in a college education for girls, and we couldn't afford it anyway.

"So, I moved here to Porterfield and stayed with my old maid aunt, Marjorie. I got a job at Patterson's Bakery, working in the back, baking cookies and special-order cakes. I was good at it, although I never approved of Mr. Patterson's recipe for cookies. I knew my mother's recipes were better, but I never said anything. I was just grateful to have a job and to be living in town. Farms could be mighty lonely places back then, especially during the war when gas was rationed.

"Anyway, come Valentine's Day, Mr. Patterson got it in his head to bake and sell heart-shaped cookies. He even put an ad in the paper, then put me in charge of baking up dozens and dozens of cookies. Well, I knew all sorts of lazy, last-minute types would be pounding down the door for those cookies, and I just couldn't abide the idea of using his recipe for them. So, the night before, after he'd gone for the day, I made those cookies the way my mother had taught me. I figured what he didn't know wouldn't hurt him none.

"Come the next day, and we were selling those cookies right and left. Mr. Patterson was just beside himself, congratulating himself on his great idea, and I was in the back, as usual, laughing to myself about the whole thing. I just knew those cookies wouldn't be selling if I'd made them his way.

"About lunchtime, Mrs. Patterson, who considered herself the real boss of the place, hollered back at me to made another batch; they were almost gone. I hauled them up front to the display case the minute I had the red icing on them. A young, handsome, dark-haired man was standing there, waiting on them. Said someone had brought some into work earlier in the day, and they were so good he wanted some more for his lunch.

"He looked at me and said, 'Are you the girl who made those cookies?' I said I surely was, and he smiled at me. That man was Ed's father, and we had our first date that night when we were both done with work."

Rick was staring at her, the food on his plate all but forgotten. "Now, *that's* romantic," he said, smiling.

"Humph. I don't know about romantic, I just know that Tim Stephens knew a good cookie when he tasted it." Norma laughed.

"Still, I'm glad Laurie got you to bake them again," Ed said. "I've kind of missed them the past few years."

Norma sighed wistfully. "I suppose I have, too. I just didn't seem to have the heart to make them, but I s'pose doing it again is a good way of remembering your father." She shook her head, and returned to her usual self. "Eat up, boys, eat up. You might as well, 'cause what you don't finish I'm sending home with you. Honestly, after that story, I'm not about to see good food go to waste."

⊰•⊱

"Considering how big Valentine's Day is for your family, I guess I should get busy with some seriously romantic plans for this weekend," Rick said.

They were parked in Ed's driveway, sitting in Rick's car, a container of leftovers on the floor at Ed's feet.

Ed shrugged. "You don't have to get all crazy about it on my account. Valentine's Day isn't that big a deal to me."

"What?" Rick was surprised. "Shit, you probably wouldn't even be here if it wasn't for your folks meeting on Valentine's Day."

"I know. That's the point. I heard that story every year, growing up, and then spent every Valentine's Day of my adult life alone. All it did was depress me. I got to thinking that Valentine's Day was just an excuse to make lonely people feel lonelier. Well, I'm not lonely anymore, but I don't want to be a hypocrite and make a big deal over it. Besides," Ed said, taking Rick's hand, "every day with you is Valentine's Day."

"Aw," Rick groaned, smiling at him. "I know what you mean, though. It can be a painful, lonely day. Still, I think we owe it to Cupid to do something on Saturday, just to say thanks for getting us together."

"I've got an idea," Ed said, grinning at him.

"Hmm. I'm not sure I'm ready for this, but go ahead."

"Let's go to Fort Wayne. There's a movie showing I want to see, and it's perfect. It's called *My Bloody Valentine*."

"*My Bloody Valentine*?" Rick repeated. "Yuck! Sounds like a slasher movie."

"It is," Ed said. "It's exactly what I would want to see if I was alone and depressed for Valentine's Day."

"So, since you've got me this year, you're gonna drag me to see it? Thanks a lot."

"Oh, c'mon. It'll be fun. Look, darlin'. I don't need Valentine's Day to tell you how much I love you. Let's go watch a bad horror movie and thumb our noses at the whole thing. Then we can come back here, eat Mom's cookies, and if you want, I'll play all my lovey-dovey records on the stereo."

"Horror movies are one thing," Rick said, unconvinced. "Slasher movies are something else all together." He shook his head. "Well, considering the horror show my first Valentine's Day with Jack was, it could be appropriate. I can sit in the theater, watch people get hacked up, and be grateful I've got you instead of him. Okay, baby, it's a date."

"What happened with Jack?"

Rick shuddered. "Oh, I'll tell you Saturday night, if you really want to know. Right now, I need to get home. It's late."

Ed pouted. "You're not gonna come in at all?"

"No. If I take one step in that house, I won't get away from you until it's time for me to go to work in the morning." Rick leaned over to kiss him. "My handyman is too big of a temptation."

Ed sighed. "Okay. I've got a love song for you then. Remember 'Precious and Few'? That one describes our relationship during the week."

"Well," Rick said, kissing him again. "You go in the house and play it, and think of me. I promise, when I come over this weekend, I'll do my best to make every one of those precious and few moments the best they can be."

⋄•⋄

Ed spent the next few days debating what to do about Rick's Valentine's present. Ed had meant what he said in the car; being in love did not make him more inclined to celebrate Valentine's Day. If he had his way, he would boycott the whole thing in support of all those people who hadn't been blessed with a Rick in their lives. However, the mention of Jack spurred him into action.

Ed told himself repeatedly that Jack was not a threat to his relationship with Rick, but every time Jack's name came up, Ed noticed the play of emotion across Rick's face. Jack may have broken Rick's heart, but somewhere in that organ Ed was doing his best to repair, Rick still held some sort of feeling for Jack.

That being the case, he determined to erase any bad Valentine's memories Rick had with something special. He suspected Rick would prefer something traditional and sentimental, so he decided, after consulting Laurie, to go with roses. Lots of them. He vetoed candy on the grounds that his mother's cookies were sweet enough, and certainly more unique than anything an ex-lover could provide.

He was ready when Rick arrived Saturday afternoon to begin their usual weekend together. Rick carried a paper bag, and after an extended Valentine's Day kiss at the door, he insisted Ed open it.

Ed looked in the bag, grinned, and pulled out a small, flat, beautifully wrapped gift. It was the exact size and shape of a 45 rpm record.

"Gee, I wonder what this could be," he said, kissing Rick.

"Yeah, it's kind of hard to disguise," Rick said sheepishly. "Claire did the wrapping job. She took it away from me, saying that I may be a gay man, but I'm the worst present-wrapper she's ever seen."

"It's incredible," Ed murmured, fingering the perfectly sculpted red ribbons. "I almost hate to open it."

"Well, baby, you know it's a record, but you don't know what song it is. Wanna take a few guesses while you're undoing those ribbons?"

"Hmm. Let's see. It can't be 'Precious and Few,' even though I mentioned it the other night. I already have that one."

"You're kinda warm. It's older, something from our high school years. It's a song I look for whenever I go through your 45s, and I've never found it. I've always wanted to play it for you."

Ed slowly untied the ribbons, thinking. "Damn, you've got me stumped, darlin'. I give up." With that, he pulled the ribbons aside and ripped open the paper to find Blood, Sweat & Tears' "You've Made Me So Very Happy." Ed laughed in delight. "Oh, I do have this one, but it's on an LP. It's upstairs in a box. I never play it because I played it so much in high school it skips through this song. Thank you."

"I had to special order it at the Record Rack," Rick said, pleased with Ed's reaction. "I told Andy it was for one of his favorite customers, and he promised to get it before Valentine's Day. Put it on, baby. I wanna hear it with you."

Ed jumped up and put the record on the turntable. As the record began to play, he sat next to Rick on the sofa.

"You have, you know," Rick said, kissing him. "You've made me so very happy. Like he sings later in the song, all I want to do is thank you, baby."

Ed kissed him back, one hand gently stroking Rick's face. "Thank *you*, darlin', for the record, and for making *me* so happy. I . . . oh, I am so happy with you, Rick. Thank you."

They sat, holding each other close, as the record played, then repeated.

Ed sighed. "This is great, but I've got something for you, too. Aren't you curious?"

"Oh, maybe just a little," Rick said, kissing him again.

"Okay." Ed stood up. "You stay here, but close your eyes."

"I gotta close my eyes?" Rick complained.

"Yeah, I couldn't wrap this. You close your eyes, and I'll bring it in from the bedroom, okay?"

"Oh, okay." Rick did as he was told.

Ed hurried into the bedroom, picked up the vase crammed full of red roses and baby's breath, returned to the living room, and stood in front of Rick. "Okay. You may now open your eyes."

Rick's eyes slowly opened, then his mouth fell open in surprise.

"I don't believe it," Rick whispered.

"Happy Valentine's Day, darlin'," Ed said, grinning from ear to ear. He handed the vase to Rick.

"Baby, this must have cost a fortune. That's the biggest bunch of roses I've ever seen!" Rick sniffed at one of the roses. "You shouldn't have spent all your money on this, but I love it. I absolutely love it."

Ed sat next to him. "Well, Ruth Dorsey finally coughed up the money she owed me, so I thought, what the hell? I know we're supposed to be saving for our future, but I decided our first Valentine's Day together was too special to worry about money."

"I can't even count them all." Rick shook his head. "How many are there?"

"Thirty-seven."

"Thirty-seven! How'd you ever get that number?"

Ed took the vase from Rick and set it on the floor. "One rose for every time we've made love."

Rick smiled, pulling Ed close to him. "You kept track all this time, huh?"

Ed kissed him. "Well, I just kinda guessed. It seemed like a good number, and I thought I should leave some in the florist shop for the other customers."

Rick hugged him, hard. "Thank you, baby," he murmured against Ed's ear. "Nobody's ever given me flowers before. This is probably the nicest thing you could have done for me."

"Remember when you brought me roses on our first date?" Ed asked.

Rick nodded.

"I wondered then if anyone had ever brought you flowers, so I was hoping I'd be the first at something."

Rick sniffed. Ed was surprised to see tears in his eyes.

"You're the first, baby, and the best. Always the best. Thank you for loving me enough to waste so much money."

Ed smiled. "It was worth every cent, seeing the look on your face. For what it's worth, I'd spend every penny I have in this world to show you how much I love you."

"Well, don't do it," Rick said, wiping his eyes. "You don't have to prove anything to me. Just know I love you that much, too."

"I do, darlin', I do."

Rick kissed him softly. "Do you s'pose we have time to make it thirty-eight before that movie starts?"

"We can always go to the second show."

"That sounds like a very good idea, because right now *I'm* gonna show you how much I love you, and it doesn't cost a thing."

⋘●⋙

After a stop at Gino's for baked sub sandwiches, they were in Rick's car and on their way to Fort Wayne. Ed had his hand possessively on Rick's leg, thinking about what a sellout he was where Valentine's Day was concerned. He hoped all the lonely people in the world would forgive him, because he was extremely happy, and he knew the romance of Valentine's Day had something to do with it.

He looked at the contented expression on Rick's face and wondered about that bad Valentine's Day he had with Jack. Ed didn't want to spoil their day by bringing it up, but curiosity got the better of him.

"So tell me about that awful Valentine's Day with Jack. What happened?"

Rick grimaced. "It was bad all right. You sure you wanna hear this story? All it will do is make you feel sorry for me."

"Oh, go ahead. If I feel sorry for you, you'll just get more kisses out of me."

"Well, in that case, okay, I'll tell you." Rick sighed. "Hmm. Well, I know I always start out my Jack stories by saying I was young and stupid, but I was. I really was.

"We'd been living together for a few months when Valentine's Day rolled around. I was excited, thinking how great it was to be celebrating it for the first time with a man I loved. I admit it, I went overboard. In addition to cards and candy, I had flowers delivered to Jack at our apartment while I was at work. I also made reservations at a very pricey, very romantic restaurant for that evening.

"I was looking forward to it all day at work. I could just see me coming in the door and Jack throwing himself at me in gratitude for the roses he'd gotten while I was away. So I drove home like a maniac, ran up the stairs, and threw open the door. Well, the roses were there, sitting on the coffee table, but Jack wasn't.

"I figured he'd gone out for an errand, maybe to buy something for me, so I sat down and waited. And waited. And waited some more. Finally I started calling his friends, wondering where he was. I got dressed to go to dinner, and he still didn't show up. By that time I was getting nervous, convinced something had happened to him. I mean, he wouldn't forget these huge plans I'd made for Valentine's Day, right?

"The time for our dinner reservation came and went. He finally showed up about an hour after that. He was bombed. He'd been sitting in a damned bar just down the street, hanging with some new friend of his. I was very hurt, and very angry, and all he could say was, 'I'm sorry, honey, I just forgot.' Not only that, but he didn't do anything for me. He thanked me for the flowers and candy, but that was about it. I should've known right there and then that I was wasting my time with him, but I was, I repeat, young and stupid. I will say this much: He didn't get jack shit from me the next year on Valentine's Day."

"Oh, darlin'." Ed squeezed his leg. "That doesn't make me feel sorry you. It just makes me want to track him down and beat the shit out of him."

"Yeah, there's a part of me that would like to do it myself, but it's all in the past. He can't hurt me anymore, and being with you has made up for any bad times I ever had with him." Rick took one hand off the steering wheel and grabbed Ed's. "I love you, baby. You know what? I thought I was in love with Jack, and maybe I was, but I swear I didn't know what real love felt like until I met you. From that very first kiss, I knew you were the one. Just that kiss alone made Jack seem like a bad dream."

Ed leaned across the gearshift and kissed Rick on the cheek. "Did I ever tell you what I was thinking about during that kiss?"

"No. What?"

"I was so . . . so surprised by it. My mind just kinda . . went blank, but suddenly I remembered *Gidget*. Did you ever watch that on TV, with Sally Field? Not the movies, but the TV show?"

"Hmm. I kinda remember it."

"Well, Laurie and I watched it every week. It came on right after *The Patty Duke Show*. I don't think it was on very long, but we both loved it. In one episode she was dreaming about Jeff, and she was wondering what kissing him would be like. So she started writing fake diary entries, and she imagined Jeff kissing her, and she wrote, 'I sank into nothingness.'"

Rick laughed, loud and hard. Ed hit him on the arm.

"It's not funny. All these years I've waited for a kiss like that, and that's what it felt like, kissing you that first time. It was like I'd never been kissed before at all."

"Damn, and I left my surfboard in Indy," Rick cracked, still laughing.

Ed crossed his arms across his chest and sulked. "Fine. Laugh all you want, but it was a big deal to a teenage boy who didn't give a rat's ass about kissing Sally Field, but dreamed about kissing a handsome man someday."

Rick pulled Ed's arms apart, taking his hand. "I'm sorry, baby. I wasn't laughing at you, really. I was laughing about the role models we had. Wouldn't it have been great if one of the surf boys on that show had been gay and had a beach boyfriend? Or if, say, that hot guy on *Petticoat Junction,* the one that married Betty Jo, had turned out to be gay? I remember dreaming about kissing him."

Ed felt slightly better. "Okay, I know what you mean. Anyway, *that's* how moved I was by our first kiss."

Rick pulled Ed's hand back to his thigh. "Thank you, baby. I just remember hoping that you were feeling what I was feeling. I'm glad to know you were, because I can promise you, I was sinking into nothingness myself. I couldn't believe a kiss could be so amazing. Thing is, you could probably get that *Petticoat Junction* guy here in the car and I could kiss him, but it still wouldn't be as good as kissing you."

That did it. Now Ed felt better.

"First red light you hit," he told Rick, "I'm going to give you a kiss that will make you forget Jack, *and* that guy from *Petticoat Junction* forever."

Rick smiled at him. "You already have, baby. That's what that first kiss was all about."

◈●◈

A collective gasp went out from the audience in the theater as a woman's mangled body slid out of the Laundromat dryer that was decorated with the upside-down heart.

"Ugh," Rick groaned. "Ed, this is disgusting. Let's go home. Now!"

"No," Ed replied, working his way through a box of popcorn, eyes glued to the screen. "I'm not leaving till I find out who the killer is."

Rick sighed, reaching a hand into the popcorn box. "Thank God you don't have a pickax at home."

"Sssh!"

After another hour of gory murders and mayhem, most of it at the bottom of a coal mine, the killer was revealed.

"Finally," Rick snorted. "Can we get outta here now?"

"Yeah, yeah." Ed got to his feet. "Man, that was really gross."

"No kidding. Damn, Ed, this is a side of you I've never seen, or even suspected. Slasher movies."

"Oh, I love horror movies," Ed enthused. "They're supposed to be making a sequel to *Halloween* later this year. I can't wait."

"Great." Rick sighed, rolling his eyes.

Rick was still grumbling as they walked across the parking lot to his car. "At least there aren't any coal mines around here. Christ, I'm gonna go to sleep tonight thinking about someone coming into your room and cutting my heart out."

Ed stopped and looked at Rick, a very smug look on his face. "It made you forget everything bad in your life for an hour and a half, didn't it?"

Rick was unmoved. "So do shock treatments, and you don't see me lining up for those, do you?"

"Okay, okay." It was Ed's turn to grumble. "I won't drag you to any more slasher movies. I'll get someone else to go. I made Laurie go with me to see *Terror Train* last fall, and she still hasn't forgiven me."

"Baby, I like *good* horror movies: *Psycho, Rosemary's Baby*—"

"How 'bout *Night of the Living Dead*?"

Rick scowled at him. "Okay, I admit it. I liked that one. Maybe 'cause it was in black-and-white. I couldn't see the blood." He stopped by the driver's side of his car. "That movie wasn't about the gore, it was just plain scary. I think . . ." Rick patted his pockets. "That's funny. Where are my keys?"

"Fell out of your coat, maybe?"

"No, I always keep them in my pants pocket, but—oh, no! There they are." Rick pointed inside the car.

Ed leaned over and peered in the window. Yes, there they were, still in the ignition. Ed pulled on the passenger-side door handle, remembering, even as he did, that he had locked it earlier.

"Aw, crud. Don't worry, darlin'. All we need is a wire hanger."

Rick shook his head, disgusted with himself. "Yeah, baby, I always carry one of those on me, right in my wallet." He slammed a fist on the car hood. "Where the hell is Joan Crawford when you need her."

"Didn't she make Christina throw away all the wire hangers?" Ed looked around the parking lot. They seemed to be the only people left. "Man, what a movie that book would make. Look, let's just go back inside. The manager will probably loan us a coat hanger. This is where you get to hug and kiss your handyman in gratitude. I know just how to unlock the car, but I need a hanger."

"I will hug and kiss the handyman *after* he unlocks the car, and after I kick myself in the ass for being so stupid," Rick said, following Ed back to the theater.

A movie was still in progress on the other side of the twin theater, but the lobby was deserted. Ed figured all the ushers had been sent to clean the crap out of the theater showing the horror movie. He hoped so. His sneakers were still sticky from the cola spill by his seat. Ed walked to the refreshment stand, where a young woman with JODY on her name tag was rearranging Junior Mints and Milk Duds in the display window.

"Excuse me," Ed said to her. "Could we see the manager, please?"

Jody looked around the empty lobby. She leaned over her counter, scowling. "There he is." She pointed to a short, skinny guy exiting the ticket booth.

"That's the manager?" The kid didn't look a day over sixteen.

"He is tonight," Jody said, rolling her eyes.

Ed walked over to the young man, Rick trailing him.

"Excuse me, sir," Ed said, feeling a little foolish. "We've got a bit of a problem. My friend here locked his keys in the car. I was wondering if you could let us borrow a wire hanger."

The young man with MARK on his name tag pushed his glasses up his nose. "What do you need a hanger for?" he asked suspiciously.

Ed sighed. "I can untwist the hanger and use it to pull up the lock button on the door. Haven't you ever seen anyone do that?"

Mark frowned, crossing his arms across his chest. "How do I know you aren't trying to steal it?"

"Look." Ed pointed out Rick's beat-up Monte Carlo. It looked worse than usual, covered with winter road grime. "Who the hell would want to steal *that*? We just wanna go home." He turned to Rick with an apologetic look. "Sorry," he muttered.

Rick laughed. "I hate to admit it, but it really is my car, kid, uh, sir. If you want, I'll show you my driver's license, and my registration after we get it unlocked."

"I think we should just call the police," Mark said. "I have no way of knowing whether you're telling the truth."

"Look, kid," Ed said, getting annoyed. "Do you have a wire hanger or not? It's getting late, and I'll just go somewhere else if you're gonna be a jerk about this."

"Ed!" Rick said.

"The fact that you locked your keys in your car is not the problem or the responsibility of the Westside Cinema," Mark said loftily. "If you had lost your keys in the building, I could help you, but I'm afraid this is a matter for the Fort Wayne Police Department."

"The theater owns the parking lot, doesn't it?" Ed asked, resisting a strong urge to shake the little twerp.

"Actually, no. It's part of the Westside Shopping Plaza, and their office would be closed at this hour," Mark said with a tight smile.

"Oh, brother," Ed snorted. "C'mon, Rick, let's get out of here. I think there's a gas station down the street. Maybe it's still open." He turned to leave, shaking his head.

"Hey," Jody hollered at him. She walked out from behind the candy counter. "Is this dork giving you a hard time?"

Ed turned to her in relief. "Look, we just locked the keys in the car and need a coat hanger to get it unlocked, that's all."

Jody, who was a good three inches taller than Mark, not to mention about twenty pounds heavier, glared at the young manager. "You asshole," she hissed. "C'mon, guys," she said, waving a hand at Ed and Rick. "I've got a hanger in my car. I lock my keys in it all the time. I'll take care of it for you."

"You've already had your break," Mark growled, doing his best to look managerial. "If you leave the building, I'm going to write a note on your timecard."

Jody handed him the scoop from the popcorn machine. "Here, dork. Why don't you get busy shoving this up your ass while I give these guys, *paying customers,* a hand with their car." She turned to Ed and Rick. "Hang on while I get my purse."

Mark shook the popcorn scoop at her retreating figure. "You have no authority to do this!"

"Kid," said Rick, laying a comforting hand on his shoulder. "She may not have any authority, but she's a hell of a lot bigger and meaner than you. I'd let this one go."

"Humph." Mark sniffed and walked behind the candy counter, then pointedly washed the scoop before replacing it in the popcorn machine.

Jody reappeared and led Ed and Rick to her car. She paused long enough to pull a pack of cigarettes out of her purse. She lit up, blowing smoke in the direction of the lobby.

"Up yours, dumb ass," she muttered. "I'm sorry, guys. He's not really the manager. The real manager called in sick, and for some dumb reason he put Mark in charge for tonight. He must have one hell of a fever."

She bent over next to her worse-for-wear Camaro. She felt inside the left rear tire well, then pulled out a rusty hanger.

"If you want, I'll unlock your car," she offered. "I'm such a spazz about locking my keys inside, I've gotten really good at it."

Jody expertly manipulated the hanger inside the window of Rick's car and easily pulled up the lock button. Ed had to admit she was better at it than he was.

"Whew," Rick said in relief, reaching for his wallet. "Thanks. Can I give you—"

"No, no," Jody said with a smile. "My reward was being able to piss that little shit off. He's been driving us crazy all night. Heck, the ushers are fighting over who gets to give him a wedgie when we close up."

"Thanks, Jody. You're the best," Ed called to her as she walked toward the theater door.

She waved at them. "Come back some time and I'll slip ya some free Milk Duds."

Rick, keys securely in his hand, began to laugh. "Thirty-seven roses, a gory slasher movie, and hearing her tell him to shove that popcorn scoop up his ass. Baby, this is a Valentine's Day I'll never forget."

Ed laughed with him. "And the *Petticoat Junction* guy."

"Him?" Rick smiled at Ed over the top of the car. "I dumped him after our first kiss, remember? You're the only valentine I want, baby, tonight and for always."

"Well, why don't you get in the car, where it's nice and dark, so your valentine can kiss you again?"

Rick jumped in and slammed his door. Ed did the same. Ed leaned over the gearshift and gave Rick a long, passionate kiss, hoping Mark was watching from the lobby.

"Happy Valentine's Day, darlin'," he whispered.

⊰•⊱

They were getting ready for bed when Rick suddenly disappeared into the living room. He returned, carrying the vase packed with thirty-seven red roses.

"I want to see them, first thing, when I wake up in the morning," he said, kissing Ed.

They pulled the covers back and settled in. Ed reached for the light, then stopped.

"Did you want to read for a while before you go to sleep?" he asked.

"No, baby. I'm beat. Let's just call it a night."

"Okay." Ed turned off the lamp, then lay down, curling up next to Rick. A thought suddenly came to him. "You know what, darlin'?"

"What?"

"I just realized. When you're here, I go to sleep with your arms around me, and when I wake up, either my arms are around you or yours are around me."

"Something wrong with that?"

"No, not at all. But I was wondering, doesn't my thrashing around keep you up all night?"

"Oh! No, you don't do that anymore."

"I don't?" Ed asked, turning around to face him.

"Well, a little bit," Rick conceded with a grin. "But if it's bad enough to wake me up, I just whisper 'I love you, baby,' and you settle down. Works every time."

"Huh. How 'bout that."

"Yeah." Rick kissed him. "How 'bout that."

With one last smile, Ed turned his back to Rick, whose arms immediately encircled him. Rick kissed Ed's neck.

"Good night, baby," he whispered.

"Good night, darlin'."

Chapter Nineteen

The rest of February passed quickly. Ed soon found himself hard at work on his usual end-of-the-month chore of preparing and mailing invoices. By the last day of the month, which also happened to be a Saturday, he was nearly finished. He spent the early part of the afternoon licking envelopes and stamps until his tongue went dry. He wanted the work finished before Rick arrived to begin their weekend together.

He smiled as he sealed the envelope addressed to Herb and Gwen Hauser. Their invoice was marked "paid in trade." Herb Hauser, an accountant, had agreed to take over Ed's tax preparation in exchange for snow removal services. Ed loved the barter system and used it whenever possible. Considering his frustrations with the tax code and arithmetic in general, he felt he was coming out ahead on this deal.

Despite the purchase of thirty-seven red roses for Valentine's Day, February had been a good month financially. Ed looked forward to his next stop at Porterfield First National, where he'd recently opened an additional savings account. He called it his Super Secret Savings, or Triple S for short. Into this account went every extra dollar he earned. It was, in his mind, money saved for his future with Rick.

Although they hadn't discussed it since that cold night at the cemetery, Ed was constantly thinking about the day he and Rick would merge their lives and their incomes. He agreed with both Mrs. Penfield and Rick that, financially speaking, a good offense was a good defense. Every dollar deposited into his Triple S, he felt, was a dollar protecting Rick and himself against anyone who might object to their relationship.

Ed's financial plans for 1981 had changed considerably. Before Rick came into his life, Ed had thought about buying a new truck and a new stereo and blowing a huge wad of cash on some kind of exotic vacation. The only big expenditure he would even allow himself to think about these days was the purchase of the coveted snow blower at the lumberyard. He had a hunch they'd mark the price down when spring arrived. Because its purchase would allow him to take on more snow removal work, he planned to buy it and be ready for next winter. By the time the snows of 1982 arrived, Ed was convinced he and Rick would be together, working toward their dreams.

Ed had even been doing a little snooping in his mother's basement, investigating boxes of his father's tools. The idea of working with wood, making things good enough to sell, had captured his imagination. He did not mention this to Rick, nor did he tell him about his Triple S account. They had agreed to table any discussion about their future until spring, so Ed kept his plans close to his heart, their warmth as comforting as Rick's love. When spring arrived, he would tell Rick, showing him with both words and actions how much their life together meant to him.

With a big sigh of accomplishment, Ed placed the last stamp on the last envelope. He went to the refrigerator for a can of Pepsi, chugging a good third of it over his dry tongue. He wanted his mouth refreshed and ready for the kissing soon to come.

He stole a quick look into the living room and smiled. He had another surprise for Rick, but this one couldn't wait. Rick would see it the moment he arrived.

He turned at the sound of Rick's car in the driveway. He stretched in contentment, watching Rick pull his usual overnight bag out of the car. Oh, this was his favorite time of the week. Every job, every chore, every movement of the past five days led to this moment, the beginning of his weekend with the man he loved.

Rick burst through the back door, smiling broadly. Ed's own smile was just as relaxed and happy. It was now officially Ed and Rick time.

After greetings, kisses, and hugs had been exchanged, Rick glanced into the living room. His eyes widened in wonder.

"Is that what I think it is?"

Ed laughed. "You bet. Come meet my new roommate. I was kind of hoping it would be you, but he'll do for the time being."

He took Rick's hand and led him to the sofa, where a young black tomcat was yawning, awakened from his nap by all the commotion. He looked at Rick with suspicion at first, but then relaxed for the hand eager to pet him.

"Where in the hell did you get this?" Rick stroked the soft, black fur.

"Mrs. Ilinski. He was a stray she took in over the winter because she felt sorry for him. Every time I went over there to shovel her walks she'd say"—Ed imitated the old woman's voice—"'Now, Ed, I just can't afford to keep this cat around. Why don't you take him home? You live all alone, and he'd be good company.' Well, I didn't have the heart to tell her I wasn't short on company these days. I've been stalling her for the last month, but today when I was over there, getting her TV antenna reanchored to the roof, the cat kept hanging around the bottom of the ladder, staring up at me. So I thought, what the hell, and brought him home with all the cat food she had on hand. She was thrilled."

A thought suddenly occurred to Ed. "You're not allergic, are you?" he asked anxiously.

"Nope."

The cat tested Rick's lap. Apparently he found it hospitable, as he settled there and began to purr.

"Cute little guy," Rick remarked. "What's his name?"

"Mrs. Ilinski was calling him Blackie. I was hoping, between the two of us, that we could come up with something a little more interesting."

"Hmm." Rick stroked the cat, looking thoughtful. "How 'bout Jet? He's jet black, and we could say it was after that old Paul McCartney song."

"Jet," Ed said, nodding. "I like it. Hey, we could spell it with two T's, make it like Jett Rink in *Giant*."

"Ah," Rick said, chuckling. "James Dean. Indiana's favorite son. Oh, that's too perfect for a cat owned by a Hoosier gay man."

"Jett it is, then," Ed said, pulling the cat out of Rick's lap. "Hey, Jett. You like your new name?"

The cat kicked away from Ed with annoyance and stalked to the end of the sofa, where he licked his disturbed fur with great disdain.

"Even acts like a gay man," Rick noted with a raised eyebrow.

"Well, then he'll fit right in around here, as long as he keeps the drama to a minimum." Ed turned his attention to Rick. "Man, am I glad to see you. And I get you all to myself until tomorrow night."

"I don't know, baby," Rick said, still looking at Jett. "Looks as though you'll have to share me from now on."

Ed gave him a lusty look. "There are some things I can do for you that the cat cannot."

Rick reached out, pulling Ed to him. "Now, how did you know I spent the day dreaming about my handyman all warm and naked. Come 'ere, you. It's been a long week."

Ed began unbuttoning Rick's regulation work shirt. "What do you say we go take a little nap in the bedroom and leave the cat to his?"

"Now, there's an idea."

It wasn't long before clothes were shed and they were stretched out on the bed, engaged in some passionate necking. Rick suddenly broke away, looking toward the door.

"Uh, Ed?" he tentatively asked. "Tell me. Have you ever had an audience before?"

Ed followed Rick's glance. Jett was standing by the bedroom door, calmly watching them. Ed began to giggle.

"I don't think so."

Rick shook his head. "Not only is the cat queer, he's a voyeur."

They looked at the cat, then at each other. Ed shrugged, reaching once again for Rick.

"Oh, what the hell. I've waited all week for this. As long as he keeps his paws to himself, I don't give a shit."

⋘•⋙

Their weekend progressed happily and affectionately, the novelty of Jett adding to their enjoyment of being together. Saturday afternoon's exuberant lovemaking seemed to kick them into a higher gear that only rock and roll could satisfy. Their mushy love songs were banished to the record cabinet, and Ed keep the record player stacked with everything from the Rolling Stones and Cream to Boston and Foreigner. By midafternoon on Sunday, however, they had both calmed down and were stretched out at opposite ends of the couch, legs intertwined, reading. Jett, unable to find a comfortable spot between them, had staked out one of the easy chairs for himself.

Rick was engrossed in his latest mystery novel, and Ed was struggling a bit with an Agatha Christie mystery Rick had brought him from the library. The combined influence of Rick and Mrs. Penfield had Ed turning to books for entertainment more often these days. On the evenings he spent alone, the television was usually quiet as he curled up with a book either Rick or Mrs. Penfield had suggested. He had to admit, though, that he found Dame Agatha rather challenging. So many of the British idioms and customs were unfamiliar to him that he had to disturb Rick occasionally for clarification.

Ed looked up when he felt Rick change positions on the sofa. Rick glanced at his watch, sighed, and his "Thinking about Going Home" look, as Ed privately called it, spread across his face. Rick returned to his book, the look fading slightly.

Ed's eyes were on the book in his hands, but his mind wandered elsewhere. He knew Rick hated to leave on Sundays, and his self-imposed guilt at ignoring Claire and the kids usually propelled him out of Ed's house earlier than was really necessary.

Ed enjoyed their cozy domesticity as much as Rick did, and hated to see the weekends come to an end as well. However, the pragmatism that had steered Ed well through his life allowed him to accept the situation for what it was. Rick, on the other hand, seemed to feel constantly torn between his responsibilities at home and his desire to be with Ed as much as possible.

Ed sighed softly, not wanting to grab Rick's attention. That same pragmatism told Ed their weekends together were not unlike romantic getaways, or even a grown-up version of playing house. He knew that when they decided to cohabitate, some of the heat of their relationship would cool in the day-to-day routines of living together. Ed wanted very much to sustain the heady excitement they had shared these past four months, but a part of him also longed to wake up next to Rick every day.

Even as practical as Ed was, he had known he was in love with Rick almost from the moment they had met, and after four months, no doubt remained in his mind that he wanted to be Rick's partner in life, for life. He was certain that Rick felt the same about him, but their mutual fears—exposing their relationship to the small-town eyes around them, Rick's potential abandonment of Judy, Josh, and Jane so soon after their father had abandoned them, and the plain old fear that they would find themselves making a mistake—were keeping them in this holding pattern. Oh, it wasn't a bad place to be, Ed thought; two guys in love spending as much time together as they could, but it was a holding pattern all the same.

Ed watched Rick absentmindedly scratch his nose. *Don't worry about it*, Ed told himself. *Right now I've got more than I ever really allowed myself to hope for. Enjoy it. We said we'd talk about it in the spring, and we will.* Ed knew, though, without looking at the calendar, that the first day of spring was less than a month away.

Rick slapped his book shut, startling Ed. "I think it's time for a cookie break," Rick announced, pulling his legs away from Ed's.

"Boy, it's sure a good thing Mom dropped those off yesterday," Ed teased, following him to the kitchen. "You've been hoovering 'em down like crazy."

"You can't beat your mother's chocolate chip cookies." Rick dug into Ed's panda-shaped cookie jar. "Norma could start her own bakery on the strength of her cookies alone."

"Yeah." Ed went to the refrigerator for the milk. "Mom has her talents, all right. Just steer clear of her fudge, though. For some reason, she's never quite gotten the hang of that."

They settled at the kitchen table with their snack. "I s'pose I should think about going home pretty soon," Rick said, chewing slowly.

"Yeah," Ed mumbled, knowing what was coming next.

"Man, I hate to leave, but—"

Ed waved a cookie in Rick's face to stop him. "Enough. You play this guilt scene every Sunday. Geez, we oughta set it to music." He dropped the cookie, stood up, and went around the table to Rick, putting his arms around him. "Darlin', I love you so much that watching you bash yourself with guilt every week kills me. You're just going across town to the Westside Hills subdivision, not around the world. Do the handyman you love a big favor, and let it go, okay? Besides," he said in a softer tone, "with you grabbing all the guilt, there's none left for me."

Rick played with a cookie, looking at the table. A faint grin twitched his mouth. "What do you have to be guilty about?"

"Oh, just my own selfish thoughts where you're concerned."

The grin widened a bit. "I have some pretty selfish thoughts about you, too, baby."

"There, you see? If we're gonna share our lives, we need to share the guilt, along with everything else." Ed's hand snuck into Rick's cookie pile. "However, I see you are *not* sharing the cookies, so permit me to take these to my side of the table."

"Hey," Rick shouted, grabbing for the cookies.

Ed tried to get away, but Rick tripped him. Ed stumbled and fell, sprawling into Rick's lap.

"Oof," Rick exclaimed as Ed's dead weight hit him. "Damn, baby, when did you get so heavy? I think you've had enough cookies."

They broke into laughter, holding on to each other, covered in cookie crumbs. Rick reached a sticky hand to Ed's face, stroking it, pulling Ed to him for a chocolate chip kiss. Ed returned the kiss, thinking that even five minutes with Rick was worth five days of waiting.

⋯●⋯

Monday morning found Ed back at work, installing a series of shelving units in the garage of a younger couple, the Rhodeses, who had just moved into his neighborhood. Ed seldomly found himself working for people near his own age, and he enjoyed Becky Rhodes's lively personality, and even more so, her teasing but wicked comments about how inept her new husband was with all things mechanical. Ed couldn't help it; he felt smug every time he learned of a straight man who was hopeless with tools. It always seemed a victory of sorts over their supposed superiority.

Ed finished the job by lunchtime, and with Becky Rhodes's fervent thanks, payment, and promise to call the next time she needed help, he drove home for a bite to eat, basking in an exceptionally good mood for a Monday. The air was still cold, but fresh with a hint of spring. March was, Ed thought, coming in more lamb than lion.

The phone was ringing as he entered the house, and he ran to answer it, assuming it was a call for more work. Much to his surprise, the caller was Gordy Smith.

Ed hadn't seen Gordy since his confrontation with Jim Murkland at the post office. Back in January, Ed had tracked down Gordy's home phone number, had called to thank him for his backup that day, and had invited him to join Rick and himself for a meal sometime. He'd heard no more from Gordy, however, and had just assumed Gordy was uncomfortable with the idea of spending time with them, although he was now Rick's favorite co-worker. Rick had told Ed they usually shared a cup of coffee and conversation before Rick left on his mail route each day.

"Ed, I was wondering, are you free for lunch today?" Gordy asked now. "I feel a little stupid about this," he continued with obvious embarrassment, "but I could really use someone to talk to."

"Sure," Ed said cheerfully. "You're more than welcome to come over here. We can talk in private that way."

"Well . . ." Gordy seemed to be weighing that idea in his mind. "Okay," he finally said. "Tell you what, though, I'll make a McDonald's run for us. The least I can do is bring the food. What would you like?"

"Oh, just grab me a Big Mac and fries. That oughta hold me. I've got lots of pop to drink here, or stronger stuff, if you like."

"Not while I'm working," Gordy said, sounding more like himself. "Hell, the last thing I need is to sell stamps with beer breath. Thanks, Ed. I'll be over in about a half hour."

Ed hung up the phone, puzzling over the unexpected turn of events, wondering what was on Gordy's mind. Jett came out of the bedroom, meowing for attention. Ed picked him up, amazed at how quickly he was getting used to having a cat around the house.

"We've got company comin', cat," he said, petting Jett. "So behave yourself. No drama, and whatever you hear, keep it to yourself."

By the time Gordy arrived, Jett was parked in a living room window, enjoying the sunshine, and Ed had, as usual, another stack of nostalgia on his turntable. It seemed appropriate, as most of Ed's memories of Gordy were from high school.

Gordy Smith, Porterfield High class of '68, had not been one of the standouts on the football team, but had been a strong and enthusiastic player. Ed, two years behind him, had always admired Gordy, not for his athletic ability, but for his general all-around nice-guy attitude, a definite departure from the behavior of the other jocks in school. They'd never been more than acquaintances, but Ed was eager to make friends with the only other gay man in Porterfield he was aware of, other than Rick and himself. Oh, he knew there had to be others, but small towns being what they are, he'd never made an effort to seek them out.

Gordy came into Ed's kitchen rather tentatively, and Ed did his best to make him feel at home. They spread their lunch over the table, and Ed went to the refrigerator to fetch a couple of cans of Pepsi for them. Gordy nodded toward the music coming from the living room. "Time of the Season" by the Zombies was playing.

"Man, that sounds great. I can't decide, though, if it makes me feel ten years younger or ten years older. 'Who's your daddy!' I always loved that song," he said with a grin, apparently beginning to relax.

"I pulled out all my old 45s right after Rick and I got together," Ed said, opening his Big Mac box. "He likes those old songs as much as I do. Sometimes we talk about what it was like for us in high school. I think the only thing we really enjoyed from that time was the music."

Gordy munched on some fries, looking thoughtful. "Yeah, I know what you mean. Oh, high school was great for me. I wasn't any brain, but I didn't mind the classes, and I liked playing ball. But I'll tell you," he said, shaking his head, grinning again, "that locker room could really be a problem for me. All those naked guys. Man! And they're all talking about pussy, and there I am, trying not to look at their dicks, eyes always on the floor. Now, that sucked."

"I'll bet." Ed remembered his own gym classes. "But how did you deal with it, other than that?"

"I didn't," Gordy replied flatly. "I went out with girls, made out with 'em, and pretended nothing was wrong." He rolled his eyes at the song that came on after the Zombies, "Tracy" by the Cuff Links. "Jesus, now, there's a memory. Remember Tracy Pettibone? Hell, I dated her all through senior year. We'd make out in my car, and she always thought I respected her 'cause I didn't want to go all the way. We broke up when she went away to college, and, man, I was more relieved than anything. I remember when they starting playing this song on the radio. I'd think about her, wondering if she'd met some guy who wanted the real thing. And I'd think about me, trying to tell myself that I just hadn't met the right girl yet. Then I met Laura Kendall. Gawd, what a disaster that turned out to be."

Ed nodded. "Yeah, I remember that. Weren't you two engaged?"

"Oh, yeah. Engaged, never married. By that time I was drinking a lot, and she wouldn't tolerate it. She finally dumped me for some asshole car salesman over in Wabash. Best thing that ever happened to me."

"Then what did you do?"

Gordy shrugged. "Oh, turned into a hermit, I guess. Went to work. Came home. Drank too much. Beat off a lot, thinkin' about guys I saw on

TV or who came into the post office. I finally met this guy in Fort Wayne. Nelly kinda guy, so I figured he was queer. That was the first time I ever did it with another guy. Damn." He shook his head, food forgotten, lost in the memory. "He wasn't my type at all, but I was over there all the time, making up for *lost* time, I guess. Of course he fell for me, but I wasn't ready for that. At all. But I learned a lot from him, and I owe him just as much. Stan, his name was. He finally met a nice guy, and they've been together for a long time. I'm glad about that.

"So I guess that's how I kinda came out—although I stopped going to Fort Wayne, afraid someone from town might see me. I go to Indy or Chicago for long weekends, which is great. No shortage of guys wanting to get laid there. But I get pretty bored around here. When Rick started at the post office I wondered about him, but was afraid to do anything. Then I figured out what was going on between you two. Man," he said, and laughed. "Good old Ed Stephens, under my damned nose this whole time. If I'd only known."

Ed laughed with him. "Yeah, me too. You know, though, I'm still not sure Rick and I would have gotten together if we hadn't've bumped into each other at Carlton's. I had such a big crush on him, and I couldn't believe he was feeling the same thing for me."

"Rick's a good man," Gordy said, nodding and smiling. "I think it's great, you two. I really hope it works out, but if it doesn't . . . ," he said, leering at Ed.

"I'll keep that in mind." Ed smirked at him. "But I'm hoping it won't be an option."

"Seriously, though." Gordy sipped his Pepsi. "You guys are an inspiration. If you can make it in this town, there's hope for me. I guess that's why I wanted to see you. I'm tired of hiding, tired of being alone. I thought about it a lot after that day at work, with Murk the Jerk. I realized I was being all careful because of assholes like him. Shit. I guess I'm getting old enough that I don't much care what people like him think anymore. So I was kinda hoping," he said, looking up at Ed, "that maybe we could get to be friends. All three of us. I think it's time I started living my life the way I want."

"Deal."

Ed stretched a hand out for Gordy to shake. Gordy did, gratefully.

"I wanted to talk to you first. Rick's the greatest, and I love working with him, but I've known you for so long, well, I just thought this might be easier," Gordy said, going back to his lunch.

"I understand. Rick and I both kinda hoped we'd be seeing more of you. We're kinda short on friends around here, too."

"Yep, I guess all us Porterfield fags could use a little support. It's funny," he said thoughtfully. "I used to keep up on all the job openings in the big-city post offices, but I never really made an effort to do anything." He shrugged apologetically. "This is home. I don't see why I have to leave, just for being gay."

"Yeah. But you know, it's 1981. Things are a-changing, at least a little. And for what it's worth, you're still as big and nasty as you were in school. I can't imagine anyone messing with you."

"Big, yes. Nasty, no," Gordy said ruefully, patting his belly. "Maybe hanging out with some new friends, getting out more, will make me want to get rid of some of this. I get too fat and no guy will want me."

"Oh, I wouldn't worry too much," Ed said, looking at the still attractive Gordy, but seeing a younger, slightly trimmer Gordy, complete with letter jacket. "A lot of guys out there have football player fantasies. I don't think you'll have too much trouble, either way."

⋘●⋙

Gordy had gone back to work by the time Rick stopped with Ed's mail. He dropped his mailbag to give Ed a hug.

"So how's your day been so far?"

"Pretty good," Ed answered, with an extra squeeze for Rick. "That job with the new people went great this morning. And you'll never guess who was here for lunch."

"Oh?" Rick reached out for Jett, who'd come over to greet him. "Who would that be?"

"Gordy Smith. He called and asked if we could talk. So he came over with some crap from the Mac Shack. It was really nice, though. We had a long talk about being gay in a town like this, and he wanted to know if he could hang out with us sometime. I said it was cool, since we'd already talked about it. Isn't that great?"

"Yeah," Rick said, intent on petting the cat. "How 'bout that."

Ed noticed a distinct lack of enthusiasm in Rick's voice. "Oh, come on. You're not still worried about *that,* are you? You don't have a thing to worry about. Gordy and I talked about it. He even called us an inspiration. There's no way he's going to try anything."

"An inspiration, huh?" Rick remarked—rather sourly, Ed thought. "He'll see how inspired I am if he ever lays a hand on you."

Ed rolled his eyes. "Oh, brother. Not only is he your best friend at work, he's a lonely gay guy who wants some nice guys to hang out with. Geez. Like I'd even look at another guy with you around."

Rick dropped the cat to the sofa and looked at Ed for a moment. A grin slowly came onto his face. "Yeah, while I'm around," he said cryptically.

Ed decided the subject needed to be changed, and fast. "So am I going to see you at all tonight? I'm going through withdrawal from the weekend."

"Oh," Rick said, grabbing his mailbag, "I don't know. Maybe for a while after supper if things are quiet at home. I'll call you, okay?"

"Hey," Ed said as Rick moved toward the door. "Aren't you forgetting something?"

Rick stopped, turned around, and finally smiled his warm and tender special. "I'm sorry, baby." He grabbed Ed for another hug, a wonderfully tight one. "I guess I've just got the Monday blahs. Don't pay any attention to me. I love you, baby," he whispered, then backed it up with a kiss.

"I love you too," Ed whispered, clinging to Rick, rubbing his back through his heavy coat. "Call me, okay?"

"I will. I promise," he said, letting Ed go. He paused for a moment, looking at Ed, then he smiled again. "You know, as far as I'm concerned, you are one hot guy. Maybe no one's beating down this door to get you to pose for some stupid magazine, but you're still the cutest handyman in this town and probably the whole state of Indiana." He opened the door. "I'll call you right after supper. I promise."

Ed watched him cross Grant Street and walk to the next house on his route. He knew Rick was still bugged about Gordy for some reason, but he couldn't understand why. Handsome as Gordy was, Ed wasn't particularly attracted to him.

Since he'd met Rick, he hadn't paid any more attention to other men than any average gay guy would. Rick was exactly what he'd always wanted, and he knew Rick felt the same way about him. Their intimate time together over the weekend had to have shown Rick the fire between them was burning just as hot, if not hotter than in the beginning. The awkwardness and tentative motions of their early lovemaking had disappeared. These days, when they reached for each other, it was with total trust and confidence; all of their individual desires could be, and always were, satisfied within their mutual boundaries.

Unlike some gay men, Ed had a tendency to think with his brain and his heart, as opposed to his dick, so he was mystified that Rick could possibly think he'd have any interest in another man. He thought of Jack, who'd routinely cheated on Rick. Maybe that was it, he thought. Maybe he worried that Ed would turn out to be like Jack. Ed sighed. All he could do, he supposed, was let time show Rick that Ed was not like Jack, and that he was stuck with Ed for life, if he wanted to be. Ed certainly hoped he did.

⋘●⋙

Ed had about given up on Rick that night when the phone finally rang around eight o'clock.

"Geez," Ed said, with some relief. "I was beginning to think you were mad at me or something."

Ed could hear Rick's deep sigh over the phone. "I'm sorry, baby. Things got a little crazy around here. The dentist told Judy that she really needs to get braces, which is a major tragedy for a twelve-year-old girl. She's been throwing a fit all evening, fighting with Claire, who's upset enough about the expense, let alone knowing how awful Judy feels. I mean, Claire went through the braces thing, too. Hell, that's where Judy got those teeth. I've been trying to play peacemaker, but let's face it: I'm no expert at calming down women. I think there's been a cease fire, though, so I was wondering if I could come over for a break."

"Get your sexy ass over here," Ed commanded. "There's no women here, just a lonely handyman and a bossy cat."

⋘●⋙

"Poor Judy," Ed said, once Rick was settled on the sofa, Jett in his lap. "I had braces, too. I know just how she feels."

"Well, that's just it," Rick said, one hand on the cat, the other around Ed's shoulders. "I don't. I didn't go through it. All I remember is how much Claire resented me, because she had to have them and I didn't. All in all, I don't think I was much help tonight, except to reassure Claire that as long as I was around, the money part wouldn't be a huge issue. The good thing, though, is since Claire's a dental hygienist, she'll be able to get a good price with this orthodontist who gets all of Dr. Wells's referrals. That should help."

"Sounds to me like you had enough—what did you call it?—'vicarious fatherhood' tonight." Ed pushed Rick into position so he could rub his shoulders. "I'm really glad you could come over here. I think you need a little attention for yourself."

"Yeah," Rick muttered. "Oh, that feels so-o-o-o good." He relaxed under Ed's hands. "And, baby, I'm sorry about earlier today."

"Sorry?" Ed turned his shoulder rub into a full-fledged back massage. Jett, dislocated and bereft of attention, fled to his easy chair. "Sorry about what?"

"Oh, being such a jerk about Gordy being here. I just get so insecure sometimes, thinking about what you have to put up with. Then I start thinking about what it would be like if I lost you, you know, to some guy who's not busy trying to help raise his sister's kids."

"Is *that* what that was about today?" Ed tried to relax the knotted muscles in Rick's back. "Darlin', how many times do I have to tell you I understand about that and how much I support you?"

"I know you do, baby. It's just sometimes I get worried that your patience with it all will end. I know you don't think you are, but I *know* how sexy and handsome and wonderful you are. Why there wasn't a long line of guys waiting to snap you up before I came along is beyond me. So, when all of a sudden there's this big, handsome guy here at your house for lunch, all that jealousy and insecurity comes pouring out of me."

"You were thinking about Jack too, weren't you?"

"Yeah. Oh, Ed, I was so stupid back then. I mean, I know that for a lot of guys, being gay is all about the sex. Hell, do you know how many guys I knew in Indy who didn't really have friends, they just had fuck buddies? I always wanted more than that, though. Problem was, I thought Jack wanted what I wanted. At least he said he did, but I wasn't enough for him. Then here I am, years later, living in this Nowhere-ville, and I just happen to meet a guy I'm crazy about, who just happens to feel the same way I do. And what's even better, since it's Nowhere-ville, I don't have to worry about him running around, screwing every guy in town."

"Oh, Rick, for cryin' out loud, you know I wouldn't do that," Ed said in disgust, rubbing a little harder.

"Ouch! Calm down, okay? I know that. But Gordy shows up, this big, macho ex-football player who just happens to be gay, and I guess all those old feelings came back. I feel like a lion, protecting his pride, ya know? You're mine, the life we're building together is ours, and I don't want anybody messing with it. I know I don't have a right to be that possessive where you're concerned, and it probably isn't all that healthy, but that's how I feel."

Ed eased up on the rubbing. "I understand. I feel the same way about you. Darlin', you know I think you're the most handsome man in the world, and it scares me to think of other guys being attracted to you, too. Hell, if I saw some guy making eyes at you, I'd probably kill him. But you do understand that you don't have anything to worry about with Gordy, don't you? He'd never disrespect your friendship by making a move on me. Plus, he knows I love you too much to even consider it."

Rick sighed. "I know. You're right. And I think the world of Gordy, really I do. I also have to remind myself that when it comes to sex, the two of us are so . . . compatible, that I don't think either one of us would be happy with another guy. Baby," he said, twisting his head to grin at Ed, "making love doesn't even begin to describe how I feel about what we do together."

Ed felt himself blushing. "I know. Sometimes I worry about us getting tired of each other, but then I also can't imagine that ever happening."

"Me too. I know all of that, but sometimes it scares me, how right we are for each other. I was unhappy for so long, I'm afraid something will happen to ruin it, and oh, boy, it's off to the races."

"Huh?"

"Oh, the mind games I play on myself. I start worrying about all the time you spend here alone, wishing I was here with you. You know what? Sometimes I lie in that bed, in that little room I share with Josh, and I think about you here alone, and I can't sleep. Then I'll hear Josh wheeze in his sleep from that stupid asthma the doctor keeps saying he'll outgrow, and I'm so glad I'm there for him. I'll think about how much happier he is these days, how much better his grades are since I've got him reading so much. But then I'll roll over, and you're not there. And I'll want to feel you next to me so bad, I swear, baby, it almost hurts. So then I think: Am I being fair to anyone?"

Ed paused his massaging for a moment, thinking. He felt as though he was playing out Rick's usual Sunday guilt scene on a Monday. He might have been annoyed, but instead he felt a tenderness for Rick he didn't know he was capable of. Perhaps the stand-in Dad lying on Ed's sofa needed a little parenting himself occasionally.

"Well," Ed said softly, "Josh is a little boy. He needs his uncle Rick right now, and the fact that you're there for him at all is pretty amazing. He's a lucky kid. As for me, well, I'm a grown man. I can handle the nights you're not here because I know you will be eventually. And Josh isn't stupid. I think he knows there's something more than just friendship between us. Thing is, he likes me, and I think he trusts me enough to know that when you're here with me, you're just across town, and if he needs you, you'd be there in a heartbeat.

"It's funny, now that I think of it. I mean, I just said I'm a grown man, and I am, running my own business, taking care of this house, and being all responsible. But I think a part of me was still a dumb kid up until the time I met you. I think watching you deal with this, and having to deal with it myself, has helped me grow up a little."

"Hey, why'd you stop?" Rick teased. "More."

Ed resumed the massage.

"You're amazing, baby, you know that? There are a lot of guys who wouldn't put up with the situation, wouldn't even bother to see it that way."

"I'm not just any guy. I happen to be the guy that loves you. Darlin', I didn't know I was capable of loving someone as much as I love you. One of the reasons I love you is because Josh and the girls are so important to you. If they weren't, I don't think you'd be nearly so wonderful. It hurts, though, to watch you tear yourself up over it. I guess I have to just keep telling you it's okay. Kids don't stay kids forever. The day will come when you and I are together full-time. Geez, then we'll have a whole new set of problems."

Rick chuckled. "Yeah, you're probably right. I know I'm being too hard on myself, but finding you, being so much in love—shit, it scares me, like I said. I'm afraid I'll screw it up."

"You mean you're human, too? Crud, I thought it was just me."

"Oh, I get scared, too. And insecure. And my self-confidence takes an occasional dive. I just hide it better than you do."

"Well, you don't have to hide it from me," Ed said, still feeling rather parental. "That's what I'm here for, to be your confidence when yours fails, just like you do for me."

"Thanks, baby. For that *and* the massage."

The last of a stack of records that Ed had put on the stereo earlier slapped into place and began to play. Three Dog Night's "One Man Band" poured out of the speakers.

"What can I say, darlin'?" Ed said, turning his man around for a kiss. "'I just wanna be your one man band.' And if I can't play for you all the time, I'll play for you when I can."

"Me too, baby," Rick murmured. "I just wanna be your one-man band too. And you know what? I could really use a little music right now."

Ed looked at Rick's watch, noting it was almost Rick's usual bedtime. He sighed. He sometimes felt every minute of the time he was allowed to have with Rick was measured by that timepiece. Despite his wise, comforting, parental words, he had a childish desire to rip it off Rick's arm and throw it out the front door.

"I want to make some music with you, too," Ed found himself saying, "but it's late for you. I suppose you should go home." Goddamned watch, he thought.

Rick looked at his watch, obviously thinking much the same thoughts. Ed watched him struggle to make a decision between what he wanted to do and what he needed to do.

"You know what, darlin'?' Ed smiled at him. "Spring's only three weeks away."

Rick looked puzzled, then smiled back at him in comprehension. "How 'bout that."

"I guess what I'm saying," Ed continued, "is you don't have to stay here and make love to me tonight to prove anything. I think they need you at home, and someday I'm going to have you full-time. I know that because I know how much you love me."

"Baby, when you talk like that, I wanna pack up and move in here right now."

Ed kissed him softly. "I know, but we agreed. We'd wait until spring. It's so close, and"—Ed shrugged helplessly, trying to express himself—"I just know something's gonna happen that will let us know it's time. So go on home, okay?" He kissed Rick again. "We'll be together this weekend. Are you forgetting? You turn thirty this week. We've got your birthday, and your parents are coming up. Besides, there's something I want even more than making love with you tonight."

Rick's warm and tender special was glowing on his face. "What's that, baby?"

"I want my lion to go home and get a good night's sleep, knowing his pride is safe. That's all."

It was Rick's turn to go for a kiss. "I don't think any lion who ever lived had a more beautiful pride than I have." He hugged Ed as tightly as he could. "Okay, baby. I'll go home, and I promise to sleep worry-free. I'll see you when I deliver your mail tomorrow, okay?"

"Okay."

Ed watched Rick climb into his car and drive away, back across town to the sister, nieces, and nephew that he loved—as big a part of that pride as Ed was. He knew that Rick was a good man, as only a good man would worry he wasn't caring deeply enough for those he loved.

Ed shook his head, looking out into the frosty night. Was it even remotely possible for him to love Rick more now than he did just a few hours ago? He wasn't sure, but he knew seeing Rick's vulnerability somehow increased a love that was already bigger than anything Ed had ever imagined.

Jett came up from behind him, meowing at the door. Ed scooped the cat up for a light hug.

"Ya know what, buddy? I think we're gonna have another roommate soon. I predict it. Before the tulips in the yard bloom, you're gonna have another lap to sit in and someone else to bug for food."

He set the impatient cat down and opened the door for him. Jett walked into the yard, sniffing the night air. Ed stepped outside and took a good sniff himself. Yep, no doubt about it. Spring was on its way.

Chapter Twenty

Ed danced around the kitchen as Honey Cone's old hit, "Want Ads," blasted from the living room, and since no one was around he allowed himself to sing out loud for a change. Well, Jett was around, and he made his reaction to Ed's singing voice quite clear. He asked to be let out. Ed didn't care; he was in too good a mood.

Damn, was there ever a more cheerful breakup song? he thought. If he and Rick broke up, he'd probably slit his wrists. He did a little shuffle of his own invention as he boogied toward the stove. He pulled open the oven door for a quick check. Yep, all was well for his birthday dinner for Rick. He slammed the door shut, spun around, and nearly collided with his mother.

"Mom," he yelled, grabbing on to her before he fell down. "Jesus Christ, don't you know how to knock?"

"Knock," she hollered over the music, pushing Ed away and depositing a bag on the kitchen table. "Why would a person bother to knock with this racket going on? And what business do you have, taking the Lord's name in vain?"

Ed was about to remind her she hadn't attended a regular church service in almost twenty years, but she wasn't finished.

"As for your singing, Ed Stephens, now I know why you were kicked out of sixth-grade chorus. Aren't you worried the neighbors will hear this ruckus? Why, I'd call the police."

Oh, Mom," he groaned, throwing his hot pad on the counter. "I'm having a good time. Give me a break already."

"Good time," she huffed. "With that noise? Honestly, I had hoped your taste in music might improve as you got older, but I was sadly mistaken. Who is that caterwauling, anyway? That Diana Ross you like so much?"

"No, but I think she's on next," he said, trying to tweak her and succeeding. "Sorry, Mom. Fresh out of Glenn Miller and Tommy Dorsey over here."

"Honestly. There hasn't been a decent recording made since Elvis shook his pelvis. Turn that noise down right this very minute."

Putting on his most wounded look, Ed went to the living room and took the needle off Diana Ross's "Surrender," which had just dropped onto the turntable.

"That's better," Norma remarked in a normal tone of voice as he reentered the kitchen. "Well, here's your cookies. You tell Rick I hope he had a happy birthday today."

"Actually, yesterday was his birthday." Ed peered into the bag. "Thanks, Mom. Rick loves your cookies, you know. I thought two birthday cakes would be a bit much."

"Yesterday? Two cakes?"

"He spent his actual birthday, yesterday, with Claire and the kids," Ed clarified. "They had a big cake and a party for him. Since today is Friday, and he doesn't have to work tomorrow, I'm celebrating his birthday with him tonight."

"I see." She nodded. "What do you have in that oven there?"

Ed sighed. *Here it comes,* he thought. "Meatloaf, baked potatoes, and green bean casserole. It's one of his favorite meals."

"Meatloaf?" Norma queried, eyebrows raised. "I don't seem to recall you asking for my meatloaf recipe."

"I called Rick's mother for her recipe. That's the one he's used to."

"Humph." Norma stalked over to the oven, hot pad in hand. "I'd just better see this meatloaf." She pulled the door down and stuck her nose as close to the pan as she could. "Well, it looks all right," she conceded. "Let me see the recipe."

Resigned, Ed handed over the scratch pad page with his scrawled notes on it.

"Bread crumbs," she read, scandalized. "Why, I never stretched a meatloaf with bread crumbs in my life. Your father would turn over in his grave."

"Guess what, Mom? Dad's not coming to dinner tonight. And neither are you. And I don't think Katharine Hepburn or Sidney Poitier are either, so you don't have to worry about it."

"Watch your mouth," she warned him, handing over the paper. "Well, if that's what the poor man is used to. I'll just have to have him over sometime for a real meatloaf. Speaking of dinner guests, though, I thought you said his parents were coming to town."

The Handyman's Dream 249

"They are, tomorrow. They're stopping here in the morning, and then we're supposed to go to lunch at the Wood Haven. Then they're going to spend the afternoon with Claire and the kids."

"Hmm." She inspected the newly scrubbed kitchen floor. "I thought it looked awfully clean in here for a change."

"Yeah," he confessed, "I was at it all day today. I was really glad no one called for a job."

"Humph. You'll clean for strangers, but not for your mother. That figures."

"Mom-m-m-m!"

"Well, just the same, you make sure you make a good impression on these people."

"I've already met them, Mom, you know that. I'm just a little uptight 'cause they're coming here."

Norma, scowling, rubbed at a grease stain Ed had missed on the wall. "Just like meeting your in-laws," she grumbled. "Can you beat that?"

"Well, that'll be one to tell 'em at garden club."

"The garden club won't hear about this, believe me. I still haven't told them about you. I figure what *they* don't know won't hurt *me*."

Ed was ashamed. Norma had been wonderful about his relationship with Rick, so he knew he really shouldn't tease her.

"I'm sorry, Mom. I know this is all pretty weird for you."

Norma turned around from the wall and looked at her son. "Yes, it is. Your father had his mind pretty well made up about you a long time ago, but actually seeing you with some man is still a little shocking for me. And I'll tell you, if it were anyone other than that Rick, I don't know how I'd feel. But he's a good man, and better than you deserve. You just see to it that you treat his parents with respect. Even with that awful meatloaf, they did a good job with him."

"I will, Mom," he said, smiling at her.

Norma sighed and shook her head. "Sometimes I do wonder what your father would say about all this. Oh, well. I'll just be on my way. I'm due over at your sister's to babysit while they go bowling in that silly league."

"Just keep your hands off their Froot Loops, okay?" He walked with her to the door.

"Oh, you. Think I'm such an ogre. I baked cookies for them, too." She turned around, hand on the doorknob. "Well, tell Rick 'happy day after' or whatever, and I hope he likes the cookies."

"He will. He always does. Thanks again, Mom. I really appreciate it."

He closed the door behind her, sighing. Bossy and domineering as she was, Norma was doing her best to accept a situation she had not wanted for

Ed, and he appreciated it much more than her cookie-baking. He wished he had a better way to show it, but nothing immediately came to mind. After all, tonight was for Rick, he thought, returning to his stereo. He'd pull a Scarlett O'Hara and worry about that tomorrow.

⋘•⋙

"The cookies were inspired, baby," Rick said later that evening. "In fact—"

"No! You've had enough. We are dancing. Shut up and dance."

"Yes, sir, but I thought it was my birthday."

"It's your birthday, but it's my house."

"But are you my man?"

"Absolutely. But sucking up to the host will *not* get you more cookies, at least not until this song is over."

The lights were dim, the Stylistics were singing "Stop, Look, Listen," and Ed and Rick were indeed dancing, or at least holding each other close, swaying from side to side. Rick had thoroughly enjoyed his birthday dinner and Ed's present of a gift certificate to the Bookworm Nook in downtown Porterfield, and he had managed to eat his way through half of Norma's cookies.

"You know the reason I really love those cookies so much tonight?"

"Why's that?"

"No candles. I thought the kids were gonna set the house on fire last night. Thirty-one damned candles blazing on that cake. One for each year and one to grow on. It took them so long to light 'em that we ate candle wax with the icing."

"My mailman is getting old."

"Oh, yeah? Take those clothes off, baby, and get into bed. I'll show you a thing or two about age and experience."

"Sure you don't need a shot of Geritol first? Ouch," Ed exclaimed as Rick purposely stomped on his foot.

The Stylistics faded out. The record changer clicked, and Gordon Lightfoot began to mournfully sing "If You Could Read My Mind."

"I'm wounded. I need to sit down."

Ed dragged Rick to the sofa. They collapsed in a heap, one big tangle of arms and legs.

Rick sighed. "Thank you, baby, for tonight. This has been the nicest birthday I've had in years. I don't even care that I'm thirty. Last night was great, but tonight is . . . really special." He put a hand to Ed's face, then gently pulled him close for a kiss. "If you could read my mind right now, what do you think you'd find?"

Ed giggled. "Probably wax from all those candles. No," he said, suddenly serious. "I think I'd see how much you love me, if the look on your face means anything."

"That's right. That's the tale my thoughts would tell, all about you and how wonderful you are. I love you, and that's all I care about right now. Well, that and the fact I think you missed your calling. Sometimes I think you should have been a deejay."

"I don't have the voice for it."

"Well, you certainly have the records for it."

"Any special birthday requests?"

"Yeah, more cookies."

"Aw, crud." Ed hauled himself off the sofa and walked to the kitchen for the cookie jar. "Another romantic moment ruined by my mother's cookies. Next year you get cake, with thirty-*two* fucking candles on it."

Rick joined him at the cookie jar. "I hope my mom doesn't bring any sweets tomorrow. Hell, if I keep this up, I won't be able to squeeze into my uniform on Monday. Are you nervous about tomorrow, baby?"

Ed took a cookie for himself. "No, not really."

Rick smirked. "Then why is this house cleaner than I've ever seen it?"

Ed scowled at him. "There is nothing wrong with trying to make a good impression."

"That's true," Rick conceded. "I just didn't want you to get all worked up again, like you did last time."

"I'm not, really. At least I don't think I am," Ed said thoughtfully. "I was more worried about the meatloaf drying out. No, your folks were easy to be with, and as long as Jett behaves himself, tomorrow should go fine. Speaking of that cat, where is he?"

They made a quick search of the house and found Jett crashed in the middle of the bed.

"Oh, great," Rick said. "Another three-way tonight. Does he always do this, or just on the nights I'm here?"

"Well, I have to admit he's good sleeping company when you're not around," Ed said, teasing him, "but I'd much rather have you."

"Is that so? Well, he's sleeping on the chair tonight. I want you all to myself. In fact"—Rick grabbed Ed's sweatshirt and began to pull it over his head—"I'm pretty damned tired. How about we lie down for a while?"

"You old men, always going to sleep earlier and earlier," Ed mumbled through his shirt.

Rick knotted the shirt around Ed's neck.

"In the first place," he said, pulling it tighter, "I was up very, very early today, a fact of which you are well aware, smart-ass. In the second place, who said anything about sleeping?"

"Argh! Get this thing off my neck or sleeping is all you *will* do tonight."

Rick disentangled Ed from his shirt and tossed it on the floor. One hand cupped Ed's head to bring him closer for a kiss, while the other hand unfastened his belt.

"Damn, you old guys know all the moves, don't you?" Ed said, smiling against Rick's lips.

The jeans were removed, the Jockeys followed, and then the socks, one at a time.

"Look at you," Rick said, admiring. "Now *there's* a birthday present."

With some help from Ed, Rick was quickly out of his own clothes. The cat was rudely awakened and deposited on the easy chair. They fell onto the bed together, kissing softly, holding each other loosely. Ed heard the last record fade out in the living room and made a move to get up, but Rick stopped him.

"Don't worry about it, Mister Deejay." He stroked Ed's hair. "This one-man band has lots of music to make right here. We don't need any more."

Ed kissed Rick slowly, tenderly. "Happy birthday, darlin'," he whispered.

Rick pulled him closer. "Baby, you remember that first night, right here in this bed?"

"Yeah. Why?"

"'Cause. I remember how bad I wanted you, how I had wanted you since I first saw you. I remember lying here with you that first time, and I don't think I ever wanted a man as bad as I wanted you. And you know what? I still do, want you that bad."

Ed glanced away from Rick's face. "I can see that."

"What're you gonna do about it, baby?"

"I can think of lots of things, but it's your birthday," Ed said, gently squeezing, moving himself farther down the bed. "I'll do whatever you want me to do, 'cause I want you just as bad."

Rick's eyes closed as he moaned under his breath.

"Happy birthday," Ed repeated, this time with a smile.

<∋•∈>

Ed sighed, pulling himself into a much nicer outfit than his usual Saturday grubbies.

"Geez. Nothing like the cold light of morning, and the fact that your boyfriend's parents are on their way, to bring reality home with a bang."

"Oh, it's only a few hours. Once they're over at Claire's we can do anything we want," Rick said as he made the bed.

"Yeah? You really think we could top last night?" Ed smiled, remembering.

"Not until your birthday, baby."

Ed put one arm around Rick from behind, his other hand gently stroking the seat of Rick's khaki pants. "Are you okay, darlin'?"

"Oh, baby, I'm way better than okay. That's a birthday present I'll never forget."

"Hmm. We could pretend today is my birthday, or it's yours again."

"Stop that. Don't you even think of getting me in this kind of trouble with my parents on their way here," Rick scolded with a smile, pulling the comforter tight. "I'll go make some coffee. I know my dad. After that long drive that's what he'll want, first thing."

The smell of fresh coffee soon wafted through the house as Ed rushed around, trying to remove as much of Jett's discarded fur from the furniture as possible.

"As much as it costs to feed you, you could at least clean up after yourself," he told the cat, who sneered at him, stalking away to his morning perch in the living room's east window. "Man, I've met drag queens who don't have as much attitude as that cat," he shouted toward the kitchen.

Rick laughed. "Well, he's your cat."

"Hey, I thought he was *our* cat."

"When he acts like a drag queen he's *your* cat, baby."

"Battle stations," Ed stage-whispered. "I just saw a car pull up front."

Rick came into the living room and peered out the front door. "Yep. That's them. Now, relax."

Ed and Rick warmly welcomed John and Vera Benton into the house. A quick tour—all that was really possible for Ed's small house—followed. Soon all four were settled in the living room with coffee and the last of Norma's cookies.

"Your mother's quite a hand with these cookies, Ed," Vera commented. "They're really good."

Ed smiled, trying to not laugh, remembering Norma's horror over Vera's meatloaf recipe. "I'll be sure and tell her you said so. I apologize, though, for spoiling your appetites. Rick and I want to take you both to the Wood Haven for lunch. It's a really nice place on the north side of town."

John shook his head. "No, we'll do the taking. After all, you only have one thirtieth birthday. How's it feel, Rick, hitting the big three-oh?"

Rick shrugged, smiling. "No big deal, Dad. I don't feel a day over twenty-nine."

"That's the spirit."

As it had at their first meeting, conversation moved well and easily, but Ed felt an undercurrent, some kind of tension between Rick's parents. Vera seemed a little too animated and John overly hearty, at least from what he remembered of the Indianapolis trip.

He puzzled over it, as John pulled out a birthday card for Rick. Rick opened it, and a check fell out. He glanced at the amount, then warmly thanked both his parents. Oh, it all seemed just fine on the surface, but unless Ed was imagining things, something was definitely going on.

Ed's feeling persisted through lunch at the Wood Haven. With some subtle scrutiny, he finally realized that Vera had something she wanted to say, but that John kept giving her guarded looks to keep her quiet.

He was eaten alive with curiosity by this time. What kind of bombshell could she possibly drop? Frankly, Ed had never met a more "Donna Reed-ish" mother, and the thought that she was concealing something shocking was intriguing. For once he wished he had inherited his mother's conversational boldness, until it occurred to him that whatever Vera had on her mind might have something to do with him. Then he was glad John was keeping her quiet. He glanced across the table at Rick, who was telling post office stories. If Rick had picked up on anything, he didn't show it.

Ed resigned himself to remaining in the dark when lunch ended with no revelations. They drove back to his house in Rick's car, and he assumed that John and Vera would immediately head over to Claire's place, but to his surprise Vera asked if they could have "a little talk" before they visited the grandchildren. Ed looked at Rick, his heart sinking. He'd never yet been invited to "a little talk" that he'd liked.

They reassembled in Ed's living room, John and Vera in easy chairs, Ed and Rick on the sofa. Ed nervously watched Vera make herself comfortable in the chair Jett usually used for naps. He hoped he'd gotten all the cat hair off of it.

"Boys," Vera said, smiling at them. "I've been thinking a lot about your future. Rick, from what I've seen, it's obvious that you and Ed are prepared to make a serious commitment to each other. Oh, I couldn't be more pleased," she added hastily. "I'm genuinely relieved that you've found such a wonderful companion. Ed's a good man. You don't have to convince me of that."

Rick looked at his father, who shrugged helplessly. "Well, I'm really glad you like Ed, Mom. Yes, I believe we'll be together for a long time. At least, I hope so. Are you worried about that for some reason?"

Vera looked solemnly at her son. "Frankly, dear, yes, I am. I worry about the two of you in this town. Do you really think this is a good place to build a relationship like yours?"

Rick's eyebrows shot up in surprise. "Whether it is or not, this is where we live. Ed has a business of his own here, I've got a job, and in case you've forgotten, I moved here to be close to Claire and the kids. What are you saying, Mom? That Ed and I should break up for the sake of Porterfield?"

"Oh, no," she exclaimed, flustered. "I didn't mean that at all. But I worry about you here. Don't you think you'd be more comfortable in a larger city?"

"Such as, I don't know, Indianapolis?" Rick asked sarcastically.

"That would be a good option, yes," Vera said, smiling nervously.

Rick looked back at his father. "Are you in on this, Dad?" he inquired.

John shifted uncomfortably in his chair. "Your mother is simply concerned for your safety. And on a more selfish note, I'm sure she'd like to have you—have you both—closer to home. That's a mother's prerogative."

Rick sat up straight, clasping his hands tightly together. Ed, knowing the volcano that was about to erupt, laid a restraining hand on his arm. Rick ignored it.

"So let me be sure I have this right," Rick began, staring at both his mother and father. "Mom here thinks that because her sissy son has met another sissy man, they aren't safe on the mean streets of Porterfield, a place where most people don't even bother to lock their doors, but would be safer in a big city, full of crime, corruption, and murder. Do I have that right?"

"Richard," his father warned.

"Small towns are notoriously full of prejudice," Vera said, staring back at him.

"I see. And because we're both sissy men, we can't take care of ourselves, right?"

"That's not what I'm trying to say," Vera said sharply. "I just don't see any reason for either of you to open yourselves to . . . to the abuse you're sure to get here."

"Hell, if that's the case, then why don't you ship us off to San Francisco? Shouldn't we go off into exile like all the other fairies?"

"Rick," John said impatiently. "There is no reason to lose your temper, nor take this the wrong way. Have the two of you thought what might happen if you choose to live together in this town? Are you sure Ed's old folks would be approving of such a relationship? And what about your job, Rick? You've built up close to ten years with the postal service. Are you prepared to lose the benefits you're in line to receive because of the person you chose to love?"

"I could lose my job just as easily in Indianapolis or San Fran-fucking-cisco as I could here," Rick hollered.

"Richard, watch your language! Don't talk like that in front of your mother," his father shouted back.

Rick, who was almost standing by this point, sank back to the sofa. "I'm sorry, Mom, Dad. That was uncalled for," he said in a much quieter tone of voice.

He took a deep breath before he continued. "I'm shocked and hurt, though, that you seem to think that Ed and I are so careless or foolish we would do anything to invite trouble. Yes, we've talked about it. Aside from my commitment to Claire and the kids, one of the reasons I'm not here every day and every night with the man I love is *because* of the very things you mentioned. We have our concerns, and at this point in time we're moving slowly and, yes, *cautiously* toward the idea of cohabitation.

"Yes, we've even talked about moving away, to a bigger city, where it might be easier for us. Mom, Dad, you can't imagine how we've struggled with this. I think it was only with the help and very wise counsel of our good friend, Mrs. Penfield, that we were able to achieve a certain amount of peace on the subject."

"Rick," his mother said, "I understand your struggle, but—"

Rick held up a hand. "May I finish, Mother?"

Vera pursed her lips, holding back her words. "Yes. Please do."

Rick nodded. "Thank you. I'm hoping you will also remember this is Ed's hometown. His family is here. His mother depends on him, and God love the old battle-ax, I don't blame her. He's about the most dependable person I've ever met."

Vera sighed. "I've no doubt of that. You don't have to sell Ed to us, Rick. We've seen what he is for ourselves. I just want you to be safe and happy. I worry. And that's a mother's prerogative as well."

Ed watched the assorted Bentons glare at one another. Mustering his shaky self-confidence, he waded in.

"May I say something?" he asked, rather timidly.

John let out a long breath. "Please do, Ed. I think we could use your input about now."

"Well," Ed said with a nervous look at Rick. "I think when he calms down, Rick will be as overwhelmed as I am at your concern for us. Most men in our situation are usually just written off by their parents, but you've made me feel like a welcome member of the family. That's means more to me than you'll ever know. My mom, even though it's been hard for her, has done the same for Rick. We've been really lucky in that respect, and maybe that's why we don't see this town as such a threat."

Ed paused. He wanted to think through his words carefully before he spoke. "Maybe we're being overly optimistic about our future here in Porterfield. Maybe we just love each other so much we can't see why anyone would have a problem with it. I know they do. We've encountered it once already, big time. But here's the thing: if it comes down to a choice between my hometown and my business versus Rick, I'll take Rick. Period. Keeping him safe, and me safe, is the most important thing. So if the day comes we feel we need to leave Porterfield, we'll leave. But I don't see any reason to move because something *might* happen. I've lived in this town long enough to know that people sometimes surprise you. Rick and I have discussed it. We're not going to give up the life we have here without a fight." Ed took a deep breath, then let it out. Aside from high school speech class, he didn't think he'd ever delivered such a sermon before.

The three Bentons looked at him silently.

John broke the silence with a chuckle. "Well put, Ed. Well put."

Ed felt Rick's hand creep into his.

"You see, Mom, it may be your prerogative to worry, but I don't think you have to worry quite so much with Ed here at my side. Yes, I'll admit, we probably get a little carried away with ourselves sometimes, but that doesn't mean we aren't watching, taking note of what's going on around us."

Vera pulled a handkerchief from her purse. She wiped her eyes and sighed heavily. "That's just it. I wish you didn't have to."

Rick shrugged. "I wish we didn't either. But we're stuck with it. But you know what? I'm not about to leave Ed and take up with some woman just to make the rest of the world happy. It's not gonna happen. And until the time the world doesn't care anymore, we'll do the best we can to coexist with it." He suddenly grinned. "Hell, Mom, we're coming up on tornado season. I could just as easily get blown away walking my route as done in by a queer basher. Ever think of that?"

Vera eagerly laughed, happy, it seemed, to break the tension. "Well, no, I can't say that I have. But thanks. Now I have something else to worry about." She fumbled her handkerchief back into her purse. "Oh, Rick, I just mean well. I wouldn't worry if I didn't care, and I only want the best for both of you."

"Yeah, Mom. I know. And sometimes meaning well is a bitch, isn't it?"

❦

Ed and Rick sat quietly together, listening to the music pour out of the stereo in Ed's living room, listening to the old songs that had begun to shape their new life together. The late winter sunlight slowly drained from the sky as dusk descended on Porterfield.

The Bentons had left hours ago, with hugs, apologies, and promises of another visit someday soon. Ed and Rick hadn't yet said much to each other about his parents' concerns. It didn't seem necessary. They both remembered that cold night at the cemetery, and the decisions they had made regarding Porterfield.

No, they didn't talk about it, but Ed thought about it, and he knew, from the look on Rick's face, that Rick was too.

Ed knew, in his mind, that he and Rick were not terribly unique and their love was no more special than any other couple's. In his heart, though, their love was more beautiful than the seven wonders, more dazzling than a perfect cut diamond.

The power of their love had enabled them to move far beyond the wounds and resentments of their past. They were already stronger, better men, as Hilda Penfield had predicted. Together, they were a force capable of creating enormous goodwill. Unfortunately, though, a great prejudice hung over them, and it was possible the potential of that goodwill would never be recognized.

Ed sighed. He would go to his grave with no understanding of why anyone would condemn a love so honest and genuine.

"Rick," Ed asked, as another record fell into place on the turntable, "when you talked about a time when the world wouldn't care about us anymore, did you really mean it? I mean, do you think that day will come, when you and I can live happily ever after without worrying what anybody thinks?"

Rick was staring into space, listening to the music from the stereo. "Get Together" by The Youngbloods was playing.

Ed nudged him. "Do you think that day might really happen?"

Rick blinked and turned to Ed. "I don't know, baby." He shrugged toward the stereo. "Maybe. People have been preaching peace and loving your brother like crazy since the sixties, but I don't know if us gay brothers will ever be included in that."

He shrugged again. "Maybe things will change for us someday." He smiled weakly. "I hope so."

Chapter Twenty-one

Early on St. Patrick's Day morning, Ed stepped outside his back door and paused, amazed at the warmth in the air. The calendar still said winter, but spring was moving in, shoving Old Man Winter aside. He shrugged his shoulders, which felt wonderfully light without his usual bulky jacket. The bright sunlight made him squint a bit, and he was grateful for the sunglasses waiting in his truck.

Near the garage he noticed green shoots, which promised first daffodils, then later, tulips. He smiled. To notice them for the first time on the day for all things green seemed appropriate. He grabbed his snow shovel and stowed it on a hook in the garage, hoping that he wouldn't be touching it again until later in the year.

Glad as Ed was to put away his shovel, he was still a little wistful to see winter come to an end. Despite the cold and the endless snow removal chores, spending the winter with Rick had been wonderful, semihibernating, getting to know one another better, and, Ed thought, falling even deeper in love than they'd been before the first snowflake fell.

His work had kept him busy enough to pay the bills and to add money to his Triple S fund, but he had also managed to have plenty of time for Rick and for dreaming about Rick. With warmer weather coming, Ed's work would undoubtedly pick up; he already had five painting jobs scheduled, and he knew more would come. Chores and repairs that folks had put off all winter always seemed to become a priority when spring arrived, and Ed braced himself for a constantly ringing phone.

Not only that, Ed thought, as he backed his truck out of the garage, but spring meant an end to people cozily tucked away in their warm homes. People would open their windows and begin to move outside once again.

Ed had felt through the winter that he and Rick were almost in hiding, keeping their growing relationship a secret inside the winter darkness. With everyone moving about freely again, would they take notice of the two men blissfully sharing their lives together at 427 East Coleman Street? The words of Rick's mother and father still haunted Ed. He wanted nothing more than to share Rick's love and companionship without worrying about community disapproval.

Ed rolled his window down, and the warm air blew against his face. He wondered if John and Vera's visit would have any effect on their future plans. He hoped it wouldn't, but he knew that Rick had been just as shaken as he that his mother felt they should move away before moving on with their relationship. He wistfully remembered telling Jett that Rick would be with them before the tulips bloomed. It was something he wanted with all of his heart, but he wanted it only if Rick could commit to it with no reservations.

Ed gave his head a good shake as he pulled up in front of Mrs. Heston's house. Such gloomy thoughts on such a beautiful day! Nope, he was going to appreciate the warmth and the sunshine for what it was worth, and he had all day to look forward to seeing Rick in the evening. Ed and Rick were meeting Gordy downtown at the Cozy Hearth Café, which stayed open late every St. Paddy's Day to serve their corned beef special. Despite Rick's earlier jealousy pangs, the three were beginning to enjoy a warm friendship.

Ed managed to keep the darker thoughts at bay throughout the day and felt downright festive when he met Rick and Gordy that evening. They were both laughing together over a screwup Jim Murkland had made earlier in the day, bringing the wrath of Don Hoffmeyer on him. Ed was glad to hear that Murk the Jerk was too busy covering his ass these days to make trouble for anyone.

"What goes around, comes around," he remarked as their drinks arrived at the table.

"Ah, where's the green beer when you need it?" Gordy asked sadly, observing his glass of Pepsi. The Cozy Hearth didn't serve anything stronger. "What's St. Paddy's Day without hoisting a few, huh?"

Ed glanced around the crowded restaurant. Few genuine Irish lived in Porterfield, but apparently plenty of folks had decided to pretend for the day.

"Well, if you want," Ed said, "come by the house after we're done here. I'll give ya a beer with some green food coloring in it. I'm not sure, though, I'd like to see this crowd tanked up. I think we're better off."

Gordy almost choked on his soda pop. "Ya gotta point. Hell, half of 'em will probably be across the street at Buck's before this night is over with. The streets of Porterfield won't be safe tonight."

"Then I'm glad I go to bed early," Rick said. "Wasn't it a great day, though? I swear, for the first time in months I didn't walk that route hunched over from the cold."

They all agreed Mother Nature had indeed been kind to them for St. Patrick's Day.

"Here's to spring," Gordy proposed, holding up his glass.

They all clinked glasses and drank to spring.

"Course, it means I have to go through with my threat," Gordy said, setting his glass aside. "I vowed when the weather warmed up I'd start jogging again. I'm gonna lose this gut or else."

Rick watched Gordy reach for his cigarettes. "Now, that should be something to see," he remarked as Gordy lit up.

"Hell, I'll make sure I head by your house every night," Gordy retorted, exhaling. "You can stand out there with a cup of water, like they do for marathon runners."

"Yeah, and an ashtray," Rick shot back, waving smoke away. "And a respirator. Shit, don't you think you oughta give those up first?"

"One thing at a time, good buddy, one thing at a time," Gordy said, relishing a deep drag.

Rick rolled his eyes at Ed, who smirked at him. Ed was learning that getting under Gordy's thick skin wasn't an easy thing to do.

"So what are you two gonna do with warm weather coming?" Gordy asked as their food was put before them.

Rick and Ed looked at each other and shrugged.

"Beats me," Rick said, picking up his fork.

"I'll probably be busier than shit with all the work people have put off all winter," Ed said. "And I'm guessing Rick will be chasing after three kids with a bad case of spring fever."

Rick groaned. "You're probably right."

Gordy stared at them, chewing thoughtfully. He swallowed and said, "You guys need a break."

Ed snorted. "You gonna give us one?"

Gordy leaned back expansively and smiled. "I just might be able to do that."

Ed looked at him, puzzled and curious.

"Whatcha got in mind, Gordy?" Rick asked. "You got a time-share in the Bahamas we don't know about?"

"Nope. Something even better. A cabin in the woods."

"Huh?" Ed asked, food temporarily forgotten. "What cabin?"

"Well, it's my dad's, actually," Gordy said, forking up corned beef. "It's just a little three-room place on a small lake, across the line in Michigan. He uses it for fishing trips, and to get away from my mom, although you didn't hear me say that. Kitchen, living room, bedroom—it's pretty basic, but there's a great fireplace, and plenty of wood to keep it going."

"How 'bout indoor facilities?" Rick asked with narrowed eyes.

"Hell, yes, Benton, you can pee indoors! You don't have to worry about waving your dick at some damned tree." Gordy laughed at his own wit. "Anyway, it's out in the middle of nowhere, and I mean nowhere. Nothing but woods and water, 'cause those damned real estate developers haven't found it yet. I just wish I had someone to take up there. Thing is, it'd be perfect for you two. Give you a chance to relax before the shit hits the fan, so to speak."

Ed looked over at Rick. "You know, I've never been with you in front of a roaring fire."

"That's 'cause we make our own fire, baby."

"Listen to him." Gordy snorted. "Seriously, though, it'd be great. Rick here can get away from the kids and the post office, and, Ed, you could have a weekend without hearing from every old lady in town. This time of year no one would be around, and you two could probably do it out in the woods for all anyone cared."

Ed flashed back to his thoughts of earlier in the day. "You have to admit, Rick, that being alone, I mean really alone, sounds pretty good. Once I settle in with all those painting jobs I have, I won't have any time for fun, and even if I do, I'll smell like paint thinner. I think it sounds great."

Rick looked dubious. "Are you sure it's okay for us to use it?"

"Sure! I've got a key for when I want to go up there, and since the ice is gone, Dad won't be back there till Memorial Day. He's been up there with his buddies off and on all winter for ice fishing, so the wood box'll be full and the place will be aired out. Oh, you may stumble over a few empties, but other than that, it should be fine. Bring your own blankets, though. Knowing my dad, the beds are probably down to bare mattresses."

Rick sighed. "I just had a Saturday off. I'm not due for a whole weekend off for another month."

"Aw, geez," Gordy protested. "With you being Don's pet, do you think he's really gonna holler if you ask for a weekend off again this month? Even if he does, I'll take your route. Hell, I'd love to get outside again. Be a great way to get some exercise. Now, can you think of any other objections?"

Rick looked at Ed, whose eyes were already bright with anticipation.

"Well, if you don't talk me into it, Ed will. And you're right, baby, it would be nice to get away somewhere quiet together. If I can work out something with Don, then sign me up."

❧●❧

The details were hammered out over the next few days. Don graciously agreed to Rick taking off the last weekend in March, and Ed managed to stall the first of his painting jobs until early April.

The weekend prior to their getaway was spent in the usual way at Ed's house, and talk naturally turned to the following weekend.

"Remember that Saturday in December when you said we'd go away some Saturday to a place neither one of us had been?" Ed asked Rick, putting records on the stereo.

Rick was stretched out on the sofa, Jett purring on his chest. "Yeah, I remember, baby. I hope this is just the first dream we talked about that day to come true."

"Do you know what today is?" Ed asked, as "Come Saturday Morning" began to play.

Rick scratched his head, doing his best to look mystified. "Gee, I don't know. Did I forget someone's birthday?"

Ed tickled him. "It's the first day of spring, you dork."

Rick pushed his hand away, giggling. "Watch it. You'll upset the cat. I know it is, baby. I've been thinking about it all week. Do you s'pose, next weekend, maybe we can take a break from making nonstop love in the woods long enough to talk about a few things?"

Ed's bright smile was Rick's answer. "I'd like that. I've got some things to tell you about."

Rick's mystified look was now genuine. "What things?"

Ed lifted Jett to his usual perch in the window. He crawled on top of Rick, holding him close, kissing him.

"Oh, I've been doing some thinking and planning of my own over the winter. Next weekend is a perfect time to share it with you. We'll be all alone, living one of our dreams, thanks to Gordy. And we can talk about the next ones that need to come true."

Rick kissed him back, sighing happily. "I'm all for that." His arms went around Ed, and the two men held each other tightly. "Speaking of remembering things, I've been remembering the first time I told you I loved you, right here on this very piece of furniture. I remember thinking that it was way too soon, but I couldn't wait any longer. I told myself I'd have to wait a lot longer to start thinking of you as my lover or my husband. I'd have to wait until I knew for sure what I was thinking was right, that we'd be together forever."

Rick smiled at him a little sadly. "Thing is, baby, so many people, gay or straight, say 'forever' and it doesn't work out that way. I *thought* that night I'd be lovin' you forever, but I wanted to know for sure first. You understand?"

Ed nodded.

"I think I know all I need to know, Ed. So, yeah, next weekend I'm ready to start talking about forever with you."

Ed buried his face in Rick's neck, telling himself not to cry. He couldn't get over how many happy tears he had shed in the past five months—certainly more than had fallen from his eyes in the whole twenty-eight previous years.

Rick lifted Ed's head for a kiss, warm and tender special in place. "Don't be embarrassed, baby. That just shows me you're as happy and excited as I am. It also lets me know I've found the right guy, okay?"

"One Man Band" began to play on the stereo. Rick laughed, hugging him.

"You've made your one-man band so very happy," he said. "Ya know what? If we ever get crazy enough to stand up in front of our friends and families and make vows to each other, I want this song playing. I'm sure we're not what the guys who wrote it had in mind, but there's so much joy in the lyrics and the music. It makes me want to shout and dance, the same way loving you does."

Ed smiled, wiping his eyes. "Are you saying, after all the sappy, slow love songs we've been playing for each other all this time, you want our song to be a noisy, upbeat rock number?"

Rick nodded. "Definitely. Because there is nothing slow or sappy about my feelings for you. The joy I feel being with you *is* noisy, upbeat, and something worth shouting about, like they shout in the song: 'I just wanna be / I just wanna be / Your one man band.'"

Rick rolled out from under Ed, jumping to his feet. "'Ain't no two ways about it. / I just got to shout.' And I will, baby, next weekend. When we're all alone on that lake, I'll shout it to the goddamned heavens."

He pulled Ed to his feet. "Will you shout it with me, baby?"

Ed hugged him. "I'll shout it till I'm hoarse, darlin'."

⋘•⋙

The next week passed with painful slowness for Ed. He moved from job to job, day to day, mentally counting down the hours until he and Rick would be alone together.

Thursday afternoon, after a stop at the hardware store downtown, Ed drove east on Commerce Street, heading for home, when an impulse made him turn south three blocks early at Race Street. He hadn't seen Mrs. Penfield for a while, and it occurred to him she might be pleased to hear about the upcoming weekend.

As Ed's truck rolled into her driveway, he spied Mrs. Penfield in her backyard garden. He tooted the truck's horn, and she looked up. Seeing who it was, she smiled and waved.

"Mrs. Penfield, one; arthritis, zero," Ed exclaimed as he joined her. "You must be feeling pretty good today."

Mrs. Penfield smiled victoriously. "I do indeed. It seemed a wonderful day to check the progress of my spring flowers and start making plans for annuals. Oh, it's way too soon to plant, but even thinking about the colors we'll see out here soon makes my old joints feel younger."

She led him to a bench inside the small rose arbor. "Effie Maude just cleaned and moved this into the garden today. We must sit down and officially christen it for the season. Tell me, Ed. How's Rick? It's been much too long since we've had a visit. Could I talk you into bringing him over this weekend?"

Ed chuckled, sitting next to her. "Not this weekend, I'm afraid. Actually, that's what I stopped to tell you about. We're going away for the weekend. Gordy Smith is letting us use his dad's fishing cabin on a lake up in Michigan. We're leaving tomorrow night. I'm so excited. We've never really been away together, unless you count a trip to Indy to see his parents."

Mrs. Penfield beamed at him. "Good for you. I'm glad to see things are going so well. I worried a bit, this past winter."

"Me too. You know what, though? I really believe everything you said to us. I really believe that incident with Murk the Jerk made us stronger, made us love each other more."

"I'm glad to see my faith in you two wasn't misplaced," she said with a wry smile. "I was confident you'd see past the unpleasantness with Jim, and with Porterfield's potential disapproval in general. This town doesn't know it, but it needs you and Rick much more than *you* need *it*."

Ed looked at her in gratitude. "I keep wondering if there is some way we can thank you for your support and everything you've told us. Just knowing you're behind us helps a lot." Ed frowned suddenly. "Thing is, why are you behind us? I mean, you've always been the most tolerant person I've ever known, but aren't you, well, a little shocked by the idea of me and Rick?"

Mrs. Penfield looked thoughtful. "Oh, perhaps at first. I think, though, that any surprise I had in discovering the object of your affection was a man was lost in my happiness for you."

She put a hand, cruelly ravaged by the arthritis, gently on Ed's arm. "I've never made a secret of my fondness for you, Ed. In many ways you remind me of George Junior. If it were he in your place, I'd like to think I would be just as accepting."

She giggled, surprising Ed. "Plus, I am what they call a sucker for the sight of a young man in love. Seeing you and Rick together, so obviously in love, is simply double the pleasure."

Ed put his hand on hers. "You're the best, Mrs. Penfield. As much as I love my own parents, I'd be honored to have you for a mother."

"Thank you, Ed. That means a great deal to me." With some effort, she squeezed his hand. "Now, I must admit I'm curious about your future. Do you and Rick plan to continue as you are indefinitely? I would assume that conventional mating rituals do not apply to young men such as yourselves. How do you signify a deeper commitment to one another?"

Ed shrugged. "Well, you're right, we can't get married. I think the next step is to live together. Remember back in the sixties when the hippies made fun of marriage, calling it just a piece of paper? Well, I'm glad of that, really. I don't need a piece of paper, or a minister's blessing, to be married to Rick. When we're living together, I'll feel just as married as Laurie does to Todd."

"I see. Ed, can you make me a promise? When the two of you are ready to take this step, will you pay me a visit?"

Ed looked at her, puzzled. "Why, sure. We probably would anyway. Any special reason?"

She smiled. "Oh, maybe, maybe not. First and foremost, I will want to be among the first to extend my congratulations. I may also," she added mysteriously, "have some sort of a wedding present for you as well."

"You've given us enough already," Ed protested.

She patted his arm. "Well, then consider it a gift on *your* part to indulge the romantic notions of an old woman. Do you think this 'living together' step might be any time in the near future?"

Ed sighed. "I sure hope so. I'm ready, and I think Rick is, too. I think his concern about leaving the kids is the only thing holding us back. We're going to talk about it this weekend. We'd decided, weeks ago—after we talked to you, as a matter of fact—that we'd make some decisions come springtime."

"Ah, springtime," she said wistfully. "George and I were married in the spring. He proposed in late summer and wanted to get married as soon as possible, but I had my heart set on an early May wedding, when the lilacs are in bloom. Of course this was during the Depression, and we certainly didn't have the money for a lavish celebration of any kind, but I knew I wanted to become his wife at the time of year when the air is filled with so much promise." She smiled, rather sadly, Ed thought, assuming she was thinking of her late husband. "I hope this happens in this season for you and Rick as well."

"You'll be the first to know." Ed smiled back at her.

"Good. I expect to hear good news when you return from your weekend away."

⸻•⸻

Late Friday afternoon found Ed preparing for the weekend at the cabin. He gathered up bedding and warm clothes, while Three Dog Night's "Out in the Country" played over and over again on the stereo. Jett followed him around the house, full of suspicion.

"I'm sorry, cat, but you're on your own this weekend. Mom's coming over to feed you, and that'll probably be more company than you want."

Rick arrived, and soon the car was loaded and ready to go. After a fast-food stop on the edge of town, they headed toward the interstate. Although the weather was cool once again and the skies threatened rain, the two men were in high spirits. They sang along with their new favorite radio song, "Morning Train."

"You know, baby," Rick said, slowing down for a semi ahead of them, "it's a good thing neither of us can sing worth a damn, or one of us might get offended by the noise."

Ed laughed. "You got that right. But you know, I wish one of us had a portable cassette player. It would have been great to have all those tapes you made from my records. 'Morning Train' and the other stuff on the radio is great, but it's just not right for this weekend. I could do with some of those mushy love songs we listen to at home, and 'One Man Band.' Just think: two whole days, all to ourselves."

"Well, I could sing to you, baby, but I might scare off all the deer."

They bantered lightheartedly as they rolled north on I-69, Rick ignoring the 55 mph speed limit. After they crossed the Michigan border, Ed consulted Gordy's directions, and eventually they were on a narrow, two-lane county road, looking for Spruce Lake. A few left and right turns later, they pulled into the rutted drive next to the cabin, almost invisible in the pitch-black night. As Gordy had promised, the place was deserted.

"Wow," Rick exclaimed, peering into the gloom. "I'd hate to have to call for help out here. You'd be long dead before anyone found you. Good thing Gordy, at least, knows where we are."

Leaving the car lights on to guide them, they carried supplies to the door. Ed unlocked it with Gordy's key, then fumbled for a light switch. The lights came on, and the two of them looked around, shock and surprise on their faces.

"Not exactly something you'd see on a travel brochure, is it?" Rick remarked.

Ed took in the cheaply paneled room, sparsely furnished with a lumpy sofa, a La-Z-Boy that had definitely seen better days, a castoff coffee table, and a few kitchen chairs. A threadbare Oriental rug covered the plank floor in front of the promised fireplace. The fireplace—a huge, almost ornate stone affair—managed to make the rest of the room look even shabbier.

"Well, I wasn't expecting an Aspen ski lodge," Ed said, gingerly stepping inside, "but I have to admit I was picturing something a little more romantic than this. Oh, well, what do you expect from a bunch of straight guys who come up here to fish?"

Rick carried their provisions to the kitchen. "A few empties?" he inquired, pointing to the litter of beer cans and bottles scattered near the sink. "Hell, it looks like Laverne and Shirley's brewery blew up."

"As long as Lenny and Squiggy aren't around, I can deal with it." Ed righted a fishing pole he'd knocked over.

"At least the water runs," Rick commented, trying the sink tap. "And it looks like someone left the gas on, so we can cook. Probably so wasted on Bud they forgot to turn it off."

They inspected the rest of the cabin, stopping at the tiny bathroom.

"I don't know, baby," Rick said, gazing at the toilet that hadn't been cleaned in some time. "I may pee in the woods after all."

The bedroom was a nice surprise, well-paneled and cozy, with two double beds, a nightstand, and a lamp. The bare mattresses were in surprisingly good condition.

"How much you wanna bet it was *Mrs.* Smith who furnished this room?" Ed said, bouncing on one of the beds.

"Yeah, did this one and gave up," Rick said, looking out the window. "What do you know, there is a lake out there. I can see a path leading down to the water. Wanna go check it out?"

"Let's go check out that fireplace first." Ed was shivering a bit. "It's cold in here."

They walked back to the living room. Ed stuck his head up the chimney to locate the damper. Rick opened the big wood box, located off to the left side.

"Full wood box, my ass," he roared. "Look at that. Nothing more than some kindling. Hell, I'm not gonna go looking for wood in the dark. I guess it's the kerosene heater for us tonight."

Ed sat down on the hearth, head cocked. "Do you hear that?"

Rick looked up. Sure enough, rain had begun to patter on the roof. They both began to chuckle.

"Baby," Rick said, sitting down next to Ed. "I think your roaring fire just got drowned out for the weekend."

⋘•⋙

Later that night they lay huddled together in one of the double beds. The lamplight provided a nice glow to the room, and despite the cold, Ed felt quite comfortable.

"So, how's your romantic weekend so far?" Rick teased.

Ed pulled Rick closer, grateful for his body heat. "Darlin', the only thing I need for a romantic weekend is you. The setting doesn't matter at all."

"It's a good thing," Rick cracked. "'Cause I can think of more romantic bus stations than this."

"Oh, cool it." Ed gave him a playful knock against his head. "Just think of how nice it was for Gordy to do this for us. You know he's lonely, and for him to think of us was really nice."

"Probably his way of getting even with us."

"Will you quit, already? Besides, are you forgetting that for the first time ever we are really alone? No phones, no neighbors, no work, no kids. We can love on each other all we want, and not be looking over our shoulders for a change. I think that's pretty incredible."

Rick smiled, rubbing against Ed. "You're right. I'm just having some fun at Gordy's expense. It was nice of him, and you're right about another thing: All I need to make this a wonderful weekend is you."

"Keep rubbing on me like that, and you're gonna get plenty of me."

"I'm merely keeping warm, baby."

"Yeah? Well, you know what happens when you rub two sticks together long enough. You get a spark."

"Listen to the boy scout," Rick said softly, rubbing harder. "You want ignition, baby, you got it."

⋘•⋙

Saturday morning dawned wet and gloomy. The rain had stopped, but the trees outside the cabin were weeping water, and the ground was cold and muddy. Ed was glad they had brought books and a deck of cards. It didn't look too promising for exploring.

Rick, either finished ragging on Gordy and the cabin or keeping his thoughts to himself, cheerfully made them a big breakfast. Ed swept the beer empties into a garbage bag they'd brought for their own trash, then set the splintery table with mismatched plates and cutlery.

"You know," Ed remarked, "I always wondered what people did with their old plates and beat-up kitchen stuff. They stock lake cabins with them."

"Or peddle them at garage sales." Rick flipped bacon onto Ed's plate. "I gotta admit, though, this stove is great, and that fridge looks almost brand-new. Oh, well. That's probably just to keep the beer cold."

"Listen to that quiet, though. I'm not even missing the stereo right now. I never realized how much noise there is until now." Ed paused for a moment, listening. "Here that? You can hear the trees dripping. If we were at home, I'd have records going, Jett would be hollering for his breakfast, and we'd both be waiting for the phone to ring with either an emergency for me or a Claire-and-the-kids crisis for you."

Rick nodded, sipping, and grimacing a bit, at his instant coffee. "You're right, baby. I can't believe how well I slept last night." He glanced out the kitchen window, where a patch of lake was visible through the trees. "What do you say, after breakfast, we pull on some boots and go skip a few stones? I don't think I'm up to a hike in this weather, but I'd like to see the lake."

"Deal."

Boots, coats, and caps on, they carefully followed the path to the lake, avoiding the biggest puddles. Ed was surprised to see lingering snow in the darker parts of the woods. Spruce Lake loomed up before them, as small as Gordy had promised, but Ed guessed it would be a fair hike around its perimeter.

The water lay still and gray under the windless, cloudy sky. The trees, still winter bare, stood thick and tall around the lake, seemingly protecting it from the rest of the world.

"I feel like I'm a million miles away from everyone." Ed sighed. "Isn't it great?"

"Yeah," Rick said, taking Ed's hand and leading him to the shore. "Funny, though, calling it Spruce Lake. Where are the spruces?"

"Over there."

Ed pointed to the other side, where indeed a large stand of spruce trees rose up, their dull green the only color in the monochromatic setting. Worse-for-wear boat docks dotted the lake, and if Ed squinted, he could see other cabins and cottages behind the trees, apparently all deserted.

Rick took Ed in his arms for a hug. He kissed him softly, lingeringly, then sighed with contentment.

"I swear I will never second-guess Gordy Smith again. He was right. This was exactly what I needed, a quiet, peaceful place where I can hug and kiss my man, hell, even strip down and make love to him by the water, and no one would see or care."

They stood, locked in each other's arms, gazing at the stark but beautiful scene before them.

"Beats the hell out of Coleman Street, doesn't it?" Ed commented.

"Would you like something like this someday, baby? A cabin by the lake? A place where we could hide from the world?"

"Yes," Ed answered, his eyes on the water. "A place we could escape to when we need it. A place where the only things I fix would be my own, 'cause I wanted to, 'cause it would make it better for us. And no mail for you to deliver. Just a little place like this where we could sit and listen to the quiet, and forget about everything." He sighed. "A place where your parents wouldn't have to worry about us loving each other as much as we do."

Rick turned Ed's face back to his. "Are you still thinking about that?"

Ed shrugged. "A little bit."

Rick squeezed him tighter, and they rocked back and forth on the cold ground.

"Don't worry, baby, at least not now. No one can hurt us here. We've got the whole rest of this weekend to ourselves, and I promise I'm gonna love you enough, and good enough, that it will last until we get another chance like this." He kissed Ed again, and the love he promised flowed from his lips to Ed's. "Someday, baby, we'll have a place like this, if you want. Don't throw out those old plates. We'll need 'em for then, okay?"

Rick kissed him one more time for good measure before letting him go. He bent over, picking up a stick that had washed ashore. He used it to carve RICK LOVES ED in the mud by the lake's edge.

"That oughta get someone's attention," Ed remarked with a smile.

"Maybe," Rick said, unsatisfied. He threw his head back and yelled. *"Rick loves Ed. I just wanna be his one-man band."*

The sound of his voice bounced against the trees on the far shore, echoing back to them. They stood, hand in hand, listening to the silence that followed.

Ed pulled Rick to him for a kiss. "That got my attention, darlin'. Do we really need anybody else's?"

"No." Rick dropped the stick so he could hold Ed with both arms. "I'd planned to do a lot more shouting, but I guess I don't need to. As long as you know, that's all I care about."

⋘•⋙

The weekend passed quietly from Saturday to Sunday. They remained indoors mostly, reading, fixing snacks, enjoying the peace of their surroundings and each other's company. They played a ridiculous, cheating game of gin Saturday night, which ended completely when, laughing hysterically, they began throwing the cards around the room. They spent another night sleeping close together after a long, lazy lovemaking session. It was, despite the lack of Ed's hoped-for fire, a perfect weekend filled with relaxation, contentment, and love.

Early Sunday afternoon, Ed sprawled on the thin carpet in front of the fireplace.

"I can at least pretend," he told Rick, who flopped down beside him, laughing.

"Next time we bring our own wood, baby," he said, a hand over his eyes, pretending to shield them from the fire's glare.

"I hope there is a next time. We owe Gordy big time for this, you know."

"Well, I can't imagine wanting to be here this summer, when that lake will be filled with boats and probably screaming kids, but maybe next fall, when it gets all quiet again like this, we can come back. That big, soft heart of Gordy's? Hell, he'll probably have a key made for us."

"Something to look forward to," Ed said, smiling at him.

Rick leaned over for a kiss. "There's lots of things to look forward to. Are you ready to talk about it?"

"Yes. You wanna go first?"

"No, baby. I'm awfully curious about what's going on in that head of yours. In fact, I've been wondering about it since last Saturday. What did you want to tell me?"

Ed pulled himself up so he could sit leaning against the battered sofa. He pulled Rick next to him and held his hand. "I wish I had some sort of . . . speech prepared. I'm not as good with words as you are."

"You do just great, baby. Just say what's in your heart. I'll have no problem understanding that."

"Okay." Ed sighed. "Here goes. Rick, you know I love you. I hope you also know that I can't imagine my life without you."

"I feel the same way," Rick murmured, kissing Ed's cheek.

"Good. 'Cause every thought I have about the future now is about us, not just me. Remember that night at the cemetery?"

Rick nodded.

"I really thought hard about the stuff we talked about, and the things Mrs. Penfield said. Right after that, I went into the bank and opened another savings account." Ed grinned, rather sheepishly. "I call it my Super Secret Savings. I didn't want anyone to know about it until we had this talk. I've been depositing every extra dollar I have in it. Every penny of it is for us and our future. Oh, it's not very much, but it's a start.

"I see us using that money to buy our own house, or anything we think will make us happy. It's not my money, Rick. It's *our* money."

"Oh, baby," Rick whispered, rubbing his head against Ed's. "I love you so much."

"I've also been going over to Mom's, digging around in the basement. She pretty much dismantled Dad's workshop. I understand why she did it. The reminders hurt her too much. She didn't throw anything away, though. She boxed everything up and shoved it aside where she didn't have to see it. It's all there, though. If I can find a place for it, I'd like to rebuild the workshop and start messing around, making things. I don't know if I'd be any good at it, but I'd really like to try. I'm also hoping to find someone who can . . . can kinda take Dad's place. Someone who can teach me what I need to know.

"See, I remember what you said about me building cabinets to sell. If I turn out to be any good at it, we can be self-sufficient, like Mrs. Penfield said. We won't have to depend on anyone else for our income. I'm also thinking about chairs, or chests, or whatever. The first thing I want to make is a bookcase, just for you, so you can get all your books out of boxes.

"I see that bookcase in a wonderful study for you someday, but for right now, I'd like it to be in my living room. Our living room. 'Cause there's nothing more I want in this world than for you to move in with Jett and me. All I've wanted for months now is to wake up next to you every day. Would you do me the honor of sharing my house and my life, Rick?"

Tears were rolling down Rick's face. "Oh, God," he whispered. "How did I get so lucky? What did I do to deserve such a good, wonderful man?"

He kissed Ed, and Ed could taste his tears.

"Yes! Yes, yes, yes. I'll share your house, and your life, and anything else you want to share with me."

Ed kissed him back and wiped away Rick's tears. Strangely, there were none of his own. He felt moved even beyond tears, if that was possible. "Thank you, darlin'. That's all I need to know."

"Well," Rick said shakily. "There's a lot I want to tell you, if it's okay." He wiped his nose. "Damn. I need a Kleenex. Would you get me one of those paper towels, baby?"

Ed jumped up and returned with the roll they had brought with them. Rick blew his nose, shaking his head.

"Oh, baby, you've made me cry before, but never like this. There's so much I want to say, but now I'm the one who can't seem to put it into words. Bear with me, okay? I'll probably get this all mixed up."

Ed, laughing softly, kissed him again. "I'm not going anywhere."

Rick took a moment to compose himself. "Well. I've been thinking about our future, too. I'm really excited about you wanting to try to build things. I have a feeling it will make you very happy, and I want that more than anything.

"I've been thinking about a new career for me as well. I think I really kicked into gear after my parents' visit. Oh, baby, I was so mad at them that day. I could go on and on about it, but I won't. That's why I haven't really talked about it since. Here's the main thing, though. I decided right then and there we were gonna show 'em. We were gonna be together, and we were gonna take care of ourselves, and to hell with everyone. What my dad said, about possibly losing my job with the postal service for being gay, really hurt. Every day since then, I've been walking that route, thinking about what I could do instead. And it finally came to me. Thing is, I don't think it would have, without you. Are you ready for this?"

Ed grinned. "I think so. What have you got in mind?"

"Well, one of the reasons I love being outdoors, walking every day, is because I enjoy all the different houses I get to visit. I've always been interested in houses, and architecture, and all that stuff, but I never really gave it much thought. Spending time at Mrs. Penfield's, though, really steered me in this direction. I've decided, if you approve, to look into getting a license to sell real estate. I know you have to take classes, but I don't know much more about it. What do you think?"

Ed nodded, smiling. "I think it's a great idea, darlin'."

Rick smiled back at him, excitement in his eyes. "It'll be hard going for a while. I mean, I can't quit my job. But I figure, between the two of us, we can put together a plan, moneywise and timewise, that will work. See, I don't know if anyone in Porterfield will let a faggot sell their house, so that's where you come in. I'm thinking we buy a house, one that's not in the greatest shape, dirt cheap. Then we'll fix it up and sell it. You know enough to do most of the work, and I'll be your grunt, fetching tools, or whatever you need me to do.

"See, we can sell that house for a profit, and move on to another one." He laughed. "We can beautify Porterfield one house at a time. Eventually, we can work ourselves up to the house we really want. I know this is throwing most of the hard work on you, but I'll learn by watching you, and hopefully I can take over a lot of it as we go. What do you think?"

Ed shook his head in amazement. "I think it's great. Why, there's no end to what we can do together, if we just use our own skills. You're right. To hell with everyone who doesn't approve of us."

"I'm so glad you like my ideas, baby." Rick leaned over for a kiss. "Oh, I don't see this happening right away. First, I want to move in with you. I think we need time to get used to each other, living together, but when we've got everything figured out, the sky's the limit. Baby, I feel like I could move mountains when I'm with you."

He took Ed's hand, holding it tight. "So, Ed Stephens. Yes, I'll move in with you, but will you be my lover, my husband, and maybe someday my business partner? Will you marry me?"

Now it was Ed's turn to cry. "Yes," he whispered, looking at his hand tightly clasped in Rick's. "Yes, I will."

Rick kissed him, a kiss that promised a lifetime full of kisses. "I'll do everything I can to be worthy of the title of Ed's lover. Being your boyfriend has been the greatest experience of my life. I can only imagine how wonderful being something more will be."

Ed was glad the paper towels were still in reach. "This is . . . is . . . all so much more than I even hoped for, but I'm so happy." He laughed through the tears. "Just so damned excited. Oh, darlin', we're gonna have a wonderful life together, I just know it."

"Me too, baby." Rick threw his head back and hollered at the ceiling. *"Ya-a-a-a-ay! He said yes. He wants me as much as I want him."*

Ed decided to do some hollering himself. *"I'm Rick Benton's one-man band, world. I'm the luckiest guy on the whole damned planet."*

Rick jumped to his feet. "C'mon. I don't care how wet or cold it is out there. If I don't run, and jump up and down, I'm gonna explode. C'mon, baby!"

Rick grabbed Ed's hand, and together they ran outside, whooping and hollering. They ran through the woods, shouting for joy, jumping over puddles, and swinging from convenient tree branches. They finally paused by the lakeshore, arms around each other, panting and laughing.

"Oh, Ed," Rick whispered, holding Ed tight. "I promise you, even through the bad times, even through the times we get so disgusted we almost hate each other, I promise I'll love you as much as I do right now."

Ed didn't answer him. Instead he picked up the stick Rick had used the day before to carve their names in the mud. He added his own words, below Rick's. ED LOVES RICK 4 EVER.

"'Cause I do, darlin. I really do."

Chapter Twenty-two

It sucks, but all good things must come to an end. By dusk that Sunday night, Ed and Rick were back in Rick's car, heading south. When Rick had them safely on the interstate, they began to talk, getting specific about their immediate plans.

"At some point," Rick was saying, "I want us to rent a U-Haul and head down to Indy. I sold almost all of my furniture before I moved up here, but I have a few things stored at my parents' house. The rest of my books, my records"—he grinned at Ed—"which aren't nearly as cool as yours are; my kitchen stuff. I also have my favorite reading chair and floor lamp, which I think will go great in the west corner of your—I mean, our—living room."

"Anything you want, darlin'," Ed said, reaching for Rick's hand.

"I've also got my bed, which isn't any bigger or better than yours, but we might as well haul it up here. When we can afford it, I'd really like to get a bigger bed for us. I know we usually end up right next to each other, but we're big guys, and I think a bigger bed would be more practical, especially if my back goes out again."

Ed laughed. "Yeah, I didn't exactly like bunking on the couch."

"I really want us to sit down before this happens and go over your budget, too. I intend to pay for half of everything, but I was thinking, since you're already doing fine with the mortgage payments, maybe instead of paying half, I'd made an *extra* mortgage payment every month. That would get us out of debt faster."

Ed shook his head in wonder. "You've really thought this all out. I think that's a great idea."

"Well, things will be a little tight for a while, because I still want to send some money Claire's way to help with stuff for the kids. I've given up on the idea of a newer car for me, and I don't suppose we'll be able to do any of the traveling I'd like us to do when my vacation kicks in, but I'm willing to sacrifice it all, if it means being with you and building toward our future together. What do you think, baby?"

"I feel the same way, darlin'. It all sounds great, except for one thing."

"What?"

Ed leaned over the gearshift and whispered in Rick's ear. "When."

Rick sighed heavily. "I know. That's the only sticking point. I meant to talk about it this afternoon, but I got so carried away with the other stuff, I let it go." He sighed again, taking his hand away from Ed's to rub his eyes. "I'm worried about the kids' reaction to all of this. I mean, it was just a little more than a year ago that Hank took off. I don't want them to think they're being abandoned again."

"Darlin', you're just moving across town."

"I know. I want to break the news to Claire first, then sit down and have a really good talk with the kids. Fortunately they're crazy about you, and I want them to understand they're not losing an uncle, they're gaining one. I also want to reassure them they can call or come over anytime they need me. Baby, please understand. I can't leave until I know they're okay with it. I just can't."

Ed looked out the window, barely seeing the WELCOME TO INDIANA sign and the lights of the Indiana Toll Road ahead. He thought about how much he had hoped to have Rick with him before the tulips bloomed. Now he wondered if that would happen. Already, it seemed, the warm glow of their weekend together was fading.

He took Rick's hand, determined to keep his disappointment to himself. "I understand, darlin'. I want you to do exactly what you need to do, because I want you to move in happy and guilt-free. But do you think"—he chuckled—"you can give me a *guess* as to when? Not to be pushy or anything."

Rick glanced at him, his warm and tender special reassuring Ed it would work out in their favor. "Soon, baby," he said. "Soon."

<the>◆<the>

Rick dropped Ed off at his house, telling Ed he didn't want to come in, as it was late and he had to get to bed for work the next day.

"Soon we'll be together all the time, I promise," he said, kissing Ed in the car.

Ed could feel Rick's longing in the kiss, a longing that matched his own.

"We're not just building castles in the air, baby." Rick stroked Ed's hair. "We just gotta get through a few details."

Ed piled his stuff by the back door, then watched Rick drive away. He opened the door to a meowing Jett, a note from his mother telling him he was out of milk for the cat, and—he couldn't believe it—a ringing phone.

"Aw, crud," he muttered, kicking a pile of bedding across the kitchen floor. "I guess I'm home."

Was he home, he wondered as the evening wore on, or in hell? He took no less than four calls for jobs that had to be done, "as soon as you can get here, Ed, I really need you." His mother called from the warpath, complaining that Jett had tried to bite her when she stopped by the house to feed him, and told Ed he could just find some other fool to feed that beast the next time he took it into his head to run off. Ed was about to take the phone off the hook when Norma called back to tell him she'd smelled something funny in the refrigerator and just when had he last cleaned it? He finally crawled into bed, setting the alarm an hour earlier than usual, hoping to get a jump start on Monday's work.

Rick called Monday morning. Two people were home sick with the flu at the post office, and he'd been assigned extra work. Not only that, he said, but Josh had put off a project for school until the last minute, so now Rick's next two evenings would be spent helping the boy build a desert landscape for his geography class.

"Way things are going, baby, I probably won't see you until Wednesday, but I'll try to call you tonight, okay?"

Ed was stretched out on the sofa when Rick finally called late Monday evening.

"It may have taken God only six days to create the world," Rick sighed heavily over the phone, "but how He got the deserts done so fast I'll never know. I think Josh's ambitions for this thing outreach his artistic abilities. Mine too, for that matter. I am wiped out, baby. I'm going to bed as soon as I finish talking to you."

"I probably will too," Ed commiserated. "I can't believe how much crap broke down in this town while we were gone."

"You're just the glue that holds it together, baby," Rick teased.

"Some glue," Ed said, wincing at the sound of Jett sharpening his claws on the sofa. He reached over to swat him away. "The only thing I could stick to right now, besides you, is my bed. And as for this cat, he's going to end up losing either his claws or his balls. He's really being a pain in the ass. Mom did nothing but bitch about him, and I'm waiting for one of the neighbors to come to the door with a paternity suit."

Rick chuckled. "Ah, things are indeed back to normal, only more so, if that's possible."

Ed's mind wandered back to the quiet lake, the uninterrupted time they'd had together, and their talk on Sunday afternoon.

"Rick, were we fooling ourselves?"

"No," Rick said emphatically. "Things are going to work out in time. We're just back in that damned Real World everyone talks about. Oh, we might have gotten a little carried away, being alone in such a peaceful place, but something tells me no matter what we end up doing, things are still gonna break down, people will still get sick, and at some point you'll probably get mad at me over something and throw a hammer at me. Romantic weekends are great, baby," he sighed, "but it ain't Christmas every day."

"Ain't that the truth," Ed agreed.

Still, he felt a little reassured. Rick was right. He was simply overreacting to a bad Monday. Things would soon calm down.

Or so he thought. Tuesday afternoon, after his usual Tuesday morning with Mrs. Heston, was a repeat of the day before, as he found himself running from job to job, repairing everything from broken windows to leaky faucets. He ended the day at Mrs. West's, who had insisted he stop by and rehang a bird feeder that had been knocked out of her maple tree by some hungry squirrels. He climbed her stepladder, bird feeder in hand, feeling, as Rick would say, wiped out. He clung to a tree limb for a moment, trying to gather the energy to descend the ladder without repeating his disaster at Rick's parents'.

"Ed?" Mrs. West called from her back steps. "Look at this banister." She gave the wrought-iron railing on her steps a good shake. "See how loose this is? Can you reinforce this for me today? I can just see myself taking a tumble like poor Gladys Mertzel, breaking a hip."

Ed slowly climbed back to earth and said apologetically, "Mrs. West, I am really beat right now. Can I take care of it in the morning?"

Mrs. West squinted at him. "Why, Ed, you don't look very good. You coming down with something? There's lots of flu going around, you know."

"Yeah, so I've heard." He grabbed the ladder, which seemed to weigh a ton.

"You just stick the ladder in the garage," Mrs. West commanded. "I don't want you coming in the house if you're sick."

"Oh, I'm just really tired," he replied. "It's been a long week, and it's only Tuesday."

"Still," Mrs. West said doubtfully. "You go right home and get some rest. You call me tomorrow before you come back over here. Last thing I need is to be around a sick person."

"I'm not sick," he mumbled. "Just tired."

By midevening he'd changed that tune. Yes, he admitted, he was sick, but surely it was no more than a cold, probably brought on by the cold, damp air at the lake cabin. He told Rick as much when he called before bedtime.

"We're up to three people off with the flu at work. Are you sure it's just a cold? Maybe you should check in with your doctor."

"Aw, crud," Ed muttered. "Why is everybody so determined to give me the flu? I'm a little run-down, and I caught a cold. No big deal. I'll stay home tomorrow, take some aspirin, and I'll be back at it on Thursday."

Rick sighed. "Well, I sure wish I was there to play nurse for you, like you did for me that time with my back, but we're so swamped at work, I'm not gonna have any time to myself tomorrow. Thank God this desert is built. It ain't no Sahara, but it'll do."

"Don't worry about it. I'm probably better off here alone anyway. No sense in you catching my cooties." Ed paused to cough. "Hell, there's enough of 'em floating around that post office."

"Baby, you don't sound well at all," Rick said, a trace of worry in his voice. "You take it real easy, you hear? I promise to stop by sometime tomorrow afternoon, or tomorrow night."

"With some butter pecan?" Ed teased.

"If that's what you want, you got it."

"No, I want rocky road. Bring me some ice cream, and I'll relieve you of any guilt for not being here."

After canceling his Wednesday jobs, Ed went to bed, falling asleep almost before he had the covers pulled back. He tossed and turned more than usual, and finally woke up at three to take more aspirin. The phone woke him up five hours later.

"Ed? It's your mother. What's this I hear about you being sick over there?"

"Oh, Mom-m-m," he groaned. "Who told you that?"

"Rick called here this morning, all worried about you. I knew he was a good man. He said he couldn't get over there to see you until tonight, and wanted me to check up on you. I already made an appointment with Dr. Weisberg. You be in his office at ten-fifteen, you hear? Do you want me to take you?"

"Aw, crud," Ed moaned. "Dr. Weisberg? Mom, I'm not that sick, I just have a cold."

"I'll just bet you only have a cold," Norma barked. "Oh, I know you, Ed Stephens. You never admit when you're sick. Just like your father. This town is full of flu right now, and you've got it, you just won't admit it. I'll be over there at ten to drive you to the doctor's. Honestly. How would you survive if I wasn't looking out for you?"

"I don't have an answer to that question right now, Mom," he said, raspy-voiced, clinging to the wall. Standing upright seemed to take an enormous effort. "But if you insist on hauling me off to Weisberg's office, I'll be ready. Like I have a choice."

Ed managed to get himself dressed and ready by ten o'clock, but it was quite an effort.

"Everyone wanted me to have the flu," he grumbled, feeding the cat, "so now I've got it. Okay, everybody, are you happy?" He coughed long and hard, almost scaring Jett away from his bowl. "Damn," he said to the cat, "I feel like shit."

As usual, Dr. Weisberg was running late. Ed sat slumped in a chair, wanting to stretch out on the floor. His coughs echoed around the room along with those of several other miserable patients.

"Oh, this place is just a disease pit," Norma hissed to him. "Why doctors stopped making house calls, I'll never know. Why, I remember that ear infection you had in kindergarten. I called Dr. Weisberg and he came right over. The state of medicine today is a disgrace."

"I'll be sure and tell the doctor that, Mom," Ed whispered, giving up on the magazine in his lap. He couldn't seem to concentrate on it.

"Humph. Old goat should be retired by now anyway," Norma mumbled. "They'll probably carry his dead body out of this office, still wearing his stethoscope. Still," she allowed, "he's done right by our family all these years. Why, I remember the night you were born, him standing over me chewing gum of all things. Held you up and told me you were a boy. Now look at you. Sick as a dog."

Ed didn't quite follow that, but chalked it up to either his mother's usual ramblings, or the fact that the flu that had taken over his thought process along with everything else.

The nurse, who was almost as old as Dr. Weisberg, called his name. He stumbled into the examining room she indicated, and collapsed on a chair. In here, at least, he was safe from more of Norma's comments on modern medicine and family history.

Dr. Weisberg shuffled in a few minutes later, his usual kindly doctor's expression on his wrinkled face.

"Well, there, Ed," he said cheerfully. "Looks like the flu to me. I can tell that from here. You're the fourth one I've seen today."

Great, Ed thought. He had gotten out of bed and put up with his mother for an hour to be told what he already knew.

"Nasty strain moving through town right now," Dr. Weisberg continued, shoving a thermometer under Ed's tongue with a palsied hand. "Bad time of the year, early spring. People think it's behind them, but it's still hanging around to knock them down."

The doctor checked Ed's blood pressure, then put his cold stethoscope on Ed's chest. He removed the thermometer, squinting at it through his glasses.

"A hundred and two," he murmured, shaking his head. "Not good, there, Ed. Still, you're young and strong, you'll beat this off in a few days. I'm going to write you a prescription, though. Thing I'm worried about with the late winter flu is pneumonia setting in. People think it's warm and they can do whatever they want. I can just see you out there with that toolbox before you're healthy enough for work. I don't care who calls you, you stay home and tell them to wait, or call someone else, for at least a week. No sense spreading this around anymore."

"How am I suppose to pay you if I'm not working?" Ed asked sourly.

Dr. Weisberg laughed. "Oh, we'll get the money out of you one way or another. You just stay in bed, drink lots of fluids, and keep up with the aspirin, along with this antibiotic."

The doctor hobbled over to the sink to wash his hands. Ed had to admit that Norma was right about one thing: Dr. Weisberg was way past normal retirement age. The doctor had never been anything but kind to Ed, and Ed genuinely liked the old man, but watching him fumble with the paper towel dispenser, Ed knew he'd want someone else if stitches or surgery were required.

"You come back in a week if you're not any better," Dr. Weisberg said on his way out of the room. "But I'm sure you'll be just fine."

Norma deposited Ed at home, then took off for the drugstore. She returned with a bottle of pills and brought one in to Ed, who was in bed, Jett by his side. She gave the cat a dirty look, but managed to keep her thoughts about him to herself. Ed took the pill and gratefully sipped the orange juice she had brought as well.

"Thanks, Mom," he said, trying to smile at her. "I feel like I'm ten years old again."

"Humph. Sometimes you act like a ten-year-old. Well, unless you need anything else, I'm going home. You can call me. Honestly, this family would go to hell in a handcart if I wasn't around."

She marched out of the room, while Ed shook his head, finally managing a smile. Oh, Norma was a bossy, opinionated old broad, but Ed realized he hadn't done bad at all in the mother lottery.

He fell asleep, but woke up sometime later to the sound of someone moving around his kitchen. *Aw, crud*, he thought, sitting up. *I'm sick in bed and now I'm being robbed.*

"Hello?" he rasped.

He heard footsteps, and much to his surprise, Laurie appeared in the doorway.

"Hey, you. Mom asked me to come over and heat up some soup for you, since I'm not working today. After Todd and the kids got this mess and I didn't, I'm guessing I must be immune or something. Mom's at home, washing her hands thirty times, bitchin' up a storm about being in Dr. Weisberg's office with all those sick people."

They shared a laugh, Ed's ending in a cough.

"Oh, Lord, I'm sorry," Laurie said, handing him his juice glass. "No more Mom cracks. I swear! I'll be back with your soup in a minute."

Laurie returned with a bowl of chicken noodle on a bed tray she'd brought with her. Ed sat up, gratefully spooning the hot soup down his sore throat.

"This is great of you," he murmured, "coming over like this."

"No problem." Laurie shrugged it off. "I tell you, though," she continued, petting Jett, "after seeing Todd and both kids through this, I'm about half tempted to go back to school and see about a nursing degree. I still can't believe I didn't get it." She shook her head.

"Hey, maybe you're like those people in that Stephen King book Rick's reading," he said, putting his spoon down. "Almost everyone in the world dies of the flu, then this handful of survivors has to go about rebuilding society."

Laurie shuddered. "Rebuild *our* society? No, thanks. I'd rather be one of the dead ones. Hey, I can take off if you want to be alone. I know how crummy you feel."

"Actually, it's kind of nice to have some company." Ed went back to his soup.

"Well, then." She smiled. "If you're up to it, tell me about your weekend."

Ed, in between spoonfuls of soup and coughing fits, managed to fill Laurie in on the plans he had made with Rick.

"I'm so glad, Ed," she said, nibbling on one of the crackers from the tray. "I remember last fall, telling you that you'd know if you were really in love with him or not. Well, you don't have to convince me. You guys are completely perfect for each other. I mean, watching the two of you together? It's like reading a romance novel where the main characters are both men. So what's the bottleneck? Why isn't he moving his stuff over here?"

Ed explained Rick's concerns about the children's feelings. Laurie shrugged impatiently.

"The kids will be fine. He'll only be a phone call away, for God's sake. Maybe I'm being selfish for your sake, but I think dragging it out is a mistake."

Ed shook his head. "No, I don't want him moving so much as a pair of socks in here until he's right in his mind about it. You don't know him as well as I do, Laurie. He's such a responsibility freak. I know those kids will be a part of our lives for a long time, and I'm okay with that. If he's gonna be here with me, though, I want him with no guilt."

Laurie frowned. "How long is this gonna take?"

"Soon, he says."

"It'd better be," she grumbled.

Ed sighed, shifting around under the covers. Every bone and muscle in his body ached, and he couldn't find a comfortable position.

"It will be. If either one of us had any doubts about us, they're gone now. I know we just spent two days away in an incredibly romantic setting, and I know it's not day-to-day life, but, Laurie, I knew. I knew, talking with him on Sunday, that we'd be together, probably forever. Am I crazy?"

She shook her head, a faraway look in her eyes. "I remember one time when Todd and I went over to Cedar Point. He hadn't asked me to marry him, but I was sure he was going to. I'd thought about it, and I wasn't sure if I wanted to, wasn't convinced he was just the right guy or whatever. Anyway, he dragged me on the Blue Streak. Remember how that roller-coaster scared me when we were kids?"

Ed managed a chuckle without coughing. "Oh, how I tortured you on that thing. Telling you I saw the support beams coming loose and all. Remember Mom threatening to send me back to the car for making you cry? Oh, that was a day. I never got you on a roller-coaster ever again."

Laurie giggled. "I was so mad at you that day. Still, I got even with you. I made Dad make you take me on the Scrambler ten times in a row. But the thing was, here was Todd making me go on that thing again. I was scared, and I didn't want to admit it. But he knew, without me saying anything. You know how those ride guys tell you to hold on to the safety bar and stuff? Todd didn't. He put his arm around me, told me to relax and just enjoy the ride. And for the first time ever, I did. I loved it. Can you believe it? I wanted to go on it again. Anyway, we got off, and I looked at Todd, saw his smile, and all of a sudden I knew. Don't ask me how, I just *knew*. And two weeks later when he showed up with a ring, I was ready to take it."

"Hmm. I'd love to go on the Blue Streak with Rick, but I doubt they're open for the season yet."

"Ha, ha, smart-ass. What I am trying to tell you, and I guess I'll have to spell it out for your fevered brain, is that, no, I don't think you're crazy. I fully intend to be with Todd, until death do us part, and I'm predicting it will be the same with you and Rick. I know gay relationships are different, but I also know a thing or two about love. You guys are the real thing. Period. Just tell him to get his butt over here, and start making those dreams come true."

Laurie had been smiling, but her face went very serious. "When Dad died, so young like he did, I realized that life is damned short. Don't put off anything that'll make you happy. That's why I'm making Todd take me to Hawaii next winter."

"Hawaii!"

"Yeah. I've always wanted to go, so why wait until we're too old to appreciate it?"

Ed thought about that. He shrugged painfully. "Soon, Laurie. That's all I can say."

"Okay, okay," she said, taking the tray. "But you can tell him for me I fully expect to have a brother-in-law by summer, you hear?"

❧•❧

Ed went back to sleep after Laurie left. He didn't know how long he'd been dead to the world when he felt a hand on his forehead. He pushed his eyes open, and saw Rick sitting on the bed, smiling at him.

"How ya doin', baby?" Rick asked softly.

"I've had better days." Ed groaned, trying to sit up, but Rick wouldn't let him. "What time is it?" he asked, looking toward the clock.

"It's time for some supper, if you want any. Looks like you managed some soup at lunch. You want some more? I brought the ice cream, like I promised."

Ed blinked at the clock. It was almost six, he noted, surprised he'd slept so long. "Laurie came over and fixed the soup. Sure, I can probably eat some more. Why aren't you at home?"

"I told Claire I had a sick kid of my own to take care of. She shooed me out of the house and told me to stay over here as long as you needed me."

Ed coughed, then coughed again. "Damn! Darlin', you know your being here is great, but I don't want you to get sick, too."

"I'll take my chances," Rick said, stroking Ed's hair. "If I was living here, it'd be no different. Now, what kind of soup do you want? I'm not sure what's in the cabinet."

Ed thought about his earlier conversation with Laurie. Yes, if Rick was in permanent residence, getting sick from each other was a chance they'd take, just like any other couple. *Geez. Why am I protesting?*

"I think there's some vegetable soup out there," he rasped. "I bought a bunch of it while it was on sale."

"You got it." Rick kissed Ed's cheek. "I may hold off on a real kiss for a few days, if you don't mind."

Ed just rolled his eyes. Rick got up.

"Eat all your soup," he said, trying to imitate Norma's voice, "and you'll get some ice cream. Honestly."

"Oh," Ed moaned. "Don't make me laugh. It hurts."

Ed managed to eat all of his soup, so Rick brought him a bowl of rocky road as a reward. The cold ice cream felt as comforting as the hot soup had.

"Can you believe this?" Ed sighed. "I couldn't even tell you the last time I got the flu. Man, am I paying for it. I'll be honest, I feel like strung-out shit."

"You look it, too," Rick said, and smirked.

"Oh, thanks. I really needed that."

"Don't worry about it. I've seen worse, living with three kids. Hey, you want me to sleep on the couch tonight?"

Ed looked at him surprise. "You're spending the night?"

Rick nodded with his warm and tender special. "I spent this whole day worrying about you. How would I get any sleep, not knowing how you are?"

"Geez, it's just the flu. I'm not dying. I may feel like it, but I'm not."

"People have been known to die of the flu," Rick said sternly. "I'm sure you're not going to be one of them, but all the same, I'll stay here where I can keep an eye on you. Someone has to. You want me to call your mother?"

Ed coughed in alarm. Rick laughed.

"I thought so. Now, bed or couch for me?"

Ed thought about it. "I'd rather have you here, next to me, but if I can't handle it, then I'll throw you out. I have a feeling you may be better medicine than those pills Dr. Weisberg gave me."

⋈•⋈

Rick spent most of the evening in the living room, engrossed in his Stephen King novel. Ed thought about joining him, but instead stayed in bed, eyes closed, letting his thoughts ramble. At one point he heard Rick moving around, and soon after soft music came from the stereo. Ed smiled, recognizing the song, Mercy's "Love (Can Make You Happy)." As awful as he felt, Ed had to admit that love, indeed, had made him happy.

Rick's face appeared around the door. "Is that bothering you?" he asked anxiously.

"Not one bit," Ed assured him. "But hold off on the rock-and-roll records, okay?"

Rick smiled and nodded. "I thought of that. Nothing but slow and easy stuff. I just wish you were up to another dance."

"The minute I'm better," Ed promised. He noticed Rick was holding on to his book. "How's the state of the world?"

"Not good," Rick said. "It seems to be setting up for some epic battle between good and evil. It's good reading, but scary to think about. I tell you though," he said, shaking his head, "all these characters sitting back and watching their families die around them. Baby, I don't know what I'd do if I lost you. I'd probably end up on the evil team, just out of spite."

"You couldn't be evil if you tried."

Ed motioned for Rick to sit on the bed. The record changer clicked, and New Colony Six came on with "Things I'd Like to Say."

"This song is so sad," Ed murmured. "But I love it. Always have. You think of me dying, well, I can't imagine you leaving me for someone else. Trust me, that would make *me* evil."

"The guy in the song is so *resigned*," Rick said. "I mean, listen to the words. He's just letting her go marry some other guy. I can't imagine doing that. I'd fight like hell for you."

"Well," Ed said, "he's asking her, really, if this guy's good enough for her. I mean, he was hoping she loved him enough to marry him, but she loves this other guy that way. I just can't imagine my heart breaking like that." Ed felt tears in his eyes. "Oh, don't mind me," he said, embarrassed. "It's just the flu making me all weak and stupid."

"You may be temporarily weak, but you're anything but stupid." Rick wiped away the tears. "I love you, baby, and you're the only man I want to marry. You don't have to worry about that."

Ed sniffled, then coughed. "Yeah, I know," he croaked.

Rick laughed softly. "I think you've had enough for one day. Why don't you try and go back to sleep? I'll do my best not to disturb you when I come to bed."

Rick left the room, closing the door behind him, muting the music from the living room.

Ed lay back against the pillows, sighing. He didn't really think Rick would ever leave him for someone else. However, the mere thought of Rick looking at another man the way he looked at Ed made him ache even worse. He shook his head, trying to knock such thoughts out of his head. He knew his illness was making him gloomier than he needed to be. Still, Ed wondered how he would feel if he was in a position to sing "Things I'd Like to Say" for real. He figured it would hurt a hell of a lot more than the flu.

He fell into a fitful sleep, and barely noticed when Rick crawled into bed beside him. He came fully awake later, surprised to see Rick there next to him. Ed got up for more aspirin and a glass of water. When he returned to bed, Rick was still asleep, snoring away as he usually did. Ed quietly slid in, carefully putting his arms around him. Ed snuggled against Rick and sighed happily, in spite of the pervasive ache in his body.

No, darlin', he thought to himself, *I wouldn't just turn evil if someone tried to take you away from me, I'd kill 'em.*

⋘•⋙

Ed wasn't feeling any better the next morning, but sent Rick off to work, telling him not to worry. His mother called, but Ed assured her he didn't need a thing, that Rick was taking care of everything.

"I tell you," Norma said. "I don't know what you did to deserve that man, but you just thank your lucky stars, Ed. I hate to admit it, but he's probably better than any girl I would have picked out for you. When you're through coughing up all those germs, I want the two of you over here for dinner, you hear me?"

"Yes, Mom," he said, coughing into the phone.

"Oh, honestly. Get back to bed. I'll check on you tomorrow," Norma barked before slamming the phone down.

Rick returned after work and fussed over Ed all evening.

"I could get really used to this," Ed teased, holding out his bowl for more ice cream.

"Well, don't you even think about getting sick on a regular basis. I probably shouldn't say it, but, baby, you're about as sexy as that pile of beer cans from last weekend."

"Man," Ed exclaimed, not coughing for a change. "Now that's the incentive I need to get better."

"See that you do," Rick said, leaving the room with the ice cream bowl. "I want my handyman back in full form for other things besides sleeping in that bed, ya know."

The phone rang. Ed heard Rick answer it, but couldn't quite make out the conversation. Rick reappeared a few minutes later.

"That was Mrs. Penfield," he told Ed. "She heard through the grapevine about you being down with the flu. I swear, baby, every old lady in this town is pulling for you. Anyway, she sends her best wishes, and wants us to come for a visit when you're feeling better." Rick grinned. "She said something about a wedding present. What on earth is that all about?"

Ed chuckled and coughed. "Oh, I told her that our moving in together was the same as two straight people getting married, so she wants to do something nice for us." He shook his head, smiling. "Darlin', what would we do without her?"

"I don't know, baby. I do know one thing, though. The next time my parents come to visit, I'm sending them over to her for a good talking to."

On Friday Ed's temperature returned to normal, but he was very tired, and never far away from a box of tissue.

"Baby, I never knew you had so much snot in you," Rick said, emptying the bedroom wastebasket.

Ed threw a pillow at him. Rick ducked, laughing, and hurried out of the room, whistling "One Man Band."

Saturday afternoon found Ed pacing around the house, feeling like a caged lion. He felt better, but knew he should follow Dr. Weisberg's advice and stay inside a few more days.

The weather had turned warm once again, and he stuck his nose out the front door, inhaling that unique scent of spring. The trees were in full bud, and Ed imagined the leaves that would soon sprout. Spring, then summer, then back to fall again, he thought, remembering the day he was raking leaves, hoping to meet the new mailman on his front path. *Where will we be by this fall?* he wondered.

Having Rick in the house with him these past few days had made being sick tolerable, and Ed suddenly knew that Laurie was right, they were wasting time. He slammed the door shut, determined to talk to Rick that evening, hoping to change *soon* to *now*. Apparently Claire and the children had survived without him this week, so maybe the time had come.

Rick returned from work in his usual joyful Saturday afternoon mood. He was pleased to find Ed feeling stronger, and declared an end to soup eating. He was, he said, going to order a pizza for their supper. Ed, catching his mood, stacked some records on the turntable, picking out those he knew Rick enjoyed the most.

At one point Rick cocked his head at Ed. "You trying to tell me something, baby?" he teased, as "More Today Than Yesterday" followed "This Guy's in Love with You" on the stereo.

"Who, me?" Ed asked innocently. "The pizza's here. Go pay the guy."

They were at the kitchen table, scarfing the pizza, Ed pleased to find that his appetite was truly back, when the phone rang.

"I'll get it," Rick said, starting to get up.

"No," Ed said, getting up. "I'll get it. It's probably Mom. She hasn't called yet today."

He stepped into the living room and turned down the volume on "One Man Band," anticipating Norma's demand to "turn off that racket."

He grabbed the phone in midring. "Hello?"

"Hello," said an unfamiliar man's voice. "Can I talk to Rick?"

Ed frowned, puzzled. He couldn't imagine who it was. "May I tell him who's calling?"

"This is Jack, an old friend of his from Indy. I really need to talk to him."

Ed's body went numb. He felt his knees begin to give out, and with his free hand, he grabbed the telephone table.

"Just a minute," he whispered into the phone.

Ed gently placed the receiver on the table. He turned and stepped back into the kitchen.

Rick was leaning across the table, grabbing another piece of pizza from the box.

"For me?" he asked, not bothering to look up. "Is it Claire?"

"No," Ed said quietly.

Rick looked at him, bewildered.

"It's Jack," Ed said, with a calm he didn't feel. "He says he needs to talk to you."

Chapter Twenty-three

The mournful America ballad "I Need You" poured out of Ed's stereo speakers. He told himself he was a fool to be listening to a breakup song, but the constantly repeated "I need yous" only echoed what was on his mind. He needed Rick. Badly. But at the moment, he had no idea where Rick was.

Ed sat hunched in a tight ball on his sofa, a box of Puffs nearby. The flu wasn't quite done with him, and he almost welcomed the coughing and nose-blowing as a distraction from his thoughts. He also knew if he wasn't feeling so weak, he'd be pacing the room, wearing a hole in the living room carpet.

The tone arm lifted off the record, silently moved aside, paused, and returned to play the same record. Ed didn't feel like getting up to find something else to listen to, and he hadn't heard enough "I need yous" yet.

Ed's mind returned to earlier that evening and the phone call that had led to Rick's absence. Rick had dropped a slice of pizza on his plate when Ed told him who was on the phone. He'd gone to the living room with a sigh of annoyance, muttering, "How in the hell did he track me down here?"

Ed sat down in his chair, trembling. Oh, he was still shaky from the flu, but his current condition was brought on by hearing Jack's voice on the phone. Smooth and low, it was a voice not unlike the late-night radio disc jockeys Ed had always enjoyed. Rick had once shown him a picture of Jack. Yes, the voice went with the rest of the package. Jack was compellingly handsome; dark, mysterious, and sexy. Ed had no problem understanding Rick's attraction to him.

Since his chair at the table was no more than a few feet from the phone, Ed couldn't help but overhear Rick's side of the phone call. He sat facing away from Rick, his eyes glued to his plate, his ears glued to Rick's voice.

"Hello? Hey, Jack. How did you . . . ? Oh. I see." Rick sighed again, listening. "Well, I'm sorry to hear that, but . . ." Another sigh came from Rick, this one of exasperation. "Well, if you must know, I'm eating pizza with the man I love, the man I've asked to marry me. What? Oh, fuck you. What do you know about it, anyway?"

There was a longer pause. Ed resisted the temptation to look at Rick.

"Yeah, well, I guess I don't have much of a choice, do I? As usual, your timing is impeccable. I'll be there in a few minutes."

Rick hung up the phone. "Aargh," he growled. He walked to Ed and lightly put a hand on Ed's shoulder. "Baby, I'm sorry, but I have to leave for a while. That goofball is over at Claire's right this minute. I have to get rid of him. I don't want him hanging around the kids. It sounded to me like he's half loaded."

Ed coughed. "How did he find you?"

Rick's hand tightened on his shoulder. "Well, he had come with me to visit Claire and the kids several times when we were together, so he knew the way to Claire's house. Someone I *used* to consider a friend told him I had moved here."

"What's he want?"

Rick left the room, saying over his shoulder, "I'm not a hundred percent sure, but from past experience, I'd say he's probably all alone and broke, and he's come here to see if good old Rick's still stupid enough to feel sorry for him. Well, I don't."

Rick reappeared in the kitchen, wearing the jacket Ed had gotten him for Christmas. "All I care about is getting him the hell away from my family. I also don't want him anywhere near you, although I should probably bring him over here, so he could see what a real man looks like. I won't, though. I don't want him to know where you—I mean we—live."

Rick patted his pockets, checking for his keys and wallet. "Baby, just leave this mess on the table. I'll clean it up when I get back."

He paused at the back door. Ed looked into his face. That look Rick always had when he thought of Jack was there, a look of pain and confusion. Ed knew he was being foolish, but that look had always scared him, and it scared him now.

"Don't worry," Rick said, biting his lip, something Ed had never seen him do. "I'll take care of this, and . . . oh, hell. I'll be back as soon as I can."

Rick bolted out the door, and soon Ed heard the sound of his car starting. He looked up and saw Rick's Monte Carlo pull onto Grant Street, pause briefly at the corner, then roar westward on Coleman.

Ed looked at the pizza, amazed that whatever had just happened had taken place in less than five minutes. The pizza was even still warm. Like a funnel cloud, Jack had swept down from the sky and taken Rick away from him.

Rick hadn't kissed him before he left. He didn't say "I love you, baby." Ed couldn't remember the last time Rick had failed to do that.

And so, here he was, two hours later, alone on a Saturday night with only the cat and an America record for company. He prayed for the phone to ring, but it didn't. He even checked to make sure there was a dial tone. The phone was working fine, it just wasn't ringing with a call from Rick.

Ed rocked back and forth on the sofa. When had Rick first told him about Jack? He thought back, and it came to him: It was their first official date, the night Rick had brought him roses. They had been having dinner together—ironically enough, delivered pizza—right here in this house, sharing their life stories.

"I met this guy, Jack, when I was twenty-four," Rick had said, pushing a piece of pepperoni around his plate with a fork. "He was handsome, witty, charming, popular. I fell for him like a ton of bricks. My God, what a fool I was. I pursued him like crazy. I was tired of being alone, and I was convinced he was the man for me. I finally convinced him that we should get an apartment together. He somehow convinced himself that he was in love with me. I don't know, maybe he was for real.

"Thing was, I didn't understand a lot of things. I didn't know that most of the guys who hung around those bars where there mostly for sex. I hadn't been out very long, and I was completely green where the gay scene was concerned.

"I had gone through this whole long struggle with myself about being gay and how I was going to live my life. It was like I had to have a . . . plan in mind before I really acted on it. So I thought, when I finally got the courage to go to those places, that I'd meet some guy, we'd fall in love, and that would be it. I met a lot of guys and had a lot of sex, but I really wanted love. I guess when I saw Jack, I decided the time had come.

"It wasn't until after we moved in together that I found out why he was so popular. He was a great-looking guy, and everyone wanted him. Turned out Jack wanted most of them, too." Rick sighed. "And he drank a lot and smoked a lot of dope. I'd never been much of a partier, and it drove me crazy. I'd come home from work, and there he'd be, half wasted at three in the afternoon, usually some of his loser friends hanging around. And poor, old, stupid Rick, why *he* thought Jack had been out looking for a job all day.

"It went on like that for a long time. Oh, occasionally he'd get some half-assed job, but he'd end up losing it 'cause he was always late to work, or didn't bother to show up at all. I didn't want to see it, but the truth was he was using me. I had a good job, good pay, and I took care of everything. He had a place to live away from his parents, a place to party, and, hell, some guy to play with when he wasn't being pursued by every other guy in town.

"I finally woke up the night he totaled my car. He'd gone out with some of those worthless friends of his and had gotten drunk, and ran my car right off I-465 into a ditch. He was afraid he'd get busted for drunk driving, so he ran off, leaving the car. He came home about four in the morning and told me it had been stolen. The cops called and told me where my car was, and blah, blah, blah. Jack was a pretty good liar, and I fell for some of his shit, but not this time. I just knew he was lying. All of a sudden, all the anger I'd held in exploded. I threw him out of the apartment."

"Then what happened?" Ed asked, captivated by the story.

"Oh, of course he apologized, said he'd make it up to me, and all that shit. I took him back. Nothing changed. I threw him out again. Took him back again. Threw him out for the third time. Finally, when the lease was up on the apartment, I moved out without telling him and took an apartment closer to work. I really thought I was done with him, but he tracked me down on my mail route, tried to make a big emotional play for me, right there on North Delaware, in this sweet little suburban neighborhood." Rick smiled bitterly at the memory. "Two crazy gay guys, arguing there on the street, right in front of Beaver Cleaver's house. But I was done. I told him to fuck off, once and for all, and that I never wanted to see him again."

"Did you?"

Rick snorted. "Yeah, like a bad penny, he'd turn up from time to time, usually wanting something, maybe money, or a place to crash. I let him stay over, once or twice. What can I say? I was lonely, and some part of me still loved him. Last time I saw him was about, oh, seven months or so ago. I was talking with Claire about the possibility of moving up here, if something opened up in the post office. I remember thinking that Porterfield may suck for a gay man, but at least I wouldn't have Jack around."

And so now the bad penny had turned up in Porterfield. Ed blew his nose, wondering what Jack's reason was for tracking Rick down this time. Was he looking for a handout? A place to hide, maybe? Or, and this was what Ed feared the most, Jack wanted Rick back, wanted him back so badly he'd leave Indianapolis and travel a hundred miles to find him.

Ed's common sense told him he had nothing to worry about. Jack was a loser, and Rick was well shed of him. He knew, he *knew* that Rick loved him, wanted to build a life with him, but he kept seeing the look on Rick's face when he had left the house. Ed couldn't even begin to imagine what kind of charm Jack possessed, but he knew from that look that some part of it still worked on Rick.

Abruptly Ed got up and shut off the stereo. He walked into the kitchen to see what time it was. Just past eight.

He looked at the mess on the table, Rick's pizza lying cold on the plate. Rick had said he'd clean it up, but Ed assumed he'd be back long before this. He threw the pizza in the box, then shoved it in the refrigerator. He poured himself some Pepsi over a glass full of ice. The cold, sweet drink comforted his still scratchy throat.

The phone rang. Ed almost dropped his glass. He slammed it on the table, sloshing Pepsi over the side. He ran to the phone and grabbed the receiver.

"Hello?" he gasped.

"Ed? It's Claire."

Ed closed his eyes. "Hi, Claire," he managed.

"I'm sorry, Ed. Rick asked me to call you right after he left, but Angie's here for a sleepover with Judy, and Jane's being the typical, bratty little sister. I've had my hands full trying to keep her away from the girls."

"Where is he?" Ed asked, clutching the receiver.

Claire sighed. "He's on his way to Indy."

"What?"

"Don't freak out, Ed, *please*," Claire pleaded. "I swear everything is okay. That jackass took a bus up here from Indy. I didn't realize that when he came here, or I'd probably never have let him in. Truth is, I still wish I'd slammed the door in his face, then called the cops."

"He came up here on a bus?" Ed asked, his brain still moving slow from the flu and fatigue.

"Yes. He showed up here, insisting I get ahold of Rick for him. Oh, I've always hated that guy, Ed. He's such a jerk. Anyway, he showed up right when Angie was arriving for supper. I hauled Jack into the living room by the phone. He doesn't know your number, Ed, or your last name. I dialed the phone myself, then left the room.

"I was getting the kids their supper when he came in the kitchen, saying Rick was on his way over to talk to him. He smelled like he'd been drinking, so I told him he could just wait out on the driveway. I didn't want him around the kids, and I had to answer enough questions as it was.

"Rick showed up a few minutes later. They sat talking in Rick's car for, oh, I don't know how long. Finally, around seven, Rick came in the house. He said since there weren't any more buses through Porterfield until Monday, he was driving Jack back to Indy. It was either that, or put him up here in town, or drive him to Fort Wayne and look into bus connections there. I think he just wanted to get rid of him as soon as possible. Anyway, he asked me to call you, and he told me to tell you not to worry, that everything's fine. He also said that if he was too tired to drive home, he'd stay at Mom and Dad's and drive back in the morning."

Ed tried to take it all in. "Do you have any idea why he came all the way here?"

"No, and I don't care. He never did anything but make Rick unhappy. Ed, you . . . well, you just can't imagine how glad I am that he's found you. Rick's always been kind of a broody type, but he's been so happy since you've been around. I've never seen him more full of life. Jack is just a user and a loser. Rick knows that, and I'll bet you anything this is the last time Jack ever comes near him."

Ed sighed, relieved to know where Rick was, but still worried. He knew he'd worry until Rick came home. "So you think he'll really stay over in Indy tonight?"

"Actually, I hope so," Claire said. "I'm sure you want to see him, but it's been the usual long day for him, getting up so early for work like he does. I'd feel better if he waited until morning to make the trip back. I'm sure, though, that he'll call you when he gets to Mom and Dad's. He would have called you himself, earlier, but he was really anxious to get going. I don't blame him. That guy gives me the creeps. I probably would have told him to hitchhike his way home, but you know Rick."

"Yeah." Ed managed a weak smile. "My responsibility freak."

"Exactly. He takes that sort of thing so seriously. You know what? I blame Jack for that, too. I think Rick vowed he'd never be like that. I think he's never really forgiven himself for Jack either. He seems to feel he made the same mistake I did with Hank. So what did he do? He moved here, to get away from Jack, and tried to clean up the mess I had made. I love my brother, Ed, but sometimes I just want to kick him. I wish he wouldn't be so hard on himself."

"Me too."

"Hang on a minute, Ed," Claire said impatiently. He heard her talking away from the phone. "Yes, sweetie, go ahead and set up the game. I'll be over just as soon as I finish talking to Uncle Ed. No, I don't care what color I am. Just pick one."

She returned to Ed. "It's Chutes and Ladders for me again tonight. I wish the kid was old enough to understand Monopoly."

Ed chuckled, remembering Rick telling him what a ruthless Monopoly player Claire was.

"Thank heaven Josh is keeping himself entertained," she said. "Rick has him reading *Paddington Bear*, and he loves it." She laughed. "I suppose I should thank you again for that Abba album you gave Judy for her birthday. It's blaring from her room right now. I'm surprised she hasn't worn it out.

"Ed," she continued, "it means so much to Rick, and to me, that you seem to enjoy the kids."

"Oh, I do," he assured her.

"Thanks. They think you're the greatest, and believe me, I can't imagine them ever thinking something like that about Jack. This whole incident tonight, with Jack, really has me thinking. You know, there's no reason why Rick can't do what I know he wants to do, move in with you. We're fine over here, and I think it's time he did something for himself, something good."

"Really?" Ed asked. "Has he spoken to you?"

"Oh, he mentioned it when he came home from the lake last weekend. He said he wanted to talk to me about moving in with you. He"—she giggled—"got all red-faced under his beard, said he'd ask you to marry him. Oh, it was so sweet, Ed. I know I shouldn't laugh, but if you'd known him when he was younger, you'd know how much this means to me, that he's found the right person.

"Anyway, seeing Jack tonight, made me realize that he needs to be with you. I don't know what he's waiting for."

"I do," Ed said. "He's waiting for your approval, and for the kids' approval."

Claire snorted. "Is that all? Well, he has it. We're fine here, really. Josh can have his room to himself again, and now I've got two uncles to tap for babysitting."

Ed's legs gave out on him again. He sank to the floor, dragging the phone with him. "Thank you, Claire. I want him here with me more than you know, but not until he feels right about it, where you and the kids are concerned."

Claire giggled again. "Tell you what, since you'll probably talk to him before I will, tell him his clothes will be in a pile on the front lawn. I'm throwing him out. There! He has no choice but to be with you."

Ed was able to laugh as well. "I'll do that. Thanks again."

"No problem. Ed, you still sound sick to me. Do yourself a favor, and go to bed. Don't worry. Rick will be home in the morning, and when I say he'll be home, I mean at your house. For good. Okay?"

"Okay. Good night, Claire. I hope you beat the pants off Jane at Chutes and Ladders."

He hung up the phone, leaning his head against the wall. He suddenly remembered telling Rick weeks ago that something would happen in the spring, something that would tell them the time was right to officially bring their lives together. It seemed Jack's sudden appearance was that thing.

"I'll be dipped in shit," he muttered. "Who would've ever thought?"

He looked around the quiet room. He tried to remember living there before Rick had come into his life, but couldn't. Every room, every piece of furniture seemed a part of their life together. Even Jett, asleep in his easy chair, seemed as much Rick's cat as his own.

Claire was right; he was exhausted. But he knew he wouldn't sleep, couldn't even consider crawling into that bed without Rick. He looked at the records scattered on the floor near the stereo. He didn't want to listen to them until Rick was back, ready to dance with him again, calling him "baby" with love in his eyes. The common endearment had almost annoyed Ed at first, but now he was so used to it, he couldn't imagine not hearing it every day, hearing the love in those two syllables.

He looked at the clock. If Rick had left Porterfield around seven o'clock, it would be after nine before he reached Indianapolis. Would he stay over or come home? Ed supposed there was nothing to do but wait.

By nine-thirty he was about to climb the walls. He didn't want to go to bed, and he didn't want to be alone in the house. He couldn't stay there without Rick. The hell with doctor's orders, he had to get out of there. He picked up the phone and called Gordy.

"Hell-lo," Gordy answered.

"Hey, Gord, it's Ed. Whatcha doing?"

"Me? On a Saturday night? Oh, I'm having a hell of a good time. Got an orgy going, what do ya think? I'm sitting here in front of the tube, waiting for that shitty new *Saturday Night Live* to come on. Man, that show has sucked since the original cast left."

Ed found himself smiling. Gordy's nonsense, his usual bitching, sounded reassuringly normal. "Well, I was wondering, could I come over for a while?"

"Sure. Hell, I'd love the company. But where in the hell is Rick?"

Ed let out a long breath. "*That* is a very long story. I'll tell you when I get there, okay?"

He slowly pulled himself together, putting on his sneakers, hunting down his truck keys. He knew he should hang around if Rick should happen to call, but he'd been cooped in that house for over four days. He wished he had an answering machine so he could leave a message for Rick, but he'd never had to worry about it before. Everyone else seemed to be getting them these days, so he supposed he would too now that Rick was moving in. Yes, he told himself, Rick was moving in.

"Oh, God," he whispered. "Bring him home safe. Don't let him crash the car on I-69. Please let me see his face, let me tell him that everything's okay for us now."

With one last, lingering glance at the silent phone, Ed left the house.

⟨≋•≋⟩

Shit," Gordy exclaimed when he'd heard the whole story. "Why didn't Claire call *me* when that bastard showed up? Hell, I'da hauled his ass down to the post office, dumped him in a box postmarked Anywhere But Here, and let him sit there in the dark until Monday."

"Well, I'm sure she didn't think of it, Gordy, but maybe she will next time," Ed said wearily.

"Next time! Ed, there's not gonna be a next time, trust me."

"What do you mean?"

Gordy, sighing impatiently, reached for his cigarettes. "The minute Rick dumps that guy in Indy, hopefully in a ditch somewhere on 465, he'll never see him again. There's no way in hell that guy is gonna bother Rick again after tonight." He lit a cigarette, blowing smoke. "Rick may have put up with that shit before he met you, but he won't now."

"I wish I felt as sure as you do," Ed said, coughing.

"Aw, geez, I forgot you've been sick." Gordy reached for an ashtray to stamp out the cigarette.

"No, no." Ed waved his hand. "I'd be coughing, smoke or no smoke. Enjoy it. Please. Hell, I'm half tempted to ask you for one."

Gordy brought the cigarette back to his lips, looking relieved. "Okay, I'll smoke, but you're not. Damn. Rick would kill me if I gave you one of these."

Ed smiled. "Yeah, I guess he would. If he was here."

Gordy shrugged impatiently. "He will be. Don't worry. Rick will be back when he's taken the trash out. And, yes, I am sure there will be no next time. Don't you have eyes in your head? Don't you see the way that guy looks at you? Shit, sometimes, watching him looking at you, I almost get jealous, wondering if any guy will ever look at me like that."

Ed felt a little better, hearing Gordy's confidence. "I can't think of anyone who deserves it more than you do, Gord. I know there's a Rick out there for you somewhere."

"Well, my luck being what it is, I don't s'pose he'll come walking into the Porterfield Post Office, but I guess maybe you're right. Lightning struck big time for you in this town. I don't know if it'll strike twice."

"I got lucky," Ed said, a part of him still not believing it. When he thought back to last fall, when he wondered if the new mailman was gay and how he couldn't imagine that he was, but also couldn't imagine him being attracted to Ed if he *was,* he sometimes felt the last five months had been nothing but a dream. "I don't know why I got so lucky. Rick says sometimes you just get lucky. I don't know, maybe you'll have to look a little harder, but I know there's a guy out there for you."

Gordy blew out a long trail of smoke, watching it float away. "Yeah. I almost drove into Fort Wayne tonight, to Carlton's. I don't know why I didn't. Guess I just didn't feel like going alone, then coming home alone."

"You want Rick and me to go with you some Saturday night?"

Gordy snorted. "Yeah, sure. The big tough guy here needs his friends to hold his hand. No, thanks for the offer, but I can do it on my own. Far as I'm concerned, that place is no place for you two. It's just packed with assholes, like that Jack, who are so miserable and jealous that they'd love nothing more than to come between you, break you up, and make you as miserable as they are. I've seen it in Indy and in Chicago. No, you guys stay home where you belong. When I meet a decent guy, I'll bring him over for dinner, okay?"

"It's a date," Ed promised. "And I bet it'll happen sooner than you think." He coughed again, then yawned.

"Look at you," Gordy said, disgusted. "Still sick, about half-asleep, and driving over here because you're worried about your guy. Hell, if there's one person in this world I wouldn't worry about, it's Rick Benton. Why don't you take your sorry ass home and go to bed?"

Ed shrugged. "It's just so damned quiet there, and I . . . oh, don't bawl me out, Gordy, but I can't help wondering—"

"Bawl you out? Hell, I'm gonna beat you up," he roared. "Get off this, Ed. I know this has been a big surprise and all that, but it don't mean anything. Absolutely nothing. Rick just had a dirty job to do tonight, and he's doing it. He'll be back in the morning, and you'll feel like an asshole, wondering why the hell you were wasting good sleeping time over at my place."

Ed looked at his friend with great affection. "You know what, Gordy? I think I love you."

Gordy threw his hands up in the air, almost throwing his cigarette across the room. "Now he tells me," he exclaimed, eyes heavenward. "Why the hell didn't this happen six months ago?"

Gordy shook his head, then began to laugh. "Oh, what the hell, I love you too, you asshole. I can't tell you how much it's meant to me, having you and Rick for friends lately. It's made a big difference in . . . well, in everything. But since you love me, and since I'm you're new best buddy, I'm gonna tell you something for your own good. Go home. Now."

Ed stood up. He was suddenly incredibly tired, but also at peace. Gordy's words had penetrated the fear he had carried with him all evening. He even thought he could go home and sleep in that bed alone.

"Okay. I'll go home. But do you s'pose I could get a big ole football player hug before I go?"

Gordy stubbed out his cigarette, got up, and approached Ed, arms outstretched. They hugged, tightly, for a long time.

"Thanks, Gordy," Ed said softly.

"Anytime, buddy," Gordy said, just as soft. "Anytime."

Ed stumbled across the parking lot of Gordy's apartment building on Stratton Avenue. He made it into his truck and started for home, braking for the stop signs at every intersection on Grant Street, almost wishing he'd taken the long way around to his house.

As he approached his own block he rubbed his eyes, convinced he was hallucinating. Rick's car was in his driveway. He hit the gas and spun the truck crazily into the driveway next to Rick's car, not bothering to put it in the garage. He jumped out, slamming the door. His weak lungs ached as he ran to the back door. He managed to get through both doors and staggered into the kitchen. He almost collapsed with relief. Rick was on the sofa, Jett in his lap. The stereo was on, "One Man Band" playing softly.

"Well, sick boy, what the hell are you doing out running around in the middle of the night?" Rick asked him, that beautiful, wonderful warm and tender smile on his face.

Ed gasped, then coughed. "I—I was at Gordy's," he choked out. "What are you doing here? Why aren't you in Indy?"

Rick shrugged. "I told you I was gonna clean up the pizza, didn't I?"

Ed couldn't help it. Those damned tears that had been betraying him ever since he got sick returned. He felt them slide out of his eyes, and he put his head down, hoping Rick wouldn't see.

But he did, of course. He pushed the cat aside, leapt to his feet, and had his arms around Ed in a heartbeat.

"Baby, baby, don't cry," he murmured.

Ed took a quivering, almost choking breath. "That's a song by Smokey Robinson and the Miracles, isn't it? I don't have that one."

Rick laughed, holding him tight. "Oh, baby, what I went through tonight. Being away from you just about damn near killed me, but I'm back. I'm about ready to drop dead from being so tired, but I'm back."

Suddenly, Rick began to cry as well. "Look at me, blubbering, and I don't have being sick as an excuse. Oh, I love you so much, baby. I'm so glad I'm here, and you're here. When I came in the house, and you weren't here, why . . . oh, I couldn't imagine where you'd gone, or what you were doing."

"But—but—you told Claire you were staying with your folks tonight," Ed managed to get out.

"I know. I told her that so she wouldn't worry, and so you wouldn't worry about me driving back. But I never had any intention of doing anything but coming right back here."

"I went over to Gordy's," Ed repeated, wiping away his own tears, then Rick's. "I just didn't want to be here alone."

"I thought so, or at least I did when I calmed down. I almost called, but I was sure you'd come home eventually. Plus, I knew if you were with Gordy, I didn't have to worry. He'd take care of you for me."

"I think I need to sit down," Ed said.

Rick led him over to the sofa, then sat next to him, one arm tightly across his shoulders.

"What happened?"

"Oh, baby," Rick sighed. He shook his head and sighed again. "Baby, I promise to tell you every last dumb detail tomorrow when I'm not so tired. Bottom line, the minute I saw him, all I wanted to do was get rid of him. I wasn't even mad at him. All I could think of was to get rid of him, as soon as possible. So I did. And something tells me, from what I said when he got out of the car, that I'll never hear from him again."

"Gordy said you'd be back when you finished taking the trash out."

"He was right. I got rid of the trash, and now I'm back." Rick looked around the room. "Where's that box of Puffs you've been carrying around all week?"

Ed grabbed it from the table next to the sofa. Rick took one and blew his nose.

"Thanks." He tossed it toward the wastebasket and missed. "Still ain't no basketball player, huh, baby?" He laughed.

Ed laughed, too. "I suppose I could tell you I'm glad to see you, but I guess you already figured that out."

"Yeah, I kinda noticed," Rick said, kissing him, the first real kiss he'd given him since Ed had been sick. "Man, that drive home, though. Talk about endless. All I could think about was you. Well, that's not true, you and me, actually. I thought about all that stuff we talked about last weekend at the lake, and how I've been here all week, taking care of you. Don't get mad at me for saying it, but I'm almost glad you got sick. It—it changed something for me. Taking care of you, knowing you needed me, that you wanted me here, even as lousy as you felt. It made me realize that I need to be here with you, all the time. In fact, I was gonna talk to you about it tonight, before I was so rudely interrupted."

"Did you talk to Claire about it tonight?" Ed asked. It was something he needed to know.

"No," Rick said, puzzled. "Why would I, or when would I have had the time?"

"So, you really want to be here, with me, all the time. Move in, change your address, the whole thing, right?"

Rick kissed him again. "I swear, there is nothing more I want in this world. Will you have me?"

Ed threw his head back and laughed. "Yes! Yes, I'll have you. And by the way, when you go home, your clothes are going to be on the front lawn. Claire's throwing you out."

Rick roared with laughter. "She is, huh? Well, then one good thing came out of all of this: I can move in here with no guilt. Nope, no guilt, just love. Lots and lots of love, baby."

Ed sighed happily, safe once again in Rick's arms. Oh, he still felt like shit from being sick, but in some other way, he'd never felt better in his life.

"I don't have anything to say," he admitted, shrugging helplessly.

"How 'bout 'I love you, Rick,'" Rick teased.

"I love you, Rick," Ed said obediently.

"And how 'bout 'I'm really glad you're home.'"

"I'm really glad you're home."

"And 'I want to be with you for the rest of my life.'"

"I want to be with you for the rest of my life. Forever. Or as long as forever is. 'Cause I do, darlin', I really do." Ed pulled Rick to him for another kiss, and this one seemed to seal the deal.

They sat quietly for a moment. Rick looked up and frowned at the stereo.

"Damn, I wanted that song playing while I told you about all of this."

He went to the stereo and started the turntable. He put the needle down on the record, and "One Man Band" began to play once again.

"You see, baby," he said, returning to the sofa, grabbing Ed, "I am, and always will be, your one-man band. Not only that, but I am your one-man-only one-man band. There isn't anyone else in this world I want to play for."

Ed heard Rick's words, heard the song playing that he'd loved for years, but had begun to love in a different way recently. He smiled at Rick.

"Don't forget, though. I'm your one-man band, too, ya know."

Rick hugged him tightly. "I know, baby, I know. And I look forward to hearing your music for the rest of my life."

Ed couldn't think of the date. He'd lost track of the days while he'd been sick. All he knew was that it was sometime in early April 1981. He'd have to look at the calendar in the morning, because he wanted to remember the date. Straight people had their wedding anniversaries, so couldn't he and Rick have one, too? As far as he was concerned, he was now as married to Rick Benton as two men could possibly be. He sighed.

"How'd we get so lucky?" he murmured against Rick's neck.

"I don't know, baby, I don't know. Sometimes you just get lucky."

Ed hugged Rick as tight as he could. He didn't say it, but he knew it was the realization of that very first, that biggest dream he'd had over six months ago, the dream the handyman had about the mailman. It had come true. He knew in his heart more dreams were waiting to be realized for both of them, but he was willing to wait on those dreams. His Dream Man was in his arms to stay, and for right now, that's all he cared about.

> Ain't no two ways about it
> I just can't live without ya
> Let's get together
> I can't wait forever
> Here I am,
> Take my hand,
> I'm your man.
>
> I just wanna be,
> I just wanna be,
> I just wanna be,
> Your one man band, oooooooooh.

About the Author

Nick Poff is a life-long Hoosier. After a long career in radio broadcasting he decided to pursue his first love: writing stories. To be on the safe side, though, he still does on-air work and writes the occasional radio spot to pay the bills. He currently lives in Fort Wayne, Indiana. *The Handyman's Dream* is his first novel. To learn more about the book, the book's soundtrack, and the author visit www.nickpoff.com. or www.writermen.com.